DATE DUE

FOLLETT

THE

DRAGONS

OF

SPRINGPLACE

STORIES
BY
ROBERT
REED

GOLDEN
GRYPHON
PRESS

Copyright © 1999 by Robert Reed

LIBRARY OF CONGRESS CATALOGING–IN–PUBLICATION DATA
Reed, Robert.
    The dragons of Springplace / Robert Reed. — 1st ed.
      p.   cm.
    Contents: The dragons of Springplace — Waging good — To church with Mr. Multhiford — Stride — Chrysalis — The utility man — Guest of honor — Decency — The remoras — Aeon's child — The shape of everything.
    ISBN 0-9655901-6-X (hardcover : alk. paper)
    1. Fantastic fiction, American.   2. Science fiction, American.
I. Title.
PS3568.E3696D73   1999
813'.54—dc21   98-37689

TO SHIRLEY AND BUD
MY PARENTS

CONTENTS

THE
DRAGONS
OF
SPRINGPLACE_____

THE DRAGONS OF SPRINGPLACE

THE PLATEAU was an island of glass, green and warm—a piece of eternal summer surrounded by the Great Ice. Its jungle was home to many strange creatures, including the famous dragons. But what brought learned people over the Ice was the bizarre, oftentimes lovely statues. What did they mean? Why were they built? And who were the vanished, wondrous masters who must have fashioned them? These were questions over which any good scholar could strip off his or her clothes, then wrestle!

The plateau's most famous statue was its largest—a vast hunk of smooth pink glass depicting a powerful man battling an ill-defined many-headed monster. A pair of dragons were etched into the man's bulging forearms. His face was twisted with exertion and titanic pain. His pose was heroic; every scholar, novice, and simpleminded workman was equally certain of the man's heroism. Yet no two observers could agree as to what he was fighting, or if, as some suspected, the man was using his great hands to strangle a host of opponents.

An apocryphal story concerned that dragon-man statue.

Not long after the plateau was discovered, it was said, a young novice saw an unexpected glow in the night. He took it to be another campfire, and naturally, he walked toward the light, assuming that a second party had come across the glacier. Yet instead of scholars and novices, he found only a tiny woman kneeling before the glass hero.

"She wasn't any taller than this," he reported to his companions. His flattened hand reached barely halfway up his calf. Wasn't it said that before the Great Ice, people were smaller than children? "And she spoke to me," he claimed, pressing everyone's patience. "She told me that I was magnificent—no, really!—and that she was my friend, and she was happy to see that we had made this plateau into a place of honor. And then with a flash of light, she vanished."

No one believed the young man, of course.

The others challenged him to wrestling matches, but those contests proved unsatisfactory—he fought like a man who believed his own words—and the scholars decided to return to the dragon-man and see for themselves.

Tracks smaller than any child's lay scattered before the statue, but no tiny girls were lurking about.

A garland of strange flowers had been hung on the hero's neck, yet not even the wisest scholar knew that the flowers were alien, plucked lovingly from plants on dozens of strange far-flung worlds.

On the dragon-man's throat, melted into the pink glass, was a miniature handprint. The skeptics asked how a waif, or anyone else, could have climbed that high, and more importantly, how she could have left that mark. And worse still, here was evidence that someone had broken the greatest taboo, defacing one of the plateau's statues—an abomination that left the scholars outraged —and of course they grabbed the novice, preparing to give him a furious, righteous beating.

But before justice could be done, the statue turned its great head, gazing down at everyone with fire-filled eyes, and a glorious booming voice from across two hundred millennia roared at its trembling audience:

"Listen to me! This is my story!"

Daniel was five when he saw his first dragon.

He didn't know where they were going. It was after Xmas, and his father wanted to take the new car for a drive, and the boy rode with him. Daniel would always remember how the city lay under a fresh Xmas snow, bright and clean, and how the city gradually grew trees until there was nothing but trees, and the forest dissolved suddenly into an empty plain, and as they drove north there was less snow and somehow the air looked warmer. Then he saw Springplace on the horizon, saw it for the first time, and Dad was laughing, saying it didn't look so special. He said it looked like a fucking office building on steroids, and he gave the boy a pop on the shoulder, then another, then said, "Shit, we'll take a peek anyhow. What do you think?"

Daniel said nothing. The plateau was huge, its smooth glass walls bright in any light, the summit flat and covered with a green-black jungle. He knew very little about Springplace. People had built it; they called themselves Artists. The Artists also built the dragons that lived in that jungle — he knew about dragons — and the plateau was hot year round, and very dangerous, and Daniel was thrilled. Which was dangerous, too. Dad liked to change his plans, particularly if the boy was too eager. Which was why Daniel didn't smile or say anything, watching the snow vanish and the glass walls grow taller and brighter, and when the old man was distracted, he would dip his head, watching hard for monsters.

They left the highway and passed through a tall electragel fence. The plain was flat and brown and dead. Smiling holoprojections danced on the car's hood, welcoming them to Springplace. Then came the warnings: The Luddite field would begin in another two kilometers. People with artificial hearts, spines, or other vital organs should turn back immediately. Computers and other standard equipment wouldn't operate inside the field. Unshielded engines risked permanent failure. Human DNA and intellectual processes were reasonably safe, but precautionary doses of antioxidants were available at the agency headquarters. Without exception, visitors were to be accompanied by an agency employee, and any attempt to trespass on the plateau would lead to a mandatory sentence of not less than three years.

The headquarters were larger than some towns, but the dormitories and laboratories were abandoned, the roads between almost empty of traffic. Shielded tour buses left on the hour. Dad bought tickets with e-cash that came with his new car. A warm damp wind was blowing off Springplace, and it felt pleasant but dusty. Two men sat in the rear of the bus, holding hands. Dad went back and spoke to them, and they said something, and Dad said something else, almost whispering. Then the men stood and left, walking past Daniel, their faces empty and their eyes getting wet.

"Come on, boy," said Dad. "I cleaned things out for us!"

Tourists climbed aboard. Since it was Xmas break, there were plenty of kids with parents, and almost everyone looked into the back before taking the first empty seat. Dad made fun of the kids, particularly the youngest ones. They were Savants, always exceptional at some sweet skill. A few of them were big. Physical Savants, probably. The pretty ones who couldn't stop chattering were Social Savants. The quiet ones with the big eyes were the Intellectuals, which was most of them. But none were worth a good brown shit, Dad promised. He said so until Daniel smiled, feeling better about himself, and he said it loudly enough to be heard everywhere, and sometimes people glanced back at them, but not often and never for long.

The bus had a driver, a man, and their guide was a woman. She arrived late, and as soon as she stepped aboard, one of the big-eyed Savants said, "Ma'am! Why is the ground so dead down here?"

"Springplace needs the water, my dear." Her voice was made loud by hidden speakers, but loud in a soft, close way. "The facility borrows from two rivers and the aquifer," she explained, "and a network of fine tubes lets it absorb whatever snow and rain falls nearby."

Daniel listened to every word.

Their guide was tall and mostly young and sort of pretty. She was wearing bright clothes, a name tag riding on her left tit, and her face was painted up like a whore's.

The driver had his hands on the steering wheel, which was strange to see. And the bus's engine sounded angry, roaring and shivering and spitting dirty fumes out the back.

With her sort-of loud voice, their guide welcomed them. She couldn't stop smiling, telling them how big "the work" was, and why it was humankind's greatest achievement. When they passed a tall glass marker, she mentioned, "We've entered the Luddite field." Then she was comparing Springplace to pyramids and great walls and other small wonders, and everyone stopped listening, her words tiny next to the simple sight of the plateau.

Springplace began in disaster. Evil men destroyed a nearby reactor, and a sarcophagus of concrete and glass was thrown up around the ruins. But leaks formed, and no one was safe until a wondrous new glass was invented. Poured on-site, the glass wouldn't age or ever leak. A glass sarcophagus swallowed the porous one, and to pay its debts, the facility became the world's repository—old reactor cores and dismantled weapons encased for the ages; each new sarcophagus thicker and taller; the Earth's crust eventually bowing under the weight of so much glass and dirty plutonium; and from all that genius and hard work, the modern Springplace was born.

Tourists could see only the newest, outermost sarcophagus.

A human-made hill stood near the south end, a service road snaking its way up the barren slope. Their bus attacked the grade, and as they climbed, their guide finally got tired of talking, begging for questions.

Dad raised his hand.

She pointed to a closer hand. The big-eyed girl was six, maybe. "Are you by any chance an Artist, ma'am?"

The woman laughed, sort of. "No, I'm much too young to be in their noble ranks."

A few adults thought the question was funny.

"We call them Artists," said their guide, "but do you know why? Why is Springplace considered an artistic masterpiece?"

The girl showed everyone her big eyes, then said, "Those fish."

"Which fish?"

"Coelacanth fish." She had a know-it-all voice and a smirky smile. "There's only one real coelacanth. But the Artists made eleven new species, big ones and little ones, and they took them to museums, in big tanks, showing them off like famous paintings—"

"Exactly. Thank you." The painted face nodded. "Tailoring was new, and the coelacanths were part of a touring exhibit. The best geneticists had crafted them. Like the King James Bible and the first *Citizen Kane,* they're still considered classics in the field."

Nobody spoke. Then an adult asked, "How many sarcowhatnots are there?"

"Twenty-seven." Their guide leaned back as the bus struggled with the grade. "But only the inner twenty-three sarcophagi have wastes. Hot springs and geysers release the pent-up heat. Which, by the way, is where the name 'Springplace' comes from."

Dad was waving both hands.

A little boy went next. "Will we get to see dragons, ma'am?"

"I'm sorry. No." The answer was quick. A lot of people probably asked the question. "The plateau is huge, and we see only a sliver of its outermost ring."

"Hey, miss," Dad called out. "My arms are getting tired here!"

She hesitated, then said, "Yes, sir?"

A careful pause. Dad smiled and waited for everyone to look at him. Then with a smooth voice, he said, "You know, I worked for the Artists."

Doubt stiffened every face.

"Honest, folks," he said, laughing off their disbelief. "Hey, someone had to put that nuclear crap in the ground. Am I right, miss?"

Their guide had to nod, saying, "Thousands helped."

"I drove diesel rigs." He was very charming, very certain. "They were shielded, and the Luddite field still wasn't at full strength. Each man did one run each day, then took a big shot of vitamins and whatnot. Every night. In the butt."

The story was a total surprise to Daniel, but he knew better than to look surprised. He just stared at his father, unable to tell what, if anything, was the truth.

Their guide was impressed, sort of. She managed to smile, saying, "Then you should know this hill—"

"And this lousy damned road, too!" He gave a bright long cackle, then told everyone, "The hill was built in a rush. The UN found secret bombs in China, and the plutonium guts had to be put somewhere safe." Everyone was watching Dad, and he was happy. "We drove up the hill, then crossed on a narrow bridge. Put up fast, and only one truck at a time."

The guide was walking along the aisle, hands grabbing at the seats.

"The jungle was short," Dad claimed. "And sometimes we'd see baby dragons. Not much bigger than me."

"Do you remember your unit number, sir?"

He gave it, then named names. "Recognize them, do you?"

Their guide took a deep breath, then told the others, "It's all true. Some very special volunteers made those last runs."

"Is that what I was? A special volunteer?" Dad giggled. "And I thought I was a kid doing five-to-ten for burglary."

It was part confession, part lie. Dad had gone to prison, but for things bigger than taking someone's property.

Yet the people believed him. It showed in their faces, in the way they relaxed and sat easier. The big, dangerous-looking man had admitted what he was, and it wasn't too awful.

"I drove trucks," Dad told them, "and I paid off my debts to society faster. And, miss, I'd like to think I did some real good, too."

Their guide said, "You did," with her loud-soft voice.

People were smiling back at the two of them.

"A lot of good," she kept saying. And she meant it, stepping up close, the name on her tit suddenly legible.

Jaen. Daniel read it slowly, with a five-year-old's clumsy care.

"Thank you," she sang, winking at a man more dangerous than

any truck full of plutonium. "For helping make all of us sleep better, thank you."

A glass-paved parking lot covered the hill's windy crest. Jaen lost her praising voice long enough to tell people to stay together and obey every warning, then with a practiced flourish, she opened the door and set them free.

The weak winter sun was at their backs, and the wind blew straight at them, carrying the heat away from a tremendous furnace. Springplace rose up like a great temple, too vast to seem real. Their simple dirt hill wasn't as tall as the plateau. The bridge that Dad may or may not have driven across would have had a steep pitch. Nothing remained of it but tangled girders moored in concrete, a bright red barricade warning the curious to stay back.

Nobody visited Springplace anymore. Except in the most incredible circumstances, Jaen conceded.

The glass wall was seven hundred meters tall, milk-colored and slick, and perched on top, between blocks of scrap glass, were a few brilliantly green ginkgo trees.

Jaen asked everyone to listen, then she spoke only to Dad, talking about the artistry before them. "What if civilization fails?" she asked, her voice full of practiced importance. "Society collapses and dies, and all knowledge is lost. Then in a little while, or a very long while, ignorant souls stumble upon Springplace. How can we keep them from digging up the hazards in the glass?" She paused. "That was the Artists' mission. How can the innocent be kept from harming themselves and their world?"

Young Savants had ready answers: The glass wall was a barrier. And the barren ground below was another barrier. And there was the Luddite field, generated by the plateau itself, disrupting electrical currents and causing refined metals to corrode at a horrendous rate. The Industrial Age couldn't linger here for long, which was the intent.

Yet there was much more. An old man mentioned the statues, and Jaen nodded, telling her audience, "The day's great sculptors all contributed. Psychological barriers, we call them. In fact, one of the works is visible from here. You see? At first glance, it looks like any glass boulder, but it's actually the image of a human head in excruciating pain."

Daniel squinted, seeing nothing but a lump of bright glass.

Then a four-year-old girl, eyes bigger than big, said what everyone already knew. "And there are the dragons, too. They help protect Springplace."

"Absolutely." Jaen smiled, confessing, "I have a special fondness for the biological barriers. Being a geneticist, by training and by outlook."

Whatever that meant, thought Daniel.

"Genetic tailors have existed for more than a generation," she continued. "But Springplace remains unique. A self-contained human-made ecosystem, isolated by climate and other factors. Until we terraform Mars, no one will have the room or resources that were brought to play here."

Jaen named species, stressing their dangers. Every snake was venomous, as were spiders and scorpions and the other vermin. Every plant was inedible or outright toxic to humans. The namesake springs were mineral-laden and undrinkable. The giant central lake was warmer than bathwater, saltier than the Atlantic, and filled with foul-tasting lungfish and coelacanths, plus crocodiles bigger than any bus. And finally, the superheated jungle was full of giants, including the famous dragons —

"Komodo lizards," the Savant interrupted, proud of her knowledge. "They've been tailored to be large and fast, and they're as smart as cats, too. That's what I've read."

Some Savants could read at two years old. Daniel was jealous.

Jaen pretended to listen, then smiled and asked, "Do you know why the Artists used reptiles?"

"They're scary," the girl reported.

"That's part of it. But what else?"

Silence. Daniel realized that the girl hadn't read that answer.

"Reptiles are ectotherms, dear. Cold-blooded." Jaen arched her eyebrows, explaining, "Cold-blooded means a slow metabolism. Slow means that hundreds of full-grown dragons can live on Springplace. They're wondrous predators and efficient scavengers, and they will live up there for the next half-million years, guarding our poisons."

Savants and ordinary people contemplated those words.

"I adore the dragons," Jaen confessed. "They're large. Fearless. Powerful and swift. And when there's something they want, they are relentless."

There was a long pause.

Then an elbow dug into Daniel, and Dad whispered, "What do you think? Sounds a lot like you and me."

Maybe the dragon was always there.

It lay sprawled out on a huge slab of scrap glass, looking dark and very thin and small with the distance, basking happily in the sun. Nobody had noticed it, just as nobody noticed Daniel climbing over the red barricade, walking out on the old glass girder, then sitting with his feet dangling in the air. Squinting, he watched the dragon, waiting for movement. But it was still as stone, and spellbinding, and Daniel glanced over his shoulder, ready to alert his father.

Dad was busy charming Jaen.

Saying nothing, Daniel looked back just as the dragon lifted its head, its mouth opening and its tail swinging over the edge, making it obvious.

The tourists noticed. A few at first, then everyone.

Daniel heard their happy chatter. Then someone said, "Careful," and he looked back again, Jaen stepping over the barricade, not quite smiling, looking down to make certain where she placed her feet.

Watching the dragon was more fun than watching people.

When her shadow fell over Daniel, he asked, "How big is it?"

"How big is what?"

Jaen hadn't seen the dragon. *Good.*

Kneeling, she said, "I'm curious. How old are you?"

Daniel didn't look at her. "Five years, five months."

"Really?" she said.

Then she said, "You must be an exceptional boy."

Every child born today was exceptional. Always.

"You're quite an athlete, I understand." She waited a moment, then added, "I can picture you in the Olympics."

He had a Physical's skills, and other genetics, too.

"You're a quiet boy," she observed. "Not like your father at all."

She wanted to be his friend. Dad's women always tried to be his friend, but usually only after Dad had fucked them once or twice.

"He says that your mother died."

Before he could say it was true, that a pissed-off trick kicked her to death, Jaen told him, "I'm sorry for your loss."

The dragon moved again, sliding out of sight. Daniel watched the long head vanish, then the body, and the tail rose up in the air like a flagpole, then suddenly wasn't there.

"You know, Danny. You shouldn't sit out here."

His name was Daniel. Daniel Costas.

"Let's go find your father. Shall we?"

She touched his shoulder, and he let loose a long wet hiss, grabbing her hand and shoving it into his mouth, then biting down on the meat between her thumb and forefinger, calmly watching the pain reach her face, twisting it into the most amazing shapes.

After that day, awake or asleep, Daniel would dream of Springplace.

He searched the Net for programs about the glass plateau, poring over old videos and photographs, plus images taken by satellites. He couldn't read well, but he attacked every book on the subject, particularly everything written about the fabled dragons. He learned about dragon habits and habitats, and he even struggled with the incomprehensible genetic charts. Anything useful was worth stealing, and he hid his treasures from his father, unsure what the old man would do with them during one of his black moods.

On his ninth birthday, Daniel marched into a body parlor and ordered a matching pair of tattooed dragons. No one questioned his age. The boy was ninety kilos of quick-twitch muscle and heavy bone. His curly black hair was already thinning, and a soft beard clung to his bulldog chin and jaw. The tattoos were his own design, every detail authentic. Sitting stoically, never moving, he watched the newborn dragons spread over his huge forearms, scaly black skin lustrous, eyes like night, and flame-shaped yellow tongues tasting the air for delicious anythings.

Daniel paid with stolen e-cash and walked home, wondering what his father would say, and if they would fight, and if he would allow the old man to beat on him again.

But as it happened, there was no fight.

One of his dad's ambitious deals had gone sour, and some disappointed partners had visited while Daniel was at the body parlor. Using fishhooks and wire, they had lashed the old man to the floor, then carved him up the middle, extracting guts and information.

Daniel stood in the drying blood, staring at the body for a long while, his face empty and very simple and very calm.

He never wept.

But the tiny brown eyes looked very much like a nine-year-old's, gazing out at a world suddenly made vast and unknown.

For two years, Daniel bounced between foster families.

His longest placement was with a bodybuilder and his doelike wife. The wife seduced Daniel, promised to spend eternity with him, then, with calculated vengeance, confessed what she had done and how much she had enjoyed herself. Her husband struck her twice before Daniel interceded, yanking the man's arm out of its socket and shattering his jaw. Yet no one regarded him as the hero. The bloodied couple blamed the boy for their troubles, and his lover even attacked him with a knife. Daniel broke her cheek with a slap, then took to the street, and he lived on his own for several months before the police finally captured him.

Another family agreed to take the feral boy, if only temporarily. It was simple coincidence that their name also was Costas. A soft couple racked by rich guilt, they gave Daniel an enormous room and spelled out their laws, then rattled on about misfortune and how adversity can always be overcome. As if they'd ever beat anything worse than bad breath. But the boy remained quiet, appreciating his sweet luck. These people were fat with money and possessions, and he intended to wait, biding his time until he could harvest some of both, knowing they wouldn't miss either.

The couple had one son. Like Daniel, he was eleven, his face boyish, smooth, and handsome. And he was tall for any age, maybe not as thick as Daniel but endowed with a graceful easy strength.

"Call me Mink," he said, offering his hand. And when it wasn't taken, Mink simply pointed at the tattoos, saying, "Pretty well done."

"I know," Daniel told him.

The kid laughed and said, "Come on. Let me show you something."

The world's longest hall ended with a cavernous playroom. A dragon lay at one end of the room, half-grown but still enormous. Daniel stopped in the doorway, astonished. Mink giggled and gave him a sudden shove, then kept giggling as the dragon lifted its head, tasting the air, a slow first step followed by faster steps, soulless black eyes tracking their quarry.

Daniel jumped for the door, colliding with Mink. It was like striking stone. Then Mink said, "Coward," and shoved him into the open. "Dinner, girl. Come get dinner!"

The dragon trapped Daniel between a VR chamber and a weight machine.

It hissed and squealed, then shut its jaws on a flailing arm. The long white teeth were soft rubber. The dragon was a fancy toy, foam laid over a robotic skeleton. Watching Daniel pound on its snout for a minute, Mink said, "Back, girl," and the toy returned to its corner, lying still as death.

Daniel felt like smacking Mink, but he didn't want to lose two fights in the same day.

"I love those lizards," Mink confessed. "I love to stand on Observation Hill and watch for them."

"Ever see one?"

"Twice," he said, with pride.

"I've been there once, and I saw a dragon." Daniel grinned. "Bigger than your toy, too."

"You're lying," said Mink.

"You're wrong."

"I saw your files. You always lie." The face wore a perpetual smile. "Your dad hired an unlicensed lab to tailor you. He made you . . . what's the word? He made you a sociopath."

Daniel didn't answer him. His father used to claim that no matter what changed in the world, no matter how smart or good people got to be, there always was room for a mean son of a bitch. Looking at Mink's angelic face, he changed the subject. "What about you? What did your father pay for?"

"Me? I'm just an ordinary Physical." The humility couldn't hide the cockiness. Suddenly the smile seemed very slick. "Your dad was murdered, wasn't he?"

"And I found him."

"I've never known anyone whose father was murdered."

"Jealous?"

He shook his head, then said, "I bet your dad deserved to die."

For the next week, Daniel would be obedient, and quiet, and glancingly polite, and after some coaxing by Mink, the Costas family would agree to keep him indefinitely. But he wouldn't stay because of their wealth or because Mink shared his fascination with Springplace. It was that one harsh comment that proved to the boy that he belonged there.

"I bet your dad deserved to die."

And without hesitation or doubt, Daniel said, "Yeah, he did." He shrugged his shoulders, then added, "He was a mean-fuck. They're supposed to die messy. Always."

It was Mink's idea to climb Springplace.

At least it seemed like Mink's idea. The boys were fourteen, nearly full grown and tired of hunting digital dragons in the VR chambers. Wouldn't it be lovely to kill a real dragon? Daniel would pose the question, then describe cutting off its head and bringing it home as a trophy. They could pry out the white teeth, and what would girls at school do for just one tooth? Daniel knew how much his foster brother liked the girls. Then after mentioning them, Daniel would shake his head, smile sadly, and admit, "It's just too bad we can't make that trip."

Mink didn't believe in the "can't" word. After enough times, he got sick of it, shouting at the ceiling, "Who says we can't?"

"Climbing the plateau is illegal," Daniel replied.

"Unless we're not discovered."

"And worse," he pointed out, "it's impossible. Only people who work for Springplace can get up there. And even if we did it, we'd die. In about two seconds, probably."

Mink couldn't let challenges stand. His expensive meat was laced with more than just the best synthetic genes. He also carried DNA pulled from great athletes. And even better, he had talents that no tailor can plan. Mink had never lost any contest of physical skills or will. Long odds just made him work harder, his life one great string of sweet uninterrupted successes.

Mink gave a snort and half-smacked Daniel on the shoulder, saying, "We'll find a way up. Soon."

"You really think we can?"

"Easily," said Mink. But he wasn't a fool, and after some careful reflection, he amended himself. "Not easily. But eventually. And it'll be even sweeter when we get there."

Buses ran up to Observation Hill on the quarter hour.

Each bus and its passengers were examined by sensors run by paranoid AIs—the world's best when they were installed. But that was three years ago, and the software hadn't been updated in eight months. The day's last bus held four boys inside its tiny luggage compartment, and the AIs had been selectively blinded until the stowaways were safe inside the Luddite field. The road began to rise, and the boys cracked the hatch. When the bus slowed on the tightest turn, they grabbed their gear and rolled free, hitting the pavement, then bare dirt, tumbling like gymnasts into a deep wind-worn gully.

The two other boys were Physicals. Big amiable kids, they believed instinctively in sweat, team play, and obeying the quarterback. As a team, everyone lay out of sight until the bus came back again, heading home. Then the October sun set, pulling darkness and the stars out of hiding. And Mink gave a signal, the four of them rising, working their way downhill and across the powdery flat ground, reaching Springplace as two moons rose— the genuine moon and its reflected twin caught swimming within the towering glass.

Each boy carried a portion of a rocket. Normal rockets wouldn't fly beside the plateau, the field scrambling any computer or gyro. But Mink had hired a Savant, and this rocket was her invention. Tall and narrow, with precise little wings set at odd angles, it held a thousand separate computers sleeping inside shielded chambers, each with its own electronic eye.

Daniel stood watch while the others assembled the rocket.

With a calm little *whoosh*, it lifted off. Vanished. The first computer was cooked, triggering the next to come on-line. Another microsecond, and it was replaced by the third. And the fourth. And the rocket began to fall, its final computer aiming its reinforced nose at a good strong ginkgo.

At the predicted moment, a black cord dropped at their feet. Mink grabbed hold with special gloves, then told his team, "Climb like madmen. There's nothing to lose!"

It was relentless hand-over-hand work, and it was scary fun, and it took almost two hours to scale the wall, everyone collapsing into a communal heap afterward—easy food for any dragon sauntering past.

But there was no dragon, and young muscles recovered swiftly. The boys rose and huddled up, congratulating themselves before heading for the interior. Each carried a gun. Mink had his father's Italian shotgun, every slug laboriously hollowed out and filled with a neurotoxin. His two buddies had hunting rifles, minus laser sights and computer safeties. But the prize was Daniel's savage weapon—twin clips and explosive bullets, enough ammunition on board to slaughter a brigade. He had taken the monstrosity from a neighbor's home, and since just holding the weapon was a federal offense, he didn't expect anyone to bitch.

The four boys moved into the wind, into the heat. Trees became tall and full. The air turned tropical, humid and close, the final traces of October dispelled.

Mink carried his shotgun in his right hand, toy-fashion. When they found the old truck road—a narrow claustrophobic tunnel walled with cycads and towering ginkgos—he began pressing the pace, outrunning the others, eventually vanishing into the secret land.

Daniel found himself shouting at his brother, anger mixed with strange unpalatable fears. Yet Mink was fine, waiting beside a pile of rubble—a dead truck, judging by its outline. The Luddite field and the humidity had obliterated its body and heavy engine. Impressed, Mink wondered aloud, "What's the field doing to us?"

Touching the metal grit, Daniel said, "You know, my father probably drove this thing."

He had never mentioned the possibility before. The response was pure Mink. A hand clasped him by the shoulder, squeezed hard, then a grave voice warned him, "Save the lies for later."

Was it a lie? Daniel didn't know, and he didn't argue. What mattered was killing a dragon, then taking the trophy teeth, and he could tell any story he wanted afterward, and every flavor of Savant would have no choice but to respect him for what he had done.

The boys kept moving, but more slowly. A gentle slope led down toward the central lake. Suddenly over the buzz of insects came a sound, a not-distant, not-loud roar spreading through the canopy.

On its heels, silence.

Even the insects held their voices, Daniel realized.

Drenched in sweat, they drank their first canteens dry, took baths in useless bug spray, then began their second canteens, their water stocks looking rather meager.

The jungle was alive. Biting, stinging nothings came from everywhere. Beetles as big as fists marched underfoot. Tortoises bigger than rooms lay asleep, safe in their knobby shells. On the old road, a giant, achingly slow iguana stood propped against a burly tree, on its hind legs, steadily consuming fan-shaped leaves and tender limbs. The iguana would dwarf an elephant, and the Artists had endowed its ancestors with beautiful spines and intricate horns. Yet despite its costume, the creature was defenseless. One of Mink's friends aimed at an indifferent eye, laughed and said, "Boom."

"Leave it alone," Mink warned. "We came for a fair fight."

A statue of milky glass appeared before them. A warning for the ages, it showed a man in the throes of agony. Poisoned, near death, his flesh and face were melting, his ruined hands raised high, warning the boys to flee and save themselves.

Beyond the statue was a hot spring, water bubbling vigorously in a glass-lined basin. The air stank of mineral salts and sulfurous bacteria; the boys imagined the metallic taste of leaked plutonium. The spring's overflow slid across a long open slope, the jungle opening up around them, and off in the distance they could see the central lake, slick and silvery in the ageless moonlight.

Eventually, the water's stink gave way to something more awful. Mink hesitated. Spoke.

"Look there," he whispered.

A second iguana lay in the stream, obviously dead. The boys crept closer, then Mink lifted his free hand and stopped again. Daniel noticed urgency in his stance and heard it in his voice. Then Mink turned slowly, and with a strange slow gentleness, he announced, "We have our dragon."

The monster shuffled out of the jungle. It was low to the ground and looked small until Daniel gauged the distance. A full-grown female or a small male, its head was longer than Daniel was tall, the body and stiff tail making for a creature fifteen meters long, and if well fed, sixteen thousand kilograms, or more.

The wind had fallen off, and the dragon was alert, following their scent through the vivid stinks of water and rot. Long clawed feet splashed and the belly rose and a deep *hiss* escaped from it, sounding like steam, and then all at once it was running, charging straight for them.

Explosions rang out.

The boys with rifles were firing at the head, aiming for a brain buried deep inside dense bone.

The dragon kept running, then suddenly, without fuss or apparent pain, it collapsed. And the two hunters laughed and slapped each other on the back, then began to run, even when Mink was shouting at them, "Wait! Not yet!"

A second dragon appeared, climbing from behind the dead iguana. It was five meters longer than the first dragon, and it was protecting its dinner. The running boys were too busy celebrating to notice the danger, and their rifles were empty, and they were exactly between the monster and their friends, neither Mink nor Daniel having a clear line of fire.

The dragon accelerated, half-galloping, its wagging head allowing one giant eye, then the other, to track its prey.

With detached fascination, Daniel watched the boys die. They finally fled, but it was too late. They kept together, which was stupid, and one boy slipped in the greasy water, falling hard. Then his friend offered a hand, dooming himself. They were running again, and they were dead, and Mink screamed and fired his shotgun for the sake of noise. And the dragon took the nearer boy, shaking him into two unequal pieces, then dropping him only to grab the second boy from behind, repeating the slaughter with deft, amoral precision.

Mink fired a second blast. And a third. His gun sounded distant, ineffectual. Then he turned to Daniel, and with a crazy lost expression on his face, screamed, "Open up on it! Now!"

Daniel saw Mink, and heard him.

But a sudden enormous terror had taken hold of him.

Daniel began to run. It wasn't a decision. He felt like a passenger inside his own body. It took all of his remaining will just to look over his shoulder, just once, and see Mink—a swifter runner on any day—charging the dragon, fearless genes or his trust in his brother compelling him to fire until his gun was empty, fighting on with a desperate incandescent rage to save, of all things, the dead.

Sensors far out on the plain felt the concussion of gunshots.

Agency guards were waiting when Daniel reached the plain. He was dehydrated and bruised, his weapon lost in the jungle. The arrest occurred without incident. No attempt was made to rescue the other boys or recover their bodies, even though Mink belonged to an influential family. It was a Springplace policy: The moral codes of the human world, including charity and forgiveness, ended where the high glass began.

The lone survivor seemed distant and icily calm, even when he was sentenced to three years in the state's boot-camp academy.

Daniel Costas served his time without serious incident.

But his barrack mates complained of the boy's periodic nightmares, arms thrown toward the ceiling and a desperate wail coming out of his belly, then lingering in the air like a toxic fog.

Staff psychiatrists found Daniel to be a fascinating subject. When they asked about his dreams, the boy claimed to remember none of them. When they asked about any aspect of his waking life, he spun elaborate and unlikely, yet utterly convincing lies, and no tool at their disposal could separate the truth from his fictions.

"Mink!" he would shout while dreaming. "Run, Mink!"

The other boys guessed what had happened on Springplace, but only one boy risked teasing Daniel about his cowardly flight from a stupid lizard.

That boy was beaten and left crippled, and a hundred others had watched the beating, and not one witness ever came forward.

In later years, there was a lucrative market for dragons and their parts.

Elderly Chinese paid dearly for sexual organs. Nigerian businessmen fashioned charms out of the scales and wore them in secret places. Latin cultures preferred the claws and teeth, adorning themselves with predatory pretties. But the people of the North, too civilized for superstition, simply ate the meat—lean and exceedingly bitter, but laced with rare antioxidants, plus the chemical harbingers of strength and true courage.

Most product was cultured from tissue samples, usually in one of the world's ten million unregistered labs. But some collectors demanded authenticity, and at most there were a handful of reliable sources.

Daniel worked for years as an enforcer in order to raise the necessary cash, then another eighteen months passed while he made arrangements with one supplier, only to have him arrested days before the final transaction. Another six months passed before he could find a new entrepreneur, and after electronic negotiations and a fat down payment, Daniel's luck seemed to have changed.

The anonymous supplier wanted to meet near the city's north edge, in an anonymous park.

Daniel arrived early.

When he was a boy, this land was forest. Now it was manicured ground surrounded by cylindrical apartment buildings, a midcity bustle taking him by surprise.

Though Daniel was only in his late twenties, testosterone had already stolen his hair, and surgery had radically altered his face. His blood signatures and left thumb belonged to an Antarctic rare-earth miner, in case someone demanded cell samples. But Daniel's build hadn't changed, nor had the dragon tattoos, and his eyes regarded the world with the same tireless suspicion, a hundred people enjoying the park and not one of them worth trusting.

Children outnumbered adults at least five to one.

Daniel found himself staring at the youngsters. New genes came on the market every day, and the unborn were being radically tailored. He knew that. But he had been living under the ice cap, in a realm without children. He hadn't realized that his species was changing itself so much, and in so many directions at once.

A voice, close and musical, said, "Pretty."

Daniel wheeled, finding a little girl smiling, staring up at him. How old? Judging by her attitude and the wise eyes, he guessed nine or ten. Giving a little growl, he said, "Nothing here's pretty. Go away."

"Oh, sir, but yes. Pretty, yes." She had long hands that didn't quite touch him. "I was referring, sir, to your lovely skin paintings."

The tiny body carried a tall, tall head, and like most of the young children, she wore a protective helmet, thick padding decorated with colorful abstract shapes. A lot of money and hope went into her fancy brain, and her folks obviously didn't want her losing fifty IQ points when she tripped over her own tiny, quiet feet.

"Your dragons are very well done," she assured him.

Another growl. "I know."

She stepped in front of him, utterly fearless. "You seem, sir, a little startled. By us, I think."

"Get away."

"Are you twenty-eight years old?"

"No," he lied. Immediately, without flinching.

The girl had a narrow and oddly pretty face with enormous almond-shaped eyes. When Daniel was a boy, he believed in flying saucers piloted by aliens wearing that exact face. "Then perhaps," she said brightly, "you are twenty-nine, perhaps."

"Why should you care?"

"This is my hobby," she replied.

"Guessing ages?"

"Not precisely. I like to identify famous genes." A long finger pointed. "Your baldness and the dimple in your left ear, and that peculiar knuckle hair . . . they are indicators of the PU99/585 gene. A powerful strength enhancer."

"I'm thirty-one," he assured her.

"You're mistaken," she said. "The crenelations in your nails are a clear sign of KU112/31, which was used for just a few months. It helps with muscle repair, but not very well."

"Listen," Daniel began, ready to threaten.

"Did you, sir, know? This is not your thumb!"

In exasperation, he asked, "What's your age?"

"In a week," she replied, "I will be five and a half."

Shock seeped out of his face. In frustration, Daniel confessed, "I didn't know you little shits were so smart."

"Oh, sir, but I'm not smart."

He glared at her.

"Oh, no! My little sister is going to be much smarter than me. She has nothing but the new triple-G series of neural enhancers."

"Yeah? How old is she?"

With pride and sibling jealousy, the girl reported, "She will be born in three weeks."

Daniel didn't speak for a long while.

"You have other genes," the girl observed. "Artificial, I mean. But frankly, I don't recognize them. Which is interesting."

A woman was strolling into the park, alone, carrying a small box in both hands, navigating with too much caution between the running, screeching geniuses. And with a genuine smile, Daniel told his new friend, "I have to go now. I've got business."

"With that lady over there?"

"No," he lied, by reflex. Then with his best intimidating voice, he added, "And leave us alone, stupid girl."

She gave a giggle, then jumped. "Okay, dragon-man!" she sang. "If that's what you want!"

The woman was new to the business, and her heart still wasn't in it. Wary eyes tried not to look at Daniel, and she held the precious box on her lap, hands clinging to the plastic handle. Sealed and locked, the box appeared booby-trapped. With a nervous flinch, she could incinerate its contents, leaving nothing but ash for prosecutors to use as fertilizer.

"First," Daniel told the woman, "I need to look inside that box. Before you get another dollar."

She was sitting on a bench, gray-haired, gray-fleshed, the face still recognizable and nearly sick with worry. "No," she whispered, "I don't think that's a good idea."

He sat beside her, the park bench twisting to accommodate his enormous frame. Then Daniel slowly and gently placed a hand on her nearer hand, prying it off the handle and holding it toward the sun.

"What's wrong?" she sputtered.

"No scar." He released the hand, adding, "I would have thought my teeth would still show."

Her face turned to wax, pale and slick.

"Open the box, Jaen."

A punched code and her thumbprints deactivated the self-destruct mechanism. Inside the box, nestled in a bed of moldy ginkgo leaves, was a long white leathery egg.

"Good," he muttered.

"I want my money," she said, her voice tight. Frightened.

"What would happen, Jaen? An anonymous complaint to the Springplace agency, and a lifelong employee is suddenly under suspicion—"

"No," she gasped.

"Today," he said, "you're having a half-price sale."

She wasn't meant for this work. Staring at Daniel, she whispered, "It's nearly impossible to get a viable egg. I earned the money!"

"Lady," he said, "you owe me."

"Owe you? Why?"

"If I hadn't bit you, you would have screwed my father. Which would have been a nightmare, believe me." He laughed and closed the box, leaving it unlocked. "Half-price. Or I'll pay full. But if I do, you have to let me chew on your hand again. Huh? Which'll it be?"

The dragon was born yellow and black, and capable, and with mice or slow fingers, it was vicious.

An abandoned salt mine became the nursery. Xenon lamps ran on timers, the heat flowed from the surrounding salt, and plastic foliage stood around pools of mineralized water, lending shade. As the dragon grew, Daniel moved barricades to give it more room, and he found larger prey. Rabbits and small pigs worked well. Speed and intelligence were no match for instinct and patience. Daniel used cameras to keep tabs on the dragon, and he recorded its attacks, playing and replaying them at all speeds, studying the angles of the head and how the slashing teeth tore at the living meat.

Small animals died immediately. But the largest boars would escape into the fake jungle, their wounds laced with a wide array of patient, murderous bacteria.

Daniel never spoke to the dragon, or pretended it was sentient, nor did he make the mistake of naming it.

He lived in the mine's old machine shop, the surroundings spartan, and appropriate. Twice each week, he went to the surface for supplies and diversions. With his remaining savings, he could afford clean hotel rooms and whores. They were his only luxuries. For the most part, the whores were his age. Younger girls didn't work his haunts, though he assumed they were somewhere, giving perfect pleasure to the brilliant babies.

Daniel's favorite whore was a Social Savant. She wasn't just lovely, she was synchronized to his moods, sensing his desires before he knew them, and with a Social's mystical skill, improving his mood with the right word or touch or the respectful silence.

He would pay to keep her for the entire night, and because he wasn't young anymore, he sometimes slept.

Sometimes the old dreams came.

Suddenly he would scream and leap to his feet, hands raised high.

The Social asked about the dream. Just once. He told her that he didn't remember it and it was nothing, and besides, he was working on the cure. Then he warned her never to mention it again.

One early morning, Daniel found the Social in his belongings. There was no e-cash or jewelry to steal, but that didn't matter. He took her lovely face, another man's thumb pressed against the cheekbone, then with chilling precision, he described what he was prepared to do.

She crumbled. Begged. Explained.

She had a sponsor. A Physical, powerful and violent. The Physical had decided that Daniel was rich and too interested in her time. She was under orders. Come home with something of value, she was told, and what choice did she have?

Daniel conceded that there was a dilemma. Then he smiled and gave her a story to tell, and before releasing her, Daniel lent the story authenticity, carefully and thoroughly bruising her entire face.

He waited for a while in the hotel room, then rose and dressed, leaving by the likeliest route. In the predawn streets, the Physical was easy to see—a younger man, smaller than Daniel but certainly stronger. In the last few years, Daniel had butted against those exact genetics, and he respected them, if not the idiots they carried.

In the darkness, Daniel rounded a corner and sprinted, then hid in the first alcove.

The Physical had no chance. One moment, he was a tough little pig marching in the forest, and the next brought misery, blood, and a pitiful thirst for a quick, merciful death.

A robot patrol found the battered man and took him to the nearest clinic on life support.

Three days later, the Social was praising her hero, saying it would be a long time before the bastard could walk again, and Daniel was amazing, and she would gladly work for him instead, giving him her body for free. . . .

He shrugged and half-grimaced. "No, thanks."

But she kept staring at his face, enthralled. With a quiet, knowing voice, she told him, "I think you are a good person."

What was that?

"You heard me," the Social chimed.

Daniel threw her on the hotel floor. Then, for emphasis, he kicked her, just once and almost softly, shattering three ribs and a vertebra.

The dragon reached five meters and nearly five hundred kilos.

Daniel found more difficult prey: stray dogs, guard dogs, two cougars, and a full-grown grizzly stolen from a private collector. The bear was the last meal, and for the next few weeks, the dragon feasted and slept; its wounds healed before it was hungry again, before it began to prowl the confines of the salt cavern, searching for its next challenger.

In those last weeks, the dream came more often. Every night, then several times in a night.

Daniel wasn't surprised. The dream was a living thing, a monster in its own right, and it was being threatened. Lashing out, the dream intended to rob Daniel of his courage, his fortitude. Which he wouldn't let happen, he vowed. He waited, keeping his focus until the dragon was crazy with hunger, then he stripped down and entered its lair with no weapon but a knife, the serrated blade as long as his forearm, glittering in the bleak glow of the xenon lamps.

The dragon caught his flavor and, without stealth or the smallest caution, began to hunt him.

Daniel let loose an enormous piercing scream.

The dragon accelerated, lifting its head in the standard bluff.

The moment was syrupy-slow. Daniel began to run at the dragon, watching its nearest foot step and plant, step and plant, and he leaped and took a hard swipe at the long scaly neck, a sweet resistance slowing the blade.

A roar; a purging fountain of blood.

Then the tail found Daniel, delivering a mammoth blow and dropping him, shattering his free arm, and the jaws spread over him as the body shoved him flush against the smooth white floor. But he kept slashing, kicking hard and slipping under the dragon, and with a desperate focus, he placed the blade's tip against a likely spot, driving it upward with his good arm, probing and probing until the cold heart was punctured and the dragon was slumping, dying with a peaceful smoothness.

Daniel felt free. Weightless. Supercharged.

He managed to crawl out from under the carcass and reach the elevator that carried him to the surface. Clothed in two kinds of blood, he drove himself to the nearest clinic, then collapsed, a dozen robot nurses struggling to save his life, then his arm.

The euphoria passed.

Exhaustion pulled him under, and he found himself on the dream plateau once again.

Mink was waiting for him there, still firing his father's shotgun, still pleading for Daniel's help. The dragon was missing, replaced with a borderless night. But if anything, the terror was worse than before. Mink still charged the blackness, thinking that his brother was with him. And in the dream, Daniel fled again. And in life, he kicked and wailed, soaking his clean sheets with urine while the nurses pumped him full of chemical wonderlands that did nothing but make the dream last all night.

Jaen saw him coming.

She was meeting with a client—a tiny Chinese man, older than old, probably desperate for a hard-on. When she spotted Daniel, she rose and began to run, dropping the precious box in her panic.

Even battered and with his arm in a therapy cast, Daniel caught her easily. Both the client and box had vanished. No matter. "Listen to me," he told Jaen. "Are you listening?"

"Go away," she whispered.

Children stood around them, quiet and curious faces trying to decipher the bizarre scene.

"Please," she mouthed, her face stricken. Pitiful.

"Listen," Daniel repeated. Then he leaned close, speaking into her ear. "You don't like this work. What you need is a partner, which is me—"

"No."

"Pay attention." With his good hand, he took her by the neck, gently, and assured her, "You have one choice now. One. Which is more choice than I need to give you."

"A partnership," she whispered, as an experiment.

"Fifty-fifty. And you're going to teach me. And whenever I want, I'm free to buy out your fifty share."

"Teach you what?"

"All your secrets. What else?"

With the help of his hand, Jaen nodded.

Daniel gave her a few more instructions, then sent her home. With a certain majestic finality, he sat on the bench, smiling to himself and watching the park return to its normal vibrance.

"Mr. Dragon," said a familiar voice.

He hadn't heard her approach. Turning, Daniel said, "Stupid Little Girl." She was six and a half years old now. Taller, but still tiny. Surely smarter, but he realized that he had no way to measure the skills that lay behind those vast, seemingly wise eyes.

"I'm glad, sir, that you got my message."

He had asked the girl to call a certain number when she saw the old woman in the park. A hundred e-dollars seemed like too much, but Daniel was in a charitable mood, placing the chip into her delicate long hand. "I'm glad you decided to help."

"And might again, sir. If you need."

For an instant, against his nature, Daniel considered telling her, "You'd be smart to stay away from me."

But instead he grinned, asking both of them, "Why not?"

The children in the park knew him as the Dragon.

Sometimes he spoke to them, weaving spells of half-truths and utter lies. The Dragon told them that he lived on Springplace, inside a dragon's abandoned burrow, and that he came down to the world only to sell his humble wares. He ate nothing but raw turtle meat and fat kicking beetles, and in place of water, he drank berry juice and bat urine. He wasn't even pure human, he claimed. Reptile genes made him grow like a dragon, becoming larger and stronger as the years passed, and he promised he would someday be five meters tall, and the ground would tremble as he walked.

Sometimes, particularly after a lucrative sale, Daniel allowed an audience to gather around his park bench, then with his flat, always serious voice, he would tell them true stories about his brother dragons.

The babies lived in the trees because their larger siblings would eat them without blinking. Adolescent dragons, too large to climb, dug temporary burrows and hunted in the heat of the day. The giants slept in deep caves dug over the decades, and they rose at dusk to hunt and to screw. Daniel told quiet, riveting stories about the adult monsters—the chilling look of their eyes and their easy anger and how if the agency didn't catch him someday, he would certainly die in a dragon's gaping jaws, swallowed whole and digested at its leisure.

The children thought the Dragon was scary and fun, but most important, he was utterly unlike everyone else in their world.

The Dragon changed Stupid Little Girl to Little, which evolved into Lilt. Lilt became his assistant and chief lookout, and she was in charge of recruiting help from among her friends. With the years, she also became paymaster for their burgeoning staff, handing out money and what the children liked best—the anonymous, untraceable gifts of dragon scales and the enormous shearing teeth.

Daniel never inquired about the girl's family. He didn't want to know or appear to care. Yet he had the impression that Lilt's sister—smarter by plenty—was her parents' favorite, which was why she had the time and freedom to help the Dragon.

One good day, he mentioned the old road on top of the plateau, and how he had just finished walking it from end to end. Then, on a whim, he told Lilt to research the road and the men who used it. He expected nothing, which was why he offered a fat reward; but when he returned to the park, Lilt handed him a thick collection of prison and agency records, including a photograph of a man with Daniel's hard little eyes. It was his father leaning against the fender of a massive truck, rust already gnawing at the metal, a wall of young ginkgos standing behind him. The story had been true after all. Who would have guessed? Daniel paid in full, added a bonus, and with a dose of true feeling, thanked Lilt.

That next year, Daniel got careless and let a young dragon chew on him. Despite antibiotics, his wounds became infected, and in a feverish daze, he staggered into the park, threw an elderly couple out of his bench, then fell like a big tree.

He woke in his own bed, under clean sheets. Of course he didn't live in a dragon's burrow, instead keeping a very ordinary apartment in one of the nearby towers. His home was supposed to be a secret. Yet Lilt came into the bedroom smiling, happy to see him feeling stronger, and she told how she had found him on the bench and hired two Physicals to carry him, and she'd paid them out of petty cash, then hired a med student whom she met in one of her advanced classes, and he wouldn't tell anyone, either. Then she shut her big eyes and held them closed, asking, "Did I, sir, do anything wrong?"

How did she know where he lived?

Astonished, she opened her eyes. "I've always known," she replied, hurt that the Dragon would underestimate her. "I never, sir, tell what I know. But it's in my head nonetheless."

She loved him. It had taken Daniel a long time to notice her feelings, but when he was done being disgusted, he began to culture that love. He offered winks and smiles, and sometimes he allowed her the honor of sitting next to him on the bench. Sometimes she was mothering; sometimes she was a little girl trying to be alluring. Daniel let her play her games. And in turn, she ignored the professional young beauties whom he hired, the best of them tailored to offer men wondrous distractions worth any price.

Eventually, Lilt found a genuine boyfriend; Daniel was furious.

He had his reasons, most revolving around his own security. But when she sat on the park bench, talking about the boy, a genuine rage began to build. He didn't understand the feeling or even give the problem the simplest reflection. Instead, he staked out the boy's home and waited, and when his rival appeared, walking back from Lilt's after dark, Daniel squatted in the shadows, ready to ambush him. He fully intended to shatter his body and leave him for dead. But at the last instant, he hesitated, and the boy was past him and safely home, never aware of his incredible fortune.

Eventually, the boyfriend was gone. Another boy replaced him, and after him, another. Lilt might be a genius, Daniel realized, but she also was an adolescent girl who barely knew her own mind—an insight he found useful, and oddly troubling.

Lilt remained his lieutenant and a constant flirt, happy for his attentions and the occasional half-compliment. Looking at her,

Daniel would secretly marvel at the knotted ways that his life had organized itself. Who could have guessed that he would make a living through Springplace? Or that every week or two, he would sit with his gang of babies in the public park, entertaining them with stories? And how could he have known that the constant in his life would be a tiny, severely mutated girl-creature who would sit on the bench beside him, legs kicking as she discussed where they would put his profits and if they should put up a jamming field in the park, and what pretty boys she liked today, and why he should be careful tomorrow when he returned to the plateau, going home again to see his brothers. . . .

"I want to walk on Springplace," said the prospective client.
  "Fat fucking chance."
  "And I want to slay a dragon, too."
  "Now that," said Daniel, "I can help you with. Maybe."
  The prospective client stood before him, laughing gently, a bright smile beneath dark impenetrable eyes. Then with a careful pride, the young man said, "I can pay. Don't doubt it. What would be a reasonable fee for a guided tour of the plateau?"
  "I'm not a guide," said Daniel.
  "I know exactly what you are, Mr. Costas." A pause. "Ten years of selling stolen biological materials. Two arrests, no convictions. As it happens, your competitors weren't as fortunate. That's why you enjoy your current monopoly in this very specific industry." Another pause. "Yet the sad truth, Mr. Costas, is that your client base has shriveled. Fashions change faster than genes these days, and the new generations don't share the traditional awe for Springplace."
  Daniel shrugged, saying nothing.
  It was early spring, damp and chill, but that didn't keep several dozen children from enjoying their park. The youngest were incandescent wonders, the metabolisms of hummingbirds coupled with tiny swift minds. Lilt and the other teenagers looked ancient by comparison, sitting together on a nearby bench, their skulls nestled inside helmets adorned with painted iguanas and cobalt blue coelacanths. There was also a trio of twenty-plus-year-old men: Physicals as large as Daniel, brought by the prospective client and standing at attention, indifferent to the children's screams and songs, but watching their rubber balls and carbon gliders with a sleek, professional suspicion.
  "You're awfully young," Daniel observed. "Why do you care about the big lizards?"
  "I hunt. An authentic Springplace dragon, acquired in authen-

tic surroundings, would make a stellar addition to my collection."

"What's your name?"

"You need to know your clients' names?"

Daniel stared at the boyish face, his tall skull covered with Brazilian armor and a necklace of dragon claws. "In this case, absolutely."

"Portion. Portion Kalleen."

The name felt genuine, and vaguely familiar.

"If we can agree on a fee, you get a third now. And a third more when we reach Springplace. 'We' includes my assistants to help carry home the skull, of course." Portion showed Daniel his best smile, then added, "The last payment comes with a successfully slain dragon."

Daniel glanced at Lilt. With a look and a whisper, the girl urged him toward caution.

He quietly and firmly named an impossible figure, one that would allow him to retire.

Immediately, Portion said, "Agreed."

Then Daniel put up another wall, adding, "I'll need that down payment before we can start planning—"

"It's being done." Amusement and a worrisome light showed in the eyes. "I know about your orbital accounts, Mr. Costas."

"You know almost everything."

"If that were the case," said the amiable voice, "why would I have use for you?"

There were flaws in the great plateau.

Mammoth projects are destined to suffer the occasional flaw, materials and workmanship falling short of lofty goals. Springplace was built as a series of concentric rings, most flaws buried deeply; and the agency, to its credit, had done a superlative job of patching the exterior. But years ago, Jaen reopened an old patch, knowing that the glass behind it held a labyrinth of bubbles, and if someone climbed with determination, making the correct turns, she would eventually reach the green summit.

The hunting party stood in the reopened patch, and when one of Portion's bodyguards began to hang back, Daniel had simultaneous thoughts: "I'm getting careless in my middle age," and "This trip hasn't shit to do with hunting dragons."

Daniel faced the man, asking, "What do you want?"

Save for a contemptuous glance, there was no answer.

Daniel turned to his employer, and with his hardest voice asked, "Who else is coming?"

"A few more associates. Is that a difficulty?"

Each man carried a bioluminescent lamp, the feeble glow of bacteria focused into blue-green beams. Daniel shone his beam into Portion's face, telling him, "You're going to explain this to me. What are you really chasing?"

Like a little boy who enjoyed his games, Portion said, "Guess."

Something biological? But every endemic species had been smuggled off the plateau. Daniel had removed hundreds of them. There was nothing left that was unique, except the crap buried in the glass . . . and with an amused scorn, he laughed and said, "What would you want with plutonium?"

Again, in delight:

"Guess."

Daniel couldn't. "You can't pry it out by hand, and machines don't work in the field. And even if they did, you can't just walk out of here with nuclear bombs strapped on your backs."

Portion blinked, then said, "I know what you are, Mr. Costas. As long as you're paid, and as long as it's enough money, you won't care what I'm doing."

Daniel almost spoke, almost agreed.

Then he saw something move on the empty plain. Rising up out of the barren ground came a platoon of armed men, each wearing a ghost suit and a bulky pack. And between two of the men was a familiar figure. Tiny. Probably exhausted. And no doubt terrified.

He was very careful with his voice, asking, "What's she doing here?"

"What do you call her? Lilt?" Portion shook his head. "She's been investigating me, which I don't like. Bringing her seemed like the responsible precaution."

Lilt had done research, but what had she learned? Almost nothing, the truth told. Portion was a Savant's Savant. He had hobbies beyond number, including blood sports. But there was no criminal past. And, of course, he was wealthy. The sole heir to a famous tailor's fortune, he was likely the richest twenty-two-year-old in history.

"Bringing the girl," said Daniel. "Why go to the trouble?"

The young man smiled, then admitted, "It's possible that I might not know you as well as I thought." Then he glanced at his bodyguards, saying, "Mr. Costas looks weary. Carry his weapons for him, please."

Daniel avoided Lilt: her piercing gaze. The reaching hand. Then the sound of her voice, ragged and slow, answering a question that he hadn't asked, telling him, "I am, sir, pretty much fine."

Even in his thoughts, she wasn't welcome.

Obeying Portion, Daniel led the little army to the summit. Then at Portion's insistence, he changed into self-cooling overalls, sprayed himself with odor-masks, and crept out into the first light of morning, unarmed, making sure that the dragons and agency guards were elsewhere.

Standing alone, gazing up at a tall old ginkgo, Daniel considered running. But without water or a weapon, his chances were poor. Which was the only reason not to escape, he told himself.

Portion opened an agency map, his destination already marked.

"The last of the plutonium went here," he explained. "What's the best route?"

Daniel drew a curved line with his fingernail.

"Not straight across?"

"We want open ground. Clear skies mean plenty of heat, and the dragons will be keeping to the shade."

"Stupid, primitive lizards," said Portion scornfully.

Daniel remained silent.

"Lead away. I want to be there by this evening."

The group followed a cycad-studded ridge. Below them, the forest was broken with hot sulfurous ponds and the occasional geyser. Claw-winged hoatzins circled above something dead. Daniel paused to watch them and to let the others catch up, then he turned to look for Lilt, unaware that he was doing it until too late. The girl was just managing to keep up. A tiny body, but tough enough. Tougher than he would have guessed, and he felt something, and he stood there wrestling with whatever he was feeling. It made no fucking sense. Lilt wasn't useful to him anymore. And when he made his break, he wouldn't look over his shoulder again.

He wouldn't make that mistake a second time. . . .

The day passed without major trouble. A few young dragons lashed out from the shadows. Some men were bit, but not deeply. The dragons were killed swiftly with silent guns, the wounds were treated with clotting agents and preprogrammed antibodies, and just in case they smelled of blood, the injured were ordered to walk behind the others, keeping a safe distance.

Portion's goal was a large clearing, smooth glass unmarred by vegetation or soil. A statue—one of the vaunted psychological barriers—stood at the far end of the clearing. Abstract and intentionally ugly, its twisted angles and gibbous rings were meant to warn the future of the dangers underfoot. But Portion thought the statue was beautiful. While his men began unloading their packs, he strode over to the artwork, fondling the malevolent red-black glass as Daniel was brought to him. Then with genuine curiosity, he asked, "Have you ever been *here?*"

"No," Daniel lied.

"Never?"

"It's a big plateau."

"Isn't it?"

The old truck road lay behind a stand of dawn redwoods. Daniel didn't look in its direction. Instead, he turned just as Lilt collapsed on the glass, thoroughly spent. His face remained calm and indifferent. Perhaps even a little scornful. Gesturing at the very peculiar contents being pulled from the nearest pack, he risked the obvious question:

"What do your toys do?"

Portion was amused, and proud. He picked up what looked like a piece of ornate jewelry, allowing his guide to hold it. Dense and cold to the touch, the object was at least as unsettling as the statue behind them.

"Its housing contains a hot superconductor," said Portion. "Carefully shaped, fully charged. That's what protects the machine's guts from the Luddite field."

"What do the guts do?"

"Ingest plutonium, of course." He took back his treasure, then with great care said, "What this 'toy' is, in fact, is an unfueled nuclear weapon. It can burrow through almost any substrate. It absorbs fissionable materials, swelling a thousandfold. And once fueled, it waits. Patiently. A coded seismic shock wave would cause it to detonate. If I wish."

Daniel glanced at the girl, for an instant.

"And now you know everything about me, Mr. Costas."

"No." He shook his head, adding, "I'm just a stupid lizard."

Portion appreciated the humor. He was grinning, his face very young and utterly simple. "What happens if an individual gains control of these plutonium stocks? The proverbial finger is on the light switch, and there are no limits to what he can demand."

Daniel stood motionless, saying nothing.

Prodded by silence, Portion added, "A few hundred atomic weapons will be buried in the glass, protected by Springplace's own defenses . . . and if they're detonated, at once, and all of the surrounding glass and poisons are vaporized. . . ."

Under his breath, with feeling, Daniel said, "The dragons, too."

"Oh, it won't happen. For the most part, people act in their own self-interest."

Daniel waited for a few moments, then made a pistol with his hand.

He lifted his hand, pointing at Lilt. "She could be a problem for you."

"Do you think so?" Portion asked doubtfully.

"She may have warned her parents, or the other children."

"There's a cover story explaining her absence, and besides, those people are being watched." Portion shook his head. "I know how to take precautions, too, Mr. Costas."

But Daniel pretended not to hear him. "Let me ask her some questions. If the kids back home are worried, they'll contact the agency."

Portion hesitated, then said, "I don't believe you."

With a dry, angry voice, Daniel said, "Listen. I'll keep helping. I will. But you have to give me a bonus."

"What sort of bonus?"

"Life. Let me out alive."

"That's always been my plan, sir."

The young man was lying, but he did a pretty job of it.

"The thing is," Daniel lied, "if Lilt managed to warn anyone, then my kids will contact the agency. They're supposed to invent any crazy story that'll put a thousand armed soldiers up here, hunting for me." He waited for an instant, then added, "My standing orders: Prison time is a lot sweeter than dead time."

"The girl is a little burden," Portion allowed.

"I'll ask her questions," Daniel said. "Then I'll unburden us."

"Would you do that for me?"

He nodded.

"Right now," Portion urged.

"But not here." Daniel scratched his bald scalp with his huge hands. Then with an expert's omniscient authority, he announced, "It's evening, and that's when the big dragons come hunting. A whiff of blood is all it takes to put them in a mood."

In delight, the monster said, "So I have heard."

"I'm thirsty," said Lilt. Twice.

Daniel was leading the murderous group into the jungle, paralleling the old road. Two bodyguards hung behind him, Portion between them, and a third walked point, helping to block Daniel's escape route. The girl was directly behind Daniel, close enough to touch. "I'm thirsty," she said, and he pretended not to hear her. Pointing in a likely direction, he said that the underbrush there looked easier. But Portion was suspicious, or at least unwilling to leave him with every decision. "No," he said, "keep going. Just a little farther, I should think."

Again, louder this time, Lilt said, "I'm thirsty."

And Daniel said, "Too fucking bad."

A pair of canteens rode his belt. When she grabbed a canteen and pulled, he spun and slapped the hand away. And for the first time that day, he found himself staring at her face.

It was worse than he could have guessed. Lilt was bruised beneath the left eye, and she looked very angry and tired but not scared. She looked like a kid on a long uncomfortable hike. Her padded helmet with its iguanas and coelacanths was ridiculous. He felt sick and very nearly weak when he looked at the helmet and at her purpled face, and he responded by taking his left hand and smacking her once, in a clean crisp motion, driving her into thorny brush, a matching bruise blossoming and Daniel standing over her, telling, "Don't touch my goddamn water."

Everyone was impressed, including Daniel.

It was Portion who helped her up, playing the role of the understanding ally. "Don't look so mortified," he advised the girl, draping a friendly arm over her shoulder. "You have no right to feel surprised."

She was stunned, and terrified.

Daniel had won a measure of latitude. He said, "Up there would work. Up in that bowl, out of the wind."

Portion agreed.

The light was fading. Shadows had spread and merged, obscuring whatever lay inside the bowl.

It had been years since Daniel last walked here.

He couldn't be sure what was waiting in the shadows. He barely knew what he was planning. One moment, Daniel was walking, the lead bodyguard almost reaching the bowl's earthen cusp, and the next moment he reached back and grabbed the girl, shaking her like a doll as he screamed, "Did you warn anyone?"

"Warn who?"

"Does the agency know? Did you tell them?"

"No," she promised. "I would never—!"

He slapped Lilt's helmet, then tossed her to the ground. Then she was crying, which just about ruined him. He watched her curl up and weep, hating that sound. Break her neck, and he would be done with her. Why not? He grabbed the girl by that frail thread of meat and spine, and he lifted her, something in his face utterly convincing, wild hot eyes blazing as Lilt dangled before him, tears coming fast. And that was when Daniel did a half turn, spying a sudden smooth motion from inside the bowl.

From the shadows came a tongue, yellow as fire and impossibly long, rising higher than a man, tasting the night's first air.

Daniel took Lilt's ear into his mouth, biting down, hard enough to make her wince.

Everyone watched him, spellbound.

Into the bruised ear, Daniel whispered, "The old road. Run."

"What'd you say?" asked Portion.

Then Daniel grabbed the girl's tiny bottom with his right hand, and he wheeled suddenly, using his arm and legs, and with a solid grunt, he threw Lilt, a long smooth arc carrying her out of sight.

The bodyguards seemed curious. Was this part of the interrogation?

Then the dragon exploded from its burrow, roaring, a thunderous crimson voice splitting the air, the world trembling.

I'm dead, thought Daniel.

Help me, Mink. . . !

Then he leaped, grabbing Portion by his armored helmet, and with thick hard fingers, Daniel stabbed upward, piercing the toy jaw and the sinuses, then the tissue-thin skull, reaching deep inside the cavernous skull.

Here's where the real dragons lived.

The first tourists of the day spotted Lilt.

Exhausted and badly dehydrated, Lilt stood beside the Miserable Man statue, waving her arms and shouting out a warning. Some of the tourists waved back. Wind-thinned voices said, "Hello, darling!" They couldn't hear her. Perhaps if she climbed higher, she thought with a fatigued logic; but halfway up the anguished glass face, she lost her grip, and it was as though she fell for hours, ending up inside a warm black nowhere.

Agency officials raised a narrow prefabricated bridge, medics found Lilt in the statue's mouth, and the ranking officer grudgingly sent armed patrols into the interior, on the unlikely chance that her incredible story was even partly true.

The unfueled bombs and a few terrified young men were found. But the only trace of Daniel and Portion was bone fragments in a dragon's wastes, both of their DNA identified by forensic experts.

The girl was subsequently arrested and given a quick trial.

As the main accomplice in a string of felonies, she was threatened with a fifty-year sentence. But as her heroic role in a much greater crime became apparent, the public forgave Lilt. She was given a ten-year sentence as a compromise, and it was reduced to time served, and for a little while, without her consent, the bright and very fortunate young woman was subject to an international fame.

In the aftermath, the agency strengthened its Luddite field, plugged every minuscule gap in the plateau, then trucked away the entire Observation Hill; the public forbidden to pass within ten kilometers of the nuclear repository. And in a final, excessively paranoid gesture, Lilt was placed under permanent observation, her movements and transactions studied in depth, investigators looking for any sign of Daniel's missing wealth or any warning that the girl, despite outward appearances, was returning to her old ways.

Lilt continued living quietly in her home city.

She eventually married and gave birth to twins, and on occasion, for private reasons, she would visit the little park, sitting on one of its new benches, watching her children play the mysterious indecipherable games popular among their generation.

It was twenty years after Daniel's death when a team of Savants found the means to easily and cheaply marry the human mind to immortal AI machinery, freeing memory and intellect from the limits of genetics and the vagaries of death.

The Age of DNA was finished.

Within six months, the public was being transformed by the new process.

Within two years, the world's sentient organisms had come to the obvious conclusion: The Earth was too small and too dull to hold their interest any longer.

The sole exceptions were a community of Luddite-inspired ultra-Physicals. Funded by a secret sponsor, they were able to win the right and public approval to remain behind, serving as caretakers for the homeworld. Everyone else packed and began to board the bright new starships. People working for the Springplace agencies were the same as anyone else, excited by the prospects, their attentions divided by change and opportunity. Which was why on a cool autumn morning, Lilt could leave home, scheduled to finally undergo her marriage with the machines, but she somehow slipped away from her usual watchdogs, never arriving at the clinic.

A general alert was called, as a precaution.

Even so, Lilt reached the plateau without incident.

Unobserved, she returned to the place where Daniel had died, the scene thoroughly unremarkable, nothing left to show that here, on this ground, her species and the world averted disaster. In one hand, she carried a shapeless lump of pinkish glass. On tiny quiet feet, Lilt walked up to the dragon's vast burrow, and she paused, watching the darkness, listening hard until it seemed that she could hear the monster's slow strong breathing. Then she threw the lump of glass, threw into the darkness, and she turned, walking away slowly, pushing tears back up into the big almond-shaped eyes.

"Listen to me! This is my story!"

Without pause or the illusion of breath, the dragon-man statue spoke through the night. Then at first light, it told how Lilt emigrated with her children; and how the ultra-Physicals — the noble ancestors of today's noble giants — had encased the Earth in a powerful Luddite field, dooming every conceivable machine; and how Lilt's apparently simple lump of pink glass was actually coated with tailored diatoms that accreted new layers over the centuries, the statue emerging gradually, shaped with nothing but patience and the cells' own sturdy genetics.

Then with a last flourish, the statue's voice grew soft, announcing, "I will talk no more. My story is done."

Then the machinery installed by Lilt, bathed in the withering Luddite field, died quietly.

True or not, the statue's tale would have been an enthralling thing to share with others. Eventually, the entire world would have heard it told and retold.

Yet as it happened, the scholars and novices heard nothing more than those first thundering words.

"Listen to me! This is my story!"

It was impossible, insane. A statue was speaking to them! As one, they turned away, and in utter panic, they ran through the jungle like scared little pigs.

No one heard the story. Except, that is, for a single passing dragon that paused just long enough to taste the air, finding nothing there worth eating.

Today, and forever, the dragon-man statue stands mute and motionless, the dimensions of its heroism left to the imagination of the young.

But, of course, that may be for the best.

With heroes and children, it usually is.

WAGING GOOD

THE SPACEPORT resembled a giant jade snowflake set on burnished glass. Not a year old, it already absorbed much of the moon's traffic. That's what Sitta had heard. Unarmored and exposed, the port didn't have a single combat laser or any fighting ships at the ready. The fat new shuttles came and left without fear. A casual, careless prosperity was thriving beneath her. Who would have guessed? In the cold gray wash of earthshine . . . who could have known. . . ?

When Sitta was growing up, people claimed that Nearside would remain empty for a thousand years. There was too much residual radiation, they said. The terrain was too young and unstable. Besides, what right-thinking person would live with the Earth overhead? Who could look at that world and not think of the long war and the billions killed?

Yet people were forgetting.

That's what the snowflake meant, she decided. For a moment, her hands trembled and she ground her teeth together. Then she caught herself, remembering that she was here because she too had forgotten the past, or at least forgiven it. She sighed and smiled in a tired, forgiving way, and blanking her monitor, she sat back in her seat, showing any prying eyes that she was a woman at peace.

The shuttle fired its engines.

Its touchdown was gentle, almost imperceptible.

Passengers stood, testing the gravity. Most of them were bureaucrats attached to the Earth's provisional government — pudgy Martians, with a few Mercurians and Farsiders thrown into the political stew. They seemed happy to be free of the Earth. Almost giddy. The shuttle's crew were Belters, spidery-limbed and weak. Yet despite the moon's pull, they insisted on standing at the main hatch, smiling and shaking hands, wishing everyone a good day and good travels to come. The pilot — three meters of brittle bone and waxy skin — looked at Sitta, telling her, "It's been a pleasure serving you, my dear. It's been an absolute joy."

Eight years ago, banished from Farside, Sitta carried her most essential belongings in an assortment of hyperfiber chests, sealed and locked. All were stolen when she reached the Earth, whereupon she learned how little is genuinely essential. Today, she carried a single leather bag, trim and simple. Unlockable, unobtrusive. Following the herd of bureaucrats, she entered a long curling walkway, robot sentries waiting, politely but firmly asking everyone to submit to a scan.

Sitta felt ready.

Waiting her turn, she made the occasional noise about having been gone too long.

"Too long," she said twice, her voice entirely convincing.

The Earth had left its marks. Once pretty in a frail, pampered way, Sitta had built heavier bones and new muscle, fats and fluid added in just the last few months. Her face showed the abuse of weather, save around her thin mouth. Toxins and a certain odd fungus had left her skin blotchy, scarred. Prettiness had become a handsome strength. She needed that strength, watching the robots turn toward her, a dozen sensitive instruments reaching inside her possessions and her body, no place to hide.

But these were routine precautions, of course. She had endured more thorough examinations in Athens and the orbiting station, and she was perfectly safe. There was nothing dangerous, nothing anyone could yet find —

— and the nearest robot hesitated, pointing a gray barrel at her swollen belly. What was wrong? Fear began to build. Sitta remembered the sage advice of a smuggler, and she hid her fear by pretending impatience, asking her accuser, "What's wrong? Are you broken?"

No response.

"I'm in perfect health," she declared. "I cleared quarantine in three days—"

"Thank you." The robot withdrew the device. "Please, continue."

Adrenaline and the weak gravity made her next stride into a leap. The walktube took a soft turn, then climbed toward the main terminal. Another barrier had been passed; that's what she kept telling herself. It was a simple ride to Farside, another cursory scan at the border, then freedom for the rest of her days. It was all Sitta could do not to run to the public railbugs, the spectacle of it sure to draw all sorts of unwelcomed attention. She had to force her legs to walk, telling herself: I just want it done. Now. Now!

Two signs caught her attention as she entered the terminal. "WELCOME," she read, "TO THE NEW NEARSIDE INTERPLANETARY TRANSIT FACILITY AND PEACE PARK." Beyond its tall viscous letters was a second, less formal sign. Sitta saw her name written in flowing liquid-light script, then heard the shouts and applause, a tiny but enthusiastic crowd of well-wishers charging her, making her want to flee.

"Surprise!" they shouted.

"Are you surprised?" they asked.

Sitta looked at the nervous faces, and they examined her scars and general weathering, nobody wanting overtly to stare. Then she set down her bag, taking a breath and turning, showing her profile, making everyone gawk and giggle aloud.

Hands reached for her belly.

Pony, flippant as always, exclaimed, "Oh, and we thought you weren't having any fun down there!"

It was insensitive, a graceless thing to say, and the other faces tightened, ready for her anger. But Sitta politely smiled, whispering, "Who could have guessed?" Not once, even in her worst daydream, had she imagined that anyone would come to meet her. How could they even know she was here? With a voice that sounded just a little forced, Sitta said, "Hello. How are all of you?" She grasped the nearest hand and pressed it against herself. It was Varner's hand, large and masculine, and soft. When had she last felt a hand both free of callus and intact?

"No wonder you're home early," Varner observed, his tone effortlessly sarcastic. "What are you? Eight months along?"

"More than six," Sitta replied, by reflex.

Icenice, once her very best friend, came forward and demanded a hug. Still tall, still lovely, and still overdressed for the occasion, she put her thin long arms around Sitta and burst into tears. Wiping her face with the sleeve of her black-and-gold gown, she stepped back and sputtered, "We're sorry, darling. For everything. Please—"

Varner said, "Icenice," in warning.

"—accept our apologies. Please?"

"I came home, didn't I?" asked Sitta.

The question was interpreted as forgiveness. A second look told her this wasn't the same old gang. Where were Lean and Catchen? And Unnel? The Twins had made it, still indistinguishable from each other, and Vechel, silent as always. But there were several faces hanging in the background, wearing the suffering patience of strangers. Spouses, or spies?

Sitta found herself wondering if this was some elaborate scheme meant to keep tabs on her. Or perhaps it was a kind of slow, subtle torture, a prelude to things even worse.

Everybody was talking; nobody could listen.

Suddenly Varner—always their reasonable self-appointed boss—pushed at people and declared, "We can chat on the rail." Turning to Sitta, he grinned and asked, "May I carry this lady's satchel?"

For an instant, in vivid detail, she remembered the last time she had seen him.

Varner took her hesitation as a refusal. "Well, you're twice my strength anyway." Probably true. "Out of our way, people! A mother needs room! Make way for us!"

They used slidewalks, giant potted jungles passing on both sides of them.

Staring at the luxurious foliage, unfruited and spendthrift, Sitta wondered how many people could be fed by crops grown in those pots, if only they could be transported to the Earth.

Stop it, she warned herself.

Turning to Icenice, she examined the rich fabrics of her gown and the painted, always perfect breasts. With a voice intense and casual in equal measures, she asked, "How did you know I would be here?"

Icenice grinned and bent closer. "We had a tip."

Sitta was traveling under her own name, but she'd left the Plowsharers in midassignment. Besides, Plowsharers were supposed to enjoy a certain anonymity, what with the negative feelings toward them. "What kind of tip, darling?"

"I told one of your administrators about us. About the prank, about how sorry we felt." Her long hands meshed, making a single fist. "She knew your name. 'The famous Sitta,' she called you. 'One of our best.' "

Nodding, Sitta made no comment.

"Just yesterday, without warning, we were told that you'd been given a medical discharge, that you were coming here." Tears filled red-rimmed eyes. "I was scared for you, Sitta. We all were."

"I wasn't," said Varner. "A little cancer, a little virus. You're too smart to get yourself into real trouble."

Sitta made no comment.

"We took the risk, made a day of it," Icenice continued. She waited for Sitta's eyes to find hers, then asked, "Would you like to come to my house? We've planned a little celebration, if you're up to it."

She had no choice but say, "All right."

The others closed in on her, touching the belly, begging for attention. Sitta found herself looking upward, hungry for privacy. Through the glass ceiling, she saw the gibbous gray face of the Earth, featureless and chill; and after a long moment's anguish, she heard herself saying, "The last time I spoke to you—"

"Forget it," Varner advised, as if it was his place to forgive.

Icenice assured her, "That was aeons ago."

It felt like it was minutes ago. If that.

Then Pony poked her in the side, saying, "We know you. You've never held a grudge for long."

"Pony," Varner growled, in warning.

Sitta made no sound, again glancing at the Earth.

Again Varner touched her with his soft heavy hand, meaning to reassure her in some fashion. Suddenly his hand jumped back. "Quite a little kicker, isn't he?"

"She," Sitta corrected, eyes dropping.

"Six months along?"

"Almost seven." She held her leather bag in both hands. Why couldn't she just scream at them and run away? Because it would draw attention, and worse, because someone might ask why she would come here. Sitta had no family left on the moon, no property, nothing but some electronic money in a very portable bank account. "I guess I just don't understand . . . why you people even bothered—"

"Because," Icenice proclaimed, taking her best friend by the shoulders, "we knew you deserved a hero's welcome."

"Our hero," people muttered, something practiced in those words. "Our own little hero."

Now she was a hero, was she?

The irony made her want to laugh. She had come to murder them, and she was heroic?

"Welcome home!" they shouted, in unison.

Sitta allowed herself another tired smile, letting them misunderstand the thought behind it. Then she glanced at the Earth, longing in her gaze, that world's infinite miseries preferable to this world's tiny, thoughtless ones.

2. The war ended when Sitta was four years old, but for her and her friends it hadn't existed except as a theory, as a topic that interested adults, and as a pair of low-grade warnings when the Earth fired its last shots. But they were never endangered. For all intents and purposes, the war was won decades before, the Earth in no position to succeed, its enemies able to weather every blow, then take a certain warm pleasure in their final campaigns.

Victory was a good thing. The four-year-old Sitta could understand good and evil, winning and losing, and why winners deserved their laurels and losers earned their punishments. She also understood, in some wordless way, that Farside was a special place meant for the best people. Its border was protected by fortifications and energy barriers. Between its people and the enemy were several thousand kilometers of dead rock. Bombs and lasers could obliterate Nearside, melting it and throwing up new mountains; but on Farside, for more than a century, the people had suffered nothing worse than quakes and some accidental deaths, friendly bombs and crashing warships doing more damage than the Earth could manage.

Other worlds were fighting for survival, every life endangered; but the back of the moon was safe, its citizens able to profit by their luck. Sitta's family made its fortune in genetic weapons—adaptive plagues and communicable cancers, plus a range of parasites. Following a Farside custom, her parents waited until retirement to have their child. It was the same for Icenice, for Varner. For everyone, it seemed. Sitta was shocked to learn as a youngster that near-youngsters could make babies. She had assumed that humans were like the salmon swimming up from the Central Sea, a lifetime of preparation followed by a minute of desperate spawning, then death. That's how it had been for Sitta's parents; both of them expired even before she reached puberty.

An aunt inherited her—an ancient, stern, and incompetent creature—and when their relationship collapsed, Sitta lived with her friends' families, all pleasant and all indifferent toward her.

Growing up, she learned about the great war. Tutors spoke of its beginnings, and they lectured for hours about military tactics and the many famous battles. Yet the war always seemed unreal to Sitta. It was a giant and elaborate theory. She liked its battles for the visual records they left behind, colorful and modestly exciting, and she observed the dead with a clinical detachment. Sitta was undeniably bright—her genes had been tweaked to ensure a quick, effortless intelligence—yet in some fundamental way, she had gaps. Flaws. Watching the destruction of Nearside and Hellas and dozens of other tragedies, she couldn't envision the suffering involved. The dead were so many theories. And what is more, they were dead because they deserved their fates, unworthy of living here, unworthy of Farside.

The Earth began the war with ten billion citizens. It had skyhooks and enormous solar farms, every sort of industry and the finest scientists. The Earth should have won. Sitta wrote the same paper for several tutors, pointing out moments when any decisive, coordinated assault would have crushed the colonies. Yet when chances came, the Earth lost its nerve. Too squeamish to obliterate its enemies—too willing to show a partial mercy—it let the colonies breathe and grow strong again, ensuring its own demise.

For that failure, Sitta had shown nothing but scorn. And her tutors, to the machine, agreed with her, awarding good grades with each paper, the last tutor adding, "You have a gift for political science. Perhaps you'll enter government service, then work your way into a high office."

It was a ridiculous suggestion. Sitta didn't need a career, what with her fortune and her natural talents. If she ever wanted a profession, for whatever the reason, she was certain that she would begin near the top, in some position of deserved authority.

She was an important child of important Farsiders.

How could she deserve anything less?

3. The railbug was ornate and familiar—an old-fashioned contraption with a passing resemblance to a fat glass-skinned caterpillar—but it took Sitta a little while to remember where she had seen it. They were under way, free of the port and streaking across the smooth glass plain. Sitting on one of the stiff seats, she stroked the dark wood trim. There was a time when wood was a precious substance on Farside, organics scarce, even for the wealthy few. Remembering smaller hands on the trim, she looked at Varner and asked, "Did we play here?"

"A few times," he replied, grinning.

It had belonged to his family, too old to use and not fancy enough to refurbish. She remembered darkness and the scent of old flowers. "You brought me here—"

"—for sex, as I remember it." Varner laughed aloud, glancing at the others, seemingly asking them to laugh with him. "How old were we?"

Too young, she recalled. The experience had been clumsy, and except for the fear of being caught, she'd had little fun. Why did anyone bother with sex? she would ask herself for weeks. Even when she was old enough, screwing Varner and most of her other male friends, part of Sitta remained that doubtful child, the fun of it merely fun, just another little pleasure to be squeezed into long days and nights of busy idleness.

The railbug was for old times' sake, she assumed. But before she could ask, Icenice began serving refreshments, asking, "Who wants, who needs?" There was alcohol and more exotic fare. Sitta chose wine, sipping as she halfway listened to the jumbled conversations. People told childhood stories, pleasant memories dislodging more of the same. Nobody mentioned the Earth or the war. If Sitta didn't know better, she would assume that nothing had changed in these last years, that these careless lives had been held in a kind of stasis. Maybe that was true, in a sense. But then, as Icenice strode past and the hem of her gown lifted, she noticed the gold bracelet worn on the woman's left ankle. Sitta remembered that bracelet; it had belonged to the girl's mother, and to her grandmother before. In a soft half-laugh, she asked, "Are you married, girl?"

Their hostess paused for an instant, then straightened her back and smiled, her expression almost embarrassed. "I should have told you. Sorry, darling." A pause. "Almost three years married, yes."

The buzz of other conversations diminished. Sitta looked at

the strangers, wondering which one of them was the husband.

"He's a Mercurian," said her onetime friend. "Named Bosson."

The old Icenice had adored men in the plural. The old Icenice gave herself sophisticated personality tests, then boasted of her inability to enjoy monogamy. Married? To a hundred men, perhaps. Sitta cleared her throat, then asked, "What sort of man is he?"

"Wait and see," Icenice advised. She adjusted the straps of her gown, pulling them one way, then back where they began. "Wait and see."

The strangers were staring at Sitta, at her face.

"Who are they?" she asked in a whisper.

And finally they were introduced, more apologies made for tardiness. Pony took the job for herself, prefacing it by saying, "We're all Farsiders here." Was that important? "They've heard about you, darling. They've wanted to meet you for a long, long while. . . !"

Shaking damp hands, Sitta consciously forgot every name. Were they friends to the old gang? Yet they didn't seem to fit that role. She found herself resurrecting that ridiculous theory about spies and a plot. There was some agenda here, something she could feel in the air. But why bring half a dozen government agents? Unless the plan was meant to be obvious, in which case they were succeeding.

A social pause. Turning her head, Sitta noticed a long ceramic rib or fin standing on the irradiated plain. For an instant, when the earthshine had the proper angle, she could make out the bulk of something buried in the glass, locked securely in place. A magma whale, she realized.

At the height of the war, when this basin was a red-hot sea stirred by thousand-megaton warheads, Farsiders built a flotilla of robotic whales. Swimming in the molten rock, covering as much as a kilometer every day, they strained out metals and precious rare elements. The munition factories on Farside paid dearly for every gram of ore, and the Earth, in ignorance or blind anger, kept up its useless bombardment, deepening the ocean, bringing up more treasures from below.

Sitta watched the rib vanish over the horizon; then with a quiet, respectful voice, Icenice asked, "Are you tired?"

She was sitting beside Sitta. Her gown's perfumes made the air close, uncomfortable.

"We haven't worn you out, have we?"

Sitta shook her head, honestly admitting, "I feel fine." It had been an easy pregnancy. With a certain care, she placed a hand on her belly, then lied. "I'm glad you came to meet me."

The tall woman hesitated, her expression impossible to read. With a certain gravity, she said, "It was Varner's idea."

"Was it?"

A sigh, a change of topics. "I like this place. I don't know why."

She meant the plain. Bleak and pure, the smoothest portions of the glass shone like black mirrors. Sitta allowed, "There is a beauty."

Icenice said, "It's sad."

"What's sad?"

"They're going to tunnel and dome all of this."

"Next year," said an eavesdropping Twin.

"Tunnels here?" Sitta was dubious. "You can shield a spaceport and a rail line, but people can't *live* out here, can they?"

"Martians know how." Icenice glanced at the others, inviting them . . . to do what? "They've got a special way to clean the glass."

"Leaching," said Varner. "Chemical tricks combined with microchines. They developed the process when they rebuilt their own cities."

"People will live here?" Sitta wrestled with the concept. "I hadn't heard. I didn't know."

"That's why they built the port in the first place," Varner continued. "All of this will be settled. Cities. Farms. Parks. And industries."

"Huge cities," muttered Icenice.

"This ground was worthless," growled one of the strangers. "Five years ago, it was less than worthless."

Varner laughed without humor. "The Martians thought otherwise."

Everyone looked dour, self-involved. They shook their heads and whispered about the price of land and what they would do if they could try again. Sitta thought it unseemly and greedy. And pointless. "You know," said Pony, "it's the Martians who own and run the spaceport." Sitta did her best to ignore them, gazing back along the rail, the Earth dropping toward the horizon and no mountains to be seen. They were at the center of the young sea, the world appearing smooth and simple. Far out on the glass, in a school of a dozen or more, were magma whales. As their sea cooled, they must have congregated there, their own heat helping to keep the rock liquid for a little while longer.

Sitta felt a strange, vague pity. Then a fear.

Shutting her eyes, she tried to purge her mind of everything fearful and tentative, making herself strong enough, trying to become as pure as the most perfect glass.

4 Sitta couldn't recall when the prank had seemed fun or funny, though it must have been both at some time. She couldn't remember whose idea it was. Perhaps Varner's, except the criminality was more like the Twins or Pony. It was meant to be something new, a distraction that involved all of them, and it meant planning and practice and a measure of genuine courage. Sitta volunteered to tackle the largest target. Their goal was quickly and irrevocably to destroy an obscure species of beetle. How many people could boast that they'd pushed a species into oblivion? Rather few, they had assumed. The crime would lend them a kind of notoriety, distinctive yet benign. Or so they had assumed.

The ark system was built early in the war. It protected biostocks brought from the Earth in finer days; some twenty million species were in cold storage and DNA libraries. Some of the stocks had been used as raw material for genetic weapons. Sitta's parents built their lab beside the main ark; she had visited both the lab and ark as a little girl. Not much had changed since, including the security systems. She entered without fuss, destroying tissue samples, every whole beetle, and even the partial sequencing maps. Her friends did the same work at the other facilities. It was a tiny black bug from the vanished Amazon, and except for some ancient videos and a cursory description of its habits and canopy home, nothing remained of it, as planned.

Sitta would have escaped undetected but for the miserable luck of a human guard who got lost, making a series of wrong turns. He came upon her moments after she had sent the beetle into nothingness. Caught sooner, her crimes would have been simple burglary and vandalism. As it was, she was charged under an old law meant to protect wartime resources.

The mandatory penalty was death. Gray-haired prosecutors with calm gray voices told her, "Your generation needs to behave." They said, "You're going to serve as an example, Sitta." Shaking ancient heads, they said, "You're a spoiled and wealthy child, contemptible and vulgar, and we have no pity for you."

Sitta demanded to see her friends. She wanted them crammed into her hyperfiber cell to have them see how she was living.

Instead, she got Icenice and Varner inside a spacious conference room, a phalanx of lawyers behind them. Her best friend wept. Her first lover said, "Listen. Just listen. Stop screaming now and hear us out."

He told her that behind the scenes, behind the legal facades, semiofficial negotiations were under way. Of course the Farside government knew she'd had accomplices, and a lot of officials were afraid that the scandal would spread. Friends with pull were being contacted, he assured her. Money was flowing from account to account. What Sitta needed to do, he claimed, was to plead guilty, to absorb all blame, then promise to pay any fine.

The judge would find for clemency, using some semilegal technicality, then demand a staggering penalty. "Which we will pay," Varner promised, his voice earnest and strong. "We won't let you spend a single digit of your own money."

What were her choices? She had to nod, glaring at the lawyers while saying, "Agreed. Good-bye."

"Poor Sitta," Icenice moaned, hugging her friend but weeping less. She was relieved that she wouldn't be turned in to the authorities, that she was perfectly safe. Stepping back, the tall girl straightened her gown with a practiced flourish, adding, "And we'll see you soon. Very soon, darling."

But the promised judge wasn't compliant. After accepting bribes and hearing a few inelegant threats, he slammed together the Hammers of Justice and announced, "You're guilty. But since the beetle is missing, and since the prosecution cannot prove its true worth, I cannot, in good conscience, find for the death penalty."

Sitta stood with her eyes shut. She had heard the word "clemency" and opened her eyes, realizing that nobody but her had spoken.

The judge delivered a hard, withering stare. In a voice that Sitta would hear for years, syllable by syllable, he said, "I sentence you to three years of involuntary servitude." Again he struck the Hammers together. "Those three years will be served as a member of the Plowsharers. You'll be stationed on the Earth, young lady, at a post of my approval, and I just hope you learn something worthwhile from this experience."

The Plowsharers? she thought. They were those stupid people who volunteered to work and die on the Earth, and this had to be a mistake, and how could she have misunderstood so many words at one time. . . ?

Her friends looked as if they were in shock. All wept and

bowed their heads, and she glared at them, waiting for even one of them to step forward and share the blame. But they didn't. Wouldn't. When they looked at Sitta, it was as if she was dead. Everyone knew the attrition rate among the Plowsharers. Had Varner and the others tricked her into confessing, knowing her fate all along? Probably not, no. They were genuinely surprised; she thought it then and thought it for the next eight years. But if they had come forward, en masse . . . if another eight families had embraced this ugly business . . . there might have been a reevaluation . . . an orphan's crime would have been diluted if only they'd acted with a dose of courage . . . the shits. . . !

The Earth was hell.

A weak Farsider would die in an afternoon, slain by some nameless disease or embittered Terran.

Yet not one good friend raised a hand asking to be heard. Not even when Sitta screamed at them. Not even when she slipped away from her guard, springing over the railing and grabbing Varner, trying to shake him into honesty, cursing and kicking him, fighting to shame him into the only possible good deed.

More guards grabbed the criminal, doing their own cursing and kicking, finally binding her arms and legs behind her.

The judge grinned ear to ear. "Wage good," he called out, in the end. "Wage plenty of good, Sitta."

It was a Plowsharers' motto: *Waging Good.* And Sitta would remember that moment with a hyperclarity, her body being pulled away from Varner as Varner's face grew cold and certain, one of his hands reaching, pressing at her chest as if helping the guards restrain her, and his tired thick voice said, "You'll be back," without a shred of confidence. Then, "You'll do fine." Then with a whisper, in despair, "This is for the best, darling. For the best."

5 The mountains were high and sharp, every young peak named for some little hero of the war. Titanic blasts had built them, then waves of plasma had broken against them, fed by the Earth's weapons and meant to pour through any gaps, the enemy hoping to flood Farside with the superheated material. But the waves had cooled and dissipated too quickly. The mountains were left brittle, and in the decades since, at irregular intervals, different slopes would collapse, aprons of debris fanning across the plain. The old railbug skirted one apron, crossed another, then rose into a valley created by an avalanche, a blur of rocks on both sides and Varner's calm voice explaining how the Martians—who else?—had buried hyperfiber threads, buttressing the mountains, making them safer than mounds of cold butter.

Then they left the valley, passing into the open again, an abandoned fort showing as a series of rectangular depressions. Its barrier generators and potent lasers had been pulled and sold as scrap. There was no more earthshine and no sun yet, but Sitta could make out the sloping wall of an ancient crater and a rolling boulder-strewn floor. The border post was in the hard black shadows; the railbug was shunted to a secondary line. Little gold domes passed on their right. They slowed and stopped beside a large green dome, fingers of light stabbing at them. "Why do we have to stop?" asked one of the strangers. And Pony said, "Because," and gracelessly pointed toward Sitta. And Varner added, "It should only take a minute or two," while winking at her, the picture of calm.

A walktube was spliced into the bug's hatch, and with a rush of humid air, guards entered. Human, not robotic. And armed, too. But what made it most remarkable was the three gigantic hounds, Sitta recognizing the breed in the same instant she realized this was no ordinary inspection.

She remained calm, in a fashion. It was Varner who jumped to his feet, muttering, "By what right—?"

"Hello," shouted the hounds. "Be still. We bite!"

They were broad and hairless, pink as tongues and free of all scent. Their minds and throats had been surgically augmented, and their nostrils were the best in the solar system. The Earth's provisional government used them, and if smugglers were found with weapons or contraband, they were executed, the hounds given that work as a reward.

"We bite," the hounds repeated. "Out of our way!"

A Belter walked into the railbug, her long limbs wearing grav-assist braces. Her bearing and the indigo uniform implied a great rank. Next to her, the hounds appeared docile. She glowered, glared. Facing her, Varner lost his nerve, slumping at the shoulders, whimpering, "How can we help?"

"You can't help," she snapped. Then, speaking to the guards and hounds, she said, "Hunt!"

Sensors and noses were put to work, scouring the floor and corners and the old fixtures, then the passengers and their belongings. One hound descended on Sitta's bag, letting out a piercing wail.

"Whose is this?" asked the Belter.

Sitta remained composed. If this woman knew her plan, she reasoned, then they wouldn't bother with this little drama. She'd be placed under arrest. Everyone she knew or had been near would be detained, then interrogated . . . *if they even suspected.* . . .

"It's my bag," Sitta allowed.

"Open it for me. Now."

Unfastening the simple latches, she worked with cool deliberation. The bag sprang open, and she retreated, watching the heavy pink snouts descend, probing and snorting and pulling at her neatly folded clothes. Like the bulky trousers and shirt Sitta wore, they were simple items made with rough, undyed, and inorganic fabrics; the hounds could be hunting for persistent viruses and booby-trapped motes of dust. Except a dozen mechanical searches had already found her clean. Had someone recently tried to smuggle something dangerous into Farside? But why send a Belter? Nothing made sense, she realized; and the hounds said, "Clean, clean, clean," with loud, disappointed voices.

The official offered a grim nod.

Again Varner straightened, his skin damp, glistening. "I have never, ever seen such a . . . such a . . . what do you want. . . ?"

No answer was offered. The Belter approached Sitta, her braces humming, lending her an unexpected vigor. With the mildest of voices, she asked, "How are the Plowsharers doing, miss? Are you waging all the good you can?"

"Always," Sitta replied.

"Well, good for you." The official waved a long arm. Two guards grabbed Sitta and carried her to the back of the bug, into the cramped toilet, then stood beside the doorway as the official looked over their shoulders, telling their captive, "Piss into the bowl, miss. And don't flush."

Sitta felt like old weakened glass. A thousand fractures met, and she nearly collapsed, catching herself on the tiny sink and then, using her free hand, unfastening her trousers. Her expansive brown belly seemed to glow. She sat with all the dignity she could muster. Urinating required concentration, courage. Then she rose again, barely able to pull up her trousers when the Belter shouted, "Hunt," and the hounds pushed past her, heads filling the elegant wooden bowl.

If so much as a single molecule was out of place, they would find it. If just one cell had thrown off its camouflage —

— and Sitta stopped thinking, retreating into a trance that she had mastered on the Earth. Her hands finished securing her trousers. A big wagging tail bruised her leg. Then came three voices, in a chorus, saying, "Yes, yes, yes."

Yes? What did *yes* mean?

The official genuinely smiled, giving Sitta an odd little sideways glance. Then there wasn't any smile, a stern unapologetic voice saying, "I am sorry for the delay, miss."

What had the hounds smelled? she kept asking herself.

"Welcome home, Miss Sitta."

The intruders retreated, vanished. The walktube was detached, and the railbug accelerated, Sitta walking against the strong tug of it. Varner and the others watched her in silent astonishment, nothing in their experience to match this assault. She almost screamed, "This happens on the Earth, every day!" But she didn't speak, taking an enormous breath, then kneeling, wiping her hands against her shirt, then calmly beginning to refold and repack her belongings.

The others were embarrassed. Dumbfounded. Intrigued.

It was Pony who noticed the sock under the seat, bringing it to her and touching the bag for a moment, commenting, "It's beautiful leather." She wanted to sound at ease and trivial, adding, "What kind of leather is it?"

Sitta was thinking: *What if someone knows?*

Months ago, when this plan presented itself, she had assumed that one of the security apparatuses would discover her, then execute her. She'd given herself a 10 percent chance of surviving to this point. But what if there were people—powerful likeminded people—who thought she was right? No government could sanction what Sitta was doing, much less make it happen. But they might allow it to happen—*that woman smiled at me!*— while checking on her progress from time to time. . . .

"Are they culturing leather on the Earth?" asked Pony, unhappy to be ignored. Stroking the simple bag with both hands, she commented, "It has a nice texture. Very smooth."

"It's not cultured," Sitta responded. "Terrans can't own biosynthetic equipment."

"It's from an animal then." The girl's hand lifted, a vague disgust showing on her face. "Is it?"

"Yes," said the retired Plowsharer.

"What kind of animal?"

"Human kinds."

Every eye was fixed on her.

"The other kinds are scarce," Sitta explained. "And precious. Even rat skins go into the pot."

No one breathed; no one dared to move.

"This bag is laminated human flesh," she told them, fastening the latches. *Click, click.* "You have to understand. On the Earth, it's an honor to be used after death. You want to stay behind and help your family."

Icenice gave a low moan.

Sitta set the bag aside, watching the staring faces, then adding, "I knew some of these people. I did."

6   The Plowsharers were founded and fueled by idealists who never actually worked on the Earth. A wealthy Farsider donated her estate as an administrative headquarters. Plowsharers were to be volunteers with purposeful skills that would help the Earth and its suffering people. That, at least, was the intent. The trouble came in finding volunteers worth accepting. A hundred thousand vigorous young teachers and doctors and ecological technicians could have done miracles. But the norm was to creak along with ten or fifteen thousand ill-trained, emotionally questionable semivolunteers. Who in her right mind joined a service with 50 percent mortality? Along the bell-shaped curve, Sitta was one of the blue-chip recruits. She had youth and a quality education. Yes, she was spoiled. Yes, she was naive. But she was in perfect health and could be made even healthier. "We're always improving our techniques," the doctors explained, standing before her in the orbital station. "What we'll do is teach your flesh how to resist its biological enemies, because they're the worst hazards. Diseases and toxins kill more Plowsharers than do bombs, old or new."

A body that had never left the soft climate of Farside was transformed. Her immune system was bolstered, then a second, superior system was built on top of it. She was fed tailored bacteria that proceeded to attack her native flora, destroying them and bringing their withering firepower to her defense. As an experiment, Sitta was fed cyanides and dioxins, cholera and rabies. Headaches were her worst reaction. Then fullerenes stuffed full of procrustean bugs were injected straight into her heart. What should have killed her in minutes made her nauseous, nothing more. The invaders were obliterated, their toxic parts encased in plastic granules, then jettisoned in the morning's bowel movement.

Meanwhile, bones and muscles had to be strengthened. Calcium slurries were ingested, herculean steroids were administered along with hard exercise, and her liver succumbed as a consequence, her posting delayed. Her three-year sentence didn't begin until she set foot on the planet, yet Sitta was happy for the free time. It gave her a chance to compose long, elaborate letters to her old friends, telling them in clear terms to fuck themselves and each other and fuck Farside and would they please die soon and horribly, please?

A new liver was grown and implanted. At last, Sitta was posted. With an education rich in biology—a legacy of her parents—she was awarded a physician's field diploma, then given to a remote city on the cratered rock of northern America. Her hyperfiber chests were stolen in Athens. With nothing but the clothes she had worn for three days straight, she boarded the winged shuttle that would take her across the poisoned Atlantic. Her mood couldn't have been lower, she believed; then she discovered a new depth of spirit, gazing out a tiny porthole, gray ocean giving way to a blasted lunar surface. It was like the moon of old, save for the thick acidic haze and the occasional dab of green, both serving to heighten the bleakness, the lack of all hope.

She decided to throw herself from the shuttle. Placing a hand on the emergency latch, she waited for the courage; and one of the crew saw her and came over to her, kneeling to say, "Don't." His smile was charming, his eyes angry. "If you need to jump," he said, "use the rear hatch. And seal the inner door behind you, will you?"

Sitta stared at him, unable to speak.

"Consideration," he cautioned. "At this altitude and at these speeds, you might hurt innocent people."

In the end, she killed no one. Embarrassed to be found out, to be so transparent, she kept on living; and years later, in passing, she would wonder whom to write and thank for his indifferent, precious help.

7 Farside, like every place, was transformed by the war. But instead of world-shaking explosions and lasers, it was sculpted by slower, more graceful events. Prosperity covered its central region with domes, warm air and man-made rains beginning to modify the ancient regolith. Farther out were the factories and vast laboratories that supplied the military and the allied worlds. Profits came as electronic cash, water, and organics. A world that had been dry for four billion years was suddenly rich with moisture. Ponds became lakes. Comet ice and pieces of distant moons were brought to pay for necessities like medicines and sophisticated machinery. And when there was too much water for the surface area — Farside isn't a large place — the excess was put underground, flooding the old mines and caverns and outdated bunkers. This became the Central Sea. Only in small places, usually on the best estates, would the Sea show on the surface. Icenice had lived beside one of those pond-sized faces, the water bottomless and blue, lovely beyond words.

It was too bad that Sitta wouldn't see it now.

Looking about the railbug, at the morose down-slung faces, she decided that she was doomed to be uninvited to the celebration. That incident with the bag had spoiled the mood. Would it be Varner or Icenice who would say, "Maybe some other time, darling. Where can we leave you?"

Except they surprised her. Instead of making excuses, they began to have the most banal conversation imaginable. Who remembered what from last year's spinball season? What team won the tournament? Who could recall the most obscure statistic? It was a safe, bloodless collection of noises, and Sitta ignored it, leaning back against her seat, her travels and the pregnancy finally catching up with her. She drifted into sleep, no time passing, then woke to find the glass walls opaque, the sun up and needing to be shielded. It was like riding inside a glass of milk or a cloud bank, and sometimes, holding her head at the proper angle, she could just make out the blocky shapes of factories streaking past.

Nobody was speaking; furtive glances were thrown her way.

"What do they do?" asked Sitta.

Silence.

"The factories," she added. "Aren't they being turned over to civilian industries?"

"Some have been," said Varner.

"Why bother?" growled one of the strangers.

"Bosson uses some of them." Icenice spoke with a flat, emotionless voice. "The equipment is old, he says. And he has trouble selling what he makes."

Bosson is your husband, thought Sitta. Right?

She asked, "What does he make?"

"Laser drills. They're retooled old weapons, I guess."

Sitta had assumed that everything and everyone would follow the grand plan. Farside's wealth and infrastructure would generate new wealth and opportunities . . . if not with their factories, then with new spaceports and beautiful new cities. . . .

Except those wonders belonged to the Martians, she recalled.

"If you want to sleep," Varner advised, "we'll make up the long seat in the back. If you'd like."

On a whim, she asked, "Where are Lean and Catchen?"

Silence.

"Are they still angry with me?"

"Nobody's angry with you," Icenice protested.

"Lean is living on Titan," Pony replied. "Catchen . . . I don't know . . . she's somewhere in the Belt."

"They're not together?" Sitta had never known two people more perfectly linked, save for the Twins. "What happened?"

Shrugs. Embarrassed, even pained expressions. Then Varner summed it up by saying, "Crap finds you."

What did that mean?

Varner rose to his feet, looking the length of the bug.

Sitta asked, "What about Unnel?"

"We don't have any idea." Indeed, he seemed entirely helpless, eyes dropping, gazing at his own hands for a few baffled moments. "Do you want to sleep, or not?"

She voted for sleep. A pillow was found and placed where her head would lay, and she was down and hard asleep in minutes, waking once to hear soft conversation—distant, unintelligible— then again to hear nothing at all. The third time brought bright light and whispers, and she sat upright, discovering that their railbug had stopped, its walls once again transparent. Surrounding them was a tall, delicate jungle and a soft blue-tinted sky of glass, the lunar noon as brilliant as she remembered. Through an open hatch, she could smell water and the vigorous stink of orchids.

Icenice was coming for her. "Oh," she exclaimed, "I was just going to shake you."

The others stood behind her, lined up like the best little children; and Sitta thought:

You want something.

That's why they had come to greet her and bring her here. That's why they had endured searches and why they had risked any grudges that she still might feel toward them.

You want something important, and no one else can give it to you.

Sitta would refuse them. She had come here to destroy these people and devastate their world, and seeing the desire on their hopeful, desperate faces, she felt secretly pleased. Even blessed. Rising to her feet, she asked, "Would someone carry my bag? I'm still very tired."

A cold pause, then motion.

Varner and one of the strangers picked the bag up by different straps, eyeing one another, the stranger relinquishing the distasteful chore with a forced chuckle and bow, stepping back and glancing at Sitta, hoping she would notice his attempted kindness.

Artificial volcanoes girdled the Earth's equator, fusion reactors sunk into their throats, helping them push millions of tons of acid and ash into the stratosphere. They maintained the gray-black clouds that helped block the sunlight. Those clouds were vital. Decades of bombardment had burned away forests, soil, and even great volumes of carbonate rock. There was so much carbon dioxide in the atmosphere that full sunshine would have brought a runaway greenhouse event. A temporary second Venus would be born, and the world would be baked until dead. "Not a bad plan," Sitta's parents once said, perhaps as a black joke. "That world is all one grave anyway. Why do we pretend?"

The earthly climate was hot and humid despite the perpetual gloom. It would be an ideal home for orchids and food crops, if not for the lack of soil, its poisoned water, and the endless plant diseases. Terrans, by custom, lived inside bunkers. Even in surface homes built after the war, there was a strength of walls and ceilings, everything drab and massive, every opening able to be sealed tight. Sitta was given her own concrete monstrosity when she arrived at her post. It had no plumbing. She'd been promised normal facilities, but assuming that she was being slighted by the Terrans, she refused to complain. Indeed, she tried to avoid all conversation. On her first morning, in the dim purple light, she put on a breathing mask to protect her lungs from acids and explosive dust, then left her new house, shuffling up a rocky hill, finding a depression where she felt unwatched, doing the essential chore and covering her mess with loose stones, then slinking off to work a full day in the farm fields.

A hospital was promised; every government official in Athens had said so. But on the Earth, she was learning, promises were no stronger than the wind that makes them. For the time being, she was a laborer, and a poor one. Sitta could barely lift her tools, much less swing them with authority. Yet nobody seemed to mind, their public focus on a thousand greater outrages.

That was the greatest surprise for the new Plowsharer. It wasn't the poverty, which was endless, or the clinging filth, or even the constant specter of death. It was the ceaselessly supportive nature of the Terrans, particularly toward her. Wasn't she one of the brutal conquerors? Not to their way of thinking, no. The moon and Mars and the rest of the worlds were theories, unobserved and almost unimaginable. Yes, they honestly hated the provisional government, particularly the security agencies that enforced the harsh laws. But toward Sitta, their Plowsharer, they showed smiles, saying, "We're thrilled to have you here. If you need anything, ask. We won't have it, but ask anyway. We like to apologize all the same."

Humor was a shock, set against the misery. Despite every awful story told by Farsiders, and despite the grueling training digitals, the reality proved a hundred times more wicked, cruel, and thoughtless than anything she could envision. Yet meanwhile, amid the carnage, the people of her city told jokes, laughed, and loved with a kind of maniacal vigor, perhaps because of the stakes involved, pleasures needing to be taken as they were found.

Tens of thousands lived in the city. Children outnumbered adults, except they weren't genuine children. They reminded Sitta of five- and six-year-old adults, working in the fields and tiny factories, worldly in all things, including their play. The most popular game was a pretend funeral. They used wild rats, skinning them just as human bodies were skinned, sometimes pulling out organs to be transplanted into other rats, just as humans harvested whatever they could use from their own dead, implanting body parts with the help of primitive autodocs, dull knives, and weak laser beams.

By law, each district in the city had one funeral each day. One or fifty bodies — skinned, and if clean enough, emptied of livers, kidneys, and hearts — were buried in a single ceremony, always at dusk, always as the blister-colored sun touched the remote horizon. There was never more than one hole to dig and refill. Terrans were wonders at digging graves. They always knew where to sink them and how deep, then just what words to say over the departed, and the best ways to comfort a woman from Farside who insisted on taking death personally.

Despite her hyperactive immune system, Sitta became ill. For all she knew, she had caught some mutant strain of an ailment devised by her parents, the circumstances thick with irony. After three days of fever, she ran out of the useless medicines in her personal kit, then fell into a delirium, waking at one point to find women caring for her, smiling with sloppy toothless mouths, their ugly faces lending her encouragement, a credible strength.

Sitta recovered after a week of near-death. Weaker than any time since birth, she shuffled up the hillside to defecate, and in the middle of the act she saw a nine-year-old sitting nearby, watching without a hint of shame. She finished and went to him. And he skipped toward her, carrying a small bucket and spade. Was he there to clean up after her? She asked, then added, "I bet you want it for the fields, don't you?"

The boy gave an odd look, then proclaimed, "We wouldn't waste it on the crops!"

"Then why. . . ?" She hesitated, realizing that she'd seen him on other mornings. "You've done this other times, haven't you?"

"It's my job," he confessed, smiling behind his transparent breathing mask.

She tried to find her other stone piles. "But why?"

"I'm not supposed to tell you."

Sitta offered a wan smile. "I won't tell that you did. Just explain what you want with it."

As if nothing could be more natural, he said, "We put it in our food."

She moaned, bending as if punched.

"You've got bugs in you," said the boy. "Bugs that keep you alive. If we eat them and if they take hold—"

Rarely, she guessed.

"—then we'll feel better. Right?"

On occasion, perhaps. But the bacteria were designed for her body, her chemistry. It would take mutations and enormous luck . . . then, yes, some of those people might benefit in many ways. At least it was possible.

She asked, "Why is this a secret?"

"People like you can be funny," the boy warned her. "About all kinds of stuff. They thought you wouldn't like knowing."

Sitta was disgusted, yet oddly pleased, too.

"Why do you hide your shit?" he asked. "Is that what you do on the moon? Do you bury it under rocks?"

"No," she replied, "we pipe it into the Sea."

"Into your water?" His nose crinkled up. "That doesn't sound very smart, I think."

"Perhaps you're right," she agreed. Then she pointed at the bucket, saying, "Let me keep it. How about if I set it outside my door every morning?"

"It would save me a walk," the boy agreed.

"It would help both of us."

He nodded, smiling up at her. "My name is Thomas."

"Mine is Sitta."

A big, long laugh. "I know *that*."

For that instant, in the face and voice, Thomas seemed like a genuine nine-year-old boy, wise only in the details.

9. Icenice's home and grounds were exactly as Sitta remembered them, and it was as if she had never been there, as if the scenery had been shown to her in holos while she was a young and impressionable girl. "Privilege," said the property. "Order." "Comfort." She looked down a long green slope, eyes resting on the blue pond-sized face of the Sea, flocks of swift birds flying around it and drinking from it and lighting on its shore. After a minute, she turned and focused on the tall house, thinking of all the rooms and elegant balconies and baths and holoplazas. On the Earth, two hundred people would reside inside it and feel blessed. And what would they do with this yard? With everyone staring, Sitta dropped to her knees, hands digging into the freshly watered sod, nails cutting through sweet grass and exuberant roots, reaching soil blacker than tar. The skins of old comets went into this soil, brought in exchange for critical war goods. And for what purpose? Pulling up a great lump of the stuff, she placed it against her nose and sniffed once, then again.

The silence was broken by someone clearing his throat.

Icenice jumped half a meter into the air, turning in flight and blurting, "Honey? Hello."

The husband stood on the end of a stone porch, between stone lions. In no way, save for a general maleness, did he match Sitta's expectations. Plain and stocky, Bosson was twenty years older than the rest of them, and a little fat. Dressed like a low-grade functionary, there seemed nothing memorable about him.

"So," he shouted, "does my dirt smell good?"

Sitta emptied her hands and rose. "Lovely."

"Better than anything you've tasted for a while. Am I right?"

She knew him. The words; the voice. His general attitude. She had seen hundreds of men like him on Earth, all members of the government. All middle-aged and embittered by whatever had placed them where they didn't want to be. Sitta offered a thin smile, telling Bosson, "I'm glad to meet you, finally."

The man grinned, turned. To his wife, he said, "Come here."

Icenice nearly ran to him, wrapping both arms around his chest and squealing, "We've had a gorgeous time, darling."

No one else in their group greeted him, even in passing.

Sitta climbed the long stairs two at a time, offering her hand and remarking, "I've heard a lot about you."

"Have you?" Bosson laughed, reaching past her hand and patting her swollen belly. "Is this why you quit being the Good Samaritan?"

"Honey?" said Icenice, her voice cracking.

"Who's the father? Another Plow?"

Sitta waited for a long moment, trying to read the man's stony face. Then, with a quiet, stolid voice, she replied, "He was Terran."

"Was?" asked Icenice, fearfully.

"He's dead," Bosson answered. Unimpressed; unchastened. "Am I right, Miss Sitta?"

She didn't respond, maintaining her glacial calm.

"Darling, let me show you the room." Icenice physically moved between them, sharp features tightening and a sheen of perspiration on her face and breasts. "We thought we'd give you your old room. That is, I mean, if you want to stay . . . for a little while. . . ."

"I hope you remember how to eat," Bosson called after them. "This house has been cooking all day, getting ready."

Sitta didn't ask about him.

Yet Icenice felt compelled to explain, saying, "He's just in a bad mood. Work isn't going well."

"Making laser drills, right?"

The girl hesitated on the stairs, sunshine falling from a high skylight, the heat of it making her perfumes flood into the golden air. "He's a Mercurian, darling. You know how bleak they can be."

Were they?

"He'll be fine," Icenice promised, no hope in her voice. "A drink or two, and he'll be sugar."

Following the familiar route, she was taken to an enormous suite, its bed able to sleep twenty and the corners decorated with potted jungles. Bright gold-and-red monkeys came close, begging for any food that a human might be carrying. Sitta had nothing in her hands. A house robot had brought her bag, setting it on the bed and asking if she wished it unpacked. She didn't answer. Already sick of luxuries, she felt a revulsion building, her face hardening—

—and Icenice, misreading her expression, asked, "Are you disappointed with me?"

Sitta didn't care about the girl's life. But instead of honesty, she feigned interest. "Why did you marry him?"

Bleakness seemed to be a family trait. A shrug of the shoulders, then she said, "I had to do it."

"But why?"

"There wasn't any choice," she snapped, as if nothing could be more obvious. Then, "Can we go? I don't want to leave them alone for too long."

The robot was left to decide whether or not to unpack. Sitta and Icenice went downstairs, discovering everyone in the long dining room, Bosson sitting in a huge feather chair at one end, watching the guests congregating in the distance. His expression was both alert and bored. Sitta was reminded of an adult watching children, always counting the baubles.

As she arrived, whispers died.

It was Bosson who spoke to her, jumping up from his chair with a laugh. "So what was your job? What kind of good did you wage?"

Sitta offered a lean, unfriendly smile. "I ran a hospital."

Varner came closer. "What kind of hospital?"

"Prefabricated," she began.

Then Bosson added, "The Martians built them by the thousands, just in case we ever invaded the Earth. Portable units. Automated. Never needed." He winked at Sitta, congratulating himself. "Am I right?"

She said nothing.

"Anyway, some Plow thought they could be used anyway." He shook his head, not quite laughing. "I'm not a fan of the Plows, in case you haven't noticed."

With a soft, plaintive voice, Icenice whispered, "Darling?"

To whom?

Sitta looked at him, finding no reason to be intimidated. "That's not exactly a unique opinion."

"I'm a harsh person," he said in explanation. "I believe in a harsh, cold universe. Psychology isn't my field, but maybe it has to do with surviving one of the last big Terran attacks. Not that my parents did. Or my brothers." A complex shifting smile appeared, vanished. "In fact, I watched most of them expire. The cumulative effects of radiation . . ."

Using her most reasonable voice, Sitta remarked, "The people who killed them have also died. Years ago."

He said, "Good."

He grinned and said, "The real good of the Plows, I think, is that they help prolong the general misery. People like you give hope, and what good is hope?"

His opinions weren't new, but the others appeared horrified. "Things are getting better!" Icenice argued. "I just heard . . . I don't remember where . . . that *their* life spans are almost twenty percent longer than a few years ago. . . . !"

"The average earthly life span," Sitta replied, "is eleven years."

The house itself seemed to hold its breath.

Then Pony, of all people, said, "That's sad." She seemed to

mean it, hugging herself and shaking her head, repeating the words. "That's sad. That's sad."

"But you got your hospital," Varner offered. "Didn't it help?"

In a fashion. Sitta explained, "It didn't weather its storage very well. Some systems never worked. Autodocs failed without warning. Of course, all the biosynthesizing gear had been ripped out on Mars. And I didn't have any real medical training, which meant I did a lot of guessing when there was no other choice . . . guessing wrong, more than not. . . ."

Suddenly she couldn't breathe, couldn't speak.

Nobody liked the topic, save Bosson. Yet no one knew how to talk about anything else.

The Mercurian approached, hands reaching for her belly, then having the good sense to hesitate. "Why carry the baby yourself? Your hospital must have had wombs—"

"They were stolen." He must know that for himself. "Before the hospital arrived, they were removed."

Icenice asked, "Why?"

"Terrans," said Bosson, "breed as they live. Like rats."

An incandescent rage was building inside Sitta, and she enjoyed it, relishing the clarity it afforded her. Almost smiling, she told them, "Biosynthetic machinery could do wonders for them. But of course we won't let them have anything sophisticated, since they might try to hurt us. And that means that if you want descendants, you've got to make as many babies as possible, as fast as possible, hoping that some of them will have the right combinations of genes for whatever happens in their unpredictable lives."

"Let them die," was Bosson's verdict.

Sitta didn't care about him. He was just another child of the war, unremarkable, virtually insignificant. What drew her rage was the innocent faces of the others. What made her want to explode was Varner's remote schoolboy logic, his most pragmatic voice saying, "The provisional government is temporary. When it leaves, the Earth can elect its own representatives, then make its own laws—"

"Never," Bosson promised. "Not in ten thousand years."

Sitta took a breath, held it, then slowly exhaled.

"What else did you do?" asked Icenice, desperate for good news. "Did you travel? You must have seen famous places."

As if she'd been on vacation. Sitta shook her head, then admitted, "I was picked as a jurist. Many times. Being a jurist is an honor."

"For trials?" asked Pony.

"Of a kind."

People fidgeted, recalling Sitta's trial.

"Jurists," she explained, "are trusted people who watch friends giving birth." She waited for a moment, then added, "I was doing that job before I had my hospital."

"But what did you do?" asked one of the Twins.

They didn't know. A glance told her as much, and Sitta enjoyed the suspense, allowing herself a malicious smile before saying, "We used all kinds of parasites in the war. Tailored and sleek. Some burrow into fetuses, using them as raw material for whatever purpose the allies could dream up."

No one blinked.

"The parasites are good at hiding. Genetically camouflaged, in essence. The jurist's job is to administer better tests after the birth, and if there's any problem, she has to kill the baby."

There was a soft, profound gasp.

"Jurists are armed," she continued, glancing at Bosson and realizing that even he was impressed. "Some parasites can remake the newborn, giving it claws and coordination."

The Mercurian showed a serene pleasure. "Ever see such a monster?"

"Several times," said the retired Plowsharer. "But most of the babies, the infected ones, just sit up and cough, then look at you. The worms are in their brains, in their motor and speech centers. 'Give up,' they say. 'You can't win,' they say. 'You can't fight us. Surrender.'"

She waited for an instant.

Then she added, "They usually can't say, 'Surrender.' It's too long, too complicated for their mouths. And besides, by then they're being swung against a table or a wall. By the legs. Like this. If you do it right, they're dead with one good blow." And now she was weeping, telling Icenice, "Give me one of your old dolls. I'll show you just how I did it."

Sitta expected to leave after her mandatory three years of service. To that end, she fashioned a calendar and counted the days, maintaining that ritual until early in her third year, sometime after the long-promised hospital arrived.

Expectations climbed with the new facility. At first, Sitta thought it was the city's expectations that made her work endless hours, patching wounds when the autodocs couldn't keep up, curing nameless diseases with old legal medicines, and tinkering with software never before field-tested. Then in her last month, in sight of freedom, it occurred to her that the Terrans were happy for any help, even ineffectual help, and if all she did was sit in the hospital's cramped office, making shit and keeping the power on, nobody would have complained, and nobody would have thought any less of her.

She applied for a second term on the stipulation that she could remain at her current post. This set off alarms in the provisional capital. Fearing insanity or some involvement in illegal operations, the government sent a representative from Athens. The Martian, a tiny and exhausted woman, made no secret of her suspicions. She inspected the hospital several times, hunting for biosynthetic equipment, then for any medicines too new to be legal. Most apparent was her hatred for Farsiders. "When I was a girl," she reported, "I heard about you people. I heard what you did to us, to all your 'allies' . . . and just because of profit. . . !"

Sitta remained silent, passive. She knew better than to risk an argument.

"I don't know who I hate worse," said the woman. "Terran rats, or Farside leeches."

In the calmest of voices, Sitta asked, "Will you let this leech stay with her rats? Please?"

It was allowed, and the Plowsharers were so pleased that they sent promises of two more hospitals that never materialized. It was Sitta who purchased and imported whatever new medical equipment she could find, most of it legal. The next three years passed in a blink. She slept three hours on a good night, and she managed to lift life spans in the city to an average of thirteen and a half years. With her next reapplication, she asked Athens for permission to remain indefinitely. They sent a new Martian with the same reliable hatreds, but he found reasons to enjoy her circumstances. "Isn't it ironic?" he asked, laughing aloud. "Here you are, waging war against the monsters that your own parents developed. The monsters that made you rich in the first place. And according to import logs, you've been using that wealth to help the victims. Ironies wrapped in ironies, aren't they?"

She agreed, pretending that she'd never noticed any of it before.

"Stay as long as you want," the government man told her. "This looks like the perfect place for you."

Remaining on the Earth, by her own choice, might be confused for forgiveness. It wasn't. It was just that the dimensions of her hatreds had become larger, more worldly. Instead of being betrayed by friends and wrongfully punished, Sitta had begun to think of herself as fortunate. Almost blessed. She felt wise and moral, at least in certain dangerous realms. Who else from Farside held pace with her accomplishments? No one she could imagine, a kind of pride making her smile, in private.

Free of Farside, Sitta heard every awful story about her homeland. Every Martian and Mercurian seemed to relish telling about the bombardment of Nearside, in those first horrible days, and how convoys of refugees had reached the border, only to be turned away. In those remote times, Farside was a collection of mining camps and telescopes, and there wasn't room for everyone. Only the wealthiest could immigrate. That was Sitta's family story. Every official she came across seemed to have lost some part of his or her family. On Nearside. Or Mars. Or Ganymede. Even on Triton. And why? Because Sitta's repulsive ancestors needed to build mansions and jungles for themselves. "We don't have room," Farsiders would complain. And who dared argue the point? During the war, which world could risk offending Farside, losing its portion of the weapons and other essentials?

None took the risk; yet none would forget.

The naive, superficial girl who had murdered a helpless beetle was gone. The hardened woman in her stead felt an outrage and a burning potent taste for anything that smacked of justice. Yet never, even in passing, did she think of vengeance. It never occurred to her that she would escape the battered plain. Some accident, some mutated bug, would destroy her. It was a simple matter of time and the proper circumstances.

Then came an opportunity, a miraculous one, in the form of a woman traveling alone. Eight months into a pregnancy that was too perfect, if anything, she was discovered by a local health office and brought to the hospital for a mandatory examination. Sitta had help from her own fancy equipment, plus the boy who had once happily collected her morning stool. He was her protégé. He happened to find the telltale cell in the fetus. In a soft, astonished voice, he said, "God, we're lucky to have caught it. Just imagine that this one got free. . . !"

She heard nothing else that he said, nor the long silence afterward. Then Thomas touched her arm — they were lovers by then — and in a voice that couldn't have been more calm, Sitta told him, "It's time, I think. I think I need to go home."

Dinner was meat wrapped in luxurious vegetables and meat meant to stand alone, proud and spicy, and there were wines and chilled water from the Central Sea and milk too sweet to be more than sipped, plus great platters full of cakes and frosted biscuits and sour candies and crimson puddings. A hundred people could have eaten their fill at the long table, but as it turned out, no one except Bosson had an appetite. Partially dismantled carcasses were carried away by the kitchen's robots; goblets were drained just once in an hour's time. Perhaps it was related to the stories Sitta told at dinner. Perhaps her friends were a little perturbed by the recipes involving rats and spiders and other treasured vermin. For dessert, she described the incident with Thomas and her bodily wastes, adding that they'd become lovers when he was a well-worn fourteen. Only Bosson seemed appreciative of her tales, if only for their portrait of misery; and Sitta discovered a grudging half-fondness for the man, both of them outsiders, both educated in certain hard and uncompromising matters. Looking only at Bosson, Sitta explained how Thomas had carelessly inhaled a forty-year-old weapon, its robotic exterior cutting through an artery, allowing its explosive core to circumnavigate his body perhaps a hundred times before it detonated, liquefying his brain.

She began the story with a flat matter-of-fact voice. It cracked once when Thomas collapsed, then again when she described—in precise, professional detail—how she had personally harvested the organs worth taking. The boy's skin was too old and weathered to make quality leather; it was left in place. Then the body was dropped into the day's grave, sixteen others beneath it, Sitta given the honor of the final words and the ceremonial first gout of splintered rock and sand.

She was weeping at the end of the story. She wasn't loud or undignified, and her grief had a manageable, endurable quality about it. Like any Terran, she knew that outliving your lover was the consequence of living too long. It was something to endure. Yet even as she dried her face, she noticed the devastation and anger on the other faces. Save Bosson's. She had ruined the last pretense of a good time for them, and with that she thought: *Good. Perfect!*

But her dear friends remained at the table. No one slunk away. Not even the strangers invented excuses or appointments, begging to escape. Instead, Varner decided to take control to the best of his ability, coughing into a trembling fist, then whispering, "So." Another cough. "So," he began, "now that you're back, and safe . . . any ideas. . . ?"

What did he mean?

Reading the question on Sitta's face, he said, "I was thinking. We all were, actually . . . thinking of asking if you'd like to come in with us . . . in making an investment, or two. . . ."

Sitta sat back, hearing the delicious creaking of old wood. With a careful, unmeasurable voice, she said, "What kind of investment?"

Pony blurted, "There are fortunes to be made."

"If you have capital," said a stranger, shooing away a begging monkey.

Another stranger muttered something about courage, though the word he used was "balls."

Varner quieted them with a look, a gesture. Then he stared at Sitta, attempting charm but falling miserably short. "It's just . . . as it happens, just now . . . we have a possibility, love —"

"A dream opportunity," someone interrupted.

Sitta said, "It must be," and hesitated. Then she added, "Considering all the trouble that you've gone through, it must seem like a wondrous possibility."

Blank uncertain faces.

Then Varner said, "I know this is fast. I know, and we aren't happy about that. We'd love to give you time to rest, to unwind . . . but it's such a tremendous undertaking —"

"Quick profits!" barked a Twin.

"— and you know, just now, listening to your stories . . . it occurred to me that you could put your profits back into that city where you were living, or back into the Plowsharers in general —"

"Hey, that's a great idea!" said another stranger.

"A fucking waste," Bosson grumbled.

"You could do all sorts of good," Varner promised, visibly pleased with his inspiration. "You could buy medicines. You could buy machinery. You could put a thousand robots down there —"

"Robots are illegal," said Bosson. "Too easy to misuse."

"Then hire people. Workers. Anyone you need!" Varner almost rose to his feet, eyes pleading with her. "What do you think, Sitta? You're back, but that doesn't mean you can't keep helping your friends."

"Yeah," said Pony, "what do you think?"

Sitta waited for an age, or an instant. Then, with a calm slow voice, she asked, "Exactly how much do you need?"

Varner swallowed, hesitated.

One of the Twins blurted an amount, then added, "Per share. This new corporation is going to sell shares. In just a few weeks."

"You came at the perfect time," said his brother, fingers tapping on the tabletop.

Varner nodded, then admitted, "The deal is still sweeter. If you could loan us enough to purchase our own shares, then we will pay it back to you. How does twice the normal interest sound?"

Bosson whispered, "Idiotic."

Icenice was bending at the waist, gasping for breath.

"You can make enough to help millions." Varner offered a watery smile. "And we can make it possible for you."

Sitta crossed her legs, then asked, "What does a share buy?"

Silence.

"What does this corporation do?" she persisted.

Pony said, "They've got a wonderful scheme."

"They want to build big new lasers," said a Twin. "Similar to the old weapons, only safe."

Safe? Safe how?

"We'll build them at the Earth's Lagrangian points," Varner explained. "Enormous solar arrays will feed the lasers, millions of square kilometers absorbing sunlight—"

"Artificial suns," someone blurted.

"—and we'll be able to warm every cold world. For a substantial fee, of course." Varner grinned, his joy boyish. Fragile. "Those old war technologies, and our factories, can be put to good use."

"At last!" shouted the Twins, in one voice.

Bosson began to laugh, and Icenice, sitting opposite her husband, seemed to be willing herself to vanish.

"Whose scheme is this?" Sitta asked Varner. "Yours?"

"I wish it was," he responded.

"But Farsiders are in command," said Pony, fists lifted as if in victory. "All the big old families are pooling their resources, but since this project is so vast and complicated—"

"Too vast and complicated," Bosson interrupted.

Sitta looked at Icenice. "How about you, darling? How many shares have you purchased?"

The pretty face dropped, eyes fixed on the table's edge.

"Let's just say," her husband replied, "that their most generous offer has been rejected by this household. Isn't that what happened, love?"

Icenice gave a tiny, almost invisible nod.

Pony glared at both of them, then asked Sitta, "Are you interested?"

"Give her time," Varner snapped. Then he turned to Sitta, making certain that she noticed his smile. "Think it through, darling. Please just do that much for us, will you?"

What sane world would allow another world to build it a sun? she wondered. And after the long war, who could trust anyone with such enormous powers? Maybe there were safeguards and political guarantees, the full proposal rich with logic and vision. But those questions stood behind one great question. Clearing her throat, Sitta looked at the hopeful faces, then asked, "Just why do you need my money?"

No one spoke; the room was silent.

And Sitta knew why, in an instant, everything left transparent. Simple. They wanted her money because they had none, and they were desperate enough to risk whatever shred of pride they had kept from the old days. How had they become poor? What happened to the old estates and the bottomless bank accounts? Sitta was curious, and she knew she could torture them with her questions; yet suddenly, without warning, she had no taste for that kind of vengeance. The joy was gone. Before even one weak excuse could be made, by Varner or anyone, she said with a calm and slow, almost gentle voice, "My money has been spent."

A chill gripped her audience.

"I used it to help my hospital. Some of the equipment was illegal, and that means bribes." A pause. "I couldn't buy ten shares for just me. I'm afraid that you've wasted your time, friends."

The faces were past misery. All the careful hopes and earnest plans had evaporated, no salvation waiting, the audience too exhausted to move, too unsure of itself to speak.

Finally, with a mixture of rage and agony, one of the strangers climbed to her feet, saying, "Thank you for the miserable dinner, Icenice."

She and the other strangers escaped from the room and house.

Then the Twins spun a lie about a party, leaving and taking Vechel with them. Had Vechel spoken a single word today? Sitta couldn't remember. She looked at Pony, and Pony asked, "Why did you come home?"

For an instant, Sitta didn't know why.

"You hate us," the girl observed. "It's obvious how much you hate this place. Don't deny it!"

How could she?

"Fucking bitch. . . !"

Then Pony was gone. There was no other guest but Varner, and he sat with his eyes fixed on his unfinished meal, his face pale and somehow indifferent. It was as if he still didn't understand what had happened. Finally Icenice rose and went to Varner, taking him in her arms and whispering something, the words or her touch giving him reason to stand. From where she sat, Sitta could watch the two of them walk out on the stone porch. She kept hugging him, always whispering, then wished him good-bye, waiting for him to move out of her sight. Bosson watched his wife, his face remote. Unreadable. Then Icenice returned, sitting in the most distant chair, staring at some concoction of mints and cultured meat that had never been touched—

—and Bosson, with a shrill voice, remarked, "I warned you. I told you and your friends that she'd never be interested." A pause, a grin. "What did I tell you? Repeat it for me."

Icenice stood and took the platter of meat in both hands, flinging it at her husband.

Bosson was nothing but calm, confidently measuring the arc and knowing it would fall short. But the sculpted meat shattered, a greasy white sauce in its center, still hot and splattering like shrapnel. It struck Bosson's clothes and arms and face. He gave a flinch. Nothing more. Then, not bothering to wipe himself clean, he turned to Sitta, and with a voice that made robots sound emotional, said:

"Be the good guest. Run off to your room. Now. Please."

12 Thomas's death was tragic, yet perfect.

Nobody else knew what Sitta was carrying. The original mother thought her baby had come early and died. The hospital's AI functions had been taken offline, leaving them innocent. No one but Thomas could have betrayed her, and it was his horrible luck to inhale a killing mote of dust. By accident? Sometimes she asked herself if it was that simple. Toward the end, the boy would wonder aloud if this was what Sitta truly wanted, and if it was right. Maybe he became careless by distraction, or maybe it was so that he couldn't act on his doubts. Or maybe it was just what it had seemed to be at first glance. An accident. A brutal little residue of the endless war, and why couldn't she just accept it?

Constructed in the final years of official fighting, the parasite within her was a particularly wicked ensemble. Designed to be invisible to Terran jurists and their instruments, it carried its true self within just one in a million cells. But in the time between her first labor pains and the delivery, each of those cells would explode, invading their neighbors, implanting genetics in a transformation that would leave no outward sign of change, much less danger.

The monster would be born pale and irresistible. Perhaps the finest baby ever seen, people would think, wrapping it in a blanket and holding it close to their breasts.

That appearance was a fiction. Beneath the baby fat was a biosynthetic factory that would absorb and transmute every kind of microbe. Mothers and jurists would sicken in a few hours, their own native flora turned against them. No immune system could cope with such a thorough, coordinated assault. A village or city could be annihilated in a day, and with ample stocks of rotting liquefied meat, the monster would nurse, growing at an impossible pace, becoming for all intents and purposes a three-year-old girl, mobile enough to wander, mute and big-eyed and lovely.

It was a weapon made in many labs, including her parents'. That was no huge coincidence; Sitta had seen many examples of their work. But it helped her resolve. If justice was a simple matter of balance, then both were being achieved.

It was a weapon rarely used and never discussed publicly. As far as Sitta could determine, no medical authority had seen it in the last fifteen years, although several isolated villages had died in mysterious unnamed epidemics, one of them within a thousand kilometers of her city. What would Farside do with such a monster? she asked herself. Its people had little experience with real disease, and if anything, the moon was a richer target for this kind of horror. Where the Earth had few species and tiny populations, Farside had diversity and multitudes. Each beetle and orchid and monkey had its own family of microbes. A thousand parallel plagues would cause an ecological collapse, the domed air left poisoned, the Central Sea struck dead. Here was an ultimate apocalyptic revenge, and Sitta was astonished by her hatreds, by the depth of her feelings and the cold calculating passion she brought to this work.

Sometimes doubts made her awaken in the middle of the night, in a sweat. Then her habit was to walk under the seamless black sky, taking the wide road to the cemetery, reading the simple tombstones with her lamp, noting the dates and trying to recall who was below her feet. The Earth itself was entombed in a grave, alone, and the heated air made Sitta think of ten billion bodies, and more, rotting in the useless ground. How could she feel weakness? she asked herself. By what right?

Given such a mandate, she had no choice but to continue, turning back with a resolve, feeling her way down to the city and along its narrow streets. That's what she did on her last night in the city, the shuttle for Athens scheduled for the morning. Her bag was packed. She was wearing her travel clothes. Approaching her bunkerlike home, lost in thought, Sitta didn't notice the children at work. She was almost past them when some sound, some little voice, caught her attention, making her turn and lift her lamp's beam, dozens of faces caught in midsmile. What were these girls and boys doing here? She muttered, "You should be sleeping." Then she hesitated, lifting the beam higher still, every bunker festooned with long dirty ribbons and colored ropes and stiff old flags. "What is this?" she whispered, speaking to herself. "Why. . . ?"

Then she knew. An instant before her audience broke into song and a ragged cheer, she realized this was for her, all of it, and they hadn't expected her so soon. These were people unaccustomed to celebrations, who had few holidays, if any; and suddenly Sitta felt her legs tremble, then give way beneath her, knees into the foot-packed earth and her eyes blind with tears. Hundreds of children poured into the street, parents at their heels. Everyone was singing, no one competent and everyone loud, and what surprised Sitta more than anything was the realization—abrupt; amazing—that these were genuinely happy people.

In the hospital, she saw them wounded or ill, or dead. Those were the people she understood best.

Yet here she saw people more healthy than hurt, and more grateful than she could believe, everyone touching her, every hand on her swollen belly, every joyous shout giving her another dose of luck, the burden of all this luck and gratitude making it impossible for her to stand, much less turn and run for home.

13. Obeying Bosson, not caring what happened, Sitta climbed halfway up the staircase before she paused, standing beside sunlight, turning when she heard a whimper or moan. Was it Icenice? No, it was one of the begging monkeys. She looked past it, waiting for a long moment, telling herself that regardless of what she heard, she would do nothing. This wasn't her home, nor her world—she was here to destroy all of them—and then she was walking, watching her shoes on the long steps, aware in a distant, dreamy way that she was walking downhill, reentering the dining room just as Bosson finished binding his wife's hands to one of the table's legs.

The Mercurian didn't notice his audience. With smooth, practiced deliberation, he lifted Icenice's gown over her hips and head, the girl motionless as stone, her naked back and rump shining in the reflected light. Then Bosson stood over the table, selecting tools. He decided on a spoon and a blunt knife. Then he moved behind the thin rump, wiping his face clean with a sleeve, coughing once, and placing the blade against the pucker of her rectum.

He was twenty years her senior and accustomed to the moon's gentle gravity, and he was taken by surprise. Sitta struck him on the side of the head, turning him, then struck his belly and kicked him twice, aiming for his testicles, Earth-trained muscles making Bosson grunt, then collapse onto an elegant floor of colored tiles and pink mortar.

"Get up," she advised.

He tried to find his balance, halfway standing, Sitta driving her foot hard into his chin.

Again she said, "Get up."

"Sitta?" whispered Icenice.

Bosson grunted, rose.

She drew blood this time. A cheekbone shattered beneath her heel. Then the man lay still, hands limp around his bloody head, and Sitta screamed, "What's the matter with you? Can't you even stand up, you fuck?"

With the weakest of voices, Icenice asked, "What is happening?"

Sitta pulled the gown back where it belonged, then untied the napkins used to bind her hands. Her onetime friend looked at Bosson, then with genuine horror said, "You shouldn't have. . . !"

Knotting the napkins together, Sitta made a crude rope, then knelt and tied the groggy man's hands and feet behind him. When she stood again, she felt weak. Almost faint. When Icenice tried to clean Bosson's wounds, Sitta grabbed her and pulled her toward the stairs, panting as she asked, "Why? Why did you marry it?"

"I was in such debt. You don't know." Icenice swallowed, moaned. "He promised to help me—"

"How could you lose all that money? Where did it go?"

"Oh," she whimpered, "it seemed to go everywhere, really."

Reasons didn't matter. What mattered was bringing Icenice upstairs, the two of them moving through the shafts of sunlight.

"Everyone had debts," the girl was explaining. "I mean, we didn't know enough about modern business, and the Martians . . . they seemed very good at taking our money. . . !"

Sitta said, "Hurry up."

"Where are we going?"

"Hurry!"

Her bag was where the robot had set it, on the bed, still unopened. She unfastened the latches and threw its contents on the floor, then used a tiny cosmetic blade to cut into the thick bottom layers. What wouldn't appear in any scan was half a dozen lozenges of leather, their pores filled with hormones and odd chemicals that nobody would consider illegal. She had made them in her hospital. Hesitating for an instant, she looked at Icenice and tried to decide the best way to do this thing.

"Varner wanted your money," said the girl.

"Come on. Into the bath."

"Why?"

"Now! Hurry!" She was scared that someone was watching them. She thought of the Belter with the dogs, wondering if she had shadowed them all this way. Stripping as she walked, Sitta ended up naked, wading into the clear warm water, down to her chest before looking up at Icenice. "You have to climb in with me. Do it."

The girl asked, "Why?"

Sitta made the lozenges when she couldn't sleep one night. What if she found herself giving birth in the wrong place? The possibility had awakened her with a shudder. What if she found herself trapped on the Earth, whatever the reason, and this monster of hers was threatening the people whom she loved most?

How could she protect the innocent ones?

"I don't understand." The girl was weeping, quietly devastated by the day's events. "Why are you taking a bath now?"

One by one, Sitta swallowed the lozenges, gulping bathwater to help get each of them down.

"Sitta?"

The whole process would take half an hour, maybe less. In minutes, the first of the drugs would cross into the fetus, crippling its genetic machinery—she hoped—giving her long enough to let the miscarriage run its course. The danger was that she would lose consciousness. The horror of horrors was that the monster would live long enough to outlast the antigenetics, then somehow climb to the air and out of the bath, premature but coping regardless, its transformation happening despite her desperate best wishes. That would be the ironic, horrible end—

"Sitta?"

—and Sitta looked up at Icenice, then said, "In. Climb in."

The girl obeyed, still wearing her gown, the black fabrics

blacker when soaked, billowing up around her waist, then covering her breasts.

"You're my jurist," said Sitta, looking straight into Icenice's eyes. "When it comes, drown it. Don't let it take a breath."

"What do you mean—?"

"Promise me!"

"Oh, my." Icenice straightened, as if stabbed by a needle.

"Promise?"

"I can try," she squeaked.

"You have to do it, darling. Or the world dies."

The words were believed. Sitta could see their impact and their slow digestion, the girl becoming thoughtful, alert. A minute passed. Several minutes passed. Then Icenice attempted a weak little smile, telling her friend, "I've never wanted your money."

A single red pain began in Sitta's pelvis, racing up her spine.

"And I've always wanted to tell you," the girl went on. "When you were sentenced, and only you would be going to the Earth, I knew that was best for everyone, really."

Wincing, Sitta asked, "Why?"

"Nobody else could have survived. Not for three years!"

"And I was safe?"

"You did survive," Icenice responded, then again tried her smile. "You always had a toughness, a strength, that I've wanted. Even back when we were little girls."

Pain came twice, *boom* and *boom*.

"I'm not strong," Icenice said with conviction.

When was I strong? thought Sitta. What did the girl see in me?

Then more pain. *BOOM.*

And when it passed, she grabbed the ruined gown, pulling her friend in close to her, wrapping arms around her, and whispering with her most certain voice, "When the time comes, I'll kill it myself."

"Because I don't think I could," Icenice whimpered.

"But can you stay?"

"Here? With you?"

Sitta winced, then pleaded, "Don't leave me!"

"I won't. I promise."

Then pains began in earnest, and every pain before them, reaching back through Sitta's entire life, were just careful preparation for the scorching white miseries inside her, trying to escape.

TO CHURCH WITH MR. MULTHIFORD

T WAS everybody's idea.

Or maybe it was nobody's.

Maybe it's that ideas drift in the air like gas, and beer and boredom worked on us to where we could catch hold of that particular notion. Sometimes I think that's what happens: Ideas are invisible clouds that get trapped inside people's heads. Different-shaped heads trap different ones, which explains a helluva lot. Here in Pelican County we've got a lot of simple round heads, if you know what I mean. Here it pays to be perfectly average. And if you happen to get stuck with a fancy-shaped head—one that catches goofy ideas—then you'd best keep a hat on it.

If you know what I mean.

Habit is everything in this part of the world; nothing wants to change.

Our Saturday night habit was to go somewhere peaceful, like the cemetery, and drink beer. Which is what we were doing when the idea found us. Pat started things off, saying, "I'm bored."

Charlie belched and said, "Yeah, why don't we pull something?" A prank, he meant. Detergent in the town pool, trees dressed up with toilet paper. That's the sort of stuff we specialized in. But that night somehow felt different, and we couldn't get excited about ordinary shit.

We had ourselves another round of beers, and I stared up at the stars, feeling smaller than small; and finally, after clearing his throat of a big loud gob of something, Lester said, "I know. Let's make ourselves a crop circle."

Charlie belched again—he's famous for his gassy sounds— then reminded us, "It's been done."

Not by us, but he was right. Pelican County is famous for its crop circles, and everyone knew who made them.

Old Man Multhiford, I was thinking. And just like that I knew what we could do. The idea settled in my head, and I giggled, and I said, "Hey, let's make a circle out on Multhiford's place!"

Pat straightened, eyes getting big and round. "On *his* farm? Are you fucking serious?"

Multhiford put maybe half of the circles on his own land. That was common knowledge. It was also known that he was insane and probably dangerous. If he spoke to you, he spoke about corn. His corn; all corn. I'd seen him talking on and on about its beauty and importance and how it was holy. Field of Loopy Dreams nonsense. Myself, I tried avoiding the man. If I saw him in town, I turned and slipped away. Even when my dad, the local Methodist minister, told me I was being rude. I didn't care. Madmen scare the piss out of me. Which is why our plan sounded fun, I suppose.

And the beer didn't hurt my mood, either.

"We aren't going to do it," Pat kept saying.

"Why not?" Charlie growled. "I like the plan!"

"Yeah," said Lester, "we'll put a circle in his own damned field. Nobody ever has."

"Who lived to tell it," Pat muttered. But it was three against one, no more need for debate. We loaded up Pat's old pickup with shovels and ropes and lengths of lumber. Lester rode with the tools. I sat between Pat and Charlie. Driving out into the country, the three of us talked about how to do it and do it fast—how do you make a flattened circle in the middle of a cornfield, in the dark, on a madman's property—and it was Charlie who pointed out, "It doesn't have to be a circle. Is that some law? Why don't we mash down something simple, like a message? We can leave words in his corn."

"Take Me To Your Leader," Pat joked, laughing.

It seemed funny to them, and decided. To me words sounded a lot less pretty than a circle, but I knew they'd vote me down. That's why I didn't complain, riding quietly there between them.

Eventually, we came to a low rise, barely worth noticing, and after that the ground started dropping, sliding into what used to be marshes. Past the next corner was Multhiford's land, and Pat killed the headlights, driving by moonlight, and all of us started looking for someplace to turn off and set to work.

The mood in the cab was getting a lot more serious. On both sides of us were enormous fields of corn, green oceans of the sun-fattened stalks. Another half mile ahead was Multhiford's farm-house, set off the road in the only patch of trees on his section and a half. Where in all this nothing could we hide the pickup? Behind a little machine shed, we decided, and Pat parked and killed the engine, everyone taking a deep breath before climbing to earth.

I don't know much about corn—I'm as urban as you get in Pelican County—but Multhiford's corn looked particularly tall and happy, standing in all that rich black marsh soil, moving the way corn does at night. Big leaves were uncurling in the cooling air. Hundreds of acres were uncurling, and I stood off by myself, listening. I didn't hear the guys talking. I never noticed Charlie sneaking up on me. Grabbing my arms, he said, "Boo."

"Hey," I sputtered.

He handed me a length of pine and a dirty mess of hemp rope. "You make the F," he said. "That's your job."

"What F?" I asked.

"We took a vote. Take Me To Your Leader is too long." Probably true. "But if we make four big letters—"

"What?!" I snapped. I mean, I'm a minister's son. There are things I can sort of do, and things I can never do.

"But it won't take long," Charlie promised.

What started as clever vandalism was becoming something more ordinary, and if I was caught, no doubt about it, my punishment was going to verge on the Eternal.

The guys started walking off into the corn.

When I didn't go with them, it was Lester who got sent back. "All you do is the F," he argued, trying to sound reasonable. "Did Charlie even tell you what the letters were?"

"I figured U, C, and K," I said. Somehow innocence didn't sound like an excuse. "Unless you're going to spell farm or funk. Is that what we're doing here?"

Lester shook his head, disappointed with me. "If you want, stay with the truck." He showed me a smile. One day he's going to be a killer salesman. "If Multhiford shows, give us a couple warning honks."

F or not, I was involved. And I didn't want to wait around for that old farmer. That's why I followed the others, carrying my board and rope up close to my body, walking between the rows of tall corn. We went a couple hundred yards into the field, then huddled, deciding how to do it. "We need it seen from the air," Charlie kept saying, sketching FUCK in the soil. "Hundred-foot letters. Think they'll get noticed?"

Think they'll be easy? I thought. Cutting through the rows, I paced off what felt like the right distance, then turned and started pushing over three rows at once. I was using my pine board and my muscles, but the plants were sturdy, fighting me all the way. I kept getting tired, kept losing my breath. I'd have to stop and stand, my back aching, my ears humming, and after a few breaks like that, the others had moved out ahead of me, and I couldn't feel more alone.

What I was doing felt wrong. Plain, simple wrong. And that feeling is what made me tired, guilt having its way of sapping me. It wasn't particularly late, the moon mostly full and hanging in the east, shining through a silvery haze. The air inside the corn was still, like a breath being held. It tasted thick and humid, full of living smells and weed killers. I was a town boy out where he didn't belong, all right. Turning, I tried to see the road, but all the world was corn, and I couldn't see anything but the silky tops and the stars, and the blackness between the stars, too.

Working again, I thought I heard an engine running. But when I stopped I couldn't hear anything but Charlie moving back along the big U he was building, pushing down more rows and never stopping. I was way, way behind. I made myself finish the stem of my F, then I turned and looked up, and just then I saw the sudden bright beam of a flashlight.

"Scared enough to piss your pants." I've said those words a hundred times, but I didn't think it was possible. Until then. I almost pissed mine, I'll tell you. Urine started trying to sneak right out of me.

Then I heard a crunching sound and a voice that didn't belong to any seventeen-year-old kid. "Stop right there," it said, deep and strong. "You boys stop."

It was astonishingly loud for not being a shout, and it had the wrong effect on us. We started to run. I heard Pat shout, "It's him!" and Charlie screamed, "He's got a gun!" Then the gun was fired. Playing it back in my head, I think Multhiford aimed at the moon. I know the shot passed over me, and I was running like a maniac, heading back along the rows of downed corn. My feet caught in the bent stalks. My head pitched forward. What I'd knocked down knocked me down now, and suddenly I took a big dive into the best farmland in the world.

I can't tell you how long I was down. Fear and the beer helped keep me on my belly; my heart was pounding hard enough that I wondered if Dad could hear it. The running sounds died away, which was good news. I kept still, praying to go unseen. Then Pat laid into the horn, begging me to hurry.

Multhiford answered with a second blast—another tall one—and I realized he was standing ten yards from me. Maybe less. Which was why I got up and ran again, picking a new direction. Tearing crosswise through the corn, I ran blind, getting no closer to the pickup for my trouble.

There were more honks, then the pickup coughed and accelerated, the guys having no choice but to leave me.

And I dropped from exhaustion, rolling onto my back and no fight left in me. I lay there looking up at the towering corn plants, telling myself to keep still and wait, marshaling my energies for the walk home. It was just a five-mile walk, I was thinking. I promised myself to cut down on my drinking and study hard in the fall, and all that. Then I heard a man walking through his corn. Coming closer. And just when I needed to be quiet, I got a piercing ache in my belly, and the ache wanted to move, demanding to be let out.

That's what I was doing when Multhiford found me.

Beer can be a bad idea, and what you catch you can also throw away. The farmer found me heaving and coughing, vomit under my face. He shone his flashlight on me, and I turned, aware of his gun and his lean little body. I thought he would kill me out of hand. I just assumed that crazy men don't have trouble committing murder.

Except he didn't shoot. All he did was say, "I know you."

I coughed again, no strength left in me.

Then he said, "Get up," and gave his shotgun a twirl. "And quit the running. I know exactly who you are."

Fame is fame, no matter where it happens.

Strangers know the famous person too well, and they don't know him at all. Like with my father, for example. He's been the Methodist minister for years, and he's considered to be the most Christian man in the county. He's got what a minister should have—a pleasant wife and a good and pretty daughter—but to make things fair, he's also got a half-wild son. I guess I'm some kind of test for Dad, and since my infractions are mostly tiny, I'm a test that he's passing. Maybe not in God's eyes, but at least in the local ones.

The town doesn't love Dad, but it admires him. Which is the harder trick, if you know Pelican City.

Yet Dad's not the perfect Christian everyone imagines. I won't claim he drinks or loves the ladies or puts on Mom's makeup and pumps. What I mean is that he has doubts. About God and himself, mostly. About the things people think ministers should trust in and accept with every Christian breath, every second of their eternal lives.

Early this summer I was reading in the den, and Dad came and sat, announcing, "I just saw Clarence Multhiford." He waited for half a beat, then added, "At Wal-Mart." As if that would help me understand why this was news. Then, after a long look, he said, "We talked. We had quite the conversation."

"About corn, I bet."

"Sometimes," Dad admitted. "He said that his crop is doing well, but Henshaw planted late and the Jacob brothers are sloppy. . . ."

That's Multhiford. He always has the good luck, and he always gives big advice. Which makes him about as popular as hailstones among our local seed-cap sect, I can tell you.

Dad gave me a stare, then said, "He asked about you."

"Who did?"

"Who are we talking about?"

I dropped my book, entirely surprised. "He doesn't even know me," I sputtered. Then, "What did the son of a bitch say?"

Dad's soft face turned disapproving. "Now, John," he began. "Didn't we agree that in this house—?"

"What did Multhiford ask about me?"

"How you were doing in school and where you might go to college." Dad gave a little sigh and shrug. "He suggested one of the Big Ten schools—"

"He doesn't know me," I complained.

"If he did know you," said Dad, "he'd know that you'll be lucky to reach the community college in Lanksville." And with that he gave me his patented disappointed glare, reminding me of last year's grades. "As for his interest . . . well, he's always had an eye for you."

"A what?"

"Don't you notice him watching?"

Me? *Me?* I didn't even want to think it.

"I know he comes to Sunday services now and again. He sits in the back and watches—"

"Not me! Not me!"

Grinning now, he said, "You have noticed, haven't you?"

Maybe, and maybe that's why I kept my distance from the madman. "Has he asked about me before?"

"Never," said Dad, without doubt.

I couldn't make sense of it. I didn't want to make sense of it. "Well, he's nuts. That's what that means."

Dad lifted his gaze, looking off into the distance. Then, with a certain care, he said, "I don't believe so. I know unbalanced people—I've tried to console them, without much luck—and I don't think Clarence resembles them very much."

I growled, thinking of those bright insane eyes staring at me. "Do sane men make circles in the middle of fields?"

"Does Mr. Multhiford do that?"

Of course he did. Everyone knew it.

"I believe in fungi," said Dad. "It attacks the stem, causing the plant to flatten." He spoke calmly, with all the authority of a gardener whose tomato plants died before August. "You know, there are old reports of circles. Older than *him*. Some date back to the 1890s."

"Made by flying saucers," I snapped.

"Have you heard Mr. Multhiford ever mention UFOs?"

How could I? I didn't have conversations with him, and I wasn't going to start now. "He makes the circles," I maintained. "People have seen him doing it."

"People see him driving at night, yes. They find him watching their fields, I agree. But nobody has ever caught him flattening anyone's crop." Dad shook his head. "It's got to be a fungus."

"That loves his farm best?"

"He has the perfect soil and the best hybrids. You see? It's just what the fungi love."

I'd had enough. I stood and asked, "Why should Multhiford care about me? I'll go to college, or I won't, and it's not his business."

Dad seemed to agree, but his voice trailed off before it got started. He sighed, glanced at his open hands, then sighed again. "I'm jealous of the man."

"Of who?"

"You know who." He looked straight at me. "Really, of all the people I know . . . I don't know anyone happier than Clarence Multhiford. . . ."

"He's crazy, Dad. Lead-poisoned nuts."

"Fine. Maybe that's the answer." Dad looked up at the ceiling, then asked both of us, "Can you imagine anything more terrible?

Two human beings hope a third human is mentally ill, and why? Because he's too happy and too different for their tastes."

He gave me a sad little smile. Dad's got one of those faces that aren't real comfortable with happiness.

"Isn't that a horrible way to think?" he asked me. "Can't you feel even a little shame, John?"

"I know exactly who you are," Multhiford warned me. He didn't sound like a particularly happy man, but then again, he didn't sound angry, either. I saw the big double-barreled shotgun in one hand, then his flashlight found my eyes, blinding me. "Stand on up, John. Please."

He did recognize me. One hope was dashed.

"What were you boys doing? Why'd you hurt my corn that way?"

I swallowed, stood. Trying to talk, I discovered that my voice had abandoned me.

"What were you doing in my field, John?"

"I don't know," I whispered. "I mean, I didn't hurt much. . . ."

"Didn't you?" He stepped closer, the glare of his light hiding his face. But I could see him by memory, the face lean and hard and red from the sun, crazy eyes burning in the middle of it. I could smell him, his earth and corn mixed together with his unwashed bachelorhood. First with his light, then his gun, he pointed off into the distance. "Why don't we walk to the road, John? You can lead. And please, don't hurt my corn anymore."

My legs felt heavy, mired in an invisible syrup.

The madman stayed behind me. "What would your father think if he knew you were here? Would he be proud of you?"

I tried to come up with something smart to say, but the best I could do was squeak, "Probably not."

"Maybe we should go tell him."

My legs stopped moving. For that instant, I'd rather have been shot dead than have Dad know what had happened.

"Let's make a deal," said Multhiford. "I won't press charges. I won't even mention this to anyone. We'll settle up tonight, and you'll be free and clear."

That sounded wonderful, for about two seconds. Then I imagined all kinds of debt-settling horrors, and I started walking again, breathing faster, picking up my pace.

"Like how?" I muttered.

"You can do some work for me."

"Tonight?"

"You don't look busy," he replied, his voice smiling. I could hear the smile in it, which made me angry. He was holding a gun at my back *and* feeling happy, which wasn't fair. "I need some heavy things moved, John, and I'd appreciate the help."

"My friends know I'm here," I blurted out. "If anything happens . . ."

"I understand." He didn't sound crazy. He sounded as if he genuinely understood everything, as if he was full of wisdom. Coming up beside me, walking on the other side of a green wall of cornstalks, he promised, "I'll have you home in time for early service."

Shit, it was Sunday morning, wasn't it? Glancing at my watch, I saw that it was past midnight. Even if I escaped now, I couldn't beat my one A.M. curfew.

But there wasn't any escape. Side by side, we stepped from the corn, the air turning cool and dry. I could breathe easier. Sounds felt sharper. Multhiford broke open his shotgun, two empty shells flying. He hadn't reloaded after firing at the moon, and realizing it made me feel even more defeated. Moonlight showed me that face that I remembered, the smile too big and happy, and his baling-wire body was dressed in ordinary farmer's clothes—jeans and comfortable boots and a simple shirt. "My truck's down this way." We walked together, him carrying his shotgun broken open, and after a little while he said, "It's a perfect night."

I said nothing.

"Perfect, perfect, perfect," he was saying.

I didn't offer any opinions.

"They'll come tonight, John." He took a deep breath, then said, "In a little while. Soon."

I looked at my feet, watching them move on the graveled road.

"Who's coming, John? Who do I mean?"

We reached his pickup—a big new Chevy; a rich farmer's toy—and I heard myself answering him. "Aliens in a flying hubcap," I said.

Multhiford looked at me, and he laughed, telling me, "How much you know is so close to zero, son." He shook his narrow head, enjoying himself. "So close we might as well call it *nothing*. And how do you like that?"

There's a certain book in the Pelican City library. I've never checked it out; I sneak it into a back corner, reading it when no one will notice. It's about crop circles, and it's got pictures from around the world. Half a dozen pictures show local circles, always from the air and mostly on Multhiford's land. I won't admit it to anyone, but I like looking at them. I don't believe in UFOs. Aliens have better places to be, I think. It's just that the circles and the other marks are kind of pretty, obvious and orderly against the bright green crops. I've even secretly admired Multhiford for his skill, working by moonlight, or less light, working by himself and making Pelican County into the crop circle capital of this hemisphere.

"Investigators" come through every spring and summer — wrong-looking, wrong-sounding people from California and the shadows of Stonehenge. It's not enough to say that we watch them with a certain suspicion. But to his credit, Multhiford won't have anything to do with them. I know this: If he was making circles *and* acting as a tour guide, then I think something bad would have happened to him long ago. If you know what I mean. I mean, if you keep your oddness inside the family, all is fine. But ask the world to watch, and the locals won't be so patient.

That library book barely mentions Multhiford. Just a quick paragraph saying that one farm has more circles than the others, and its owner — unnamed — has the best yields of any local farmer.

Year in, year out.

I've read that part twenty times, in secret, and honest to God, it never occurred to me just what that means.

We pulled off the county road, driving up to Multhiford's farmhouse. It was normal at a distance, tall and angular with the usual shade trees huddled around it. But the legends made me expect more, and sure enough, it wasn't long before I was noticing the statues.

The old farmer built them out of car parts, lumber, and crap from the local landfill. Nobody knew just why. No two were the same, but they all looked like weird corn, leaves oddly shaped and cobs oversized and their stalks twisted every which way. It was just like I'd heard, down to the general spookiness. I watched the statues watch me as we drove past, and I halfway expected them to pick up and move. To chase me, maybe.

Multhiford put us in reverse, backing in between two metal buildings.

We climbed down. I found myself staring at a stack of concrete blocks and chunks, rusted fingers of rebar sticking out here and there.

The tailgate dropped with a powerful crash. Multhiford told me, "I want you to fill it for me. Agreed?"

I picked up a little chunk and threw it in. It hit the plastic liner with a thunderous *boom*.

"Here," he said, "use these."

Work gloves fell at my feet. Putting them on, I smelled their owner on leather. Then I set to work, throwing in half a dozen blocks before I noticed the voice, quiet and steady and almost sane. Except the words themselves were anything but sane.

"People didn't domesticate corn," he said. "If you think about it."

I'd rather not, thank you.

"It's corn and the other crops that did the domesticating. They took wandering hunters and made them into farmers. They tamed a scarce ape and made it civilized." A pause, then he asked, "Why, John? Why did corn and wheat and the rest of them do it?"

I didn't think I was listening, but I stopped and looked at him, trying to find some kind of answer.

The farmer was standing safely off to one side, shaking his head. "Look at the world from the corn's eyes. It finds an ape to enslave. We serve it by plowing the ground and caring for it. We bring water, manure, and propagate its children for it. And the corn rewards us with food and wealth." He paused, taking a big breath. "Farming makes cities possible. Cities make armies possible. And the armies marched off to conquer new lands to plow and plant." Another pause, then he added, "For a tropical grass with no certain parent—a bastard, that's what corn is—it sure has done awfully well for itself. Don't you think?"

If someone had asked what I'd be doing tonight, I wouldn't have pictured myself flinging concrete and suffering through a loopy history lesson.

"The old empires thrived so long as they cared for their crops. You must know that from school, John. Greece. Rome. The Soviet Union. All failed as farmers; all succumbed. That's how our crops punish us when we can't keep them happy."

I paused in my work, telling myself that the pile was getting smaller.

"You don't believe me," said Multhiford. Then he gave a big laugh, asking, "Do I take care of my corn, or does the corn take care of Old Man Multhiford?"

I looked at the shiny new pickup, then out at the perfect rows of lush green grass. Suspecting a trick, I said, "I don't know."

"The ancients worshiped their crops," he offered. "Are we smarter, or are we less aware? Maybe what's happened, John, is that we're so thoroughly enslaved that we can't even see the obvious anymore."

With a half-block of concrete in my hands, I gave a silly shout.

"I'm nobody's slave!"

"You don't eat?" He laughed again. "Well, maybe not. I can't claim to have seen you at your supper table."

I threw the half-block on the pile, watching it roll and catch.

"Do you think much about the future, John?"

I wished he'd quit saying my name. I said, "Sometimes," and wished I hadn't. I started flinging concrete like someone possessed, grunting and groaning, making my arms and shoulders start to burn.

But Multhiford spoke with a big voice, no way to ignore him. "In the future," he said, "think what we'll do for our corn. Today, this minute, scientists are learning how to change its genetics, giving it extra ears and nitrogen nodules, then fancy leaves to suck up every drop of sunlight. We'll make it grow faster. It'll be tougher. We'll give it new jobs. Making medicines. Human hormones. Fancy clean fuels." He paused, then let out a big sigh. "You're a bright young man. I can tell that for myself."

I didn't respond, but I could feel his compliment worming into me.

"What I'm saying—listen, John—is that life will get richer for the corn. And for people, too. In a few centuries, both of us will be living on Mars and the moons of Jupiter. Eventually, what with our birthrate—who knows? Somewhere someone will get rid of farmers, leaving the corn to care for itself. Simple minds grafted into their stalks, say. And just imagine if billions of plants were to start linking minds, improving themselves however they want—"

"Corn's stupid!" I shouted, with a panicked inflexibility. The block in my hands fell free, landing against my foot. But I didn't grimace or hop around, telling Multhiford, "Stupid, stupid! And we're in charge! We eat it, for Christ's sake. It doesn't eat us."

He shrugged as if to tell me my words didn't matter.

And I doubted myself, for that instant.

"Imagine the far future," he said, "and the day we meet aliens rather like ourselves. What do we give in trade, John? Our crops would be valuable. A multitude of uses, designed for a multitude of worlds. Think of how many green worlds might welcome our corn."

My anger started seeping out of me. I couldn't keep hold of it.

"Corn has spread over this planet. Why not across the galaxy?"

Not once, never, had such a loopy idea gotten inside my skull.

"Corn prospers, carried along by commerce and conquest." He said it, then paused. Then he gave a big dramatic sigh before asking, "Who survives the next billion years, John? Human beings, arrogant and blind, or the adaptable crops that we tend?"

I said, "We do," out of instinct.

"You know this, do you?"

I said, "You're insane. That's what I know."

I'd been thinking it all night, but finally saying it did nothing. I must have thought the words would be like thunder in a clear sky, the old man left shaking. Except his only reaction was to smile. And the clear sky swallowed up my words, leaving everything still and quiet.

I couldn't stand the silence. I picked up a huge block of concrete, getting ready to heave it.

"No need," said the smiling madman. "That's enough now."

At last! I dropped the block and peeled off the gloves, wiping the sweat from my hands.

But Multhiford said, "Just a minute. Now I want you up in the bed and throwing it all back down. Put everything in the same pile again."

"What?" I blurted. "That doesn't make sense."

Shaking his head, he asked, "Does spelling a dirty word in my field make sense?" He was laughing louder than ever, telling me, "You're being punished, John. Remember. Pointless is the point in being punished."

I wondered if running away would help.

"Put the gloves back on, John."

I did as I was told, flexing my hands, listening to the creaky old leather and thinking, just for that little instant, that this was what I deserved.

Multhiford said nothing during the unloading. He leaned against one of his metal buildings, his face dark against the moonlit metal wall. It was nearly three in the morning when I finished. I said, "Done," and he came over, giving the bed an examination, then pointing. "Missed some pieces."

I tossed them overhand onto the pile. Except the last bit, which I threw out into the field of stupid corn.

"And sweep it clean, too."

He gave me a blunt straw broom, then climbed into the cab. I did a rush job and jumped in the other side, thinking I was going home. I was already planning what to tell the guys, including embellishments.

Multhiford's legend was going to grow, I'd decided. The night was looking worthwhile, thinking about my own little future.

We drove maybe fifty feet, then stopped.

"What do you think of my friend?"

We were parked in front of a phony cornstalk. I was close enough to touch it. I couldn't help but stare at the thing.

"What do you think?" he repeated.

It had a cob that wasn't a cob. It was made from bits of smooth glass, each bit looking more like an eye than a kernel. The plant itself was painted black, and some kind of wiring was sewn into the stalk. Its roots weren't roots, either. They looked like worms or muscular tendrils. Scrap plastic and pounded metal had been shaped to make it seem that the plant was moving, walking on its roots. And its leaves were thick and wrong-shaped, reminding me of stubby arms.

A lot of arms, I was thinking.

"I wish I'd done a better job," said the old farmer. "I wish I was a stronger artist."

Except it wasn't bad. I mean, forced to look, I had a real feeling for the thing. I was impressed enough that I almost said so, catching my tongue just as we started rolling again.

Multhiford didn't bother with headlights. He had us on the county road, keeping it slow. Toward town, but never fast. I could see the town's lights in the distance, and I watched the field passing on my right. There wasn't any better corn in the world, I was thinking. Madman or not, Multhiford always planted the best hybrid, always on the perfect days, and all at once I was thinking about him and his noise about the future . . . thinking my own crazy thoughts . . . and I realized we were coasting, the farmer's boot off the pedal and him asking, "What if people could travel in time? I don't know how. Maybe we'd have to hammer together some dead stars, or build some wormhole doodad. But what if we could?"

I wouldn't look at him. I made up my mind, watching the field, staring out at the blurring rows.

"People might visit our hunting ancestors and thank them. Pay homage, we could. It would be a religious event, and we'd select only our finest, holiest pilgrims for the honor."

I didn't look at him, but my resolve was slipping. The rows were crawling past as we ground to a halt. I felt my heart pounding, not fast but each beat like an explosion.

"Our finest pilgrims," he said again.

It wasn't a light that I saw over the field. It had no color and made no shadows, and it didn't even have a real shape that I can name. But inside it were motions, energies. Without deciding to move, I opened my door and jumped down, gravel crunching under me. Then with a calm dry voice, Multhiford said, "Go on." He reached clear over to touch me, saying, "They're expecting you. Hurry on."

I ran. Before I could get scared, I shot across the roadside ditch and into the field. I wasn't even running, it was more like flying, everything dreamy and slow. Leaves slapped my face. I lost sight of my target. Then, just when I thought I was lost, I felt a presence, electric and close, and the air tasted of comet soils and perfect manures, working machinery and some kind of vibrant, tireless life.

The ground under me was covered with gently flattened corn-stalks.

For the third time in a night, I fell; and when I tried to get up I had hands grabbing at me, holding me down while voices sang, speaking just to me. The voices knew my name. There wasn't anything they didn't know about me. From the ends of time they told me as much, then whispered, "Be at ease." A million pilgrim voices sang, "John, be at ease."

I tried to obey, roots swirling past my nose.

Stalks of every color, thick and thin, crowded around me, leaving no room for air.

I tried speaking.

Before I could, they said, "Quiet. Quiet, quiet."

I kept perfectly silent.

Then they broke into a shared song, dry leathery leaf-limbs rolling me onto my back, giving me a larger view. The pilgrims were tall, too tall to measure, stretching into a sky full of messy colors and countless stars and swift bright ships of no particular shape; and the song deafened me, cutting through my saturated brain; and finally, after a million years of listening, my eyes closed and I fell asleep. Or unconscious. Or maybe, just for a moment, I died.

I woke when someone shook me.

It was Mr. Multhiford's hand on my shoulder, and it was his voice saying, "Almost morning, John."

I smelled normal green corn. The farmer above me was framed by the brightening sky. Three times I tried to sit up, then he helped me with my fourth try, bringing me to my feet.

"Some evening," was his verdict. "Wouldn't you agree?"

I couldn't even speak.

"I've been where you were," he confessed. "Once. Just once." He let those words work on me for a moment, then added, "Believe me. All you need is one time."

"But why?" I managed, making my parched throat work.

"Why us?" A big shrug, then he said, "They like us. With me, they get a damned fine farmer who keeps their secrets. With you? They see someone who's going to do something good for them. I don't know what exactly. I don't know when. But they told me about you—"

"Told you?"

"Years and years ago," he said, laughing again. "They tell you something once, believe me, you *remember*."

"What else did they tell you?"

"Next year is dry, and there's an early frost. For instance." He looked off into the distance, then added, "In twelve years, plus a few weeks, my heart gives out and I die."

"You know that?" I whispered.

He shrugged his shoulders as if saying, "So what?" Then he pointed, asking, "Do you see that bent stalk over there, John? Well, you and I both know it's real. It exists. It occupies a place and doesn't need us touching it to make it what it is."

"I guess not. . . ."

"Look back through time, and there's the past. There's me planting my corn, and you drinking beer with your pals. It's every instant of our lives, good and not, and lives like that can't be killed. Not by heart attacks, at least." He gave me a big wink, then added, "That's the best thing they ever told me, John. We're always here, always living this life." A big happy smile, and he said, "So do it right. Live as though you'll always live it, because you will be. Because that's just the way these things are."

We rode into town without talking, nothing worthwhile left to say.

Early risers saw us together, and they stared. When we pulled up in front of my house, Dad practically exploded from the front door, and when I climbed down he screamed at me and hugged me and gave me a sloppy wet kiss on the cheek. He'd just gotten off the phone with Charlie. He thought he knew the story. "I'm so furious with you," he told me, never looking happier. Then he glanced at Mr. Multhiford, saying, "Something awful might have happened." But he showed no malice toward the farmer, either. And then Mr. Multhiford drove away, without so much as a good-bye wave, and I was left to suffer a couple more hugs, then the unrestrained affections of my sister and weepy mom.

They thought they knew. Vandalism. Gunfire. And I was missing, presumed wounded. Maybe dead.

Feeling halfway dead, I went inside to eat and shower and put on some good clothes. Dad left for early service. I made it to the eleven o'clock service, finding the guys waiting for me on the front lawn. It was Charlie who told me that they'd just come from Multhiford's, and did I know there was a new circle?

I gave a little nod and the beginnings of a smile.

"He caught you and made you pound it out," said Charlie.

"Is that what happened?" asked Lester.

"I bet it is," said Pat.

We were all dressed for church, standing in a knot, watching people streaming inside. After a few seconds, I said, "That's it exactly. He made me pound it out."

"How's he make them?" Charlie wanted to know. "With boards and rope? Like we figured?"

"Yeah," I told them. "We were right."

"So now we know," Charlie declared, almost as happy as Dad. "It makes last night worth it, huh? Getting shot at. Being chased. We sure as hell worried about you, let me tell you."

I didn't say anything.

"After church," he said, "come over to my place. Help us finish off last night's beer."

Lester and Pat made agreeable sounds, punching me in the arm.

I still hadn't answered when Dad came outside, heading straight for me. The guys scattered in something just short of panic. Oh, well. From where I was standing I could see the edge of town, green fields stretching around the world; and just then, just for a moment, little snatches of the future became clear in my head. I saw myself in college. I saw myself grown up, changing the shapes of living molecules. Making new kinds of corn. . . .

To the corn, I'm famous.

"This afternoon," said Dad, "we'll discuss your punishment."

I blinked and turned toward him, saying, "Fine."

Then he hugged me hard once again. For a long time. People were watching, but I didn't care. I stood there and took it, only squirming a little bit, and I even came close to admitting how good that hug—and everything—felt just then.

Know what I mean?

STRIDE

PHILLIP FINDS himself awake, finds himself running, midstride and charging hard down the left rut of a little ranch road; and he stops and turns, and turns, confusion becoming panic and someone close uttering a shrill moan. Then he realizes that he's moaning. Nobody else is here. And he shuts his mouth, feeling dizzy and weak and wondering:

Where is this?

It looks like the hill country, tall brown grass moving under a gusting southerly wind. His panic bleeds into a broader, more muscular fear. The sky is high and blue-white with high clouds, the sun not far from the horizon, and which is it? Morning or afternoon? The air is hot and late-day muggy. It must be afternoon. But what day? Glancing at his left wrist, he finds that his watch is gone, a pink untanned band obvious against his brown forearm. And he remembers wearing other clothes, nothing on him now but his black nylon shorts and his racing flats with the new socks . . . *who did this. . . ?* and clenched in his right hand is a stick, short and lightweight—

—not a stick, no. A weapon. The wooden handle has knobs shaped for his fingers, for both hands, plus little symbols that resemble tiny neat and stylized bones. Under a leather sheath is a long paper-thin blade made from gray-blue metal. He touches the serrated edge once, then replaces the sheath and sucks at his own cut thumb. "Shit." And again he turns, slowly this time, examining the horizon and the grass, searching for odd motions or a certain shape. He finds neither. Yet Phillip has the clear impression that he is being watched, someone to the east. He was running west when he awoke, some piece of him lucid enough to keep him upright, legs churning; and for no obvious reason now he lifts his weapon, the axe, holding it overhead with both arms straightened, something about the stance formal, almost ritualistic, some half-remembered voice telling him:

"Once you are conscious, turn to show me. Stand this way. This way is holy. And then we truly begin. This will be our starter's pistol."

He remembers more than the voice, startling himself, dropping the axe and backing away from it. Why did he do it? A scalding and clean and focusing rage begins, telling him that he should have kept running, feigning sleep . . . and in the same instant Phillip understands that he couldn't have, that he had no choice, that the instructions were given while he was in a powerful drugged state. Then he realizes that by standing here, doing nothing, he is assuring his own death . . . and he picks up the axe again, turns and runs, almost sprinting down the little road.

"Bless you," said the remembered voice. Then in another language, with a hard chattering sound, it must have said the same words again. "Bless you, bless you."

Phillip remembers the touch of hands, claws dimpling the skin of his neck and the breath close, warm and damp and steady. And he remembers the face inches from his face, smiling black eyes staring at him, the voice deep and rough and strange as it said:

"Bless the meat."

Then:

"Run."

Like never in his life, the meat runs.

It was after high school, after his family disowned him for all time. It was after that business with the liquor stores, Phillip driving the car and testifying against his buddy to save his own ass. And it was after going through rehab twice, coming out clean at last. After all that, and he was barely nineteen, and someone said to Phillip, "What you ought to do is try running. It's better than drugs, I've heard, and it's legal, too."

The idea sounded reasonable. Phillip needed something to do with his time, and jogging would at least make him fit. But he began badly, wearing basketball shoes and training without any plan, believing that running was one thing and covering ground was all that mattered. It isn't. Yet he had help from his lean build and his youth, surviving a couple of early knee injuries and eventually improving despite himself.

The best runners are built from the same blueprints, narrow hips and long legs and deep lung-rich chests. Greyhounds and Kenyans have much in common, and Phillip resembled both in his essential lines and his strong innate stride, nothing but breathing more natural than the act of running. And despite himself, he succeeded. Entering his first race on a whim, he ran with the lead pack because he thought that was the point of racing: You run to win and for as long as possible. Phillip managed to stay with the leaders for a mile, in those basketball shoes, draining himself and collapsing into a shuffling jog. Several hundred cautious souls passed him before the finish line, cheerfully telling him, "Stick with it. You look strong." *The bastards.* But afterward Phillip finally bought proper shoes and shorts and a couple of "how-to" guides. He read about intervals and long runs and hard-days, easy-days. Then he began using his old high-school track for his intervals. In those days the track was unpaved, cinders crunching with every footfall, and Phillip usually had the track to himself. He was twenty or twenty-one, and there was an evening—a windy and muggy evening like this one—where he was running hard, an audience watching him intently.

Crows. There were a dozen big, big crows, squawking and cawing among themselves. And one crow was perched on the old drinking fountain, the black head dipping every so often. Phillip barely noticed it until he took a break, trotting over for a drink and the crow not eager to leave. It gave him a long cawing curse before settling on the nearby grass, glaring at him. Phillip has never forgotten the moment. The fountain's drain was plugged up, probably by kids, and the steel bowl was filled with cloudy pink water. Phillip froze, blinked, and stared. The crow had caught a young ground squirrel and butchered it in the bowl, blood and fur and bits of candy-bright guts making a delicious cold soup.

Disgust became a kind of disgusted fascination, the moment having a bizarre spiritual feel about it.

Bending and squinting, Phillip could see how the squirrel's eyes had been neatly chiseled from their sockets, probably eaten as delicacies. And the crow gave him another harsh caw, its voice urgent and the meaning obvious.

"Mine, mine, mine!" it was shouting.

Phillip retreated, his thirst gone. The crow picked up its prize and flew away, chased by the others; and fifteen years later, the same crows and their descendants still perch on the bleachers and high fences. Today the track is paved, runners using it almost every evening. Crows like the place because it has water and stupid ground squirrels and edible trash in big steel barrels, and because they like to watch the humans run in circles, sometimes staggering, their hope of hopes being that some evening one of the runners will collapse and die for them.

"Dibs on the eyes!" they say. Or words to that effect. "Dibs dibs dibs on the big sweet eyes!"

Deer are browsing partway up the hillside, up ahead — big mule deer enjoying the evening — and they lift their heads together, watching Phillip cruise along the ranch road. At least they look like muleys, he thinks. In principle, they could be anything that's possible, and this could be any possible place; and it's no small relief that this is his Earth, his home, maybe no more than thirty miles between here and his apartment door.

A manageable distance.

A *fucking piece of cake.*

Phillip feels strong, rested. Plenty of pop in the legs. His early pace has slowed to something more measured, more controlled, old habits emerging from the initial shock. The sun has just set, the western sky full of red dust, and he grows more alert as the light fails. Is there a moon? Yeah, for a while. It's the moon he expects, half-lit and one-eyed, and that's also reassuring. He's running on familiar ground, under his sky, following this road back to its source, hoping to find a ranch house or a larger road where he can get help.

Piece of fucking cake.

Suddenly the deer begin to run, bounding downhill with a graceful easy strength; and Phillip watches them, tension building before his mind can find the reason for tension, a gloomy internal voice asking: "What spooked them?"

Because he didn't. Because the deer are coming in his general direction, leaping over a low barbed-wire fence and crossing the road in front of him, close enough that he can hear hooves on the packed earth, then in the grass. And they're past, continuing down into a stand of wild plums and shadow, then gone, a sense of motion and residual life hanging in the air.

What spooked them . . . is over the hill. . . .

Phillip stops for an instant, squinting and gasping. And

waiting. Nothing shows itself, but he has no doubts. For a moment he thinks of following the deer, trying to hide among them; but changing direction is too difficult to consider. In the dark, in this country, he'd rather use the relatively good footing of the road. What's best is to move fast, picking up his pace, assuming that help is somewhere close and holding nothing back now.

He gives the axe to the other hand, running again; and with a downward glance he notices hoofprints in the soil, fresh as fresh can be, shaped by Nature for this kind of panicked flight.

Humans are wondrous runners.

Phillip once read that it's bullshit, pure bullshit, when people claim that people are lousy athletes. It's a lie started by and for snobs and fat-asses. The truth is that few critters can cover ground like a healthy well-trained *Homo sapiens*. Still fewer can manage it in the heat and under a midday sky, humans built for and tested on the huge expanses of African savanna, and the best human runners are born there today.

Oh, sure. Your basic cheetah is three times faster over the short haul. But it's got quick-twitch muscles, like every sprinter, and tiny lungs that can't keep the engines burning for more than a minute or two. And for half an hour after its big run, the cheetah pants like a maniac, dropping heat and gulping oxygen while some lithe and steady young Bushman robs him of his kill.

Naked flesh; abundant sweat glands; and a huge heat-radiating brain. Human beings were capable of astonishing runs long before they built fancy spears and spaceships.

For the last fifteen years, almost without exception, Phillip has run from seventy to one hundred and twenty miles every week, each of those runs recorded in a logbook, every year's mileage totaled and analyzed and criticized and enshrined.

For the last dozen years, with no exceptions, Phillip Krause has been the local champion runner. The town's races are his personal possessions. On the good days he wins the larger regional events. On his best days he has gone to the line with giants— Olympic-caliber stallions—once breaking twenty-nine minutes in a 10K, chasing Bill Rodgers into the last mile.

If only, he has thought countless times.

If he only could have been more fit, more flexible. More focused.

If only, only, only he hadn't ingested the chemicals and avoided exercise during his ugly youth.

Sometimes Phillip imagines himself running in high school, then college—a prime Division I school—with coaches who would have given him opportunities without making him burn out. Good press and racing the best Americans would have won him attention. And Phillip hasn't the feeblest doubt that he would have won in a fair world, victories bringing the spoils: corporate sponsors and shoe contracts and fat, fat appearance fees.

Could have happened and should have, and didn't.

His real fame is a smaller, more intimate kind. Almost everyone in the little city of Forrestal knows Phillip by sight, if not by name. He's the lean and strong long-legged maniac out running every day, in blizzards and hail and blistering heat, the black hair worn long and tied into a ponytail, the weathered face always serious, always focused, with eyes that local runners have dubbed: "Bruce Dern eyes."

Obsessed. Passionate. Almost crazed.

Phillip isn't exactly friendless. There are always people who gather around someone of remarkable skill, ignoring their shortfalls in order to breathe the same air. The trick with Phillip, say his admirers, is to pretend that he was raised by wolves. It's not that he's intentionally abrupt or distant, no. He just doesn't understand the subtleties of normal conversation, or its power. Having given his entire life—energy and focus and intellect—to a single pursuit, he doesn't have room for normal friendship or anything like love.

He has a famous temper, incandescent and sudden.

And the truth is that some people pity him. Phillip is thirty-five years old, muscles filling with rust and the elasticity leaving his poor hamstrings; and they watch his tantrums after bad races, wondering what happens when his times truly slow. What happens when he can't win even the local races? When some college kid, young enough to be his son, crushes him without so much as a backward glance?

That's what slower, wiser runners ask each other, watching Phillip run scorching laps at the high-school track.

How can such a creature survive being slow?

Moonlight betrays motion on his left, which is where he expects it. But when he turns his head, looking straight at his sudden companion, the cones of his eyes can't resolve anything but a long reach of whispering grass.

Phillip jerks his head forward, lifting his pace again.

And again he sees the figure running in the tall grass, paralleling him, the corners of his eyes able to resolve a general shape and the stride, both of them recognizable.

His belly tightens, almost paining him.

For an instant, Phillip wonders if he's going to lose control of his bowels, horribly embarrassing himself on top of everything. But the pressure passes with a fart, and he gasps, and he looks over at the figure, this time not quite staring at it, letting the light-sensitive rods of his eyes resolve an image.

The figure moves faster, its stride long and easy. In moonlight it seems only half-real, composed partly of ghostly substances, weightless and perfect for a runner.

It's jockeying closer to the road now.

Phillip can hear it. He hears the bare legs in the grass and the occasional grunt, and again he looks ahead, able to resolve a line of silvery somethings that become fence posts and a gate—no, not a gate, but a gap in the fence—and the quicker runner will reach the gap first, by at least fifty yards.

Phillip stops running, and he thinks to lift the axe, using both hands but forgetting to remove the leather sheath. In the wood of the handle he can feel his heart, the beats too fast to count. His opponent comes up onto the road and turns, almost strutting, holding an identical axe in one hand, the blade glistening like water.

Phillip stares at the face.

Even at this range, in moonlight, he knows what he sees. A *Terror*. The face is narrow and beaked with feathers in place of hair—a shaggy blood-colored mass of feathers growing on the head and neck and shoulders and back—and a naked body painted with ceremonial spearheads, simple and ancient. The tail is hidden behind it, abbreviated and vaguely reptilian. The legs are long, ending with long clawed feet, and the feet begin to scratch at the bare earth, kicking up dust clouds. And with a sense of ceremony the Terror lifts its axe toward the partial moon, chanting with a shrill piercing voice, the language unintelligible but rhythmic, almost familiar somehow.

Ancient gods are being invoked, he senses.

And Phillip lowers his axe, saying, "Fuck you," as he turns, sprinting north toward the nearest hill.

RUNNING LOG:
Date—6/10 Weight—145 Pulse—46
Course—Forrestal track
Description—Mile repeats (6, 10 miles overall)
Comments—Fair pace, pop; arch sore; 4:50s, 4:39 last one;
new runner, Nash something—quick, odd

There were half a dozen other runners at the track, mostly plodders, and Phillip did his usual best to ignore them. It was a cool evening for June, the air dry and smelling of newly mowed grass. It wasn't until after his first hard mile when he noticed the white Mercedes parked in the student lot. Whose was it? He tried to remember if it was there when he arrived, and he couldn't remember, finishing his one-lap rest and hitting the *Start* button on his watch, launching into his second scorching mile.

Seventy-two seconds per quarter, give or take. Phillip has a sense for pace, innate and rarely wrong. Except for the occasional hot pain in his right arch, he felt fine. Strong, smooth. He hit the *Stop* button as he finished, guessing 4:50 before he glanced at the numbers. 4:51. Not quite fast enough, he thought. He'd let his concentration slip, and yesterday's hard fourteen miles weren't helping. Trotting now, he felt a general ache in his legs, circling back around to the starting line and sometimes glancing through the high chain-link fence, the white Mercedes still sitting in the open.

Smoked glass windows, he noticed. Out-of-state plates, which made sense. Forrestal was a relatively small city, and conservative, and this wasn't any car that he recognized as local. Then he quit thinking about it, concentrating on his next mile . . . running it in his head before he began. *Beep.* His right foot ached on the first turn, his pace suffering. He didn't need his watch to know that he was a couple of seconds slow on the first lap, a flicker of anger making him focus, pushing him through the second lap, then the third one, coming around in full stride and all at once noticing that someone had emerged from the mystery car.

Even at a distance, the man looked odd. Wrong. He was tall with big shoulders and narrow hips and a long pair of legs. He was wearing some kind of warm-up, ugly green and shiny. A Ben Hogan green. The face was pale, reddish-blond hair cut short; and Phillip glanced at the face as he ran past, feeling something unsettling. Or maybe not. Maybe it was his imagination or the exhaustion. And with that he did his last lap, finishing with a surge and hitting *Stop* and grimacing as he eased into a gentle healing trot.

The stranger was watching him, apparently smiling as he shut his door with a solid Mercedes *thunk*. Phillip refused to notice. He was busy trying to bring life back into his legs, busy telling himself that he was halfway done and only three more and, God, he felt strong. And when he came around again, he realized that the stranger was running, still wearing the warm-up, taking the first turn as Phillip began his fourth mile.

Of course he'd catch the stranger. He had no doubts, hitting the first lap too fast, crushing seventy seconds and paying for it. The gap did close somewhat, but the guy had some spark in him, some power, and Phillip finished in the rear, managing a ragged 4:51 that left him shuffling in the inner lane. And then the stranger passed him, no warning given. There wasn't the usual slap of feet on the soft asphalt, the tall and lean and obviously strong figure passing on his right, never speaking, perhaps not even breathing, surprising Phillip enough to make him jump sideways, twisting in midair and lifting his hands.

He felt like a fool. Scared for no reason.

Again he started to trot along, anxiety making his legs shake. The stranger was half a lap ahead when he finally pulled up, and Phillip watched him climb partway up the bleachers, scaring off one of the eternal crows. There he sat, legs stretched out in front of him and appearing relaxed, at ease, with his eyes fixed on Phillip. Always.

Two more, Phillip thought. Almost done.

He managed the fifth mile in an anemic 4:53.

"Shit," he shouted, ignoring the audience. Staring at the track and his feet, he thought how he needed new shoes and insoles. They'd help his sore arch. Then he came back around and realized that he had company, the stranger having climbed down onto the track again, standing in his lane, still wearing the ugly warm-up—pants and a long-sleeved hoodless shirt—and watching Phillip, eyes large and dark and somehow, even through fifty yards of twilight, odd.

Phillip kept moving. The air felt cool, soothing. He concentrated on breathing, then had the peculiar thought that the stranger was going to fight him, that they must have met somewhere and he held a grudge—not the only runner who could claim that status—and just as Phillip wondered what to say, if anything, the stranger broke the silence, asking:

"May I join you?"

He had a thick voice, ragged and a little slow, with the hint of an accent. Or maybe a speech impediment.

Phillip responded by coughing, tasting iron at the back of his throat. "Guess so," he allowed. *It's a public track—*

—and the stranger stepped out of his way, almost smiling.

"I'm doing a mile," Phillip told him.

The stranger let him begin, giving him a couple of strides before engaging whatever engine it was that powered him. Phillip didn't hear him. He concentrated on keeping himself under control, feeling a deep twinge from the balky arch; then his opponent was cutting past him on the first back side, that effortless stride carrying him, the fabric of his warm-up giving a rhythmic dry crack. Phillip managed the first lap in the midsixties, he guessed. The second lap was faster and twice as painful. Then the third was slower, Phillip burying himself deep inside anaerobic metabolisms, lactic acids made by the bucket and pooling inside his rubbery old legs.

The stranger was toying with him, keeping a constant lead. And Phillip massaged his ego with thoughts of how this was a workout, not a race, and how this bastard hadn't run as far as him tonight. He was some kind of speed merchant. A track-head. And this meant nothing at all.

A sudden backward glance startled Phillip.

The narrow face grinned, the expression full of arrogance. And Phillip knows arrogance, having produced more than his share in life. *Fuck you,* he thought, and he surged, the legs driving even as they ran out of oxygen, him halving the distance on the last lap and the fucker responding by putting himself into some new, heretofore unseen gear, legs blurring and Phillip left far behind.

Frustration bled into an intense, tightly focused rage.

The stranger stopped early, perhaps forgetting where they'd started. Phillip kept pressing, thighs burning and the air useless and his tight angry voice grunting, "Track," as he streaked past, not moving far enough to his right and their elbows clipping one another, bone to bone, the pain barely worth noticing on top of every other misery.

And he finished, his hand remembering to stop his watch and the rest of him gasping, then shuffling out onto the grass of the practice field. He decided to throw up, bending at the waist in preparation; but the nausea became a general gassy sensation, almost manageable. More hard breathing cured him of the discomfort, leaving him mobile and a little ashamed. Just a little. Then he knelt and reached inside his right shoe, massaging the arch—plantar fasciitis is a brutal, long-term, hard-to-cure ailment—and only gradually did he become aware of his companion. Dark green shoes blended into the grass—what brand?—and he lifted his eyes, finding the stranger's face smiling again and a long hand extending, the mouth opening and saying, "Nash," two times.

"Nash?" said Phillip.

"And you are?"

There was an accent, plus a speech impediment—very slight—with the hard r faltering inside that blue-black voice. Phillip gave his full name, halfway expecting Nash to say, "I've heard of you." But he didn't, looking off in a random direction, not watching Phillip as he said:

"Phillip," with too much care.

What I need . . . is to move. . . .

Nash joined him, not invited but not told to leave, either. Trotting around the first turn, Phillip glanced at him several times, in profile, wondering about his nationality—German? Scottish?—and entertaining a fantasy where Nash was a world-class athlete who had come here to race him. A sweet image, wasn't it? And he wondered about his age, realizing that he looked younger than his voice and general bearing. Twentysomething? And then they were on the back side, Nash turning his head and smiling as he asked:

"Shall we drink?"

Phillip said nothing.

"I need to drink," his new friend confessed.

The old water fountain was at the south end of the track, beside the second turn. No crows on it tonight, but just the same Phillip felt uneasy. His own water was in a plastic bottle hidden under the bleachers. He could almost taste it, watching Nash step onto the grass; and Phillip had no choice but to warn him, "That water's no good."

Nash paused, asking why not.

He told the story, in brief, waiting for Nash to become disgusted. But if anything, he seemed intrigued, offering an odd little smile and a soft laugh.

The drain was plugged, as always. The broad steel bowl was filled with water, a steep nipple standing in the center, maybe an inch above the water's surface. Nash stepped on the pedal and bent at the waist, the flow short, barely sturdy enough to rise off the metal. Yet he drank, the head down for a long while, slurping and swallowing; and Phillip watched the pale slick back of the neck, his own disgust holding steady. Finally Nash stood up and belched with authority, turning to Phillip and saying:

"Have some."

It wasn't a question.

In the next few weeks, as events mounted, Phillip would recall the man's tone and expression, challenging him with that wrong-sounding voice, two words elevating this stupid act into some kind of manhood test.

"Have some," he repeated. Demanded.

Phillip made himself do it. Nash depressed the pedal for him, standing over him while he bent and drank. The water was warm and bland, and what was left over in the bowl was almost clear, Phillip telling himself that what he was drinking had to be clean and there was nothing to worry about and then noticing something move, swirling under his nose, long and thin and without color. Drifting in the bowl was a washed-out noodlelike length of artery, and Phillip stopped drinking, standing with a certain slow dignity, then managing a small inadequate belch.

Nash was smiling, and he wasn't.

That face was too thin, like a greyhound's face, and the skin was too smooth and milky and hairless as an egg; and later, remembering the moment for the thousandth time, Phillip would think of those eyes and how they reminded him of crow eyes, intense and powerful, and malicious, and black in a manner that made them glow with an inner light.

He attacks the hill, not looking back, pressing and pressing and discovering a reserve, a potent new gear, that lifts him to the crest without destroying him.

And he slows, glancing over a shoulder—

—better than a hundred yards between them, the Terror leaning into the grade where it's steepest, for an instant, and Phillip wondering if it can be tired. What if it has limits after all?

What was he taught?

This rite, this ceremony, is intended to be dangerous. When the Terror isn't assured victory at the outset, then this is the perfect and noble chase of worthy meat. . . .

Me . . . the worthy meat . . .

The grass on top of the hill has been grazed thin and dried out by the winds, the ground beneath stony and uneven. Phillip thinks of pausing over the crest, dropping and waiting to ambush the Terror, finishing everything now. But the legs vote otherwise, churning hard and extending themselves on the downhill slope, hips tilting forward, the balls of his feet and his shins absorbing the jarring impacts.

He imagines water flowing on the hillside, and he follows the imagined stream, lifting his gaze, mapping his course up the next long moonlit climb.

A couple of days after the mile repeats—after Nash—Phillip was awakened by a hard professional knock on his door. He has a tiny,

tiny apartment, ascetic and suitable. Daylight gleamed through gaps in the curtains. Posters showed famous marathoners in victory stances. What time was it? Noonish. His right foot had stiffened while he slept, like always, and he grimaced and pulled on the nearest shorts, limping to the door as the knocking quit and finding a uniformed figure smiling in the hallway.

"Hope I'm not bothering you."

UPS. The deliveryman smelled of cigarettes and industrial cologne. Until Phillip signed his name, they were the best of friends. In exchange for his signature, he received a small box wrapped in brown paper and tape, the return address smudged. Unreadable.

Phillip growled and shut the door, then tore into the paper, waking as he worked. Dark green letters spelled the word STRIDE, on top and on the sides. Inside the box was a single round canister, sealed with foil and a plastic lid. STRIDE was written on its face, in the same flowing style, and rubber-banded around it was a cover letter that began:

"A gift for you, Phillip Krause, in recognition of your talents as an athlete."

A free sample, he realized. And not the first one, either. Phillip always enjoyed this warm sense of success, as if his grueling work was aimed at these occasional gifts. STRIDE, he read, was a new and innovative electrolyte replacement drink, fructose and complex carbos mixed with essential minerals and amino acids, plus a delightful citrus taste, too. In theory.

Piss would have tasted better, he decided. But when he mixed his test batch with diet pop, it became manageable. Even palatable. He finished a big glass before returning to bed, then lay awake for a long while, aware of a warmth spreading from his belly and the steady unhurried beating of his heart.

He awoke around five o'clock, ran an easy eight, then put the bad foot into a bucket of ice water. Phillip's latest job was night watchman at a local factory, fourteen months of service being something of a personal best for him. It was easy, solitary work, and it made the rent. But that night, dressing in the ridiculous uniform, he suddenly felt dizzy and weak. The apartment took on a tilt, just for a few minutes. An illness? Or a brain tumor? Yet it passed, and by morning he was strong enough to run a solid eighteen, taking a favorite course to the east of Forrestal, past the last of the farms and into the open green hill country.

It was a warm day, even before nine o'clock.

Pausing at the crest of a long hill, at the turnaround point, he pulled his water bottle from its padded belt, sucking down a long curing dose of STRIDE.

The taste had grown on him.

Piss, but premium piss. And he turned and started home, started downhill, the right foot warm and loose and happy.

On the third hill the legs start to feel the slope and the pace, and Phillip discovers that he can take his pulse when he places his tongue against the roof of his mouth. It's a warning, an old trusted one, and he decides what to do as he comes over the crest, one more backward glance and his lead diminished to eighty yards and little choice left for him. He finds an abbreviated gully where he hunkers down low and waits, breathing too hard and watching for the Terror and not waiting for long. There is no one, then there is. It appears before him, that clean strong gait slowing in an instant, the face dropping, the eyes finding something of interest in the hard stony ground.

Moving too quickly, Phillip removes the leather sheath from the long axe blade.

Moving too surely, the Terror turns and starts to walk toward him, the head always down and Phillip telling himself to charge him now, to catch the monster before it can react—

—and the Terror pauses, eyes lifting, easily able to see everything despite the gully and its shadows. Everything is obvious and amusing, the hard mouth managing a smile, the plumage on its head lifting, the entire creature splendid and imposing in the silvery moonlight. And now the familiar voice, deep and serrated, says:

"You are not particularly tired, I think. Not yet."

Then:

"Phillip. You must have confidence. Confidence in the possibility of success."

Phillip stands, both hands gripping the axe handle. Again he considers the sudden assault, bold and probably suicidal; and perhaps his body, his stance, signal his intentions. Because the Terror places its long bare feet farther apart, telling him:

"Run. You should run."

Phillip cannot move, not in any direction.

And the Terror gives a little chant, throwing its axe into the air, into moonlight, Phillip watching the axe turn and rise and fall and turn again, caught with the same hand, the motions expert and efficient, meant as a warning to him. One of them truly knows how to use his weapon.

Phillip wheels and leaps, out of the gully and turning again, swinging at nothing. Just in case.

The Terror watches, nods, and says:

"Now run."

Phillip obeys, tracking sideways like a soccer player, following the crest of the hill and turning forward, his gait strong and the Terror right about his fatigue. He has very little of it. A minute's rest, and he feels ready to run through the night.

RUNNING LOG:
7/4 143 39
Independence Day 5–Mile
22:55
Comments — Quick and strong, fast legs; PR; *Nash*

There have been warnings, looking back.

The collective aches had vanished in the last weeks, including his foot's old miseries. And with comfort came a renewed sense of pop and purpose, Phillip's times dropping steadily through June, in the easy runs as well as the intervals.

The only bitch is that he chose this race to win.

It's a nothing event, purely local. A thousand entered, but no big money to the winner and none of the usual top dogs coming in from around the state. Lining up before the gun, watching his competition do their last surges and stretches, Phillip told himself to win before the halfway mark. Yet the first mile was enough, him streaking along at a 4:30 clip, everyone else feeling the heat and humidity and the brilliant sunshine. He ran the entire race alone, nobody pressing him; and what was strangest was the freshness of his legs and the ease with which he ate the miles. Coming back into the furnacelike downtown, on that last mile, he slowed his pace only because of a panicky sense that he was no longer running inside his own body. It was that easy, and empty.

There was the white ribbon to break, the PA system announcing a new course record. Then someone tore the tag from under his race number; and half a dozen worriers asked Phillip how he felt, if he knew where he was, and could he walk by himself.

A small impressed audience clapped, for a few moments.

Phillip ignored them. He walked past the water tables and the Pepsi van, into the town square with its grass and shade trees. Taking his pulse, he found his heart rate plummeting. Then he drank from a public fountain, taking an inventory of his muscles and joints. No pain at all. Selecting a likely tree, he began to stretch his calves and hamstrings, none of them stiff —

—and Nash said, "Hello, Phillip Krause."

He was beside Phillip, hands behind his back, wearing the same ugly green warm-up and acting as if they were the best of friends.

"My, my. You certainly ran well, don't you think?"

Phillip nearly said, "Fuck off." With anyone else he would have. But instead he shrugged his shoulders and continued the ritual stretching.

Nash moved to where he couldn't be ignored, standing too close while asking, "What do you win for winning?"

"A trophy."

Nash seemed to laugh. "A trophy. My!"

And a gift certificate to the sponsor's store. But he didn't mention that, wondering where in his apartment was there room for another lump of wood and fake brass.

"What an honor," the peculiar man was saying, his tone satirical. He was looking off into the distance, saying, "You're running much better than just a few weeks ago. I wonder why."

That made two of them.

Then Nash said, "I know why. I do."

Once again Phillip decided that the man was foreign, but now, seeing him in daylight, he guessed that he must have been injured in the past, thrown through a windshield and his face rebuilt from the pieces. It had a reasonable shape, ignoring the narrowness, but something about it was inflexible. Dead. It looked like the molded face of the runner on top of every trophy, smooth and hard and unliving.

"You should cool down," Nash assured him.

Phillip always cooled down after hard runs, but here he hesitated.

Laughing, Nash asked, "Are you afraid of me?"

"Come on," Phillip growled. He picked a direction and began to coast, taking them away from the finish line and the abrasive roar of the PA system. His legs were ready for another race, but he held back, finally asking, "So why?"

Nash echoed, "Why?"

"Am I running this fast?" he snapped.

Another pause. The man's teeth were even and white, his tongue coming out to lick at the thin lips; and after wetting them, he smiled and said, "You know very little about everything, don't you?"

What?

"I mean you, and everyone. All of you." Nash tilted his head in an odd fashion, always grinning. "When you think about science, if you ever do, does it occur to you that your finest minds don't comprehend much of this universe? That its properties and possibilities are beyond them? And whatever exists beyond this universe is entirely beyond their reach—"

"What are you saying?" Phillip snarled.

Nash tilted his head in the other direction, the milky skin bright and simple. "Universes without end. Parallel and intersecting in hyperrealms that are close, astonishingly close —"

"What?!"

"With each event, Phillip, every possible occurrence is inevitable. And every potential universe is born."

The man was insane, of course.

"This is just a single unremarkable universe, Phillip —"

"Shut up!"

Nash complied, and he stopped running without warning.

Phillip thought of continuing but couldn't, something in him curious enough to stop and turn, and stare, noticing how the man's flesh looked oily. Not sweating, but almost varnished. "Why am I running fast?" he asked once again, nearly shouting. "You said you know. So tell me. Fucking just tell me."

"Life," said Nash.

Then he said, "Health."

The man is nuts. A crazy. Phillip was relieved to think it, certain that Nash's words would lose their impact. *He's some goofy jerk who forgot to take his medication —*

"Life has its way of degrading health, doesn't it?"

Phillip nodded, thinking of softened brains.

"People acquire parasites," said Nash. "Viruses implant their toxic genes. Chemicals and radiations, natural and not, splinter our good genes, fouling up the most delicate machinery." He stepped closer and touched Phillip on the shoulder, for an instant and so softly that Phillip wondered if he had been touched. Then the long arm dropped and he said, "Imagine." In a low raspy voice, he said, "Imagine you can somehow, someway, cleanse yourself, erasing all errors, defeating every disease, and leave yourself clean and pure. At least temporarily."

"Go away," Phillip said, almost without sound.

Again Nash touched the shoulder, squeezing with an astonishing strength, and Phillip kept telling himself to move, to find people, to get away from this maniac —

—and Nash was saying, "Enjoy your victory, Phillip. Absolutely. But your success means very little, I think, and I think it would help if you knew how little it means."

"Go away," Phillip said again, louder.

And the strong hand was withdrawn, the strange man complying, turning without another word and jogging up a side street, looking back just once; and Phillip was thinking, really for the first time:

He isn't human.
Thinking:
Nash isn't.
Telling himself:
Nash is some kind of monster.

He cuts himself while climbing over a fence, a single rusted barb catching the meat of his calf, and Phillip feels it as a heat and a dull pain. It's just a cut, but he can't stop thinking about it, wondering if this little bit of lost blood and torn muscle will weaken him. He finds himself favoring the leg for no good reason, and the imagined weakness grows worse on the next slope, every motion made difficult.

The Terror has fallen back again. Spelling itself, or teasing him. Or maybe bothered by the night's heat and distance, finally.

Coming over another crest, Phillip discovers a long valley and what looks like a road, thin and straight and white; and on his right, to the north, is a block of planted trees, a single strong blue light anchored on a telephone pole.

There's a ranch house, he reasons. Down in those trees somewhere.

Phillip sprints, wondering if the Terror is unaware of this oasis. If he can get there without being cut off, he can find help. Hopefully. And the promise heals his leg in an instant, legs driving, a second fence crossed with a deft leap and then he's on the road, simple and graveled, and he hears the distant barks of dogs. Harsh and urgent. And lovely.

Phillip doesn't hesitate. He charges down the road, the dogs coming out to meet him — frantic dark shapes low to the ground — and he shouts, "No, stay! Back!" Rural dogs respect noise and bluster. He threatens them with the axe, never afraid, a threesome of snarling mutts welcome after everything else.

The blue light illuminates a long front yard. An upstairs window is lit, then the windows downstairs. Then the front porch. Phillip is almost to the stairs when a man emerges, dressed in a long bathrobe and holding a shotgun in both hands; and leaping with excitement, like a kid, Phillip cries out:

"Thank God, thank God. . . !"

The rancher responds, his voice scared and quick and mixed with gasping breaths; and very slowly, almost despite himself, Phillip realizes that the man isn't speaking English, or any recognizable language. It's complete gibberish, but with a practiced, structured feel to it.

And now the rancher becomes frustrated, aiming and firing a

single round into the air. *Wham.* The dogs leap and retreat. What kind of dogs are they? Like Labs, Phillip notices. Only broader. Stronger. With strange bony heads. And he looks at the rancher again, blinking as he retreats, some angry and stupid part of him wondering:

Why can't you speak English?

But he knows. The explanation has always been with him, and of course this isn't his Earth. Why should it be? And why would a rancher welcome some half-nude, gibberish-spouting runner who carries a vicious axe in one hand? Of course there's no help here, nor anywhere else. What was he thinking? That he was anything except absolutely alone?

The gun is aimed at him now.

Dogs creep nearer, sniffing at his feet and growling.

For an instant, in sudden stark images, Phillip pictures himself charging the rancher and being shot dead. Everything finished. And it's as if all that has happened until now is preparation, readying him for the seminal image of being on his back, bloody and cold. A crow perches on his forehead, pecking at the sightless eyes . . . and he whispers, "No," as he takes one careful step backward. With a calm and quiet and worthy strength, he says, "Like fuck I will. . . ."

The dogs escort him back to the road, into the open again.

Waiting is the Terror, feet kicking gravel backward as it utters some new chant. The wind is rising again. Phillip can barely hear the voice, but he smells the limestone dust and something vaguely animal. And the dogs begin to run toward the Terror, barking and then not, bowing their heads and whimpering as one of the long clawed hands pats each of them in turn, three tails wagging.

Phillip turns, running west again.

"Like fuck I'll die," he tells himself, leaping over another fence and up the next long hill. *No goddamn way.*

Phillip bought his new racing flats with the 5–Miler's gift certificate. When he began running he wore nine-and-a-halves, but mileage has its way of making feet longer and broader. In the store he asked for tens and ten-and-a-halves, putting on the smaller shoes first—peacock colors and feather-light—and he walked around the store, knowing they were too tight with the first step but wishing they'd fit. And just then the store manager came out of the back room, winking and saying:

"Congratulations."

Phillip gave a distracted nod, then a shrug.

The manager asked, "How'd you do it? Blood doping? Bee pollen? What's the trick?"

The manager was a gadfly and a gossip, a pudgy and occasional jogger versed in the language, and he loved to tease Phillip now and again. When brave.

"In that heat, and you still beat your best. And at your age!"

But Phillip didn't feel like boasting. Instead, he swallowed and asked, "Do you know a runner?" The manager knows everyone. "A new guy? Nash something?"

The manager pinched his face toward his nose, thinking.

"Tall. Pale. Short red hair." *And insane, or worse.*

"Legs up to his neck?"

"You know him?"

"Not really. I mean, he came in here . . . I don't know . . . a couple months back? Something like that?"

Phillip kicked off the shoes, then sat on the hard bench and let the salesgirl lace up the larger pair. "He came here?"

"On a weekday, when it was slow."

"He wears this shit-ugly warm-up—"

"—that he bought somewhere else. I know. He was wearing it then." The manager laughed at the image. "You've run with him?"

"Once. Twice."

"Any good?"

Phillip shrugged and said, "Yeah. I guess."

Two months in the past, but the manager remembered, "All he bought from me was a pair of socks."

Phillip was thinking.

"His name is Nash?"

"You talked to him?"

"For about a week, it seemed like." The manager growled. "He said he'd just moved to town, that he wanted to know about the local running scene. He asked questions."

Phillip stood. The new shoes felt like slippers, like parts of his own feet. "Talk about me?"

Swallowing, the manager looked ridiculously guilty.

"Did Nash ask about me?"

"He may have . . . I don't know. . . ."

"What'd you tell him?"

"Nothing."

"What?" Phillip felt his throat tighten. "Hey! What did you tell him about me?"

The store was silent, customers and clerks watching them. Phillip realized that he was half-shouting, that he was scared and for no clear reason, the lack of reason making it worse, his heart quickening and part of him begging for him to stop asking questions.

But he couldn't stop. He said, "Tell me. Now."

"Hey," the manager warned him, "it's nothing. I don't remember, and forget it. All right?"

On another day it wouldn't have mattered. In other circumstances it would have felt good, knowing that a stranger had heard all the usual bad-mouthing that Phillip had heard thirdhand for himself. That he was a prick, a maniac, an incandescent shit. But today he felt a vicelike pressure building, squeezing down on his heart and lungs; and he approached the little prick, ready to grab him and lift him off the ground. To threaten his buttery ass. "Didn't you notice?" he wanted to scream. "Nash is some kind of monster—!"

—but he didn't touch the man, another question occurring to him just then. He breathed, breathed again, then took a step backward. Then he asked, "Have you ever heard about a drink . . . something called STRIDE?"

The manager wiped his palms against his trousers. "Called what?"

Phillip explained, in brief. Then he added, "I'm out. And I was wondering if you're going to carry it."

"Never heard of it. Sorry."

Which he already knew, of course. Phillip was surprised by how little surprise he felt; and the manager watched him, watched his expression, and felt the most astonishing dose of empathy for Phillip.

The craziest shit of a runner, but something in that expression was so very lost. He couldn't help but feel for him.

He rests while in motion, while walking, circling the big galvanized stock pond after drinking his fill, its water cool and clear, pumped from the deep aquifer. Phillip didn't know he was thirsty until he put his mouth to the water, and now his belly is full enough to ache, his thoughts clearing, eyes fixed on the Terror. It's standing in the open, drawing shapes on the ground. A hundred yards between them, and some kind of ritual truce is in effect.

Phillip spits in the pond, then runs west again.

His legs are tight and tired, the right knee aching under the patella and another sore spot up near his left hip flexor. But otherwise, after some twenty-plus miles of hard motion, he is fine. Fine.

After a little while, the moon vanishes. To the west-northwest, taller than the Himalayas, is a wall of black clouds. And the southerly wind is roaring, hot and sticky and ceaseless. Phillip can't hear his own feet hitting the ground, much less hear the Terror. He finds himself glancing back every minute or so. Yet he's not frantic, either. Not like in the beginning. He has been doing this for what seems like years—being chased; being prey—and a kind of practiced intensity is becoming easier. The elaborate hunt has made him into an expert piece of meat.

Not pressing, he climbs the next long hill, then crosses a fence and turns and sees no one behind him.

And he turns in another few seconds, on a hunch.

The Terror is in motion against the sky, coming over the crest in a strong jog. It moves the axe from hand to hand, pausing at the fence, staring at Phillip and Phillip lifting his axe over his head, like in the beginning. The wind gusts. This is the last southerly wind before the storm front hits. And now he turns, gathering himself as he runs . . . running with measure, with patience . . . the moon gone and the land growing darker by the moment. . . .

"About your scar tissue."

"What scar tissue?"

"Exactly." His physical therapist walked down to his more thoughtful end, showing a puzzled smile. "The scar tissue in your hamstring. I think it's gone."

"It broke up," Phillip offered.

"Something's happened." His therapist is a burly woman with a butcher's hands, strong and warm. For six years Phillip has come to her, surrendering his dignity for the regular massages, her helping to hold him together with a regime of diet and stretching, massages and more stretching. "You've lost weight too, haven't you?"

"Did and gained it back."

"Stand up," she commanded.

"Why?"

"Humor me." Then she grabbed his waist, squeezing a fold of flesh.

"What's wrong?"

She released him and found her calipers, taking measurements from his thigh and waist and chest. "What were you last time?"

"Four percent." Body fat.

Consulting the chart, she said, "Two percent. Provided you're how old? Thirty-five?"

It should have been wondrous news. Next to no body fat

implies ample muscle mass, nothing extra to carry around the world. But Phillip felt a deep foreboding and an anger, taking a long moment to think about crazy nonsense. Like Nash. Somehow Nash was involved—

—and he asked, "What else can we test?"

She put him on a fancy treadmill, a hose in his mouth and his oxygen consumption measured with clinical care. Then he was run to exhaustion, the treadmill roaring at a six-minute-per-mile pace, then inclined, creating an endless hill that finally, after what felt like a week, left him spent and temporarily sore.

"Not eighty," he heard.

Oxygen over body mass. He couldn't remember the units, but eighty is Olympic caliber.

Then the therapist said, "Seventy-nine. Which might be eighty if we run you again." She gazed at Phillip with a mixture of awe and doubt. "What's that? Six points higher than last time?"

Something like that, yes.

"Are you blood doping?"

No.

"Because something's different," she assured him.

Phillip tried to imagine himself in the Olympics, hanging with the willowy Kenyans, then surging at the end and winning the marathon by plenty; yet the scene felt unreal, almost ludicrous, some instinct firmly assuring him that it would never happen.

"Run more tests," he muttered.

"For what?"

"Drugs."

"Are you taking drugs, Phillip?"

He said nothing.

"Because these are very, very effective drugs. If that's what it is."

"Can you?"

She shook her head, shrugged, and said, "We can send your urine to a lab, sure. If you think there's some kind of problem."

There was a problem, but the lab found nothing.

Clean, said the report.

Clean, clean, clean.

The wind drops to nothing in front of the storm, the supersaturated air thick enough to drink; and the booming of thunder is constant, distant but stronger every minute. The sky itself has been halfway covered with black clouds, and when Phillip looks back, just as lightning strikes at the earth, he realizes that the Terror isn't quite holding pace anymore.

Instinct says, "Fast," and he obeys, charging through a basin and up the next hill. Legs ache and stiffen, but he keeps them moving. Fifteen years of being chased tells him that the Terror is dropping back, hating this soup more than he hates it, suffering from the humidity after hours of hard motion.

No wind blows across the body; sweat rolls off him, cooling nothing; his flesh feels nearly feverish, cooking itself.

Terrors, he thinks in a lucid moment, *must be nocturnal.*

The thundering leaden air closes in around Phillip, choking him, and he fights the seductive desire to drop and vomit—

The Terror feels worse.

—and not even a backward glance now. Not once. He summons everything for this one final surge across someone else's Earth.

RUNNING LOG:
7/24 144 32
Two mile warm-up, stretching
Comments—Nash Nash Nash Nash NASH NASH NASH NASH *NASH NASH*

The track was crowded that evening, maybe two dozen joggers and serious plodders working hard, and Phillip was stretching, down on the grass and one leg out in front of him, nose to his knee with minimal effort. The white Mercedes appeared in the distance, turning off the boulevard and then into the student lot, parking exactly where it had parked last time and the driver's door opening and Phillip watching Nash, part of him icy calm and part of him anything but. But he refused to act scared. The asshole was only crazy, he had told himself for weeks. And he could handle crazy. Putting his cheek to his knee, he held the stretch for as long as it took Nash to walk to him. Wearing the green warm-up, naturally. And grinning. Then kneeling beside him, the fabric crackling and one of his knees giving a faint dry *pop.*

"Hello, Phillip."

Phillip said nothing, sitting up and taking a full deep breath. A picture of calm, yet his heart was beginning to ram against his ribs.

"Speed work, Phillip?"

So talk, he thought. And he said, "Mile repeats."

"A poor plan," the crazy man responded.

Ignore him. Phillip changed legs and dropped and held the new stretch, his face turned the other direction, looking west across the clipped and summer-browned grass of the practice field.

"You should rest now," he heard. "Relax."

Phillip asked, "Why?"

"Because," said the voice behind him. "In a few days, I think, you'll need your energy. Very soon."

Phillip sat up, breathed, and looked at Nash.

Nash wasn't smiling, but there was something serene and infinitely pleased in his expression, the pale skin of his face reflecting the ruddy sunlight, the eyes never larger.

"Go away," Phillip whispered, his voice breaking.

"Perhaps you could spend these days putting your affairs in order." The arrogance showed again, never far beneath the words and gestures. "I think it's fair to give you that chance."

Go away.

Nash leaned closer, one hand patting Phillip on the knee. "In your Arctic," he began, "wolves run the caribou for miles—"

What?

"—even though they can catch them sooner. They run them, and do you know why?"

Not breathing, Phillip waited. His mind was blank.

And the crazy man said nothing, reaching into his own mouth with a motion practiced and efficient, fingers gripping something and giving a strong jerk—gripping his tongue—and the tongue slipped free with a smooth wet squish, twisting and rolling as it lay in his upturned palm.

A new tongue emerged from between the large white teeth, thinner and long, gut-red and shiny.

The voice was distorted but recognizable.

"They chase," said Nash, "and because? Because it sweetens the meat."

Sweetens the meat.

But what truly scared Phillip—what terrified him enough to make him shiver and moan—wasn't the words and it wasn't the monster's tongue. It was him looking across the track, watching the various runners and even knowing a few of their names . . . and him realizing with a chilling honesty that nobody here cared about him. Not enough to believe him, much less help him.

He was alone.

Watching Nash walk away. Understanding that anything could happen to him. Anything. And he would never be missed.

Lightning strikes nearby, a scalding white blast of electricity followed by the immediate crash, and he presses toward the hill's crest, wishing that the next bolt will hit behind him, frying the

Terror. It's possible. Unlikely but undeniably possible, which means that in a multitude of universes it does happen—

—and he glances backward once from the crest, for an instant, discovering a lead, authentic and intoxicating. The Terror is a tiny shape almost lost against the grass, maybe three hundred yards between them. Flashes of more distant lightning show the creature in strobe-fashion, once and then again. It's laboring, if only a little bit. Bent forward and distracted by its own fatigue.

At least Phillip believes that it's tired, bolstering his own confidence, over the sharp crest and stopping again, then kneeling, facing east and working to count the seconds, guessing pace and distance and waiting, gathering himself.

The first fat cold drops of rain fall on his back.

Another blast of lightning illuminates every head of grass, every raindrop; then comes a sudden cold wind, swirling and throwing more rain. Over his shoulder he sees the storm rushing across the valley, black and fast, and roaring, and Phillip hearing nothing but a faint gray whisper, eyes dropping, hands strangling the little axe.

After Nash drove away, after the aborted intervals, Phillip went home and changed into his uniform and went to work, struggling for normalcy. Then he came home and lay in bed, never sleeping, listening to the hum of his refrigerator and anonymous thuds through the apartment walls and a car backfiring two blocks away. By noon he was up again, sitting on his sofa, trying to think of anyone he could visit in the middle of the day, or call. Who would believe him and offer to help him? It was a horrible puzzle, no good answer waiting at the end. What was better, he learned, was to pretend that Nash was just a liar using tricks to tease him. To torture him. To make him look like a madman to the world.

Phillip drifted into sleep for a few hours, then awoke in the evening. Again he dressed in the rumpled brown uniform, and he left home with seventy-two dollars in his wallet, driving toward work after nightfall, watching the traffic in the mirrors and no trace of a Mercedes shadowing him. He barely warned himself what he was planning, driving past the factory, out onto the interstate, then east, skirting the empty unlit hill country and pushing the old Datsun to better than seventy, hands clinging to the steering wheel and his eyes on the mirrors more than they looked ahead.

Nobody was following him. By dawn he was into his third state, feeling relief and even a tentative joy. He celebrated with breakfast at a truck stop—a substantial greasy egg-and-sausage breakfast—and wondered where he should stop driving. How far was far enough? And he would need a place to live, plus a job. How did a person acquire a new life?

This is best, he kept telling himself.

Now running was impossible, under any name. He imagined that Nash would be searching for an athlete matching his description, and Phillip was desperate enough to accept the loss of that linchpin. Looking at the truckers and salesmen and vacationers and waitresses, examining their tired self-involved faces, he tried to fashion some imaginary life for himself. True friends; a wife; fat pink kids. It was the kind of normalcy that he'd always seen as a trap, suffocating and final; yet nothing could feel as precious or remarkable now, Phillip assuring himself that he'd never run another step, making himself fat and slow, and old, no monster ever again taking any interest in him.

He paid and left, the urgency gone. Driving again, it occurred to Phillip that this was nothing new. Once before he had transformed his life, making himself over again, and he would do it better this time.

At the next rest area he pulled off and parked. The men's room was empty, and he took the back stall, hearing the men's room door open and close and someone cough, then the rattle of a zipper. Eventually, a urinal was flushed, and the door opened, and someone else entered as the first man left. Phillip heard a squeak of shoes. Then he rose and flushed, fastening the brown trousers. And he stepped out and around the stalls, Nash standing with his back to one of the urinals, squatting, the warm-up's trousers around his ankles and the face smiling, arrogance mixed with amusement as he said:

"These aren't designed for me."

Phillip felt almost no surprise. In that instant, in many ways, he found himself retreating from shock and fear and every other strong emotion. Of course he had been followed. Of course this creature could track him at will, no escape possible. Any other thought was ridiculous, even foolish. To have come as far as this thing had come—

—and he thought of a question, swallowing before he asked, "What are you? Really?"

A laugh came, almost musical. Nash said, "The best translation? A Terror. That's what we call ourselves."

Phillip stared at the penisless crotch and the bizarre birdlike architecture of the hips and legs. The trousers must somehow hide the differences, he realized; and he muttered:

"A Terror?"

"And my name is not Nash, I'm afraid." The Terror pulled up the trousers, then turned and began to wash its hands in the sink, hot water and strong soap swirling together. "My true name is NaaATat."

Phillip looked into the urinal. Something white and semisolid, like bird shit, was floating on the yellow water.

"Where are you from?" Phillip managed to ask.

"Didn't I tell you?" Another laugh. "From another Earth, Phillip. A separate and distinct alternate possibility."

He thought of running, but his legs refused to move. And he imagined striking the Terror, using his fists. But the creature seemed too relaxed and confident, and too large. *Wait*, he cautioned himself. *Wait.*

It dried its hands against its shirt, then said, "Here. Look." And it opened the shirt in front, proudly showing its pale muscular chest. There were no nipples, and every line was wrong, the rib cage too narrow and the arms set wrong into the wide shoulders. It wasn't a bird's chest, nor anything else that Phillip could name. He barely heard the squeak of the door, the Terror closing the shirt as a beefy fellow came around the corner, finding the men facing one another, the scene odd. Probably obscene. The man cursed in low tones, shuffling into one of the stalls; and the Terror said:

"Come with me."

Phillip followed. Again he thought of running and didn't. And of fighting but wouldn't. He was trapped. Stepping into the brilliant horizontal sunshine, he squinted and gave a long discouraged sigh. Parked beside his Datsun was the Mercedes, white as bone. The Terror opened the passenger's door for him, and he sat on the smooth warm leather seat, swinging his legs inside, the door slammed shut and locking itself. *Wait. Pick your moment.* The interior was gloomy with the smoked glass windows, the world outside left in perpetual twilight. The Terror walked around the front and climbed in and shut its door, grinning now, hands on the wheel, telling Phillip with a happy voice:

"Anything is possible."

Phillip sighed again.

"Everything is possible," he heard, "and everything happens in an endless array of living universes."

"I don't understand," he whispered.

They were driving east again, no need to hurry now. Traffic

passed them until they came to the next interchange, and the Terror—a careful, even overly cautious driver—signaled and took them off and over the viaduct, then back onto the interstate again, driving west.

Phillip's stomach hurt. He placed a hand on it, kneading the muscles.

"Within my universe, on my Earth," said the Terror, "there was a line of protobirds who never gained flight. Who never lost their hands. Whose wrists never fused, and who moved into the trees to live like lemurs and monkeys. Who survived every mass extinction for a hundred million years, eventually thriving."

Phillip worked to not listen.

"Everything is possible. And each universe is a structure built from countless unlikely events."

He took a breath and held it, his chest aching.

The Terror looked at him, saying, "Drink something. I brought several bottles. You'll want to be hydrated and fed for this."

On the backseat was a gym bag. Inside it were three water bottles filled with strong mixtures of STRIDE, plus his peacock-colored racing flats and his black shorts and a new pair of polypropylene socks, a tag dangling from the toes. Holding up one shoe, Phillip said, "You were in my apartment?"

"I took liberties," the Terror confessed. "I thought you would appreciate your own shoes."

Phillip managed a few mouthfuls of the sweet-bitter liquid, remembering the taste and feeling a tingle beneath his skin.

Then NaaATat was telling him, "My Earth is especially strange. You see, it gave rise to two intelligent tool-using species simultaneously. Both upright. One omnivorous, the other more predatory. Each with its own hemisphere. But then the seas dropped during an ice age, and each followed the wandering herds onto the other's lands."

Phillip breathed and asked, "Why tell me?"

"Aren't you even a little curious?" The Terror laughed and said, "I am very disappointed, Phillip."

"Fuck you," he whispered.

"This other species was mammalian. Primate-derived. In appearance and history and habits, it was human." Again the Terror opened its shirt, exposing the chest. One hand on the steering wheel, it pulled a small cylinder from a leather pocket on the door, air hissing as the tool applied paint to its flesh, an artful spearhead drawn on the sternum. "We competed," it explained. "For thousands of years, in every sense of the word, we competed for dominion over our Earth. Terrors and the Others. A vast sad brutal lovely holy struggle, and, of course, we worshiped one another. We carved idols with our enemy's face, and we stole each other's gods, and no honor was so great as the honor won in a fair fight. A Terror and an equal Other would chase one another to the death, everyone's gods cheering for the victor."

Phillip sat back and shut his eyes.

"Pressed by the Others, we evolved faster than we might have evolved otherwise. Otherwise? Isn't that a pun?"

He opened his eyes. The monster was peeling some kind of tape from its back, freeing a short thin tail that had been pulled flush against its spine.

"We entered our industrial age many thousands of years ago. And I'm sorry to confess, Phillip, that one of our first acts was to make our great enemy vanish. Extinct. In a century or two, we owned the entire Earth, yet part of us died with them. A vital part, I think."

Phillip looked at the door handle, trying to will himself to open it. *Fall out and roll. Crippled, I won't be worth anything.*

"Eventually, we learned about the hyperrealm and the infinite universes, Earths populated with every assemblage of life, and we have excelled. In part we have excelled because we know how to deal with strange species. We have experience, of course. Which is our special luck."

Phillip said nothing.

"Imagine our astonishment and joy, Phillip. On a portion of Earths, like yours, humans have evolved without us. Safe from us. How would you feel if an essential part of your heritage were to reappear after death? What would you do?"

"Will you destroy us?" he whispered.

"Hardly. Dear Phillip, we are civilized creatures. We make friends. We trade. We take nothing but the best. The excess. Following the ancient faiths, with a multitude of Earths in our reach, we can afford to be selective."

Phillip took a breath and held it.

The Terror had stopped painting its chest, putting down the stick and shoving two fingers into some hidden seam on the other wrist, peeling that hand free as you would a tight-fitting glove. The hand within was clawed and long and reminiscent of a chicken's foot, bony and scaled. Then that hand reached below, removing one green shoe to expose a long three-toed foot, claws painted red. Then the first hand pierced a seam on the neck, removing the face and shoulders with a hard jerk. Everything changed in an instant. Except for its eyes, Phillip noticed. And he gasped, moaning to himself, pressing against the door and jerking on the handle, the lock refusing to release.

There were bright red feathers and a bony abbreviated beak, the human teeth removed and curved white knives in their place, the beak able to move enough to feign a smile, and a changed voice telling him:

"You can win, I promise you. There is no glory in the unlosable contest."

Phillip stared at the creature, trying to gather himself.

"Not that you will have a great chance of winning, either." The laugh was huge and shrill, almost birdlike. "I'm not an idiot, after all."

Phillip reached with both hands, trying for the steering wheel, then he felt the impact of a needle plunging into his back, up through the upholstery, a cocktail of drugs making him fall asleep in moments.

"That's good," he heard. "Rest will help you, I should think."

Then he was awake again, finding himself running hard and alone across an empty windswept prairie.

Never the sprinter, he digs and drives, adrenaline and nerves helping and his arms pumping, coming back over the crest again, charging the Terror that he imagines must be on the other side . . . and wrong, by a few feet, leaping at the last instant and lightning exploding behind him and the weary shocked big-eyed Terror on his left, not his right, Phillip having to twist and swing the axe while off-balance, without ample force.

The other axe is lifted, metal striking metal, thunder masking the sound and rainwater washing over them in a wave. Phillip lands and nearly falls, twisting again, a blind quick slash at the closer arm while the Terror's axe is down—

Another fierce blast of lightning.

—and meat cut, then bone, a forearm left ruined and bloody and his opponent's scream loud as the thunder.

Another slash, nothing struck.

Then he retreats and thinks again and charges.

And the Terror changes hands, blocking the next blow with its axe, wood against wood and the blades catching and the Terror managing to focus and drive and twist, screaming again, Phillip's axe pulled from his fingers and thrown off into the swirling grass.

Phillip retreats again, trying to follow the axe's flight.

Then the Terror descends on him, protecting its bad arm and

swinging, and swinging, then shouting in its own language, invoking gods, swinging a third time and Phillip dropping back, then stumbling and falling and down on his side, momentarily stunned.

The Terror charges, and he rolls.

Stands.

The axe strikes on Phillip's shoulder but the blade missing high, a bruise and crunch and he's charging, screaming for himself, getting beneath the Terror and swinging with his fists, then twisting and driving an elbow into the ribs and falling backward, the Terror beneath him and its good arm taking aim.

Phillip grabs it by the wrist, the Terror muscling the blade down to within inches of his face. He sees the flash of lightning in the polished metal. He can't resist the pressure. Still on top of the Terror, he feels as if he is being embraced to death, breathing in gulps and screaming, "Fuck you!" and then, "You won't!" and lifting his head, twisting his neck, finding a fat long chicken finger in his mouth and clamping down hard enough to taste blood, then tendons, the teeth cutting into a white rubbery joint—

—and the Terror wails and flings the axe to one side, freeing itself. Phillip is up and turning. Lightning strikes a nearby hillside, the world lit up for miles, and something short lies in the grass, him bending fast and gripping a handle, knowing the feel of it and turning—

—and the Terror fumbling for its axe—

—and Phillip charging it and swinging, catching the lowered head with the wood and blade, the head giving a good solid *pop* as it snaps back, the body collapsing in an instant.

Then he stands over the monster, not thinking.

And again it reaches for its axe, Phillip screaming, "No!" and striking the nearest leg as if it's firewood, severing the hamstring, a deep thorough wound crippling the Terror and it screaming, grabbing what's ruined.

Phillip throws its axe as far as he can.

And he turns back, believing he is ready. He stands over the monster with his axe in both hands, and it grows silent and still, having the discipline or the fear to deny the white pain.

Phillip remembers.

With rain falling, with the Terror sprawled out in a bowl of matted grass, he remembers the crow and its butchered ground squirrel; and then the monster shouts:

"Please, please take my head!"

What?

"Set it! My head! In a place of honor!"

As a trophy? Is that what it wants?

"Promise me," the creature begs.

And Phillip thinks of that long-dead ground squirrel, feeling an aching genuine pity—

—no, not for the squirrel.

"Please," NaaATat whimpers.

Phillip leans close, asking, "How do I get home?"

"My car. Is where we began." A wince of pain. "It will take you."

"Will it?"

"With my head? Promise me?"

Phillip doesn't answer, contemplating everything. Whatever happens, he knows, his life is remade. It's reconstituted around what he chooses to do now—

"I beg you, please!"

—and he decides, lifting his axe and cutting with the long serrated blade, slicing free a handful of the brilliant red feathers, saying, "Sorry," over the sound of the wind-driven rain. "You just picked the wrong animal, I guess."

The Terror screams once again, in horror.

Then Phillip begins to run, leaving it, moving east with a gentle gait, feathers in one hand and the axe in the other.

Sometimes he stops, tipping his head back to drink rainwater.

How many miles so far?

He doesn't even guess, running with a pace that he can hold forever, laughing and then crying and then laughing again, hills to the horizon and him floating over each of them in turn.

CHRYSALIS

 HE STARSHIP embraced many names.
To the Artisans, it was 2018CC — a bloodless designation for a simple world of ice and cold tars that was long ago gutted, then given engines and a glorious purpose, carrying off the grateful survivors of an utterly inglorious war.

To its organic passengers, human and otherwise, it wore more evocative names: squeals and squawks and deep-bass drummings, plus names drawn in light, and sweet pheromonal concoctions with no easy translation.

The *fouchians*, a species incapable of exaggeration, knew the ship as The-Great-Nest-Within-Another's-Black-Soil — an honored name implying wealth, security, and a contented slavery.

The whalelike *moojin* sang about the Grand Baleen.

Home was the literal meaning of many, many names.

As were Womb and Egg and Salvation.

Two dissimilar lactators, in utterly different languages, called it Mother's Nipple, while a certain birdlike creature, in a related vein, screeched lovingly, "Our Mother's Green Vomit."

Humans were comfortable with many names, which was only reasonable. They had built the ship and its Artisans, and no other species was half as abundant. In casual conversation they called the starship the Web, or the Net, or Hope, or the Ark, or Skyborn, or Wanderer. In the ancient ceremonies, when reverence was especially in demand, it was Paradise or Eden, or most often, with enduring emotion: Heaven.

A name of chilling dimensions.

If you are admitted to Heaven, then it stands to reason that every other place in Creation is somehow flawed. Tainted. Impure.

And if you deserve perfection, shouldn't you be perfect yourself? Not just occasionally, not just where it matters most, but always, in every ordinary day, from your first sip of milk or green vomit to your very last happy perfect breath?

By any measure, the Web was a vast ship. Even small habitats were huge, particularly when you are a young girl, wonderstruck at every turn.

Sarrie was born in one of the oldest human habitats, in a village of farmers, hunters, and shop clerks. From her playroom she could see the length of the habitat—a diamond-hulled cylinder spinning for mock-gravity, not especially large but substantial enough to hold a few rugged mountains and a stormy little sea. It was a perfect home for a fledgling genius. Sarrie's foster parents were gently brilliant and happily joined—shopkeepers who weren't too smart or happy to ignore their carefully tailored daughter. From the instant of conception, the girl's development was monitored and adjusted, reappraised and readjusted, her proven genetics enriched by the peaceful village, an alignment of gloved forces steadily nudging her toward the ultimate goal: Voice.

Sarrie spoke long before she could walk. Before her second birthday, she could hold her own in idle adult conversation. Barely four years old, she wrote an awful little novel, but sprinkled through its pages were complex and lovely sentences that lingered in the reader's astonished mind. Later, she invented her own language to write a second novel, then taught the language to her best friend—an older and taller and effortlessly beautiful girl named Lilké. To her credit, Lilké read every make-believe word. "It's wonderful," she claimed. But a Voice knows when someone is lying, and why, and Sarrie forgave her best friend, the lie meant to spare her pain.

The Artisans ruled the Web with the lightest of touches. They normally didn't visit the habitats, seeing no need to intrude on the organics. But one particular Artisan made a habit of coming to see Sarrie. His name was Ejy, and he would wear a human-style body out of politeness, resembling any wise old man but smelling like new rubber, his hairless brown face projecting a perpetual smile, oversized black eyes bright in any light and blinking now and again to serve the illusion of humanness.

It was obvious that he had a special interest in the child, and Sarrie's parents were proud in appropriate ways, encouraging her to behave when he was there—as if she ever misbehaved—and to be a good audience, asking smart questions and giving prompt, perfect answers when she knew them. But only if she knew them, of course.

When Sarrie was eight years old, Ejy brought her a thick volume filled with butterflies.

"Select one," he instructed, his voice smooth and dry, and timeless. "Any species you wish, child. Go on now."

"But why?" she had to ask.

"I will build it for you," he replied. "Are you intrigued?"

Sarrie couldn't count the butterflies or find any end to the book. Reaching its final page, she flipped to the front again and discovered still more butterflies, every stage of their lives shown in three dimensions, usually in their natural size. Captions were available in every shipboard language; the young Voice understood most of the audio captions. Some of the butterflies had lived on the lost Earth, but most were alien, possessing the wrong number of legs or odd eyes, giant differences undoubtedly buried in their genetics. Lilké was going to become a geneticist; Sarrie tried to think of questions worth asking her friend. That's why she paused for a moment, and Ejy interrupted, asking, "Which one will it be?"

She blinked, a little startled, then turned the soft plastic page and pointed to the first place where her eyes found purchase.

The butterfly wasn't large, and while lovely, she didn't find it exceptional. And the Artisan seemed equally surprised by her choice. Crystal eyes grew larger and more round, thin lips diminishing the smile. Yet he declared, "It's a fine selection." With warm rubber-scented hands, he retrieved the book, then turned and prepared to leave.

Sarrie waited as long as possible, which was maybe five seconds. Then she blurted out, "When do I get to see the butterfly?"

Ejy was a tease. Glancing over a shoulder, he smiled and made laughing sounds, the dry voice warning her, "To be done well, even butterflies need a little time. Haven't you learned that yet, child?"

"A little time" to the Artisans can mean days, or it can mean aeons. But a young girl training as a Voice is too busy and happy to dwell on promised gifts.

Three weeks passed in a pleasant blur. Language lessons were peppered with general studies in science and the Web's glorious history. A Voice was a specialist in twenty areas, at least. That was why they were rare and why their training was so rigorous. Someday, in thirty or forty years, Sarrie would accompany a team of explorers to one of the nearby suns. If the team found sentient life, it would be her duty and honor to make contact with it, deciphering the alien minds. And if they were worthy, she would try to lure them into joining her, giving their devotion to the Web.

Sarrie loved her studies, and after three weeks, when her tutor quit lecturing in midsentence, she was disappointed. Perhaps even angry. The tutor told her to go to an isolated valley, and go alone. "No," it warned her, "Lilké is not invited." Of course the girl obeyed, running herself breathless and still gasping when she found Ejy waiting for her. He was in an open glade, wearing green-and-black robes over his human body, and wearing the enduring smile. The trees surrounding them were covered with gemstones, bright and sparkling in the mock-sunshine. The stones were cocoons almost ready to hatch. Ejy never mentioned them. He filled the next hour with questions, testing the Voice. Meanwhile, the day warmed and the cocoons grew dull, then split open within moments of each other. The butterflies were identical, each one a little bigger than Sarrie's hand, emerald wings decorated with white eye patches and margins black as comet tar. A colored hallucinogenic snow seemed to fill the woods, wingbeats making a thin dry sound, thunderous in the gentlest fashion.

The tailored creatures lived vigorously and fully until their fat stocks were spent. The busiest few were first to drop, but all fell within the next few minutes; and Sarrie watched the spectacle, composing poems in her head but saying nothing until it was done.

Ejy seemed as happy as any Artisan could be.

Afterward, he told her that her chosen species came from a world of insects, and that this particular species had not flown in half a million years.

Sarrie was impressed, and she said so.

"Why am I fond of you, child?"

Startled, she remained sensibly mute. "Voice" was an inadequate name. The best Voices were exceptional listeners, and even when they guessed an answer, some questions were left untouched.

"Tell me, child. If you meet strangers, what will you do?"

" 'Embrace their souls,' " she quoted. " 'Show them the Web's caring face.' "

"How many Voices are being trained today?"

Several hundred, she had heard. At least one Voice would represent each of the ship's organic species—

"Yet you are possibly our finest Voice."

It was an incredible thing to hear. Sarrie was eight years old, her talents barely half-formed, and how could anyone, even an Artisan, know who was best?

"I love humans," Ejy confessed. "More than any other organic, I do."

In a whisper, she asked, "Why?"

He touched the thin false hair on his head. "Human genius designed me. It built me. It gave me a noble mission. And when I wear this body, I do it to honor you and your species."

Sarrie nodded, absorbing every sound, every tiny cue.

"I have lived on 2018CC since its inception. Which makes me how old?" Several million years, she knew.

"If I could become organic, I should like to be human." It was another astonishing statement, yet he didn't linger on it. "Suppose you could become a different species, child. Not in the abstract, as Voices try to do. But in reality, as flesh and fluid . . . which species would you become. . . ?"

She reached down, gently grasping one of the dying butterflies. It was dusty and strangely warm, weighing almost nothing, its mouthparts adapted to suck nectar from a very specific, very extinct flower. There was a soft chirp, then it sprayed her with a mist of fragrant oils; and for lack of better, she told Ejy, "This."

Doubt shone on the Artisan's face. "And why, child?"

"It's very beautiful—"

"You are lying. To me, you are lying." His voice didn't sound angry, but a fire shone behind his eyes. "I know you, Sarrie. You don't know yourself half as well as I do, and you just lied."

Sarrie shook her head, claiming, "I did not—"

"First of all, these aren't your favorite colors." He pulled the carcass from her hand. "And more important, where's the value in becoming something that's lovely? This species has slept in our library for five hundred millennia, dead and forgotten, and if you hadn't chosen it, it would have remained dead until the end of time."

He dropped the butterfly, both of them watching it flip and spin downward like a paper glider.

"You are exactly who you should be, Sarrie." Wise, ageless eyes smiled, and the pink tongue peeked out from between narrow lips. "The universe is full of beautiful, perishable things. Butterflies, for instance. They can take infinite forms, and they are cheap. But a rare skill — the genius of a Voice, for example — is something that will be born and born again, without end."

"I didn't mean to lie," she whispered, in self-defense.

"Oh, yes, you did." Ejy laughed, then assured her, "And I know what you were thinking. I know what you would ask to become."

She said nothing.

"To be an Artisan, of course."

"No!" she roared.

"Oh, yes," he replied. "You envy our immortality. You lie awake at night, wishing you could know everything." A pause. "Given your chance, child, you would happily rule this noble ship of ours. Any human would. It is your simple nature."

He was correct, in a fashion. Deep inside Sarrie were black desires that she'd kept secret from everyone, including herself . . . and she collapsed suddenly out of shame and fear, the dead butterflies pressed against her face, threatening to choke her . . . and warm unliving hands pulled her up again, warm immortal words assuring Sarrie that she was fine, all was well, and regardless of childish thoughts, she was loved and always would be. . . .

2: Sarrie's final novel was a tribute to life on the starship.
An enormous plotless epic, it was consumed, and loved, by every sentient organic. Sarrie was barely sixteen and found herself suddenly famous. Every translation was her responsibility, regardless whether the species read with its eyes or touch or its sensitive nose. Her most avid fans would travel to the village just to give her thanks: a peculiar, but sincere, parade of well-wishers. Even the fouchians paid their respects, their massive bodies dressed in woven soil, dim little eyes squinting despite black eye shades. A social species with strict castes and an evolutionary history of slavery, they had thrived under the Artisans' care. Except for humans, no organic was as abundant, and perhaps none was as trusted. There was no greater honor than a

fouchian's squeak of applause, telling you that your work had captured the special joy in being another's treasured property. And with their nose tendrils quivering, holding tight to the precious novel, the molelike fouchians would bless Sarrie; and she in turn would squeak the proper thanks, and when they turned to leave, she would carefully sniff each of their rectums with all the formality that she could manage.

Ejy, as always, seemed pleased with her success, if never surprised. His visits remained irregular but memorable, and always intense. They would discuss her studies, her rapid progress, and the approaching future. Then as he prepared to leave, Ejy would give the young Voice an elaborate simulation, its aliens bizarre, their souls almost impossible to decipher. But Sarrie was required not just to decipher them, but to win their trust, too. That was why Voices existed. They brought new blood into the Web—new souls into Heaven—and if Sarrie was ever going to be a true Voice, she certainly needed to outwit Ejy's damned puzzles.

Successes dwarfed failures, but failures lingered in the mind. High-technology aliens were the real nightmares. One of Ejy's scenarios didn't even involve another world. Instead, there was a starship as large as the Web, and a xenophobic crew, and Sarrie tried to solve the puzzle at least twenty times, each attempt more disastrous than the last. She wept each time the Web was obliterated by nuclear fire and laser light. The situation was absurd— the Artisans had never met their equals—but she was left unnerved and disheartened.

If Sarrie couldn't charm these fictional entities, how could she be trusted out in the universe, coping with reality?

Lilké, always the friend, comforted her with jokes and buoyant little compliments. "Ejy is just keeping you humble," she would claim. "You know there's no such starship out there. Organics destroy themselves. As soon as we learn to fuse hydrogen, it's inevitable that we'll try to pound ourselves into extinction."

Humans were extinct, save upon the Web.

Millions of years ago, a brutal war left the Earth and the entire solar system devastated. More wars were inevitable. To save themselves, a small group of humans traveled into the Kuiper belt and there carved a starship out of a comet. They intended to protect what they could of their homeland and past. But they didn't trust themselves, much less their descendants: Why go to this bother today if others eventually forgot the past, and in some other solar system, in the same tragic ways, finished the obliteration?

Artisans were a desperate solution.

Frightened, chastened humans placed themselves into the care of machines—the ultimate parents—relinquishing one kind of life and freedom for a safer, sweeter existence.

And as predicted, the final War arrived.

The Web, still little more than an iceberg with rockets, escaped unseen. But it left behind robot spies, scattered and hidden, that watched a thousand more years of senseless fighting—living worlds shattered, debris fighting debris, not even a bug left behind to die in the end.

But the little starship prospered. The occasional comet was mined for raw materials. The ship doubled in size, then doubled again. When a living world was discovered, the Artisans obeyed already ancient programs, hurting nothing, taking samples of every species, adding to their cryogenic archives before wandering to the next likely sun, and the next.

An intelligent species was found eventually. How to deal with them? Machines shouldn't leave the ship, it was decided, which was how the Voices were born. But when the first mission ended in disaster, the Artisans told the survivors that the blame was theirs. They were the ship's masters, and by any definition, masters are always responsible for the mistakes of their property.

Provided it is done well, slavery can bring many comforts.

Later worlds brought success. Better talent and training made for better Voices, and they brought new species on board, enlarging the talent pool and everyone's prosperity.

The starship became the Web, moving along one great spiral arm of the galaxy. Thousands of worlds were explored, billions of species preserved in the archives, and by Sarrie's time there were more than a hundred sentient organics living in habitats built just for them, lured there, as always, by the honest and earnest and easily seductive Voices.

When Sarrie and Lilké had free time—a rare event—they liked to visit the nearby habitats, human and otherwise, or sometimes ride a bubble car back and forth on the vast diamond threads to which every home was strung.

The Web was an awesome mixture of beauty and pragmatic engineering. Thousands of kilometers across, it was sprinkled with cylindrical habitats and moon-sized fuel tanks feeding rockets that hadn't stopped firing in living memory, carrying them toward stars still invisible to the naked eye. Success had swollen the ship; new mass meant greater momentum, hard-won and difficult to extinguish. The far-off future would have to deal with those stars. What mattered to the young women was several dozen nearer suns, bright and dim, aligned like tiny gems on a twisted necklace. Each gem had its own solar system, they knew. Several centuries of work would consume generations of scientists and Voices—a daunting, wondrous prospect. And the young Voice would hold her best friend's hands, they would sing their favorite songs to praise the Web, and the Artisans, and the wisdom of their ancestors for making their astonishing lives possible.

Behind the Web, in the remote distance, was the diffused brilliance of the Milky Way. They had left its embrace long ago. Momentum was one reason. It was easiest to let the ship's momentum carry them into the cold between galaxies, finding orphaned suns and saving whatever life had evolved in that solitude. In essence, Sarrie understood, they were making an enormous lazy turn, allowing the Milky Way's gravity to help reclaim them, like some wayward child, gently pulling them back into the other spiral arm.

Sarrie could see the future from the bubble car, and the past, and she would weep out of simple joy, earning good-natured barbs from the realist beside her.

The realist was bolder than Sarrie, and more inquisitive. Lilké was the product of Artisan ingenuity, genius genes working in concert with a scientist's upbringing, which was likely why she was the one who suggested that they visit the archives. "Like now," she said. "What's the matter with now?"

There was no rule against it. None. Yet Sarrie wanted to ask permission first. "We'll go home, and I'll contact Ejy—"

"No," Lilké snapped. "This time is ours, and I want to go there."

It wasn't a particularly long journey. Their car took them to the center of the Web, to a mammoth triple-hulled wheel bristling with telescopes of every flavor, plus an array of plasma guns and lasers, the weapons meant for defense, nothing to shoot but the occasional comet.

Sarrie felt ill at ease. Stepping from the car into a small white-walled room, she held Lilké's hand as if it were all that kept her from drowning . . . and after what seemed like a long wait, though probably it was no more than a minute, the whiteness parted, a doorway revealed, and an Artisan emerged, its body unlike any she had ever seen.

It was a machine's body, practical and elegant in design, but simple, its corners left sharp and a variety of spare limbs stacked like firewood on its long back. Jointed legs clattered on the milky floor. A clean, lifeless voice said, "Welcome."

Artisans were machines. Of course they were. But why did

Sarrie feel surprise? And why did she lose the last of her poise, blurting out, "I want to speak to Ejy. Is Ejy here?"

The machine replied, "Certainly, my child—"

"We've come for a tour, if that's possible." Sarrie couldn't stop her mouth, and she couldn't begin to think. "My friend here, Lilké, is a geneticist, or she will be . . . and she wants to see the archives . . . if it's not too much trouble—!"

A soft laugh came from the rolling machine.

"Sarrie," said its voice. "Don't you recognize me?"

Ejy?

And he laughed louder, Lilké joining in . . . then finally, grudgingly, the embarrassed Voice, too. . . .

Ejy took them on a tour of the ancient facility.

Every surface was white, befitting some logic of cleanliness, or perhaps some ascetic sensibility. Each wall was divided into countless deep drawers, cylindrical and insulated and sealed, every drawer filled with the DNA or RNA or PNA from a vast array of past worlds.

First and always, the Artisans were insatiable collectors.

They walked for a long while. Sometimes they saw other Artisans, their machine bodies the same but for the details. Sarrie didn't feel entirely welcome, but then again, she couldn't trust her instincts. Voices were bred and trained to know organics, not machines, and she reminded herself that their long glassy stares and chill silences might mean nothing at all.

In one nondescript corridor, Ejy paused without warning, touching a control panel, a skeletal ramp unfolding from a wall.

"Climb," he told the women. "All the way to the top, if you please."

The archive's mock-gravity was less than their habitat's, yet the climb was difficult. Sarrie found herself nervous and weak, eyes blurring as she reached the top. Before her was a ceramic drawer, pure white save for the tiniest imaginable black dot—a memory chip—and beside it, in exacting detail, the black silhouette of a human being.

Lilké touched the symbol, lightly, a low keening sound coming from deep in her chest.

"What is within?" asked the Artisan.

"I am," Sarrie whispered.

"And everyone else, too," said Lilké, her fingertips giving it an expectant caress. "Is this where you keep us?"

"The sum total of human genetics," he affirmed, his pride

obvious, hanging in the air after the words had faded. "Every human who has ever lived on 2018CC is represented," he told them, "as are several billion from the ancient Earth. Plus, of course, the unincorporated genes, natural and synthetic, that we will implant in future generations, as needed."

Neither woman spoke. A simple drawer, yet it held their entire species. What could anyone say at such a moment?

Ejy continued, voice purring. "In addition, the walls on both sides of us encompass the Earth's biosphere. Every possible species is represented, including every possible genotypic variation."

An electric surge passed through Sarrie, bringing a clarity, a transcendent sense of purpose.

Lilké, by contrast, saw more pragmatic concerns.

"You should make copies," she warned. "Of everything, if possible. Then put them somewhere else, somewhere safe. Just in case."

The Artisan ignored the thinly veiled criticism.

Glassy eyes on Sarrie, he said, "Imagine this. Within that modest drawer are certain traits that, when combined, make perfection. The ultimate scientist, perhaps. Or our best farmer. Or maybe, a singular Voice." He paused, then asked, "If we ever found perfection, in any job, wouldn't we be wise to let it be born again and again?"

Lilké answered for Sarrie, saying, "Certainly. So long as it helps the Web, you have no choice."

Ejy only watched the Voice. "Certain qualities may vary, of course. Gender and height, and skin color, and general appearance are minor details, free to dance where they wish." Mechanical arms gestured, underscoring each word. "But the soul within is constant. Eternal. And if it is reborn today, wouldn't it be a link in the most glorious chain?"

Sarrie nodded weakly, whispering, "Yes."

Without shifting his gaze, Ejy said, "Imagine this. An Artisan finds perfection. Can you imagine it, Lilké? He finds it in the very early days of the Web, which would mean that this perfect soul has been born how many times? You are good with calculations, Lilké. How many times is she brought out of that little drawer?"

"What's her job?" asked the scientist.

"I cannot say."

Lilké shrugged and played with the numbers regardless. After a moment, she said, "Ten thousand and eleven times. Give or take." Then she broke into a quiet self-satisfied laugh.

Sarrie felt distant, utterly remote, as if watching these events from some invisible faraway sun.

"I can't even say if there is such a soul," Ejy continued. "There are rules that rule even the Artisans, which is only fair."

Both women nodded.

"If you wish to believe in a number near ten thousand, I think you would be rather close. But of course it's a hypothetical problem, and there are no ultimate answers."

It was a strange, compelling game.

The immortal Artisan crawled partway up the ramp, and with a certain quietness asked, "How many lives do you stand on, Sarrie?"

The answer bubbled out of her.

"None," she told Ejy. "I stand on no one else."

"Interesting," was his only response.

Lilké was staring at her friend, astonished and envious and almost certainly dubious of Sarrie's vaunted status. "I'm as good a geneticist as you are a Voice!" her expression shouted.

Then Sarrie, feeling a kind of shame, climbed down the ramp, wondering how many human Voices had visited this holy place, and if Ejy had accompanied all of them, and what answers they might have given to his question: "How many lives do you stand on?"

But there was only one answer, of course, and it was hers.

Then Lilké and Ejy were speaking about the techniques of gene preservation, and Sarrie stood by herself, trying very hard to think of other, more important matters. . . .

3. It was a secretly warm world.

Cherry-hot iron lay at its center, blanketed in a roiling ocean of magma. Only its skin was cold, young rock covered with water ice and a thin nitrogen snow, the face deceptively simple, glowing white and pink beneath the bottomless sky.

The lecturer, an adult male fouchian, described their target world as being formed four billion years ago, presumably in one of the local solar systems. It spent a chaotic youth dancing with its more massive neighbors, orbits shifting every few centuries, a final near-collision flinging it out into the cometary cloud. Perhaps a similar near-collision had thrown this cluster of stars out of the Milky Way. Who knew? Either way, the world today was tracing a slow elliptical orbit around a cool M-class sun, its summers barely warmer than its fifty-thousand-year winters, the original ocean of water frozen beneath a thin atmosphere of noble gases and molecular hydrogen.

Dramatic images floated above the fouchian, fresh from the Web's telescopes. He pointed out volcanoes and mountain ranges and the conspicuous absence of impact craters. Even so far from any sun, heat persisted. Tectonics and the table-smooth plains of ice were evidence of recent liquid water, which meant the possibility of simple life. And with that pronouncement, the fouchian looked out at his audience, reminding them that not every training mission had hopes of finding life. Other, less gifted teams were being sent to survey nearby comets and little plutos, the poor souls. Attempting a human smile, the fouchian lay its nose tendrils against its muzzle, then parted its thin lips, exposing incisors whiter than any ice. "Thank Artisan Ejy for this honor," he told them, his voice box pronouncing words with an eerie hyperclarity. "He specifically chose each of you, just as he selected my Nestbrother and myself to serve as his chief officers. And who are we to doubt an Artisan's judgment?"

Two dozen humans sat together in an open-air amphitheater. It was night in the human habitat, cloudless and warm and lovely. Curious people stood at the gates, straining for a glimpse. Beyond the stage was a broad calm cove, playful dolphins stitching their way through the water, trading insults as they hunted in the living sea.

"A mission at last," Lilké muttered. "We've got something to do!"

Sarrie smiled and nodded, unsure when she had ever felt so happy.

Wearing his human body, Ejy stood on one side of the stage, accompanied by the second fouchian. Sarrie wanted to dance around like a little girl, but how would that look? Instead, she punched commands into her monitor, asking for permission to view the files on this wondrous new world.

A young man was sitting in front of Lilké. Without warning, he stood, giving the fouchian a quarter-bow even as he said, "I have to disagree. There's a lot of liquid water today. More than you've predicted, I think."

He was a sharp-featured, sharp-tongued fellow named Navren. A genius with physical sciences, Sarrie recalled. He understood the periodic table better than did the elements themselves, it was said, and he never, ever let an opinion go unspoken.

"Your estimated heat flows are too small," he informed the

fouchian. "And I see a deep ocean beneath the ice plains. Plenty of vents, and heat energy, and particularly *here*. This basin on the southern hemisphere is our best bet."

The fouchian's tendrils flexed and became a bright pink. A sure sign of anger, Sarrie knew. Yet the artificial voice remained crisp and worthy. "We know the world's age and mass, and Ejy himself made these estimates, all based on long experience—"

"A volcanic pulse," Navren interrupted. "But more likely, residual heat after a major impact." He launched into a thorough analysis, intuition sprinkled over a technical mastery that astonished Sarrie. If it was an impact, she learned, then it was recent—in the last million years—and it had happened where the ice was smoother than a newborn's cheek.

When the impromptu lecture ended, a cold silence held sway.

Every team member should be grateful for expert advice. Yet only Ejy seemed genuinely pleased. His old-human face smiled and smiled, even as his first officer remarked, "No one can make such a quick analysis. I think our distinguished colleague accessed these files before you gave him permission, Artisan Ejy."

It was a serious breach of the rules, if true. Knowledge, in all its glorious colors, belonged to their masters.

But Ejy chose to ignore any offense. "The boy is eager. I see no crime." Black eyes glanced at both fouchian officers. "This is a training mission, children. A simple world is being given to us to share, and let's not forget our purpose. Our unity. Please."

Navren grinned openly, winking at the two young women behind him.

Again, Ejy said, "Children."

He meant humans and he meant fouchians, and Sarrie didn't need to be a Voice to understand the intent of that one potent word.

It had been centuries since the Web had had so many worlds to investigate; very few organics could recall such adventures, and none of them were human. In honor of their mission, the humans held a traditional ceremony, but it turned into a static, formal, and desperately dull affair. It took a party to cure the dullness. With strong drink in her belly, the mission's Voice decided to join Navren, complimenting him for being right about the new world's heat flow. Tiny probes had landed recently, sending home evidence of a genuine ocean, deep and warm and exactly where he had predicted it to be.

Compliments made Navren smile. But he wasn't prompted to

compliment her in turn, his gaze saying, "Of course I was right. Why wouldn't I be?"

Sober, Sarrie would have seen the soul inside the arrogance. But the drunken Voice persisted, confessing excitement, hoping aloud that she could help their mission, if not as a Voice, then at least as a willing worker.

"Forget worrying," was Navren's advice. "This is a useless little mission. It's nothing."

She winced, then remarked, "That seems harsh."

"We're visiting a snowball," he countered. "A big fancy snowball. This team's real work doesn't begin until we slide past the fourth solar system." His narrow brown face showed disgust. "And we'll be old people before we reach its most promising world—"

"What world? How do you know?"

"I had access to our mission files. Remember?"

"You've studied what's coming?"

"Maybe I'm guessing." A big wink, then he said, "Our best prospect is Earth-like. Warm and green. Radio-dead, but even light-years away, it shows evidence of agriculture—"

Sarrie clapped her hands over her ears, in reflex. " 'Knowledge too soon is the same as poison,' " she quoted from the Artisan code. And their mission wasn't useless, either.

Navren shrugged, then effortlessly changed subjects.

"You know," he remarked in a casual self-satisfied way, "you and I won't sleep together. You're wasting your hope trying to seduce me."

Surprise became a fumbling anger. Sarrie muttered, "I was never thinking—"

"Oh, yes, you were," Navren insisted. "You and Lilké talk about me, wondering who's to screw me first."

Astonishing, infuriating words.

And true, but only to a degree. Idle chatter, in passing, and she wouldn't let him entertain the remote possibility. . . !

"You're too conventional for my tastes," Navren continued.

"You don't know me," she growled.

"Of course I do. I read those novels of yours." He shook his head and squinted, telling her, "The second novel was your best."

"You didn't read it."

"In that silly language of yours, yes."

She felt light-headed.

"Besides," he claimed, "every Voice is the same essential creature. Human or fouchian, or whatever. Voices have an exact job, and like it or not, the Artisans build you along very precise lines."

Sarrie took a deep, useless breath.

"On the other hand, I have twenty-three untried genes inside me. I require things to be fresh. New." Emotions that no Voice could have read passed through his face, the eyes flaring. The insufferable man announced, "I think your friend—Lilké, is it?—is more to my taste."

Looking across the green paddock, Sarrie found her parents speaking to Lilké, no doubt wishing her well, and begging her to please watch after "our little Sarrie."

"Tell her what I said," Navren purred. "Tell her to come visit me."

She had enough, cursing him in fouchian and storming off. But later, when Sarrie calmed enough to laugh at the boorish idiot, she told Lilké exactly what he had said. Voices were natural mimics and entertainers, but her lovely friend didn't laugh at the appropriate moments, or even speak, her deep brown-black eyes looking elsewhere, trying to find Navren among all the young blessed geniuses.

Their scout ship was built on ancient proven principles—blunt and swift, fuel tanks and engines dwarfing the tiny crew quarters. With supplies and extraheavy equipment, there was no room left for elbows, much less comfort. Humans had to spend most of the eleven-month voyage in cold-sleep. Only the fouchian officers and Ejy remained awake, each immune to the claustrophobia.

Ten days out from the new world, the sleepers were warmed, then reawakened.

They gorged on breakfasts rich with fat and antioxidants. Then the scientists and engineers were sent to organize their laboratories and calibrate delicate instruments. Lilké found little problems that evaded easy answers. Tests supplied by Ejy? Perhaps, although not likely. Either way, Sarrie helped where possible, then simply tried to stay out of the way. By early evening, she was starving again, teetering close to exhaustion. Yet she felt like a traitor when she excused herself, making amends by promising, "I'll get our cabin in order. Come to bed soon. You need rest, too."

True enough, but her friend didn't arrive by midnight. Bundled up in bed, Sarrie plunged into her first dreams in nearly a year—intricate dreams of being alien, of meeting a human Voice who sang of some faraway Heaven. Waking, she smiled, then realized it was three in the morning and Lilké was missing . . . and of course Sarrie dressed and went to the genetics lab, trembling with worry until she saw that the lab was dark, and sealed, and she finally thought to ask the ship's computer about Lilké's whereabouts.

The computer gave a cabin number. Navren's cabin.

In the morning, after a string of nightmares, Sarrie saw her best friend sitting with Navren in the tiny galley. What she already knew became a concrete truth, as inescapable as physical law. Despite a fierce hunger, she couldn't eat near them; the next few days were spent hiding in her cabin, pretending to work at Ejy's insolvable simulation. As always, the xenophobic aliens destroyed the Web. Nothing she did seemed to mollify them. Yet it didn't matter anymore. Nothing mattered except for Sarrie's black mood, and she clung to it for as long as her nature and Ejy allowed.

The Artisan hadn't spoken twice to the Voice since she had risen from cold-sleep. She had barely wondered why. But within a few hours of their landing, he came to her cabin dressed as the old man, and he asked if she would please join him for a little stroll.

They went to the astronomical lab, empty now despite important work on hand. Empty by command? she wondered. The main screen was filled with their nameless world—a pale white ball, cold and nearly featureless. It seemed incapable of holding Sarrie's attention. She forced herself to appear interested. "Have we learned anything new?" she inquired, knowing that learning was as inevitable on this ship as breathing was.

"We've learned much," the ancient Artisan replied. "But most of it is trivial. Nuggets and details only."

The worthwhile discoveries were waiting for the humans to find them. As it was intended to be, she told herself.

A strong false hand gripped her shoulder, squeezing hard.

Sarrie refused to talk about the lovers in the nearby cabin. Instead, with a tone of fearful confession, she whispered, "I want to have a great life."

"You will," her companion replied, without hesitation.

"I want you, you and the other Artisans . . . to talk about me for a million years."

The gripping hand relaxed, almost lifting.

No voice said, "We will," or even, "Perhaps we will." Because it wasn't possible, of course. What single organic deserved such fame?

Without looking at Ejy, she said, "Thank you."

"For what, may I ask?"

"Your help. Your patience." She paused, forcing herself not to cry. "Thank you for making me into the best Voice that I can possibly be."

"You cannot be anything else," he assured her, laughing gently.

Fouchians had an insult. "Posturing-on-another's-mound-of-soil." She thought of it until Ejy, affecting a tone of concern, asked her:

"What are you thinking, child?"

She looked at the false face, crystal eyes cool and black — more alien than any other eyes on the Web — and she confessed, "I feel closer to you than to my own species."

A soft, soft laugh.

Then the hand squeezed until her shoulder ached, and the Artisan said, "Exactly as it should be, sweet Voice. As it always is. . . ."

4   The ship set down on a plain of water ice — hard as granite, smooth as sleep, and relentlessly, numbingly cold. Tradition and practicality called for an unessential crew member to be first to the surface. Ejy gave Sarrie the honor. She donned her heavily insulated lifesuit, gave a general thumbs-up, then with a musical hum of motorized limbs strode into the main airlock, waiting to descend onto the ice.

"For the Artisans, parents to all," she announced, "I claim this lovely bleak place."

Violence had created the ice. Yet Navren seemed unsure which natural process to blame. Comet impacts or vulcanism? Perhaps some combination of both, he decided, and he built elaborate simulations involving rains of comets piercing the crust, allowing plastic rock to rise to within a very few kilometers of where they stood now.

Steady chill winds had polished the ice ever since. Disturbing that crystalline perfection felt sacrilegious, but Lilké wanted deep samples, unmarred by cosmic radiation. Navren helped her erect a portable drilling rig. Their first fist-sized sample, brought up after just a few minutes' work, was sprinkled with treasure: a few dozen tiny, tiny fossils frozen where they had died, swimming in an ocean melted for a moment after a hundred-million-year winter.

Scarce, as expected, and uncomplicated, the fossils resembled bacteria in basic ways. Lilké isolated their DNA, patching gaps and decoding the naked genetics. Then in a long aquarium filling half of her lab—a cold, lightless, and pressurized little ocean—she conjured the aliens out of amino acids and lipids, watching as they began slowly to thrive.

Despite this world's poverty, life had persisted. Lilké's bugs were pragmatically sluggish, powered by anaerobic chemistries, and judging by their numbers in the ice, they were scarce. She and Navren warned the others that beneath the ice, even the ocean's secret gardens, life would be scarce. Yet these creatures were survivors and admirable because of it, existing for several billion years—outliving suns, worlds, and even their own pitiful Earth.

Ejy called a general meeting, then asked humans and fouchians to find some means to cut their way to the mysterious sea.

Navren proposed using nuclear charges, hammering through two kilometers of ice in an afternoon. But more conservative souls won out. The ship's potent reactors would pump heat into the ice cap, sculpting a deep hole, and the superheated vapor would be thrown high overhead, freezing almost immediately, then falling. For the first time in aeons, this world would enjoy a good long peaceful snow.

Sarrie was suddenly desperate to feel involved. But the hardware, fat pumps and redundant backup power systems, had been proven on thousands of similar worlds, and her help took the form of sitting inside a prefabricated hut near the borehole, watching for mechanical problems only a little more likely than another comet impact. To someone groomed for intellectual adventure, boredom was a shock. Sarrie stared out at the enormous geyser, feeling its roar more than she could hear it in the near-vacuum . . . and a secret portion of her feared that nothing more interesting than this would ever happen in her life.

The twisted necklace of suns set during her duty time. The temperature would plummet another fraction of a degree, the sense of eternal night growing worse. On her second day, Sarrie was considering tears when the Milky Way rose behind her—a majestic fog of suns, never more lovely, lending color and depth to the man-made geyser, but the geyser's magnificence all its own.

Sarrie composed a poem in the next few hours, then dedicated it to Lilké and posted it in the galley. But her friend was taking her meals in the lab, studying her bugs twenty hours a day before indulging in private fun with her gruesome boyfriend. It was Ejy who praised the poem first, applauding her imagery and the message. Only then did the fouchians and other humans read it, with seeming appreciation. But Navren, of all people, offered no opinions. Sarrie was eating a late dinner when he read it, and she braced herself for some terse, biting critique. Surely he would browbeat her for not understanding the physics of expanding gases and phase changes. But no, the gruesome boyfriend seemed to nod respectfully, even as the author sat nearby, sipping juice, pretending to be blind.

That next morning, Sarrie was walking toward her post. The borehole was several kilometers from the ship. The thin winds had abated while she had slept, icy snow falling silently on her. She was navigating in a darker-than-night gloom, using her suit's instruments to keep on course, and suddenly, without warning, a dark monstrous blob appeared before her.

A low liquid moan came from Sarrie.

It was some kind of alien, obviously. Her eyes refused to find anything familiar about it. She took a few steps backward, then paused, one hand lifting instinctively, ready to ward off any blows; and finally, at the last instant, she remembered that she was a Voice, for goodness' sake. And in a thin whisper, she told the alien, "Hello," in many languages, hoping against hope to be understood.

"Hello," the monster replied, smiling behind his crystal faceplate.

She knew him. The bulky body was a lifesuit, and she finally saw the identification symbol on the helmet — the familiar silhouette of a human — then the sharp, self-assured face.

"Navren?" she sputtered.

But he said nothing else — an uncharacteristic moment — handing her a small pad and making sure that she had a firm grip. Then he walked past, the blizzard swallowing him without sound, without fuss, his wide bootprints beginning to fill with icy grains. Perhaps he hadn't been here at all.

Sarrie reached the hut without further incident, relieving an extremely bored expert in alien neurology.

Alone and unwatched, she woke Navren's pad. It contained nothing but a long poem about another geyser on a different world. A warm blue-green world, she realized. Judging by the star-rich sky, it was somewhere deep in the Milky Way. No author was named, but clues led to obvious conclusions: The poem had been written by a human Voice. Moreover, its rhythms and imagery were nearly identical to the poem displayed back in the galley.

The same symbols, even. The geyser linked life and the stars, emotion and purpose, organics and the blessed Artisans. On and on, point by point. It was obvious — Sarrie's soul had written both versions. But what disturbed her most was that this earlier work, without question, was better than yesterday's effort. Not to mention superior to everything else that she had written in her current life.

Read once, the mysterious poem vanished from the pad, leaving no trace except in Sarrie's mind.

When the neurologist arrived at the appointed time, relieving her, Sarrie went straight to Navren.

Before she could speak, he told her, "I gave you nothing. And if you say otherwise, I'll be *extremely* disappointed."

He was working on some kind of device, possibly of his own design. The machine shop was cluttered and loud, and save for the two of them, it was empty. Yet for some reason, Sarrie found herself glancing over her shoulder.

"I expected more from you, Sarrie." The man plugged components into components, telling her, "The good Voice sees the universe through another's eyes. Am I right? Well, look at my eyes. Look! Tell me what I see!"

She hated the man.

"Leave me," he growled. "Get out of here. I'm working!"

She hated him and wouldn't do what he asked. In revenge, Sarrie refused him the simple gift of her understanding.

They reached the living sea exactly on schedule.

A quick celebration culminated with the Artisan blessing his organics for their good work. The precious water rose almost two kilometers on its own, then was grabbed by powerful pumps and insulated pipes, filling both an empty fuel tank and Lilké's pressurized aquarium. The celebrants filed through the lab for a symbolic quick glance. One of the fouchians, pulling his bulk down the narrow aisle, claimed to see a momentary phosphorescence. "Too much to drink," was Lilké's verdict — a glib dismissal of a colleague whose physiology couldn't survive ethanol. Then the nonessential organics herded themselves into the hallway, standing three-deep, talking too loudly as the geneticist tried to ignore them, starting to make the obvious and routine first tests.

The water was glacially cold and mineral-rich — as predicted — but it also carried a delicious hint of free oxygen. Not predicted, and marvelous. Navren, remaining at his lover's side, said, "Impossible," giggled, then began offering explanations. A catalytic reaction between water and metal ions? Or water and hot magma? Or water and life. . . ? Though that last speculation was absurd — where would the energy come from? — and he giggled again, for emphasis. . . .

Befitting his role, Ejy remained in the lab, standing nearly motionless, his false face showing confidence and a well-honed pleasure.

Life was easy to find, and it too held surprises. The biomass was two or three hundred times higher than predicted. But more astonishing were the natives themselves. A stereomicroscope focused on the sample. Projected images swam in the air above the central lab table. As if injured, Lilké gasped aloud. Bacteria were darting along like grains of enchanted rice, seeping a kind of firefly light as they moved. Even Sarrie, standing her ground in the narrow doorway, knew their significance: these bugs were a different species, operating on some radically different, spend-thrift metabolism.

The rest of the audience grew silent, watching over Sarrie's shoulder or using portable monitors. A baffling moment, and holy. . . !

Without warning, something else glided into view. A monster, perhaps. It was burly and vast, and powerful, remaining blurred until the automatic focus could engage, recalibrating data made from bent light, the monster suddenly defined, suddenly utterly familiar.

It was a protozoan. Sarrie knew a sophisticated organism when she saw it. That general design had been repeated on a multitude of worlds, always with great success. The nucleus and engorged food vacuoles lay within a sack of electric broth. A thick golden pelt of cilia beat too rapidly for an eye to follow, obeying the sim-plest reflexes. Without conscience or love, the monster hovered, feasting on the hapless minuscule bacteria. Then it moved again, without warning, covering an enormous distance — the width of an eyelash, perhaps — passing out of view before the lenses could respond.

One of the fouchians gave a deep moan, his voice box asking, "How? How, how, how?"

Explanations were obvious, and inadequate. The fossil ocean from a million years ago had been replaced by another ocean, richer by any measure: oxygen metabolisms; rapid growth and motility; the extravagance of trophic levels. But how could a new ocean evolve so quickly? Lilké claimed that's exactly what had happened, then she just as quickly dismissed the idea. No! Their borehole had to be situated directly above some local paradise. A volcano. A vent site. Whatever the physical cause, free oxygen was being generated in this one locale. In tiny amounts, no doubt. The bulk of the unseen ocean was exactly as the ice had promised, she maintained—cold and dark and impoverished, and content with its poverty.

Navren made fun of the free oxygen. His magma and metal ion hypotheses were jokes, nothing more. Under these circumstances, he admitted that he couldn't see any trick that would split water molecules, and his features seemed to sharpen as his frustrations grew.

Sarrie enjoyed the befuddlement, part of her wishing this moment wouldn't end.

But wise old Ejy knew exactly what to do. Obviously this new world had mysteries, delicious ones, and everyone needed to work as one to solve them. He began to move, dispensing assignments. Humans and fouchians were sent where they could contribute, or at least where they brought the least distraction. Sarrie knew enough about biological instruments to help Lilké prepare specimens for mapping; and Ejy, perhaps wishing to heal wounds between friends, ordered his young Voice into the lab, hovering nearby while Lilké gave instructions, both humans pretending to cooperate for the moment.

Sarrie worked with DNA drawn from a protozoan's nucleus, making it legible for their machinery. Lilké was already reading genes from the oxygen-loving bacteria. Silence was followed by curses. With the mildest of voices, Ejy asked what was wrong. Lilké said, "Nothing." Then after more transcriptions, she amended herself. "Somehow, I don't know how . . . I managed to contaminate this sample, Artisan Ejy. . . !"

Ejy's face was sympathetic, but his voice was all barbs and disappointment. "That doesn't sound like you, Lilké. Now does it?"

The mission's geneticist turned to Sarrie. "Is your sample ready yet?" Nearly, yes. "Let me finish up. And you get started on another bacterium. Go on."

The protozoan was genetically complex. Even in an expert's grip, interpretations took time. Lilké entered a near-trance, skimming across long, long stretches of base pairs, trying to decipher the codes. And Sarrie tried to convince herself that her friend deserved absolute control. This was Lilké's lab, after all. Only a selfish, inadequate organic would feel angry about being pushed aside. Pushed like an untrustworthy child. Yet she wasn't a child, and she was confident in her abilities . . . except for some reason she couldn't work, or think, and her hands trembled as if some degenerative condition were eating at her nervous system.

"What the fuck's wrong?" Lilké shouted.

Sarrie was startled, a vial slipping from her fingers and bouncing, then rolling out of reach.

"We've got a major contamination problem," Lilké explained, embarrassed to tears. "I'll need to clean up and start over. I'm sorry, Artisan Ejy. As soon as I can track down the problem, I'll run more samples. But I can't concentrate just now. . . !"

The Artisan did not speak, or move.

The women watched him, waiting for his sage advice or the perfect encouragement. Yet he remained silent for an astonishing length of time. The old-man face was hard and flat, inert as a mask, but behind the eyes was a flickering, hints of a swift elegant mind being applied to intricate, uncompromising programs.

Then he spoke. With the mildest of voices, he asked, "From where does your contamination come?"

"From us," Lilké muttered. "These codes and the genes . . . they're all *Terran*. . . !"

The Artisan nodded, contriving a smile. "But of course," he replied, "there's another conclusion supported by your data. Yes?"

In a whisper, Lilké said, "No."

Ejy stared at Lilké. He didn't blink or offer another word, waiting until the geneticist finally, grudgingly said, "Maybe."

"I don't understand," Sarrie confessed.

No one seemed to hear her.

"What other conclusion?" Her voice was soft, weak. Useless.

Lilké shook her head, telling Sarrie, "That there's no contamination. Our data are perfectly valid."

But if Sarrie was extracting earthly DNA, that meant . . . no. . . !

Ejy turned to Sarrie, the dead face opening its mouth, saying nothing. The eyes were what spoke, surprise and pain mixed with pity.

Why pity? she asked herself.

And then she understood everything. Not just what was in the ocean far beneath the cold hard ice, but what was in the mind of the machine, the mind behind those pitying eyes.

5 News of the discovery spread at a fever's pace.

And one fever-induced explanation was produced almost immediately: The microbes came from the Great Web. One of its earthly habitats must have sprung a leak — a common enough event in those ancient structures — and the escaping water froze, tiny ice crystals set free to wander the universe, hitching a ride on one of their probes, or maybe just carried along on the chill starlight.

It was an inventive, ludicrous explanation. Yet both fouchians and most of the humans tried to believe it just the same. Everyone knew that the Earth was far away, and dead; there was no reason to mention it. Of course the Web was to blame. That was the consensus. Improbabilities were better than impossibilities. In voices growing more feeble by the moment, the crew promised each other that aeons of tranquillity and purpose wouldn't be threatened, at least not because of some damned little bugs swimming in an ocean nobody had even seen yet.

Ejy remained quiet about the pregnant snowflake, panspermian nonsense. And quiet about almost everything else, too.

He wandered from lab to lab, then out to the borehole itself; but he rarely offered encouragement, much less advice, watching the organics with a peculiar intensity, leaving everyone ill at ease.

It was Navren who asked the obvious: What were the odds that a pregnant snowflake would come here? And how would frozen spores migrate through kilometers of solid ice? And even if they found the means, then where did the damned bugs get their energy and free oxygen? And how did they become so common so quickly?

But geniuses are nothing if not clever.

A second explanation was built from scratch. This was a training mission, people reasoned. Ejy, the great old Artisan, was testing them. The microbes had been planted. Who knew what else was falsified? Perhaps every team endured this kind of trickery. It had been generations since the last important field mission, right? Absolutely! But the sweetest advantage of this explanation was that Navren could ask any question, find any flaw, and none of it mattered. This was an elaborate practical joke, nothing else, and at some point, probably in a minute or two, Ejy would tell the truth, and everyone would laugh themselves sick.

The obvious next step was to visit the hidden ocean. A blunt diamond balloon was assembled in the machine shop. It was a submersible, crude but proven in a thousand seas. It had room on board for two cramped humans. Navren and Lilké were originally slated for the dive. But Ejy ordered the seats removed, then picked one of the fouchians to go in their place.

No explanation was necessary, yet he offered several. Experience. Expendability. And the light-sensitive fouchian eyes.

Reasonable enough, people told each other. The fouchian was probably a coconspirator in the practical joke. Suddenly a false exuberance took hold of them. The borehole out on the ice had been capped, warm breathable air beneath the tentlike structure. The chosen fouchian drove himself out in one of the mission's three big-wheeled buggies, and without the slightest ceremony forced his way through the tiny hatch—like a fat rat through a knothole. Spontaneous applause broke out in the galley. Everyone was in the galley, save for the submersible pilot. When the submersible was lowered into the hole—a vapor-shrouded puddle nearly eight kilometers deep—most of the audience cheered aloud, telling themselves that everything would be answered soon, and with answers, everything would return to normal.

Navren acted distant, and exactly like Ejy, he rarely spoke, and when he offered words, his comments were brief and remarkably bland.

In the crowded galley, Sarrie sat close to Navren, watching him, practically ignoring the banks of monitors on the far wall. Video images and raw data enthralled most of the humans. Vacuous conversation came and went. The ship's reactors were still heating the borehole's water. Its ice walls were smooth, translucent. Spotlights dove into the pure ice, shattering on ancient fissures, sudden rainbows forming and fading as the submersible continued its descent. And with that same false exuberance, people commented on the beauty of their seemingly simple surroundings, and wasn't the universe a marvel. . . ?

Navren didn't insult their sentimentality. He sat beside Lilké, holding his lover's hand with a wrestler's grip. Sometimes he would lean in close to her, making some comment about the oxygen levels or other dissolved treasures. But most of the time he just watched the monitors, his face tense yet strangely happy, his eyes missing nothing even when nothing at all happened.

Sarrie watched the monitors through his face.

When the submersible left the borehole, entering open water, there was more applause. But softer now, somehow less genuine. Navren blinked and took a breath, as if preparing for a long swim. Away from the ice there was much less to see. The spotlights reached out for hundreds of meters, finding nothing. Yet the tension in the galley doubled, then doubled again. Navren lifted

Lilké's hand as if to kiss it, then hesitated. In a smooth and astonished voice, he said, "Look at the oxygen now. Look." Then he gently took a flap of his own skin into his mouth, and he bit down hard enough to make himself wince, to make his eyes tear.

The ocean floor remained remote, unimaginable. It would take forever to reach, which was unfair. More than once, in a quiet way, someone would whisper, "I wonder what's supposed to happen next." Because it was all a test, of course. Conceived by the Artisans. Run by Ejy. An elaborate means of determining *something* about this very young, very inexperienced team.

The fouchian was still a full kilometer from the bottom when he reported seeing a distinct glow. Built from many little lights, he claimed. And probably an illusion, since the lights were arranged in a definite pattern, as regular as the vertices on graph paper—

"Have him cut his spotlights!" Navren shouted. "Tell him, Ejy!"

But the Artisan, standing at the back of the galley, must have already given the order on a private channel. At once the monitors were filled with black water. The native glow was magnified a thousandfold. Suddenly the submersible was a tiny balloon floating above a rolling landscape, narrow towers erected at regular intervals, each one perhaps two hundred meters tall, capped like a mushroom and a brilliant light thrown down from the cap at what seemed to be trees.

No, not trees. Lilké told everyone, "They look like kelp, or something similar." Then an instant later, "Growing in rows. Columns. Do you see?" Then she screamed, "It's a farm! Someone's cultivating seaweed down there!"

Sarrie looked at her best friend, then at Navren, and she felt a warm weakness spreading through her.

Navren turned, glancing over his shoulder at Ejy.

The Artisan said nothing, did nothing.

Navren opened his mouth, words framed. Carefully, slowly, he turned forward again, taking one more deep breath, then remarked with all the sarcasm he could muster:

"Goodness! I wonder whose farm this is!"

The fouchian, crammed into that tiny submersible, utterly alone, began to beg for guidance. Should he investigate the unexpected forest? Should he snip off samples? Surely no one would miss a few brown leaves, he advised. Then he adjusted the focus on his cameras, revealing that the nearest water was filled with life: clouds of plankton; schools of jerking copepods and delicate shrimp; and a single fish, long as a forearm and nearly transparent.

The placement of its fins, gills, spine, and pulsing pale heart

were exactly the same as earthly fish. Sarrie knew enough tax-
onomy to feel certain. But the transparency of its meat gave her
hope. No pigment in the blood implied an alien physiology, which
was exactly what she hoped to see . . . except Lilké quickly and
thoroughly dashed any hopes, turning to Navren to tell him and
the room, "I don't know the species, but I know their cousins. Ice-
fish. Very low-energy. No hemoglobin. They lived on the shoulders of Antarctica, bodies laced with antifreeze, oxygen dissolving
straight into their plasma."

Again, in fouchian squeaks and translated human syllables, the
pilot begged for instructions. Directions. Purpose.

Artisan Ejy was as rigid as a statue. No doubt he was hard at
work, his mind spliced directly into the ship's main computers.
The black crystal eyes were superfluous, and vacant, and seemed
to lend him the appearance of utter helplessness. But with the
fouchian's next words—"Do I continue my descent?"—he moved
again, suddenly tilting his head, smiling for perhaps half a moment too long. Then with a calmness that unnerved the entire
room, he told the pilot, "No." The old-man face was overly serene,
if that was possible. "No, you've seen enough. Come back now.
Back through the borehole, please."

The fouchian hesitated for an instant, then dropped his
ballast.

Silence in the galley became a soft murmur.

And within the murmur: excitement, confusion, and the ragged beginnings of a stunning new explanation.

A wondrous explanation, it was. Always unthinkable, until
now.

"It's Terran life," Sarrie heard, from all sides.

"And someone has high technology," people whispered. Sang.

"Who could have imagined it?" said a voice behind Sarrie.

She turned, eager to confess to a lack of creativity. But as she
spoke, she spied Navren placing both hands around Lilké's head,
pulling her close and saying a word into her ear, then two more
words, or three, and kissing the lobe softly.

Something about that tenderness was perplexing. Almost terri-
fying.

Then someone else—in the distance, from beside the tiny
beverage counter—shouted in a clear, joyous voice, "Humans!
That would explain everything! On this world somewhere . . .
could they be. . . ?!"

The word *human* held magic, potent and ancient, dangerous
beyond all measure.

As a chorus, a dozen voices responded by saying:

"Humans are extinct! Everywhere but on the Web."

But the engrained words held no life, no fire. Spoken, they dispersed into an atmosphere filled with electricity and possibilities. Two dozen youngsters were suddenly free to leap to their feet, asking the obvious:

"What if other humans escaped the Wars?"

Sarrie found herself standing, almost jumping, hands clasped over her open mouth. She couldn't speak. The great Voice was mute and lost. She could barely think, struggling to piece together clues that led to the inescapable conclusion—

Ejy moved, walking down the galley's single aisle. Only he seemed immune to the excitement, every step slow, even stately, the smile on his rubbery face never larger or less believable. It was the greatest discovery in aeons—a pivotal moment in the Web's glorious history—and he resembled a grandfather strolling down his garden path.

An engineer beside Sarrie took her by the arm, pulling hard as she jumped up and down. "What a training mission! Can you believe it? Oh, Sarrie . . . who would have guessed. . . ?!"

Again, the Voice glanced over at Navren.

Suddenly he seemed old. Older than Ejy, even. He sat among the wild children, his expression black, thin mouth trembling, the eyes tracking sideways until they intersected with Sarrie's eyes.

He willed himself to smile—a brief, bleak attempt.

Then without sound, he carefully mouthed the words:

"Our. Mission. Is. Canceled."

Ludicrous. Navren was utterly wrong. Wasn't it just beginning?

Ejy was standing under the largest monitor, facing the raucous youngsters. A radio pulse from him made the screen go black, and with a delicate firmness, he demanded silence. Then when the prattle continued, he raised his voice, saying, "Look at me now. Look here."

Ejy would explain everything, Sarrie believed.

This was the standard hazing, doubtlessly employed since the Web was born. On its first mission, every young team was tricked into believing that they'd found some viable splinter of humanity among the stars. Sarrie could believe it. Absolutely. She even felt a smile coming, anticipating Ejy's first words and his crisp laugh. "I fooled you," he might tell them. "I made you believe the impossible, didn't I?"

But the old machine said nothing about tricks. Instead, speaking with a cool formality, he repeated the words, "Look at me."

The silence was sudden, absolute.

"Before our submersible breaks the surface," he told them, "I want our ship's systems prepared for launch."

No one spoke, but the silence changed its pitch. If anything, it grew larger, flowing out of the galley, spreading over the glacial world.

"And please," said the Artisan, "prepare for cold-sleep. Each of you, as always, is responsible for your own chamber."

The second fouchian, filling the galley's far corner, lifted a powerful digging hand, pointing a claw at Ejy. "I assume this is a precaution," said his voice box. "You wish us ready to leave should the natives prove hostile."

The Artisan said, "No."

People turned and turned again, looking for anyone who seemed to understand that reply.

"No, we will launch," said Ejy. "In one hundred twenty-eight minutes. And each of you will place yourself into cold-sleep—"

"Artisan Ejy," the fouchian interrupted, "you don't mean me, of course."

"But I do. Yes."

The nose tendrils straightened and paled—an expression of pure astonishment. "But who will pilot our ship?"

"I am more than capable," Ejy reminded him, and everyone.

Sarrie found herself weak and shaky. Turning to Navren, she hoped for one of his good tough questions. She wasn't alone. But the genius sat quietly with his lover, and Lilké held his hand with both of hers, neither of them seemingly involved in anything happening around them.

Ejy admitted, "Our mission has taken an unexpected turn."

Sarrie tried to swallow, and failed, then looked at the Artisan. His smile meant nothing. The eyes couldn't appear more dead. And the words came slowly, too much care wrapped around each of them.

"It has been a wonderful day," he promised. "But you are too young and inexperienced to carry this work to its next stage—"

We're as old and experienced as anyone else! Sarrie thought.

"I congratulate each of you. I love each of you. You are my children, and I thank you for your hard work and precious skills."

Why did those words terrify her. . . ?

Then she knew why. Ejy was looking at each of their faces, showing them his perfect smile; but he could never quite look at Sarrie, unwilling to risk showing their Voice his truest soul.

With no technical duties, Sarrie filled her time shoving her few possessions into the appropriate cubbyholes, cleaning her scrupulously clean cabin, then making sure that her cold-sleep chamber was ready to use. It was. But nearly an hour remained until they launched, which was too long. Sarrie considered placing herself into cold-sleep now. She went as far as undressing, then climbing into the slick-walled chamber, fingers caressing one of the ports from which chilling fluids would emerge, bathing her body, invading her lungs, then infiltrating every cell, suspending their life processes until she would be indistinguishable from the dead.

A seductive, ideal death. Responsibilities would be suspended. She wouldn't have to prove her value to this mission and the Web, and there wouldn't be the daily struggle with loneliness and self-doubt. Even if she never woke—if some unthinkable accident killed this body, this soul—then the best in her would simply be reborn again, brought up again under Ejy's enlightened care, and why was she sad? There wasn't a day when a child of Heaven had any right to be sad.

In the end, she decided to wait, climbing from the chamber and reaching for her clothes. . .and she noticed a familiar and bulky beetlelike form standing in the hallway, watching her now and possibly for a long while.

Sarrie gave a start, then whispered, "Ejy?"

"I scared you. I apologize." The machine's words were warm and wet, in stark contrast to the mechanical body. "I came here to ask for your help. Will you help me? I need a Voice—"

"Of course." Ejy must have changed his mind. Jumping to her feet, she started pulling on her trousers. "If there are humans nearby, I'm sure I can talk to them. We should start with underwater low-frequency broadcasts. In all the dead languages. I want to send audio greetings, and maybe some whale-style audio pictures of us—"

"No." A ceramic hand brushed against her cheek, then covered a bare shoulder. "I want you to speak with Lilké. I know that you and she have been at odds, but I know, too, she still feels close to you."

"Lilké?"

"Speak calmly. Rationally. And when you can, gain a sense of her mind." He paused for a moment, then admitted, "This is unexpected, yes. Remarkable, and unfair. But when you're finished, return here. Here. As soon as possible, please."

The hand was withdrawn.

Sarrie whispered, "Yes." She knelt, unfolding her shirt, then thinking to ask, "Where is Lilké?"

"In Navren's cabin," he answered.

"Navren —?"

"Is elsewhere."

The Voice pulled on her shirt, again wishing that she was cold and asleep, deliciously unaware. Then something in his last words caught her attention. "Where is Navren now?"

"I don't know," the Artisan replied.

The machine within, linked to every functioning system on the ship, confessed to Sarrie, "I cannot see him. And to tell the truth, I haven't for a little while."

Lilké expected her arrival.

That was Sarrie's first conclusion — an insight born not from innate talent, but friendship.

They showed one another smiles, Sarrie claimed the cabin's only seat, then tried to offer some pleasant words . . . and Lilké spoiled the mood, remarking, "I guessed Ejy would send you."

"Why?"

She wouldn't say why. Red eyes proved that Lilké had been crying, but the skin around them had lost its puffiness. She had been dry-eyed for a long while.

Opening a low cubbyhole, she removed a homemade device, pressing its simple switch, a high-pitched hum rising until it was inaudible and the cabin's lights dimming in response.

"Now," Lilké said, "we can speak freely."

"Navren isn't here."

"I don't know where he is, but I know what he's doing." She took a seat on the lower bunk, always leaning forward, ready to leap up at any time. "He and the others are working —"

"What others?"

"You don't need to know."

Sarrie hesitated, then said, "I want to understand. For my sake, not Ejy's."

"I'm disappointed with you. I thought you'd be better at this game." The geneticist shook her head, a wan smile appearing. Vanishing. "Answer a question for me, Sarrie. What have we found here?"

"Earth life. High technology." She hesitated before adding, "Some evidence, rather indirect, that other people survived the Wars."

"On a ship like ours, you mean." Lilké looked at the low ceiling as if it were fascinating. "A second starship. And its crew left the sun behind, and the Milky Way, coming here to settle this hidden sea . . . is that what you believe?"

"It is possible."

"Two starships, and we cross paths *here?*"

Sarrie said nothing.

"Calculate the odds. Or I can show you Navren's calculations."

"There's another possibility." She paused, waiting for Lilké to glance her way, a thin curiosity crossing her face. "The Artisans brought us here intentionally. They heard something, perhaps aeons ago. A beacon, a leaked signal. Nothing definite, but certainly reason to come here."

"Why would humans leave the galaxy?"

Some cultures might relish the idea of this empty wilderness. An ascetic appeal; a spiritual chill; the relative safety of islands far from the galaxy's distractions. Sarrie devised her explanation in an instant, then thought again. Better to point out the obvious. "We left it behind, didn't we?"

Lilké dismissed the obvious, shrugging and changing subjects. "Why have we always been sure that our home solar system died?"

"We watched its destruction," Sarrie replied.

"How did we do that?"

"Our ancestors did. With probes."

"Machines sending coded signals, received and translated by still more machines—"

"What are you implying?"

Instead of answering, Lilké posed more questions. "But what if the Wars weren't as awful as we were taught? What if a few worlds survived, perhaps even the Earth continued on . . . and our species recovered, then built starships and colonies. . . ?"

"Our ancestors would have seen them. Leaked radio noise alone would have alerted them—"

"Who would have seen them? Who?"

The implication was absurd. Sarrie said, "Impossible," without the slightest doubt.

Yet beneath the word, simple fear was building. What if it was true? What if the Artisans, even for the best reasons, had lied to their organics? Yet she couldn't imagine them lying for simple human reasons. Certainly not for vanity, or to be cruel.

Sarrie had come here to read Lilké's soul, but suddenly it was her own hidden soul that captivated her.

"Go back to *him,*" said a quiet, composed voice.

What was that?

"Or stay here with me." Lilké touched the Voice's knee, promising, "If you do nothing against us, nothing happens to you."

A sigh. "You know I can't stay."

The hand was withdrawn.

"Ejy's waiting," Lilké remarked, eyes bright. Bitter. "Be with him," she advised. "Immortals like you should stand together."

Sarrie never reached the cold-sleep chambers.

She was running, in a panic, threading her way past empty labs until every light suddenly flickered and went out.

Sarrie halted. The darkness was seamless. Pure. But what terrified was the silence, the accustomed hum of moving air and pumps and plumbing apparently sabotaged, replaced by the galloping sound of her own breathing.

Every on-board system was failing.

"Rebellion," she whispered. An ancient word, and until this moment, useless, save as a blistering obscenity.

Days ago, in a lost age, someone had built an aquarium out of spare materials, placing it in the hallway and filling it with the deep ocean water. As Sarrie's eyes adapted, she saw the aquarium's faint glow, and she crept forward until her fingertips touched slick cool glass, their slightest pressure causing millions of bacteria to scream with photons, the thin ruddy glow brightening for a half-instant.

Someone moved. Behind her.

A great clawed hand closed over her shoulder, delicate tendrils grabbing the closer ear. "The-Nest-Is-Sour," the fouchian squeaked. No voice box gave its thorough, artless translation. With a sorrowful chirp, he told Sarrie, "The-Loyal-Must-Escape."

She turned and grabbed his stubby tail, then followed, the scent of his rectum meant to reassure.

The fouchian managed a terrific pace, squeezing through narrow hatches and turns, twice nearly leaving the tiny human behind. But Sarrie never complained, never lost her grip, and when they reached the airlock, she donned her lifesuit in record time, then helped her vast companion struggle into his bulky unwieldy suit.

Reflexes carried her out onto the ice, and there they faltered.

Two buggies were parked in the open. With heavy limbs meant for construction work, one of the buggies was expertly and thoroughly dismantling the other. Ejy filled the buggy's crystal cockpit. A radio-born voice told her, "Welcome." He said, "A change of plans, child. Hurry now."

Sarrie lost her will. Her urgency.

Despite the servos in her joints, she couldn't seem to run. The fouchian scurried past, and she responded by hesitating, pulling up and looking back at the looming ship. A lifetime of order, of knowing exactly where and what she was, had evaporated, and Sarrie felt more sorry for herself than afraid. Even when she saw a figure appear in the open airlock, she wasn't afraid. Then the figure lifted a tube to his shoulder, and the tube spouted flame, and she watched with a certain distant curiosity, observing a spinning lump of something fall on the hard ice and bounce and stop. Ten or twelve meters away, perhaps. A homemade device. She almost took a step closer, just to have a better look. Then she thought again, or maybe thought for the first time, turning away an instant before the bomb detonated, its blast lifting her off her feet and throwing her an astonishing distance, her arms outstretched in some useless, unconscious bid to fly.

"He tried to kill you," Ejy assured her. The machine and Sarrie were inside the buggy, its cabin unpressurized and she still in her lifesuit, laying on her sore left side. The fouchian was in the cockpit, protected tendrils and heavy claws happily holding the controls. "If you have doubts at all," said Ejy's earnest voice, "watch. I will show you."

A digital replayed the scene, but from the buggy's perspective. Sarrie saw herself step toward the bomb, then turn away. Then came the blast, not as bright as she remembered it. The digital also allowed her to watch as her assailant received swift justice. Ejy had used a limb that Sarrie didn't recognize—a fat jeweled cannonlike device—focusing a terrific dose of laser light on the rebel's lifesuit, melting it in an instant, then evaporating the body trapped inside.

Sarrie grimaced for a moment, then quietly, almost inaudibly, asked, "Which one? Was he?"

Ejy gave a name.

She remembered the face, the person. And with a kind of baffled astonishment, she asked herself: *Why would an alien neurologist want to murder me?*

The machine seemed just as puzzled, in his fashion.

"I'm the object of their hate," Ejy promised, ready to take any burden. "Attacking you was unconscionable. It only proves how quickly things have grown ugly. Unmanageable. Tragic."

Sarrie discovered that she could sit upright without too much agony.

"We never should have come here," the machine confessed. "I blame myself. If I'd had any substantial clue as to what we would find, we wouldn't have passed within ten parsecs of this place."

They would have missed the local suns altogether.

"What about Navren?" she inquired.

"Oh, that may be. The clever boy did notice at least one clue, didn't he? This ocean's heat is plainly artificial." A pause, then with a mild but genuine delight, he proposed, "The boy had an inkling of the truth, perhaps. Even before we left 2018CC, perhaps."

Shaking her head, Sarrie whispered, "No."

She told him, "What I meant to ask...do you blame Navren at all?"

"For following his nature? Never, no!" The faceless machine showed no recognizable emotion, but the voice seemed sickened with horror. "The errors, if there are such things, belong to the Artisans. Mostly to me, I admit. I allowed that boy too many novel genes, and worse, far too many illusions. Illusions of invulnerability, particularly." A momentary pause, then he added, "Blame is never yours, child. Or theirs. It all rests here, in me."

Mechanical hands gripped the armored carapace, accenting the beatific words. The cannonlike laser merely dangled off the back end like some badly swollen tail.

Sarrie felt the buggy slow, then bounce.

Directly ahead was the tentlike cap over the borehole, and near it, familiar and unwelcome, the prefab hut. They had bounced over an insulated pipe. They approached another, but frozen water made a serviceable ramp and the buggy was moving slowly, its oversized wheels barely noticing the impact.

The submersible and second fouchian must be near the surface by now. Yet no fouchian shape was obediently waiting for them. And the last buggy . . . where was it now?

Again they were moving, accelerating as rapidly as possible. Whatever Ejy's plan, time seemed precious.

Sarrie stood, half expecting to be told to sit down and keep out of sight. But no one spoke, no one cared. She walked carefully to the back of the utilitarian cabin, dancing around assorted machinery and scrap. From the wide rear window, she gazed out at the bleak ice, and above it, the dark bulk of their ship.

"Where are we going?" she asked. And when Ejy didn't respond in an instant, she became pointedly specific. "When can we go home?"

"The ship is dead," Ejy answered, his voice stolidly grave.

"Did Navren do it—?"

"Not entirely, Sarrie. He and his cohorts were stealing its systems, which left me with no choice. I had to put everything to sleep."

She said nothing.

"Giving him a fully functional ship was unacceptable." A pause. "You do understand, don't you?"

With conviction, she said, "Oh, yes."

Something else was visible on the ice. Something was moving toward the ship. The third buggy?

Ejy kept speaking, in human words and fouchian squeals. "But how dead is dead? Given time and the desire, someone might regain control of any ship." Both voices were trying to reassure. "That's why there is one choice, one course, and you must trust me. Both of you, do you trust me?"

The Voice tried to say, "Yes" immediately, but the fouchian driver was faster. Louder.

"We have supplies here. Power and food and air. We will rescue our friend and leave." A pause. "There is a large team of fouchians on a nearby world," Ejy reported, now using only human words. "Accompanied by another Artisan, of course. They are exploring a pluto-class world. I have already warned them about our disaster. A reactor mishap, I have called it. At full acceleration, they will arrive in eighteen days."

"What kind of reactor mishap?" Sarrie asked.

But the fouchian answered, already intimate to the details.

"The-Light-That-Blinds-Generations!"

A nuclear explosion, she understood. The ship's reactors were sabotaged, or a bomb was hidden somewhere out of reach. Either way, she realized that the rebellion wasn't too astonishing to catch the Artisans unprepared. How many times in the past had they resorted to booby traps and other outrages?

But she didn't ask, knowing better.

And Ejy made his first and only true mistake. With a mixture of sadness and burgeoning awe, he told his most loyal organic:

"The blast will vaporize much of this crust. We have very little time to waste."

Vaporize the ice, then fling it into the sky, Sarrie realized. Creating an enormous temporary geyser.

She shuddered, in secret.

Then other secret thoughts followed, one chasing after another, the universe changing in an instant.

The stars and the black between made new again.

7 The buggy stopped beside the capped borehole.

"Your Nest-brother has finally surfaced," Ejy told the driver. "Help him disembark. Help him understand what has happened. And he must, must put on his lifesuit quickly, or what are my choices?"

We will leave your Nest-brother behind, thought Sarrie. And you too, if it comes to it.

The fouchian didn't spell out consequences, much less complain. Opening the pilot's hatch, he scrambled down and crossed to the airlock, vanishing.

Calmly, quietly, Sarrie observed, "Artisans can tolerate high radiation levels and heat. If we need to remain here a few minutes longer—"

"But I won't risk *you*," Ejy promised.

"I'm willing to take that risk," she confessed. "If it means saving one or both of my colleagues, I'd do it gladly."

Silence.

But of course she didn't own her life, and it wasn't hers to sacrifice. Was it? Again, she walked to the back of the cabin, watching the doomed ship and the tiny distant buggy. The buggy was definitely moving toward them, but not fast enough. She imagined its cabin crammed with humans, weighing it down, Navren hunched over his pad, desperately trying to calculate blast strengths and the minimum safe distance.

"What would have happened to us?" she asked.

"What would have happened when?"

"After we put ourselves into cold-sleep." She didn't look at the machine, didn't expose her face to scrutiny. "You wouldn't have dared allow us to wake again. Am I right?"

Outrage, sudden and pure.

"Sarrie," said the shrill voice in her headphones, "Artisans do not casually murder. I intended the cold-sleep as a security measure, to give everyone time to prepare—"

"We couldn't go home again. We might have told the truth."

"2018CC is a large vessel," Ejy reminded her. "There are simple, kind ways to sequester."

With eyes closed, she envisioned such a future. Life in some tiny, secret habitat. Or worse, hidden within the sterile white archives. . . .

"It's happened before, hasn't it?"

"What has?"

"All of this," Sarrie replied, turning to show Ejy her face. Her resolve, she hoped. Her desperate courage. "A team finds unexpected humans. Then they're quarantined. Or they rebel against the Artisans." A moment's hesitation. "How many times have these tragedies happened, Ejy? To you, I mean."

Again, silence.

She turned, squinting at the slow, slow buggy. It was a naked fleck beneath the fine bright snows of the Milky Way. With little more than a whisper, she asked, "How many humans are alive today?"

"I have no way of knowing."

"I believe you," she replied, nodding. "If they're so abundant that they've got to come here to find a home—"

"We may very likely have found an exceptional group," Ejy speculated. "Sophisticated agriculture coupled with the lack of radio noise implies an intentional isolation."

Again, she looked at the machine. "Your telescopes watch the galaxy. You have some idea what's happening there."

"Of course." The old pride flickered. "Judging by radio noise, misaligned com-lasers, and the flash of extremely powerful engines . . . yes, we have a working model." His various arms moved apart as if to show how big the fish was that Ejy had caught. "Since the Wars, humans have explored the galaxy, and they have colonized at least several million worlds. . . ."

What astonished Sarrie, what left her numbed to the bone, was how very easily she accepted these impossibilities. Nothing was as she had believed it to be, in life or the universe, and the idea of the Milky Way bursting with her species just confirmed this new intoxicating sense of disorder.

She took a step toward Ejy. "Why lie?" she asked.

Then she answered her own question. "You were instructed to lie. Your human builders ordered you to pretend that the worst had happened, that my species was extinct everywhere but on the Web."

Ejy had to admit, "In simple terms, that's true."

"Can you see any wars now?"

"None of consequence."

"Maybe humans have outgrown the need to fight. Has that possibility occurred to you?"

A long, electric pause.

Then with a smooth, unimpressed voice, the Artisan told her, "You are a child and ignorant, and you don't comprehend—"

"Tell me then!"

"These humans aren't like you anymore. They have many forms, they live extremely long lives. Some possess vast, seemingly magical powers."

Sarrie was shaking, and she couldn't stop.

"But they remain human nonetheless," said Ejy. "Deeply flawed. And the peace you see is temporary. Temporary, and extremely frail."

With an attempt at nonchalance, the Voice stepped closer to Ejy and closer to one of the buggy's walls.

"When the peace fails," the Artisan continued, "every past war will be a spark. An incident. When your species fights again, the entire galaxy will be engulfed."

Turning, she glanced at the nearest hatch.

"Is that why you brought the Web out here?" she asked, showing him a curious face. "To escape this future war?"

"Naturally," he confessed. "We intend to circle the Milky Way, once or twenty times, and the next cycle of wars will run their course. The galaxy will be devastated, and we, I mean your descendants and myself, will inherit all of it." A pause. "By then, the perfection that we have built—the perfection you embody, Sarrie—will be strong enough to expand across millions of unclaimed worlds."

She looked straight at Ejy, guessing distances, knowing the machine's most likely response.

Ejy wouldn't kill her.

Not as a first recourse, not when she embodied perfection.

But Ejy noticed something in her face, her posture. With a puzzled tone, he asked, "Child? What are you thinking?"

"First of all," Sarrie replied, "I'm not a child. And secondly, I can save my friends, I think."

Servos and adrenaline helped her hand move. And with a sloppy, jarring swat, she caused the rearmost hatch to fly open.

Softly, sadly, Ejy said, "No."

Sarrie dove through the open hatch, fell to the ice below, then sprinted toward the prefab hut.

She might have meant the fouchians when she said "my friends," and for as long as possible, Ejy would resist that corrosive belief that his precious Voice—symbol of his goodness—was capable of anything that smelled like rebellion.

Sarrie lived long enough to reach the hut, pausing, risking a fast look backward. The Artisan's body was large but graceful, pulling itself out of the same hatch and scrambling over the open ice, already closing the gap. "No, no, no," the whispering in her ears kept saying. "No, no, no, no. . . !"

She opened both airlock doors, the tiny hut's atmosphere exploding outward as a blinding fog. Then she was inside, in the new vacuum's calm, knowing exactly what to do but her hands suddenly clumsy. Inept. Standing over the bank of monitors and controls, she hesitated for perhaps half a second—for an age—before mustering the will to quickly push the perfect sequence of buttons.

Reserve power was left in the borehole's cells, as she had hoped. She called to the pumps, waking them, then made them pull frigid seawater into the insulated pipes, the utterly reliable equipment utterly convinced that the ship wanted as much of the precious fluid as it could deliver. Now. Hurry. Please.

Through her feet and fingers, Sarrie felt the surging pumps.

More buttons needed her touch. She almost told herself, "Faster," then thought better of it. What mattered most—what was absolutely essential—was to do nothing wrong for as long as possible, and hope it would be long enough. . . .

So focused was Sarrie on her task that she was puzzled, then amazed, to find herself being lifted off the floor . . . and she just managed to give the final critical command before Ejy had her safely in his grip.

He kept saying, "No, no, no," but the tone of that one word had changed. Sadness gave way to a machine's unnatural fury.

Suddenly she was dragged outside, held by several arms and utterly helpless.

Far out on the table-smooth plain of ice, the twin pipelines closed the same key valves. Yet the pumps kept working, faithful to the end, shoving water into a finite volume and the water resisting their coercion, seams upstream from the closed valves bursting and the compressed water escaping, then freezing in an instant—hundreds of metric tons becoming fresh hard ice every second.

It was happening in the distance, without sound, almost invisibly.

But the Artisan had better eyes than Sarrie, and an infinitely faster set of responses.

Quick surgical bursts of laser light killed the main pumps.

Emergency pumps came on-line, and they were harder to kill—smaller, tougher, and set at a safe distance. Redundancies built on redundancies; the Artisans' driving principle. It took Ejy all of a minute to staunch the flow, killing pumps and puncturing the lines and finally obliterating the tiny hut. But by then a small durable new hill had formed on the plain.

If the buggy could somehow reach that new ice, reach it and use it as a shelter, then some portion of the blast would be absorbed, however slightly, its radiations and fearsome heat muted—

"Why?" cried the Artisan.

She was slammed down on her back—the almost universal position of submission—then again, harder, Ejy drove her into the granitic ice. The impact made her ache, made her want to beg for Ejy to stop. But Sarrie said nothing, and she didn't beg even with her face, and when he saw that bullying did no good, he let her sit up, then more quietly, almost reasonably, said, "Please explain. Please."

At last, the fouchians emerged from the capped borehole. They seemed small, hurried, and inconsequential.

"I know the answer," Sarrie whispered.

No surprise, no hesitation. "What answer?"

"To the xenophobes' scenario. I know how to succeed." She let him see her pride, her authority. "It's simple. They cannot be won over. Never. And it's the good Voice's duty to warn you, to tell you as soon as possible that they're malevolent, and leave you and the other Artisans time to defend the Web—"

"Yes," said Ejy.

Then he added, "It's remarkable. A Voice so young has come to that very difficult answer."

She ignored the praise. Instead, she asked quietly, "How many starships have we met, then destroyed?"

"You've destroyed nothing," the Artisan reminded her.

"Responsibility is all yours."

"Exactly."

She felt a shudder, a sudden rippling of the ice.

And so did Ejy. He rose as high as possible on the mechanical legs, measuring a multitude of useless factors, then guessing the answer even as he inquired, "What other clever thing have you done, Sarrie?"

"The plasma drills believe that we need a second borehole. Now."

Crystal eyes pivoted. The laser started hunting for targets.

"You destroyed their control systems," Sarrie warned. "You can't stop them."

Between the scrambling fouchians and Ejy, out of the ancient ice, came a column of superheated vapor, twisting and rising, a wind lashing at everyone in a wild screaming fury.

Sarrie was knocked backward. Knocked free.

She tried to climb to her feet, falling once, then again. Then she was blown far enough that the scorching wind had faded, and she found herself standing, then running, trying to win as much distance as possible.

From her headphones came fouchian squeaks begging for instructions, then Ejy himself calling after her, the voice wearing its own loss.

Sarrie allowed herself to shout:

"Thank you."

A pause.

Then from out of the maelstrom:

"Thank you for what, child?"

"The butterflies," she told Ejy, almost crying now. "I liked them best."

Later, trying to make sense of events, Sarrie was uncertain when the nuclear charge detonated — moments later, or maybe an hour. And she couldn't decide what she saw of the blast, or felt, or how far it must have thrown her. All she knew was that suddenly she was half-wading, half-swimming through slush, and the sky was close and dense, fogs swirling and cooling, then freezing into a pummeling relentless ice, and she staggered for a time, then stopped to rest, perhaps even sleep, then moved again, eating from her suit's stores and drinking her own filtered urine, and she must have rested two more times, or maybe three, before she saw the tall figure marching along the edge of the fresh pack ice.

She couldn't make out details. She wasn't even certain if it was a human shape, although some part of her, hoping against reason, decided that it was Lilké, that her friend had survived, and everyone else must be somewhere nearby.

But if it was Lilké, would she forgive? Could she forgive Sarrie for everything?

And of course if it wasn't, then it likely was one of the natives. Whoever they were. Surely *they* would send someone to investigate the blast . . . to see who was trying to shatter their peaceful world. . . .

Sarrie realized that what she was seeing was an immortal godlike human.

With the last of her strength, she started kicking her legs and tossing her arms in the air, thinking: *Whoever or whatever they are, they don't know me.*

THE UTILITY MAN

MOST PEOPLE stand up front and wait for the horn. It's Monday morning. Faces are long and tired, voices hoarse, and red eyes squint and water from too little of this. Too much of that. It's like any Monday, except for two things. First, Miller is up front with the others. That's unusual. For the last three years, without exception, he's punched in and gone to the back of the plant. He's got his stuff back there, and he reads until the horn goes off. Books. It's always books with Miller. Except today, that is. He's sitting on a heavy worktable and staring at the door, his expression eager and strange. The second oddity is visible from where he's sitting. Out on the parking lot, on the dirty white gravel, waits a camera crew from the town's only TV station. The new employee is coming this morning. But what's the big fucking deal? some wonder. There's already a couple, three of *them* working in town. Right? It's been what? Two years since that big spiderweb of metal and glass pulled into orbit, and *they* came out. The aliens. Those toothless things from Tau Ceti. There's several million of them inside the starship, right? Miller would know how many. He's got a thing about the aliens. A couple of people consider asking Miller some questions, giving him the chance to talk about what he knows. Only that's dangerous. He might not shut up. God, they think, look at him. He looks like a kid at Christmas. All eager and ready. They think, So what the fuck if the government's giving us an alien? A lot of businesses are getting them. Some sort of get-to-know-each-other nonsense, right? It's been on TV from the first, and everyone understands the basics of the thing. And nobody wants to get excited like Miller. No, they know better. All the good these aliens are supposed to do for people, people everywhere, but they want to wait and see. To keep a rein on things. Pretend it's any Monday, they tell themselves. Ignore Miller and just wait for the damned horn.

The horn screams. Miller jerks and looks at the clock; then he turns, reluctant and slow, and hopes against hope that he can work up front today. Up where he can watch for the Cetian.

Only the foreman comes over to him. He's a tall, beefy man with a fringe of dirty-blond hair, and he tells Miller that so-and-so is gone and he's got to be on the line for now. With Jacob. "Sure," says Miller. "Okay." He's the utility man. He plugs holes during vacations and drunks and whatnot. He's worked here for three years, ever since he last quit school, and he does every job in the plant without complaints. Without lapses. Miller is a small man, young-looking but with lines starting to show on his face. Around his eyes and mouth. He has the kind of face that moves from adolescence into middle age without once looking thirty; and his expressions tend to compound the illusion of youth. Dreamy. Distracted. A little lost, perhaps.

He's a prideful sort of fellow. The pride shows whenever he smiles and shakes his head at this or that.

People don't like Miller. As a rule.

It isn't any one thing. There are others in the plant with smug attitudes. And others who keep to themselves in their free time. A couple people even have college degrees. (Miller doesn't. But he's close in three different majors.) Yet nobody puts together these traits quite like he does. The book reading, the know-it-all voice. And besides, Miller is a prude. An incredible prude. He's not married, but he doesn't talk like any normal bachelor. Off-color jokes and conquest stories embarrass him. Nor does he drink or smoke weed. People have learned to tease him about these things. It's something of a game to them. They like to make him red-faced and crazy, seeing how far they can push him. For the fun of it. "You get any last night, Miller? Huh?" He hates that talk. "Come with us at lunch, Miller. Get high. What do you say, huh? Come down from that pulpit, and let's have some fun."

Fun. They call that fun, thinks Miller. Imagine!

It's the worst thing about working here—listening to the harsh, frank chatter about pussy and dope. Miller's outside life is nobody else's business, he figures. He guards his privacy every moment. Every day. That's one of his prides. He has strict, solid values, and he won't make compromises. Never. After all, he tells himself, he's not part of this place. He doesn't really belong here, and he has no intention of letting this place rub off on him. Or wound him. Not even when he goes to the toilet and reads what people have written on the walls—the Fag Professor and Virgin Miller and the rest of it. He tells himself to ignore it. He won't stoop to their garbage. Sure, he gets angry. Furious, even. But the pay here is good, and he can read while he works. At least sometimes. And most of the time, most days, they leave him alone. Which is fine.

They don't matter, after all.

He's going to make something of his life. Absolutely. He's told them that in a hundred different ways, a thousand times. Just as soon as he saves enough money, he's quitting this dump and heading back to school.

The alien arrives a few minutes after eight, delayed by who-knows-what. He's probably driving his own car, Miller knows. Something suitable. A used car purchased at one of the local lots. Something a factory worker would buy for a thousand dollars, worn tires and dripping oil but otherwise sound.

That's the way they operate.

The Cetians are coming to work and live among human beings, doing their surveying firsthand. That's what this is all about. The Cetians have a master plan, and they've explained it to all the world's nations. From the United States to Chad. They are here to dispense knowledge. An ancient race, they are wise beyond human understanding. Their technologies are eerie, almost magical, and some of them will be turned over in time. Their stardrive, for instance. And their closed ecosystems. Metallurgy. Architecture. And so on. But first they need to learn about the human species. All its facets, weaknesses and strengths. They've done this kind of thing with other alien races. Miller has read every official account. The Cetians are masters of this business. By studying a species from the inside out, they can dispense their gifts without fear of causing massive disruptions. Indeed, thinks Miller, they'll come to understand people better than people do. Maybe that'll be their greatest gift, he tells himself. And he smiles. They'll teach us about ourselves, he thinks. They're going to show us the way to peace and happiness.

Miller has studied the Cetians since their arrival—their starship a glittering webwork rushing from deep space. "They're millions of years older than us," he mutters. He's working across the table from a small pudgy black man. Jacob. "They're part of the great galactic community," he says to himself. "Hundreds of thousands of worlds . . ."

"What's that?" asks Jacob. "What're you mumbling?"

Miller blinks and says, "Nothing." He looks at Jacob for an instant. Then there's motion in the aisle, and he turns his head and sees a cameraman walking backward, a spotlight perched on a pole rising over his head. The alien is nearby. The emissary from the stars. Miller feels a tightness in his throat. He's full of emotion. This won't be the first Cetian he has seen, not hardly; but still and all, he can barely contain himself.

"Hey, Einstein," shouts Jacob. "Get that up here. Here!"

A wooden frame is on the end of the belt, only partway up on the big tabletop. Miller sighs and does what he has to do. Doesn't Jacob see what's happening? Who understands besides him? Sometimes he feels ashamed by everyone's lack of enthusiasm. By their sheer indifference. He wonders why any alien race, saintly or not, would waste precious time in trying to educate mankind. The Earth doesn't deserve the attention, he believes. It has too little imagination, too much stupidity, and he feels like shouting his opinions for the passing camera. Let everyone hear the truth. . . .

"Would ya fucking watch what you're fucking doing?"

Miller blinks and apologizes. He pushes the frame into position and Jacob uses an air gun, pounding long staples into the pine with a slick liquid motion. Jacob is famous for his thoroughness. His efficiency. He takes the frame and pushes it onto the next belt, and the next frame is already here and waiting. The alien is coming down the aisle, but Miller doesn't have time for more than a quick glance or two. He notices the human shape with the milky white skin—skin that can change into gray or black or even become clear. At will. They're beautiful, he knows. Remarkable entities. No real teeth, but a complex gizzard in place of enamel. No hair, but wearing thoroughly human clothes and not looking the least bit silly. This Cetian has faded jeans and a pale blue work shirt, plus running shoes. Miller glances again. He sees a cap riding the smooth hairless head, its brim tilted up and some seed company's emblem riding above the brim. Very natural. Very *right*. If it wasn't for the cameras and the crowd, he thinks, the figure might be anyone. It's a little bit unnerving to see how easily the Cetian fits in.

Half of the front office is helping to give a tour of the plant. For the camera. They're the ones who look misplaced, what with their suits and ties and polished leather shoes. Miller has to concentrate on his job; he can't watch the group as it moves, lingers, then moves again. He's talking to the Cetian whenever he can. In his head. And the imaginary alien asks him how he came to be here. A person of his interests, of his training, seems wasted in this place. I needed the money, Miller explains. It's just the way things fell together, you know? But the alien doesn't understand, no. So Miller, speaking inside his head, tells half of his life story. It doesn't answer everything, but he tells it with all the vigor he can muster. As if he's practicing for later. For the conversations to come.

The imaginary Cetian smiles in his peculiar fashion—the beaklike lips parting and the violet tongue showing against the roof of his mouth. Then he compliments Miller in glowing terms, telling him that he's bright and articulate, and so on. A good thing I found you, the Cetian declares. I thought I might be lonely while I'm here. And bored. But now I've got you for a friend . . . a soul mate. . . .

"Hey! You alive, Miller?"

Miller is behind again. He apologizes to Jacob and lifts the next frame, making dead certain that it's properly aligned.

And the next one, too.

And the next.

People from the office begin to file past them, and the newspeople. Their jobs are done. Smiles and amiable chatter mean everything has gone well. Miller concentrates on his job. Eventually, the foreman wanders past. He's alone, smoking and looking generally pissed at the world. Miller remembers how last week, hearing that they were getting a Cetian, the foreman had moaned something about not wanting or needing one of those goddamn chameleons. Fuck gifts from the stars and all that shit. He had a business to run. Product to get out. If he couldn't fucking hire who he wanted, then screw all the suits and their goddamn offices, too—

Miller stands on his toes for a moment, looking down the line.

The Cetian is standing at the line's end. In the plant's hierarchy, that's one of the worst jobs. The Cetian and a scruffy man are pulling the finished frames from the belt and stacking them on pallets. But what else are they doing? he wonders. Talking? The scruffy man is a drunk, Miller knows. He didn't get past ninth grade, and he's been to prison how many times? For stupid crimes.

For drugs. He's probably still stoned, Miller realizes. Red-eyed and wobbly. Yet the Cetian is talking to him, and he's answering. They're having a conversation—?

There comes a sudden wood-splitting *crash.*

"Goddamn you!" shouts Jacob. He aims the air gun at Miller's chest. "Pull your head out of your ass, Professor. The chameleon will keep, for God's sake! So let's get busy. What do you say? Huh?"

There's a horn for the morning break—fifteen minutes of rest, minus walking time. Most people go back up front, up to where the vending machines are stacked along the concrete walls. They settle down to play cards and nap on the golden stacks of lumber. And there's the talk, the constant talk, about tits and asses and blow and beer.

Normally Miller goes the other way. He has a corner, quiet and out of the way, where he keeps his lunch and books and a comfortable seat he made for himself out of scrap lumber. Sometimes when he's reading he finds a sentence or a little paragraph that he likes, and he uses a marking pen to copy it on the concrete walls. For future reference. Today, hearing the break horn, Miller's first thought is that the Cetian might wander back to his corner and pause, reading some of the carefully written wisdoms. Yes? They're from great novels and classic works of science—the crowns of human achievement. It's such a wonderful image, the Cetian and him meeting in that corner. So wonderful that Miller almost expects it to happen. He's got it all planned.

Except the Cetian doesn't know the plan. He comes forward with the general flow of bodies. It's unnerving to watch him. He seems to carry himself like any new employee. There's a tentativeness, a calculated caution in the eyes—flat and square, in this case, with tiny triangular pupils the color of new snow—and the caution extends to everyone around him. Maybe these people are scared, thinks Miller. I'm not scared, he tells himself. This is an opportunity, rare and remarkable. Miller feels singularly suited to act as a bridge between the two sides. A rush of adrenaline pours through him. He climbs under the belt and joins the flow of bodies, and it's all he can do to keep from jogging after the Cetian and calling to him. Like some long lost friend.

They're amazing, really. These aliens.

In Asia, Cetians dress in peasant clothes and enormous straw hats, bending over and shuffling through the flooded rice paddies. In Australia, in the dusty outback, they drive little 4 x 4 pickups while they do simple ranch work like abos do. In Europe, odd as it sounds, Cetians are among the protestors marching against imperialism and environmental decay; and they're also the police wearing riot gear and standing in rows, defending order and the state.

These ironies are abundant and somehow comforting.

There is a sense of utter fairness in the process.

Cetians will undergo almost anything to learn about mankind firsthand—some even dying—and Miller has to wonder how many of his coworkers appreciate their earnestness, their good intentions. He doubts any of them do. Probably not one, he thinks.

It must be lonely, dull work for them.

Miller knows.

A Cetian would welcome a friend, sure. Someone who appreciates the age and depth of the Cetian culture. Miller sees the odd white figure sitting alone on a lumber stack, the square eyes watching a cluster of men playing poker on a little table. Miller breathes and sits on the same stack, not too close but near enough that they could talk. If they want. He glances at the odd eyes and the white, white skin. What should I say? he wonders. Why am I so nervous? I shouldn't be nervous, he tells himself. His hands shake in his lap. A couple of poker players glance up at him and smile, then they mutter something rude. No doubt. Again Miller breathes, finding a quick courage. "Hello?" He sees all of the Cetian face, blank and so strange. He offers his name and smiles, extending one of his nervous hands.

The square eyes blink in slow motion. "I'm Rozz," says the Cetian, the voice deep and liquid and amazingly human. One of Rozz's four-fingered hands grabs Miller's hand, squeezing and feeling like plastic. It's smooth and cool and tough. Like plastic. Or maybe Teflon.

"Hey," says Miller, "it's great you're here. I mean it. Everywhere, I mean." He feels clumsy, his mouth spitting words at random. "I just really think it's neat."

Rozz blinks again, no expression to be read.

Miller hears a poker player laughing. Maybe at him. He gulps and tells the Cetian, "This isn't much to look at, I know," and then he glances about, his own face critical but tolerant. "Did they show you everything? I mean, do you have questions? Because I might answer them. I mean, I've been here quite a while." He feels giddy now. He tells himself that he's doing too much, he wants too much, but all he can do is listen to his own prattle. "Years," he says. "I mean, if you want to get a feel for this place and all—"

The poker table erupts in laughter. Miller jerks, not having heard what was said but imagining several things. Something tasteless and pointed at him, no doubt. Then he looks at Rozz, ready to deny anything. The Cetian is now focused on the little table — raw pine scraps stapled together — and the hunched-over bodies with cigarettes in their laughing mouths and the cards tight in their hands. Maybe fifty cents in nickels and dimes are in the middle. Everyone is looking at the alien. The laughter diminishes. Something wary and alert comes into their faces. For a long moment, nothing happens. Then Rozz says with a slow, precise voice:

"Five-card draw."

A couple players blink as if surprised. Someone asks, "You know it? The game?"

Rozz lifts a hand, flattens it, and wiggles it in the air. "A little bit," he seems to imply. "I'm not so good," he says aloud. "But I can play."

The men look at one another, not sure what to make of things. It's the foreman, sitting with his back to Rozz, who announces, "This is an open game, I guess. Anyone who wants to join, joins."

Rozz drops off the stack, leaving Miller without a good-bye glance. One of the players moves aside, giving up most of a long bench, and Rozz sits and watches a new hand being laid out. No one looks comfortable. They're judging him, thinks Miller. This is some test. Rozz picks up the five cards and finds a nickel in his front pocket, putting it into the new pot. Then he draws three cards, adds a second nickel, and loses with a pair of tens. The game couldn't be any quieter. They play again, a couple more hands, and everyone is sneaking looks at the hard plasticlike skin, at the square eyes, at the beaked and toothless mouth. Rozz pays no attention to them, and Miller stays on the stack, still marveling. An ancient race that has traveled around the galaxy, to countless wonderful places, and yet their representative has the charity and poise to sit with a backward race. A hard and graceless race. Us.

At one point, his voice cracking, Miller asks, "How's it going, Rozz? How are we doing?"

Rozz looks at him, maybe smiling. "Not too fucking bad," he declares. "Not bad at all." And he lays down the winning hand, grinning in a very human fashion, sweeping in the nickels while the other players stare, almost laughing, a few of them nodding as if they've seen something and it's something they might like.

Through the rest of the morning, Miller writes little notes on the golden wood of the frames. He uses a black marker. The frames are going to be painted, so there's no damage done. Then the belt carries them and his notes on down the line, straight to Rozz.

"The Cetian Earth," he scribbles, "is tropical and wet and covered with lemon-colored vegetation." He hopes Rozz will be impressed with his interest. "Its largest creature is a fish-analog, one hundred tons, semi-intelligent and peaceful and worshiped by the ancient Cetians." He has to write quickly, trying Jacob's patience. He wants Rozz to respond somehow, but he can't even tell if his new friend is reading the notes. "Cetian starships are powered by matter-antimatter engines, both fuels derived from the interstellar medium." The message is broken up on several frames. Still no response. No wave or smile. Nothing. "I'm interested in you," he writes finally. "And I admire your culture."

This time Rozz looks down the line and nods. Once.

Miller is excited. He looks at his watch, thinking hard. It's close to noon. "Eat with me?" he writes. "Miller." Then he waits, watching the frame travel to the end. To *him*.

But the Cetian doesn't respond. He seems to read it, yes, but then there's the horn and he's walking down the aisle, down past Miller and gone. Jacob wants to finish the frame on the table. Maybe Rozz didn't understand? thinks Miller. Maybe I should have told him where? Still optimistic, he hurries back to his corner and gets a certain book—a recently published guide to Cetian myths and legends—plus his lunch pail. But when he's up front, trotting toward the time clock, he discovers the Cetian sitting snugly between the foreman and another one of the poker players.

Disappointment starts to nag at him.

He punches out and returns. The three figures are sharing a stack of lumber. The humans eat from pails—sandwiches and hard-boiled eggs and sweating pop cans within easy reach. Rozz has a crumpled grocery sack behind him and a cellophane bag of unshelled, unsalted peanuts in one hand. No one is talking, but the humans watch the peanuts being flipped up into the mouth two at a time. Rozz doesn't chew; he only swallows. His pace is amazing. The foreman shakes his head and smiles. Miller settles at the poker table, barely hungry but pretending to chew on his sandwich. While he watches.

He feels cheated.

Coming here this morning, he had expectations. They'd been building since last week's announcement. It was the prospect of a *friend*—someone he could respect, and converse with, and learn from. Not another sweatshop goon full of harsh talk and ugly humor. But someone of culture, of learning. Someone who had been to odd and wondrous places beyond human reach. Someone he could share breaks with, and lunchtime, the two of them talking and talking and talking—

Miller bristles, thinking he might have been wrong.

He sets down his lunch-meat sandwich, his stomach churning and his breath tasting foul. The foreman asks Rozz, "So how do you do it?" and Miller waits. "Like I've seen on TV—?"

"A gizzard," Rozz answers, his tone matter-of-fact. Patient. "You know, like a chicken's gizzard? It's lined with rocks that grind up the shells, and I shit out what my body can't use."

"Huh," says the foreman. "Huh!"

"Do you want to see it?"

"What? Your gizzard?" The foreman halfway shudders, surprised.

"You've seen 'em, Pete," says the other man. "They do it on TV."

Rozz unbuttons the blue cotton shirt, exposing the white chest with its narrow, widely spaced ribs. Maybe he's smiling. Miller shifts on the hard wooden seat and watches, his thoughts jumbled. A look of utter calm comes into Rozz's face, and the whiteness weakens like milk being flooded with water. A large yellow heart, six chambers and a tangle of thick arteries and veins, is set within the long pale ribs. The gizzard is the darker bundle of round muscle beneath the heart. Miller recognizes it from all the science articles. He feels an urge to stand and point out organs, lecturing. "This is where the peanuts are now." But Rozz himself points, telling them the same thing. Then, as if to display his talents, the gizzard contracts with a sudden violence. Shells crumble and the two men give a little jump, then they shake their heads and laugh, looking at one another as if to congratulate themselves on their courage.

"All right," says Pete, the foreman. "With rocks, you say?"

Rozz turns white again, and he smiles again. "Here. Watch this." He reaches into the grocery sack and retrieves a single black walnut, rough against the smooth skin of the hand. "Watch," he cautions. The nut vanishes into his mouth, and he swallows in a theoretical way; and with Miller eating again, unnoticed and still glowering at all of them, the walnut shatters somewhere inside the Cetian's belly. It's like a little explosion. The men jump and then giggle, then turn and look around the plant, hunting for someone to show the marvel they've just found.

Rozz is moved off the line after lunch. The foreman wants him up front, up in Assembly, which is pretty much the easiest department. It's where the foreman spends most of his day. What's going on? Miller wonders. He feels betrayed and rather jealous. And maybe foolish, too. All the time he'd been building this image of the Cetians, and all the time he'd been so blind. The Cetians fit into all kinds of places, with anyone. It never occurred to him that they actually *enjoyed it!* Now the blood roars in his head and his fingers shake. He can scarcely think, barely able to do his job. Jacob glares at him several times, shaking his head but too weary to shout. Miller counts the minutes till afternoon break, the halfway point, because everything afterward will be quick. The day and the craziness will be over soon after break. Then he'll have time to go home and collect himself, to sleep and relax and get it all straight in his head.

When the break horn sounds, Miller decides a Coke would taste good.

By the time he's up front, the poker players are at it. Rozz is among them. Miller pauses and stands nearby, just watching, and then something unexpected occurs to him. Why not? he asks himself. It's an open game, isn't it? There's an empty seat. Miller takes it and looks straight across at the Cetian, waiting, feeling tight inside while he watches the white hands shuffling the deck like a pro.

How does he do it? Miller wonders. Did he practice before coming here? Or does he just pick it up along the way? Card games. The language. All of it. The humans watch Miller while Rozz deals. Miller isn't sure how to bet. He throws a nickel into the pot, takes three cards, and loses with a pair of fours. The foreman wins, grinning at Miller and sweeping up the coins. He says, "So what's the occasion? Thought you'd be social for a change?"

Miller doesn't know what he's thinking. He opens his mouth as if to answer, but nothing comes to mind.

The foreman is amused. Still smiling, he turns to another man and asks, "Have you seen what the new guy can do, Ed? Have you?"

"What do you mean?" Ed works in the paint department—an ancient simpleton with a partial beard and spooked eyes. He glances at Rozz, unsure of himself. "What can he do?" he manages. "Tell me."

"Would you?" says the foreman. "You mind?"

Rozz shrugs. No, he doesn't mind. His skin immediately turns black, like coal. Someone up on the stacks yells, "Hey, he looks like Jacob! Don't he?"

A lot of them laugh.

The foreman laughs. "But it's the other thing I wanted."

"God, I don't want to see!" Ed shivers. "Why the fuck would anyone do that to himself? I mean . . . Jesus. . . !"

"For camouflage," Miller responds. He says, "They do it so they can hide," and nods, glad to have spoken. To throw in his knowledge.

But no one is listening to him. Except Ed. And Ed doesn't like what he hears. "So how come he's not colored? You know. Green and all? Those fucking lizards are green and brown and shit. Right?"

"Cetians are color-blind." Miller smiles. He's sorting his next hand without looking at his cards, telling everyone, "They see the world in black and white and gray. Like cheap TV."

Only Ed listens, his mouth opened and his expression befuddled. The rest of the table, Rozz included, studies the cards and Ed and the little piles of change out in front of them. They aren't going to let him take part in this. Not if they can help it. Someone up on the stacks says something, probably about Miller, and he hears men chuckling. It was funny to them. He can imagine what they just said.

Nickels are tossed into the pot.

Miller glances at his cards once, then catches Rozz staring at him. The square eyes are cold and a little bit unnerving. He shifts his weight, feeling the hard wood against his butt. There's more betting and he loses again. Rozz wins. Reaching for the pot, he makes the skin of his hands turn transparent. Everyone can see his colorless meat and the fine yellow bones, and almost everyone laughs. Except for Miller and Ed. "Would you fucking stop that?" says Ed. "Goddamn, you're nuts. Can all of you . . . you people do that? Can you?"

"You should have seen him at lunch," the foreman confides. "We looked in on Rozz's heart, didn't we?" Everyone nods. Poker has been temporarily forgotten. "And his gizzard. And his guts."

"I don't want to see any guts," says Ed, emphatic. He waves his large calloused hands, telling the Cetian, "I don't even like think-ing about that stuff."

Rozz shrugs.

The foreman says, "Do it in the face. Can you do it there?" He asks, "Can you make your face go clear?"

"Sure." Rozz seems unperturbed. Amused, even.

Ed says, "No, no, no! I can't stand this shit."

The foreman waves to the men on the stacks. "Come on over. Old Rozz is going to give us a show."

They drop from the stacks, giggling and trotting over and forming a clumsy horseshoe around the poker table. Miller doesn't know what to do. He feels small and absolutely unnoticed, picking at his cards and trying to focus on their blurred figures.

People start to applaud.

He jerks and looks. He has to look. He's startled by the yellow skull—eye sockets cubic and the tongue curled against the mouth's roof and pale muscles making the small jaw move, Rozz saying, "Look, Ma. No face!"

The men start to howl. Someone says, "What's the matter, Ed? Hey! You don't look so good!"

Ed's face has turned pale. His hands push the coins and cards away from him. "I can't take it," he squeals. "You guys—!"

"What's wrong, Ed?"

"Why the hell does he have to do that? Why?" he wondered. "I don't see why he's got to turn to glass!"

Miller knows. He touches Ed and says, "It's because of sex," with a very serious, utterly sober voice.

The table becomes quiet.

Rozz turns white again, watching Miller.

Ed turns his head and looks lost. "What do you mean? What's sex got to do with it?"

No one admits they're listening, but no one makes a sound. Not the foreman. Not any of them. Miller says, "It's like with birds. Birds have bright plumage so they can show potential mates they're healthy. Strong. Virile. Cetians do the same thing by making themselves transparent. It's a very private thing." And he pauses. "Normally. It's to show their mate that they don't have internal parasites. No diseases. Nothing bad or out of place." He breathes and puts his own cards on top of the mess, feeling every eye and relishing the attention. These stupid jerks, he's thinking. And he means *all* of them. He glares at Rozz as if accusing him of some failure, some wicked crime, and he crosses his arms on his chest and says nothing more.

Says Rozz, "What do you know?"

Eyes shift to the Cetian.

"He's right, you know." Rozz nods, telling them, "When I go to bed with a girl, I really undress."

A few men laugh, uneasily.

Rozz grabs the scattered cards, arranging and then shuffling the deck. Everyone takes back their old bets. Rozz deals. When he starts to throw in a nickel, by accident, he knocks other coins to the floor. So he bends and vanishes under the table for a moment. The men are glaring at Miller. One of them says, "Professor Perfect," and several of them are laughing.

Rozz returns. The hand is finished in tense silence. Miller wins sixty-five cents with three aces, but he doesn't care. It means nothing. He's halfway tempted to leave the pot, proving his scorn for everyone. The alien is manipulating the crowd, he senses. But not me! The horn sounds, and everyone is standing. Miller starts to pocket his winnings regardless, and there comes a sudden stillness. What's happening? He notices how everyone else is looking at the floor, at his feet, and he looks down and spots a single card on the floor. A fourth ace right beneath his seat.

Says the foreman, "What's this?"

Miller looks at the smiling alien.

"What're you doing?" asks the foreman. "Cheating us for change?"

They're all watching him, waiting, their expressions stern and maybe angry. Maybe not. He's having trouble reading their faces. "I didn't do this," he argues. "I mean, you can't really believe. . . !"

Rozz shakes his head as if supremely disappointed.

"It's you!" shouts Miller. "You put that there, didn't you?"

"Did I?" asks Rozz.

Miller moves toward him. "When you went under the table, you did it! Didn't you?"

"Gosh," says the foreman. "That's a pretty strong accusation, Miller. I hope you can back it up."

"Someone must have seen him do it." Miller pivots, wanting a witness to step forward. "Who saw him put the card there — ?"

Nobody says, "Me."

Miller faces the Cetian again, waiting for a moment. Then he leaps. He shoves a handful of nickels into the bastard's face, right at its beaked mouth, shouting, "They're yours, goddamn you! You eat them! Now!" He says, "Line your goddamn gizzard with these, you shit!"

The men pull him off Rozz.

The foreman and another fellow, stern-faced and certain, march him into the little glass-walled office where the plant manager holds court. He isn't here just now. The other man goes to find him. The foreman shakes his head and says nothing. His arms are crossed on his chest.

"I didn't do it," Miller manages to say.

"I know," says the foreman. "We all know that. Rozz was just having fun with you. It was just a joke, you idiot."

Miller can barely hear him. He's looking out into the plant, into Assembly. A group of men are standing in a circle, talking to Rozz. He's so far away that he looks human. The jeans, the shirt, the seed cap. Even his motions are true. It occurs to Miller that the alien is genuinely fitting into this place. All the Cetians fit in. To them this isn't a chore, it's a joy. They wear humanity like you would a new suit—

"What's happening out there?" asks the foreman.

Miller can't tell for certain.

"Stay here. I'll be back." He shuts the door and stalks out into the plant. The men don't see him approaching. They're engrossed with whatever Rozz is telling them, both of Rozz's hands above his head, eyes wide, the hands implying some epic tale of great drama and worth.

The foreman breaks it up.

Miller watches everyone get back to work. He sees Rozz talking to the foreman and glancing toward the office. Then the foreman returns. "He gave me a message. He wants you to know something."

Miller asks, "What?"

"He said he's been sizing you up—"

"Yeah?"

"—and he doesn't like your insides."

Miller has no response. He presses his face to the glass and sighs, feeling nothing, his thoughts jumbled and slow. What I'll have to do first, he thinks, is get my stuff out of that corner. The books and the rest of it that I want. Then he remembers the quotes on the walls and wishes there was some way he could take them, too. But there's not, of course. They're there. That's where they'll have to stay.

GUEST
OF
HONOR

ONE OF THE robots offered to carry Pico for the last hundred meters, on its back or cradled in its padded arms; but she shook her head emphatically, telling it, "Thank you, no. I can make it myself." The ground was grassy and soft, lit by glowglobes and the grass-colored moon. It wasn't a difficult walk, even with her bad hip, and she wasn't an invalid. She could manage, she thought with an instinctive independence. And as if to show them, she struck out ahead of the half-dozen robots as they unloaded the big skimmer, stacking Pico's gifts in their long arms. She was halfway across the paddock before they caught her. By then she could hear the muddled voices and laughter coming from the hill-like tent straight ahead. By then she was breathing fast for reasons other than her pain. For fear, mostly. But it was a different flavor of fear than the kinds she knew. What was happening now was beyond her control, and inevitable . . . and it was that kind of certainty that made her stop after a few more steps, one hand rubbing at her hip for no reason except to delay her arrival. If only for a moment or two . . .

"Are you all right?" asked one robot.

She was gazing up at the tent, dark and smooth and gently

rounded. "I don't want to be here," she admitted. "That's all." Her life on board the *Kyber* had been spent with robots — they had outnumbered the human crew ten to one, then more — and she could always be ruthlessly honest with them. "This is madness. I want to leave again."

"Only, you can't," responded the ceramic creature. The voice was mild, unnervingly patient. "You have nothing to worry about."

"I know."

"The technology has been perfected since —"

"*I know.*"

It stopped speaking, adjusting its hold on the colorful packages.

"That's not what I meant," she admitted. Then she breathed deeply, holding the breath for a moment and exhaling, saying, "All right. Let's go. Go."

The robot pivoted and strode toward the giant tent. The leading robots triggered the doorway, causing it to fold upward with a sudden rush of golden light flooding across the grass, Pico squinting and then blinking, walking faster now and allowing herself the occasional low moan.

"Ever wonder how it'll feel?" Tyson had asked her.

The tent had been pitched over a small pond, probably that very day, and in places the soft, thick grasses had been matted flat by people and their robots. So many people, she thought. Pico tried not to look at any faces. For a moment, she gazed at the pond, shallow and richly green, noticing the tamed waterfowl sprinkled over it and along its shoreline. Ducks and geese, she realized. And some small crimson-headed cranes. Lifting her eyes, she noticed the large omega-shaped table near the far wall. She couldn't count the place settings, but it seemed a fair assumption there were sixty-three of them. Plus a single round table and chair in the middle of the omega — *my table* — and she took another deep breath, looking higher, noticing floating glowglobes and several indigo swallows flying around them, presumably snatching up the insects that were drawn to the yellow-white light.

People were approaching. Since she had entered, in one patient rush, all sixty-three people had been climbing the slope while shouting, "Pico! Hello!" Their voices mixed together, forming a noisy, senseless paste. "Greetings!" they seemed to say. "Hello, hello!"

They were brightly dressed, flowing robes swishing and everyone wearing big-rimmed hats made to resemble titanic flowers. The people sharply contrasted with the gray-white shells of the robot servants. Those hats were a new fashion, Pico realized. One of the little changes introduced during these past decades . . . and finally she made herself look at the faces themselves, offering a forced smile and taking a step backward, her belly aching, but her hip healed. The burst of adrenaline hid the deep ache in her bones. Wrestling one of her hands into a wave, she told her audience, "Hello," with a near-whisper. Then she swallowed and said, "Greetings to you!" Was that her voice? She barely recognized it.

A woman broke away from the others, almost running toward her. Her big flowery hat began to work free, and she grabbed the fat petalish brim and started to fan herself with one hand, the other hand touching Pico on the shoulder. The palm was damp and quite warm; the air suddenly stank of overly sweet perfumes. It was all Pico could manage not to cough. The woman—what was her name?—was asking, "Do you need to sit? We heard . . . about your accident. You poor girl. All the way fine, and then on the last world. Of all the luck!"

Her hip. The woman was jabbering about her sick hip.

Pico nodded and confessed, "Sitting would be nice, yes."

A dozen voices shouted commands. Robots broke into runs, racing one another around the pond to grab the chair beside the little table. The drama seemed to make people laugh. A nervous self-conscious laugh. When the lead robot reached the chair and started back, there was applause. Another woman shouted, "Mine won! Mine won!" She threw her hat into the air and tried to follow it, leaping as high as possible.

Some man cursed her sharply, then giggled.

Another man forced his way ahead, emerging from the packed bodies in front of Pico. He was smiling in a strange fashion. Drunk or drugged . . . what was permissible these days? With a sloppy, earnest voice, he asked, "How'd it happen? The hip thing . . . how'd you do it?"

He should know. She had dutifully filed her reports throughout the mission, squirting them home. Hadn't he seen them? But then she noticed the watchful excited faces—no exceptions—and someone seemed to read her thoughts, explaining, "We'd love to hear it *firsthand*. Tell, tell, tell!"

As if they needed to hear a word, she thought, suddenly feeling quite cold.

Her audience grew silent. The robot arrived with the promised chair, and she sat and stretched her bad leg out in front of her, working to focus her mind. It was touching, their silence . . . reverent and almost childlike . . . and she began by telling them how she had tried climbing Miriam Prime with two other crew members. Miriam Prime was the tallest volcano on a brutal super-Venusian world; it was brutal work because of the terrain and their massive lifesuits, cumbersome refrigeration units strapped to their backs, and the atmosphere thick as water. Scalding and acidic. Carbon dioxide and water made for a double greenhouse effect. . . . And she shuddered, partly for dramatics and partly from the memory. Then she said, "Brutal," once again, shaking her head thoughtfully.

They had used hyperthreads to climb the steepest slopes and the cliffs. Normally hyperthreads were unbreakable; but Miriam was not a normal world. She described the basalt cliff and the awful instant of the tragedy; the clarity of the scene startled her. She could feel the heat seeping into her suit, see the dense, dark air, and her arms and legs shook with exhaustion. She told sixty-three people how it felt to be suspended on an invisible thread, two friends and a winch somewhere above in the acidic fog. The winch had jammed without warning, she told; the worst bad luck made it jam where the thread was its weakest. This was near the mission's end, and all the equipment was tired. Several dozen alien worlds had been visited, many mapped for the first time, and every one of them examined up close. As planned.

"Everything has its limits, " she told them, her voice having an ominous quality that she hadn't intended.

Even hyperthreads had limits. Pico was dangling, talking to her companions by radio; and just as the jam was cleared, a voice saying, "There . . . got it!"—the thread parted. He didn't have any way to know it had parted. Pico was falling, gaining velocity, and the poor man was ignorantly telling her, "It's running strong. You'll be up in no time, no problem. . . ."

People muttered to themselves.

"Oh, my," they said.

"Gosh."

"Shit."

Their excitement was obvious, perhaps even overdone. Pico almost laughed, thinking they were making fun of her storytelling . . . thinking, *What do they know about such things?* . . . Only, they were sincere, she realized a moment later. They were enraptured with the image of Pico's long fall, her spinning and lashing out with both hands, fighting to grab anything and slow her fall any way possible—

—and she struck a narrow shelf of eroded stone, the one leg shattered and telescoping down to a gruesome stump. Pico remembered the painless shock of the impact and that glorious instant free of all sensation. She was alive, and the realization had made her giddy. Joyous. Then the pain found her head—a great nauseating wave of pain—and she heard her distant friends shouting, "Pico? Are you there? Can you hear us? Oh, Pico . . . *Pico?* Answer us!"

She had to remain absolutely motionless, sensing that any move would send her tumbling again. She answered in a whisper, telling her friends that she was alive, yes, and please, please hurry. But they had only a partial thread left, and it would take them more than half an hour to descend . . . and she spoke of her agony and the horror, her hip and leg screaming, and not just from the impact. It was worse than mere broken bone, the lifesuit's insulation damaged and the heat bleeding inward, slowly and thoroughly cooking her living flesh.

Pico paused, gazing out at the round-mouthed faces.

So many people and not a breath of sound; and she was having fun. She realized her pleasure almost too late, nearly missing it. Then she told them, "I nearly died," and shrugged her shoulders. "All the distances traveled, every imaginable adventure . . . and I nearly died on one of our last worlds, doing an ordinary climb. . . ."

Let them appreciate her luck, she decided. *Their luck.*

Then another woman lifted her purple flowery hat with both hands, pressing it flush against her own chest. "Of course you survived!" she proclaimed. "You wanted to come home, Pico! You couldn't stand the thought of *dying.*"

Pico nodded without comment, then said, "I was rescued. Obviously." She flexed the damaged leg, saying, "I never really healed," and she touched her hip with reverence, admitting, "We didn't have the resources on board the *Kyber*. This was the best our medical units could do."

Her mood shifted again, without warning. Suddenly she felt sad to tears, eyes dropping and her mouth clamped shut.

"We worried about you, Pico!"

"All the time, dear!"

". . . in our prayers. . . !"

Voices pulled upon each other, competing to be heard. The faces were smiling and thoroughly sincere. Handsome people, she was thinking. Clean and civilized and older than she by centuries. Some of them were more than a thousand years old.

Look at them! she told herself.

And now she felt fear. Pulling both legs toward her chest, she hugged herself, weeping hard enough to dampen her trouser legs; and her audience said, "But you made it, Pico! You came home! The wonders you've seen, the places you've actually touched . . . with those hands. . . . And we're so proud of you! So proud! You've proven your worth a thousand times, Pico! You're made of the very best stuff—!"

—which brought laughter, a great clattering roar of laughter, the joke obviously and apparently tireless.

Even after so long.

They were Pico; Pico was they.

Centuries ago, during the Blossoming, technologies had raced forward at an unprecedented rate. Starships like the *Kyber* and a functional immortality had allowed the first missions to the distant worlds, and there were some grand adventures. Yet adventure requires some element of danger; exploration has never been a safe enterprise. Despite precautions, there were casualties. People who had lived for centuries died suddenly, oftentimes in stupid accidents; and it was no wonder that after the first wave of missions came a long moratorium. No new starships were built, and no sensible person would have ridden inside even the safest vessel. Why risk yourself? Whatever the benefits, why taunt extinction when you have a choice?

Only recently had a solution been invented. Maybe it was prompted by the call of deep space, though Tyson used to claim, "It's the boredom on Earth that inspired them. That's why they came up with their elaborate scheme."

The near-immortals devised ways of making highly gifted, highly trained crews from themselves. With computers and genetic engineering, groups of people could pool their qualities and create compilation humans. Sixty-three individuals had each donated moneys and their own natures, and Pico was the result. She was a grand and sophisticated average of the group. Her face was a blending of every face; her body was a feminine approximation of their own varied bodies. In a few instances, the engineers had planted synthetic genes—for speed and strength, for example —and her brain had a subtly different architecture. Yet basically Pico was their offspring, a stewlike clone. The second of two clones, she knew. The first clone created had had subtle flaws, and he was painlessly destroyed just before birth.

Pico and Tyson and every other compilation person had been born at adult size. Because she was the second attempt, and behind schedule, Pico was thrown straight into her training. Un-

like the other crew members, she had spent only a minimal time
with her parents. Her sponsors. Whatever they were calling themselves. That and the long intervening years made it difficult to recognize faces and names. She found herself gazing out at them,
believing they were strangers, their tireless smiles hinting at something predatory. The neat white teeth gleamed at her, and she
wanted to shiver again, holding the knees closer to her mouth.

Someone suggested opening the lovely gifts.

A good idea. She agreed, and the robots brought down the
stacks of boxes, placing them beside and behind her. The presents
were a young tradition; when she was leaving Earth, the first compilation people were returning with little souvenirs of their travels.
Pico had liked the gesture and had done the same. One after
another, she read the names inscribed in her own flowing hand-
writing. Then each person stepped forward, thanking her for the
treasure, then greedily unwrapping it, the papers flaring into
bright colors as they were bent and twisted and torn, then tossed
aside for the robots to collect.

She knew none of these people, and that was wrong. What she
should have done, she realized, was go into the *Kyber*'s records
and memorize names and faces. It would have been easy enough,
and proper, and she felt guilty for never having made the effort.

It wasn't merely genetics that she shared with these people; she
also embodied slivers of their personalities and basic tendencies.
Inside Pico's sophisticated womb, the computers had blended together their shrugs and tongue clicks and the distinctive patterns
of their speech. She had emerged as an approximation of every one
of them; yet why didn't she feel a greater closeness? Why wasn't
there a strong tangible bond here?

Or was there something—only, she wasn't noticing it?

One early gift was a slab of mirrored rock. "From Tween Five,"
she explained. "What it doesn't reflect, it absorbs and reemits
later. I kept that particular piece in my own cabin, fixed to the
outer wall—"

"Thank you, thank you," gushed the woman.

For an instant, Pico saw herself reflected on the rock. She
looked much older than these people. Tired, she thought. Badly
weathered. In the cramped starship, they hadn't the tools to re-
vitalize aged flesh, nor had there been the need. Most of the voyage had been spent in cold-sleep. Their waking times, added together, barely exceeded forty years of biological activity.

"Look at this!" the woman shouted, turning and waving her
prize at the others. "Isn't it lovely?"

"A shiny rock," teased one voice. "Perfect!"

Yet the woman refused to be anything but impressed. She clasped her prize to her chest and giggled, merging with the crowd and then vanishing.

They look like children, Pico told herself.

At least how she imagined children to appear . . . unworldly and spoiled, needing care and infinite patience. . . .

She read the next name, and a new woman emerged to collect her gift. "My, what a large box!" She tore at the paper, then the box's lid, then eased her hands into the dunnage of white foam. Pico remembered wrapping this gift — one of the only ones where she was positive of its contents — and she happily watched the smooth, elegant hands pulling free a greasy and knob-faced nut. Then Pico explained:

"It's from the Yult Tree on Proxima Centauri Two." The only member of the species on that strange little world. "If you wish, you can break its dormancy with liquid nitrogen. Then plant it in pure quartz sand, never anything else. Sand, and use red sunlight —"

"I know how to cultivate them," the woman snapped.

There was a sudden silence, uneasy and prolonged.

Finally Pico said, "Well . . . good . . ."

"Everyone knows about Yult nuts," the woman explained. "They're practically giving them away at the greeneries now."

Someone spoke sharply, warning her to stop and think.

"I'm sorry," she responded. "If I sound ungrateful, I mean. I was just thinking, hoping . . . I don't know. Never mind."

A weak, almost inconsequential apology, and the woman paused to feel the grease between her fingertips.

The thing was, Pico thought, that she had relied on guesswork in selecting these gifts. She had decided to represent every alien world, and she felt proud of herself on the job accomplished. Yult Trees were common on Earth? But how could she know such a thing? And besides, why should it matter? She had brought the nut and everything else because she'd taken risks, and these people were obviously too ignorant and silly to appreciate what they were receiving.

Rage had replaced her fear.

Sometimes she heard people talking among themselves, trying to trade gifts. Gemstones and pieces of alien driftwood were being passed about like orphans. Yet nobody would release the specimens of odd life-forms from living worlds, transparent canisters holding bugs and birds and whatnot inside preserving fluids or hard vacuums. If only she had known what she couldn't have known, these silly brats. . . . And she found herself swallowing, holding her breath, and wanting to scream at all of them.

Pico was a compilation, yet she wasn't.

She hadn't lived one day as these people had lived their entire lives. She didn't know about comfort or changelessness, and with an attempt at empathy, she tried to imagine such an incredible existence.

Tyson used to tell her, "Shallowness is a luxury. Maybe the ultimate luxury." She hadn't understood him. Not really. "Only the rich can master true frivolity." Now those words echoed back at her, making her think of Tyson. That intense and angry man . . . the opposite of frivolity, the truth told.

And with that, her mood shifted again. Her skin tingled. She felt nothing for or against her audience. How could they help being what they were? How could anyone help their nature? And with that, she found herself reading another name on another unopened box. A little box, she saw. Probably another one of the unpopular gemstones, born deep inside an alien crust and thrown out by forces unimaginable. . . .

There was a silence, an odd stillness, and she repeated the name.

"Opera? Opera Ting?"

Was it her imagination, or was there a nervousness running through the audience? Just what was happening—?

"Excuse me?" said a voice from the back. "Pardon?"

People began moving aside, making room, and a figure emerged. A male, something about him noticeably different. He moved with a telltale lightness, with a spring to his gait. Smiling, he took the tiny package while saying, "Thank you," with great feeling. "For my father, thank you. I'm sure he would have enjoyed this moment. I only wish he could have been here, if only. . . ."

Father? Wasn't this Opera Ting?

Pico managed to nod, then she asked, "Where is he? I mean, is he busy somewhere?"

"Oh, no. He died, I'm afraid." The man moved differently because he was different. He was young—even younger than I, Pico realized—and he shook his head, smiling in a serene way. Was he a clone? A biological child? What? "But on his behalf," said the man, "I wish to thank you. Whatever this gift is, I will treasure it. I promise you. I know you must have gone through Hell to find it and bring it to me, and thank you so very much, Pico. Thank you, thank you. Thank you!"

Death.

An appropriate intruder in the evening's festivities, thought Pico. Some accident, some kind of tragedy . . . something had killed one of her sixty-three parents, and that thought pleased her. There was a pang of guilt woven into her pleasure, but not very much. It was comforting to know that even these people weren't perfectly insulated from death; it was a force that would grasp everyone, given time. Like it had taken Midge, she thought. And Uoo, she thought. *And Tyson.*

Seventeen compilated people had embarked on *Kyber*, representing almost a thousand near-immortals. Only nine had returned, including Pico. Eight friends were lost. . . . *Lost* was a better word than *death*, she decided. . . . And usually it happened in places worse than any Hell conceived by human beings.

After Opera—his name, she learned, was the same as his father's—the giving of the gifts settled into a routine. Maybe it was because of the young man's attitude. People seemed more polite, more self-contained. Someone had the presence to ask for another story. Anything she wished to tell. And Pico found herself thinking of a watery planet circling a distant red-dwarf sun, her voice saying, "Coldtear," and watching faces nod in unison. They recognized the name, and it was too late. It wasn't the story she would have preferred to tell, yet she couldn't seem to stop herself. Coldtear was on her mind.

Just tell parts, she warned herself.

What you can stand!

The world was Terran-class and covered with a single ocean frozen on its surface and heated from below. By tides, in part. And by Coldtear's own nuclear decay. It had been Tyson's idea to build a submersible and dive to the ocean's remote floor. He used spare parts in *Kyber*'s machine shop—the largest room on board—then he'd taken his machine to the surface, setting it on the red-stained ice and using lasers and robots to bore a wide hole and keep it clear.

Pico described the submersible, in brief, then mentioned that Tyson had asked her to accompany him. She didn't add that they'd been lovers now and again, nor that sometimes they had feuded. She'd keep those parts of the story to herself for as long as possible.

The submersible's interior was cramped and ascetic, and she tried to impress her audience with the pressures that would build on the hyperfiber hull. Many times the pressure found in Earth's oceans, she warned; and Tyson's goal was to set down on the floor, then don a lifesuit protected with a human-shaped force field, actually stepping outside and taking a brief walk.

"Because we need to leave behind footprints," he had argued. "Isn't that why we've come here? We can't just leave prints up on the ice. It moves and melts, wiping itself clean every thousand years or so."

"But isn't that the same below?" Pico had responded. "New muds rain down—slowly, granted—and quakes cause slides and avalanches."

"So we pick right. We find someplace where our marks will be quietly covered. Enshrouded. Made everlasting."

She had blinked, surprised that Tyson cared about such things.

"I've studied the currents," he explained, "and the terrain—"

"Are you serious?" Yet you couldn't feel certain about Tyson. He was a creature full of surprises. "All this trouble, and for what—?"

"Trust me, Pico. Trust me!"

Tyson had had an enormous laugh. His parents, sponsors, whatever—an entirely different group of people—had purposefully made him larger than the norm. They had selected genes for physical size, perhaps wanting Tyson to dominate the *Kyber's* crew in at least that one fashion. If his own noise was to be believed, that was the only tinkering done to him. Otherwise, he was a pure compilation of his parents' traits, fiery and passionate to a fault. It was a little unclear to Pico what group of people could be so uniformly aggressive; yet Tyson had had his place in their tight-woven crew, and he had had his charms in addition to his size and the biting intelligence.

"Oh, Pico," he cried out. "What's this about, coming here? If it's not about leaving traces of our passage . . . then *what?*"

"It's about going home again," she had answered.

"Then why do we leave the *Kyber?* Why not just orbit Coldtear and send down our robots to explore?"

"Because . . ."

"Indeed! Because!" The giant head nodded, and he put a big hand on her shoulder. "I knew you'd see my point. I just needed to give you time, my friend."

She agreed to the deep dive, but not without misgivings.

And during their descent, listening to the ominous creaks and groans of the hull while lying flat on their backs, the misgivings began to reassert themselves.

It was Tyson's fault, and maybe his aim.

No, she thought. It was most definitely his aim.

At first, she guessed it was some game, him asking, "Do you ever wonder how it will feel? We come home and are welcomed, and then our dear parents disassemble our brains and implant them—"

"Quiet," she interrupted. "We agreed. Everyone agreed. We aren't going to talk about it, all right?"

A pause, then he said, "Except, I know. How it feels, I mean."

She heard him, then she listened to him take a deep breath from the close damp air; and finally she had strength enough to ask, "How can you know?"

When Tyson didn't answer, she rolled onto her side and saw the outline of his face. A handsome face, she thought. Strong and incapable of any doubts. This was the only taboo subject among the compilations—"How will it feel?"—and it was left to each of them to decide what they believed. Was it a fate or a reward? To be subdivided and implanted into the minds of dozens and dozens of near-immortals. . . .

It wasn't a difficult trick, medically speaking.

After all, each of their minds had been designed for this one specific goal. Memories and talent; passion and training. All of the qualities would be saved—diluted, but, in the same instant, gaining their own near-immortality. Death of a sort, but a kind of everlasting life, too.

That was the creed by which Pico had been born and raised.

The return home brings a great reward, and peace.

Pico's first memory was of her birth, spilling slippery-wet from the womb and coughing hard, a pair of doctoring robots bent over her, whispering to her, "Welcome, child. Welcome. You've been born from *them* to be joined with *them* when it is time. . . . We promise you. . . !"

Comforting noise, and mostly Pico had believed it.

But Tyson had to say, "I know how it feels, Pico," and she could make out his grin, his amusement patronizing. Endless.

"How?" she muttered. "How do you know—?"

"Because some of my parents . . . well, let's just say that I'm not their first time. Understand me?"

"They made another compilation?"

"One of the very first, yes. Which was incorporated into them before I was begun, and which was incorporated into me because there was a spare piece. A leftover chunk of the mind—"

"You're making this up, Tyson!"

Except, he wasn't, she sensed. Knew. Several times, on several early worlds, Tyson had seemed too knowledgeable about too much. Nobody could have prepared himself that well, she realized. She and the others had assumed that Tyson was intuitive in some useful way. Part of him was from another compilation? From someone like them? A fragment of the man had walked twice beside the gray dust sea of Pliicker, and it had twice climbed the giant ant mounds on Proxima Centauri 2. It was a revelation, unnerving and hard to accept; and just the memory of that instant made her tremble secretly, facing her audience, her tired blood turning to ice.

Pico told none of this to her audience.

Instead, they heard about the long descent and the glow of rare life-forms outside—a thin plankton consuming chemical energies as they found them—and, too, the growing creaks of the spherical hull.

They didn't hear how she asked, "So how does it feel? You've got a piece of compilation inside you . . . all right! Are you going to tell me what it's like?"

They didn't hear about her partner's long, deep laugh.

Nor could they imagine him saying, "Pico, my dear. You're such a passive, foolish creature. That's why I love you. So docile, so damned innocent—"

"Does it live inside you, Tyson?"

"It depends on what you consider life."

"Can you feel its presence? I mean, does it have a personality? An existence? Or have you swallowed it all up?"

"I don't think I'll tell." Then the laugh enlarged, and the man lifted his legs and kicked at the hyperfiber with his powerful muscles. She could hear, and feel, the solid impacts of his boot-heels. She knew that Tyson's strength was nothing compared to the ocean's mass bearing down on them, their hull scarcely feeling the blows . . . yet some irrational part of her was terrified. She had to reach out, grasping one of his trouser legs and tugging hard, telling him:

"Don't! Stop that! Will you please . . . quit!?"

The tension shifted direction in an instant.

Tyson said, "I was lying," and then added, "about knowing. About having a compilation inside me." And he gave her a huge hug, laughing in a different way now. He nearly crushed her ribs and lungs. Then he spoke into one of her ears, offering more, whispering with the old charm, and she accepting his offer. They did it as well as possible, considering their circumstances and the endless groaning of their tiny vessel; and she remembered all of it while her voice, detached but thorough, described how they had landed on top of something rare. There was a distinct *crunch* of stone. They had made their touchdown on the slope of a recent volcano—an island on an endless plain of mud—and afterward they dressed in their lifesuits, triple-checked their force fields, then flooded the compartment and crawled into the frigid pressurized water.

It was an eerie, almost indescribable experience to walk on that ocean floor. When language failed Pico, she tried to use silence and oblique gestures to capture the sense of endless time and the cold and darkness. Even when Tyson ignited the submersible's outer lights, making the nearby terrain bright as late afternoon, there was the palpable taste of endless dark just beyond. She told of feeling the pressure despite the force field shrouding her; she told of climbing after Tyson, scrambling up a rough slope of youngish rock to a summit where they discovered a hot-water spring that pumped heated mineral-rich water up at them.

That might have been the garden spot of Coldtear. Surrounding the spring was a thick, almost gelatinous mass of gray-green bacteria, pulsating and fat by its own standards. She paused, seeing the scene all over again. Then she assured her parents, "It had a beauty. I mean it. An elegant, minimalist beauty."

Nobody spoke.

Then someone muttered, "I can hardly wait to remember it," and gave a weak laugh.

The audience became uncomfortable, tense and too quiet. People shot accusing looks at the offender, and Pico worked not to notice any of it. A bitterness was building in her guts, and she sat up straighter, rubbing at both hips.

Then a woman coughed for attention, waited, and then asked, "What happened next?"

Pico searched for her face.

"There was an accident, wasn't there? On Coldtear. . . ?"

I won't tell them, thought Pico. Not now. Not this way.

She said, "No, not then. Later." And maybe some of them knew better. Judging by the expressions, a few must have remembered the records. Tyson died on the first dive. It was recorded as being an equipment failure—Pico's lie—and she'd hold on to the lie as long as possible. It was a promise she'd made to herself and kept all these years.

Shutting her eyes, she saw Tyson's face smiling at her. Even through the thick faceplate and the shimmering glow of the force field, she could make out the mischievous expression, eyes glinting, the large mouth saying, "Go on back, Pico. In and up and a safe trip to you, pretty lady."

She had been too stunned to respond, gawking at him.

"Remember? I've still got to leave my footprints somewhere—"

"What are you planning?" she interrupted.

He laughed and asked, "Isn't it obvious? I'm going to make my mark on this world. It's dull and nearly dead, and I don't think anyone is ever going to return here. Certainly not to *here*. Which means I'll be pretty well left alone—"

"Your force field will drain your batteries," she argued stupidly. Of course he knew that salient fact. "If you stay here—!"

"I know, Pico. I know."

"But why—?"

"I lied before. About lying." The big face gave a disappointed look, then the old smile reemerged. "Poor, docile Pico. I knew you wouldn't take this well. You'd take it too much to heart . . . which I suppose is why I asked you along in the first place. . . ." And he turned away, starting to walk through the bacterial mat with threads and chunks kicked loose, sailing into the warm current and obscuring him. It was a strange gray snow moving against gravity. Her last image of Tyson was of a hulking figure amid the living goo; and to this day, she had wondered if she could have wrestled him back to the submersible—an impossibility, of course—and how far could he have walked before his force field failed.

Down the opposite slope and onto the mud, no doubt.

She could imagine him walking fast, using his strength . . . fighting the deep, cold muds . . . Tyson plus that fragment of an earlier compilation—and who was driving whom? she asked herself. Again and again and again.

Sometimes she heard herself asking Tyson, "How does it feel having a sliver of another soul inside you?"

His ghost never answered, merely laughing with his booming voice.

She hated him for his suicide, and admired him; and sometimes she cursed him for taking her along with him and for the way he kept cropping up in her thoughts. . . . "Damn you, Tyson. Goddamn you, goddamn you. . . !"

No more presents remained.

One near-immortal asked, "Are we hungry?" and others replied, "Famished," in one voice, then breaking into laughter.

The party moved toward the distant tables, a noisy mass of bodies surrounding Pico. Her hip had stiffened while sitting, but she worked hard to move normally, managing the downslope toward the pond and then the little wooden bridge spanning a rocky brook. The waterfowl made grumbling sounds, angered by the disturbances; Pico stopped and watched them, finally asking, "What kinds are those?" She meant the ducks.

"Just mallards," she heard. "Nothing fancy."

Yet, to her, they seemed like miraculous creatures, vivid plumage and the moving eyes, wings spreading as a reflex and their nervous motions lending them a sense of muscular power. A vibrancy.

Someone said, "You've seen many birds, I'm sure."

Of a sort, yes . . .

"What were your favorites, Pico?"

They were starting uphill, quieter now, feet making a swishing sound in the grass; and Pico told them about the pterosaurs of Wilder, the man-sized bats on Little Quark, and the giant insects —a multitude of species—thriving in the thick warm air of Tau Ceti 1.

"Bugs," grumbled someone. "Uggh!"

"Now, now," another person responded.

Then a third joked, "I'm not looking forward to *that*. Who wants to trade memories?"

A joke, thought Pico, because memories weren't tradable properties. Minds were holographic—every piece held the basic picture of the whole—and these people each would receive a sliver of Pico's whole self. Somehow that made her smile, thinking how none of them would be spared. Every terror and every agony would be set inside each of them. In a diluted form, of course. The *Pico-ness* minimized. Made manageable. Yet it was something, wasn't it? It pleased her to think that a few of them might awaken in the night, bathed in sweat after dreaming of Tyson's death . . . just as she had dreamed of it time after time . . . her audience given more than they had anticipated, a dark little joke of her own. . . .

They reached the tables, Pico taking hers and sitting, feeling rather self-conscious as the others quietly assembled around her, each of them knowing where they belonged. She watched their faces. The excitement she had sensed from the beginning remained; only, it seemed magnified now. More colorful, more intense. Facing toward the inside of the omega, her hosts couldn't quit staring, forever smiling, scarcely able to eat once the robots brought them plates filled with steaming foods.

Fancy meals, Pico learned.

The robot setting her dinner before her explained, "The vegetables are from Triton, miss. A very special and much-prized strain. And the meat is from a wild hound killed just yesterday—"

"Really?"

"As part of the festivities, yes." The ceramic face, white and expressionless, stared down at her. "There have been hunting parties and games, among other diversions. Quite an assortment of activities, yes."

"For how long?" she asked. "These festivities . . . have they been going on for days?"

"A little longer than three months, miss."

She had no appetite; nonetheless, she lifted her utensils and made the proper motions, reminding herself that three months of continuous parties would be nothing to these people. Three months was a day to them, and what did they do with their time? So much of it, and such a constricted existence. What had Tyson once told her? The typical citizen of Earth averages less than one off-world trip in eighty years, and the trends were toward less traveling. Spaceflight was safe only to a degree, and these people couldn't stand the idea of being meters away from a cold, raw vacuum.

"Cowards," Tyson had called them. "Gutted, deblooded cowards!"

Looking about, she saw the delicate twists of green leaves vanishing into grinning mouths, the chewing prolonged and indifferent. Except for Opera, that is. Opera saw her and smiled back in turn, his eyes different, something mocking about the tilt of his head and the curl of his mouth.

She found her eyes returning to Opera every little while, and she wasn't sure why. She felt no physical attraction for the man. His youth and attitudes made him different from the others, but how much different? Then she noticed his dinner—cultured potatoes with meaty hearts—and that made an impression on Pico. It was a standard food on board the *Kyber*. Opera was making a gesture, perhaps. Nobody else was eating that bland food, and she decided this was a show of solidarity. At least the man was trying, wasn't he? More than the others, he was. He was.

Dessert was cold and sweet and shot full of some odd liquor.

Pico watched the others drinking and talking among themselves. For the first time, she noticed how they seemed subdivided—discrete groups formed, and boundaries between each one. A dozen people here, seven back there, and sometimes individuals sitting alone—like Opera—chatting politely or appearing entirely friendless.

One lonesome woman rose to her feet and approached Pico,

not smiling, and with a sharp voice, she declared, "Tomorrow, come morning . . . you'll live forever. . . !"

Conversations diminished, then quit entirely.

"Plugged in. Here." She was under the influence of some drug, the tip of her finger shaking and missing her own temple. "You fine lucky girl . . . Yes, you are. . . !"

Some people laughed at the woman, suddenly and without shame.

The harsh sound made her turn and squint, and Pico watched her straightening her back. The woman was pretending to be above them and uninjured, her thin mouth squeezed shut and her nose tilting with mock pride. With a clear, soft voice, she said, "Fuck every one of you," and then laughed, turning toward Pico, acting as if they had just shared some glorious joke of their own.

"I would apologize for our behavior," said Opera, "but I can't. Not in good faith, I'm afraid."

Pico eyed the man. Dessert was finished; people stood about drinking, keeping the three-month-old party in motion. A few of them stripped naked and swam in the green pond. It was a raucous scene, tireless and full of happy moments that never seemed convincingly joyous. Happy sounds by practice, rather. Centuries of practice, and the result was to make Pico feel sad and quite lonely.

"A silly, vain lot," Opera told her.

She said, "Perhaps," with a diplomatic tone, then saw several others approaching. At least they looked polite, she thought. Respectful. It was odd how a dose of respect glosses over so much. Particularly when the respect wasn't reciprocated, Pico feeling none toward them. . . .

A man asked to hear more stories. Please?

Pico shrugged her shoulders, then asked, "Of what?" Every request brought her a momentary sense of claustrophobia, her memories threatening to crush her. "Maybe you're interested in a specific world?"

Opera responded, saying, "Blueblue!"

Blueblue was a giant gaseous world circling a bluish sun. Her first thought was of Midge vanishing into the dark storm on its southern hemisphere, searching for the source of the carbon monoxide upflow that effectively gave breath to half the world. Most of Blueblue was calm in comparison. Thick winds; strong sunlight. Its largest organisms would dwarf most cities, their bodies balloonlike and their lives spent feeding on sunlight and hydrocarbons, utilizing carbon monoxide and other radicals in their patient metabolisms. Pico and the others had spent several months living on the living clouds, walking across them, taking samples and studying the assortment of parasites and symbionts that grew in their flesh.

She told about sunrise on Blueblue, remembering its colors and its astounding speed. Suddenly she found herself talking about a particular morning when the landing party was jostled out of sleep by an apparent quake. Their little huts had been strapped down and secured, but they found themselves tilting fast. Their cloud was colliding with a neighboring cloud—something they had never seen—and of course there was a rush to load their shuttle and leave. If it came to that.

"Normally, you see, the clouds avoid each other," Pico told her little audience. "At first, we thought the creatures were fighting, judging by their roaring and the hard shoving. They make sounds by forcing air through pores and throats and anuses. It was a strange show. Deafening. The collision point was maybe a third of a kilometer from camp, our whole world rolling over while the sun kept rising, its bright, hot light cutting through the organic haze—"

"Gorgeous," someone said.

A companion said, "Quiet!"

Then Opera touched Pico on the arm, saying, "Go on. Don't pay any attention to them."

The others glanced at Opera, hearing something in his voice, and their backs stiffening reflexively.

And then Pico was speaking again, finishing her story. Tyson was the first one of them to understand, who somehow made the right guess and began laughing, not saying a word. By then everyone was on board the shuttle, ready to fly; the tilting stopped suddenly, the air filling with countless little blue balloons. Each was the size of a toy balloon, she told. Their cloud was bleeding them from new pores, and the other cloud responded with a thick gray fog of butterfly-like somethings. The butterflies flew after the balloons, and Tyson laughed harder, his face contorted and the laugh finally shattering into a string of gasping coughs.

"Don't you see?" he asked the others. "Look! The clouds are enjoying a morning screw!"

Pico imitated Tyson's voice, regurgitating the words and enthusiasm. Then she was laughing for herself, scarcely noticing how the others giggled politely. No more. Only Opera was enjoying her story, again touching her arm and saying, "That's lovely. Perfect. God, precious. . . !"

The rest began to drift away, not quite excusing themselves.

What was wrong?

"Don't mind them," Opera cautioned. "They're members of some new chastity faith. Clarity through horniness, and all that." He laughed at them now. "They probably went to too many orgies, and this is how they're coping with their guilt. That's all."

Pico shut her eyes, remembering the scene on Blueblue for herself. She didn't want to relinquish it.

"Screwing clouds," Opera was saying. "That is lovely."

And she thought:

He sounds a little like Tyson. In places. In ways.

After a while, Pico admitted, "I can't remember your father's face. I'm sure I must have met him, but I don't—"

"You did meet him," Opera replied. "He left a recording of it in his journal—a brief meeting—and I made a point of studying everything about the mission and you. His journal entries; your reports. Actually, I'm the best-prepared person here today. Other than you, of course."

She said nothing, considering those words.

They were walking now, making their way down to the pond, and sometimes Pico noticed the hard glances of the others. Did they approve of Opera? Did it anger them, watching him monopolizing her time? Yet she didn't want to be with *them*, the truth told. Fuck them, she thought; and she smiled at her private profanity.

The pond was empty of swimmers now. There were just a few sleepless ducks and the roiled water. A lot of the celebrants had vanished, Pico realized. To where? She asked Opera, and he said:

"It's late. But then again, most people sleep ten or twelve hours every night."

"That much?"

He nodded. "Enhanced dreams are popular lately. And the oldest people sometimes exceed fifteen hours—"

"Always?"

He shrugged and offered a smile.

"What a waste!"

"Of time?" he countered.

Immortals can waste many things, she realized. But never time. And with that thought, she looked straight at her companion, asking him, "What happened to your father?"

"How did he die, you mean?"

A little nod. A respectful expression, she hoped. But curious.

Opera said, "He used an extremely toxic poison, self-induced."

He gave a vague disapproving look directed at nobody. "A suicide at the end of a prolonged depression. He made certain that his mind was ruined before autodocs and his own robots could save him."

"I'm sorry."

"Yet I can't afford to feel sorry," he responded. "You see, I was born according to the terms of his will. I'm ninety-nine percent his clone, the rest of my genes tailored according to his desires. If he hadn't murdered himself, I wouldn't exist. Nor would I have inherited his money." He shrugged, saying, "Parents," with a measured scorn. "They have such power over you, like it or not."

She didn't know how to respond.

"Listen to us. All of this death talk, and doesn't it seem out of place?" Opera said, "After all, we're here to celebrate your return home. Your successes. Your gifts. And you . . . you on the brink of being magnified many times over." He paused before saying, "By this time tomorrow, you'll reside inside all of us, making everyone richer as a consequence."

The young man had an odd way of phrasing his statements, the entire speech either earnest or satirical. She couldn't tell which. Or if there was a *which*. Maybe it was her ignorance with the audible clues, the unknown trappings of this culture. . . . Then something else occurred to her.

"What do you mean? 'Death talk . . . ' "

"Your friend Tyson died on Coldtear," he replied. "And didn't you lose another on Blueblue?"

"Midge. Yes."

He nodded gravely, glancing down at Pico's legs. "We can sit. I'm sorry; I should have noticed you were getting tired."

They sat side by side on the grass, watching the mallard ducks. Males and females had the same vivid green heads. Beautiful, she mentioned. Opera explained how females were once brown and quite drab, but people thought that was a shame, and voted to have the species altered, both sexes made equally resplendent. Pico nodded, only halfway listening. She couldn't get Tyson and her other dead friends out of her mind. Particularly Tyson. She had been angry with him for a long time, and even now her anger wasn't finished. Her confusion and general tiredness made it worse. Why had he done it? In life the man had had a way of dominating every meeting, every little gathering. He had been optimistic and fearless, the last sort of person to do such an awful thing. Suicide. The others had heard it was an accident—Pico had held to her lie—but she and they were in agreement about one fact. When Tyson died, at that precise instant, some essential heart of their mission had been lost.

Why? she wondered. Why?

Midge had flown into the storm on Blueblue, seeking adventure and important scientific answers; and her death was sad, yes, and everyone had missed her. But it wasn't like Tyson's death. It felt honorable, maybe even perfect. They had a duty to fulfill in the wilderness, and that duty was in their blood and their training. People spoke about Midge for years, acting as if she were still alive. As if she were still flying the shuttle into the storm's vortex.

But Tyson was different.

Maybe everyone knew the truth about his death. Sometimes it seemed that, in Pico's eyes, the crew could see what had really happened, and they'd hear it between her practiced lines. They weren't fooled.

Meanwhile, others died in the throes of life.

Uoo—a slender wisp of a compilation—was incinerated by a giant bolt of lightning on Miriam 2, little left but ashes, and the rest of the party continuing its descent into the superheated Bottoms and the quiet Lead Sea.

Opaltu died in the mouth of a nameless predator. He had been another of Pico's lovers, a proud man and the best example of vanity that she had known—until today, she thought—and she and the others had laughed at the justice that befell Opaltu's killer. Unable to digest alien meats, the predator had sickened and died in a slow agonizing fashion, vomiting up its insides as it staggered through the yellow jungle.

Boo was killed while working outside the *Kyber*, struck by a mote of interstellar debris.

Xon's lifesuit failed, suffocating her.

As did Kyties's suit, and that wasn't long ago. Just a year now, ship time, and she remembered a cascade of jokes and his endless good humor. The most decent person on board the *Kyber*.

Yet it was Tyson who dominated her memories of the dead. It was the man as well as his self-induced extinction, and the anger within her swelled all at once. Suddenly even simple breathing was work. Pico found herself sweating, then blinking away the salt in her eyes. Once, then again, she coughed into a fist; then finally she had the energy to ask, "Why did he do it?"

"Who? My father?"

"Depression is . . . should be . . . a curable ailment. We had drugs and therapies on board that could erase it."

"But it was more than depression. It was something that

attacks the very old people. A kind of giant boredom, if you will."

She wasn't surprised. Nodding as if she'd expected that reply, she told him, "I can understand that, considering your lives." Then she thought how Tyson hadn't been depressed or bored. How could he have been either?

Opera touched her bad leg, for just a moment. "You must wonder how it will be," he mentioned. "Tomorrow, I mean."

She shivered, aware of the fear returning. Closing her burning eyes, she saw Tyson's walk through the bacterial mat, the loose gray chunks spinning as the currents carried them, lending them a greater sort of life with the motion. . . . And she opened her eyes, Opera watching, saying something to her with his expression, and she unable to decipher any meanings.

"Maybe I should go to bed, too," she allowed.

The park under the tent was nearly empty now. Where had the others gone?

Opera said, "Of course," as if expecting it. He rose and offered his hand, and she surprised herself by taking the hand with both of hers. Then he said, "If you like, I can show you your quarters."

She nodded, saying nothing.

It was a long painful walk, and Pico honestly considered asking for a robot's help. For anyone's. Even a cane would have been a blessing, her hip never having felt so bad. Earth's gravity and the general stress were making it worse, most likely. She told herself that at least it was a pleasant night, warm and calm and perfectly clear, and the soft ground beneath the grass seemed to be calling to her, inviting her to lay down and sleep in the open.

People were staying in a chain of old houses subdivided into apartments, luxurious yet small. Pico's apartment was on the ground floor, Opera happy to show her through the rooms. For an instant, she considered asking him to stay the night. Indeed, she sensed that he was delaying, hoping for some sort of invitation. But she heard herself saying, "Rest well, and thank you," and her companion smiled and left without comment, vanishing through the crystal front door and leaving her completely alone.

For a little while, she sat on her bed, doing nothing. Not even thinking, at least in any conscious fashion.

Then she realized something, no warning given; and aloud, in a voice almost too soft for even her to hear, she said, "He didn't know. Didn't have an idea, the shit." Tyson. She was thinking about the fiery man and his boast about being the second generation of star explorers. What if it was all true? His parents had injected a portion of a former Tyson into him, and he had already known the early worlds they had visited. He already knew the look of sunrises on the double desert world around Alpha Centauri A; he knew the smell of constant rot before they cracked their airlocks on Barnard's 2. But try as he might—

"—he couldn't remember how it feels to be disassembled." She spoke without sound. To herself. "That titanic and fearless creature, and he couldn't remember. Everything else, yes, but not that. And not knowing had to scare him. Nothing else did, but that terrified him. The only time in his life he was truly scared, and it took all his bluster to keep that secret—!"

Killing himself rather than face his fear.

Of course, she thought. Why not?

And he took Pico as his audience, knowing she'd be a good audience. Because they were lovers. Because he must have decided that he could convince her in his fearlessness one last time, leaving his legend secure. Immortal, in a sense.

That's what you were thinking . . .

. . . wasn't it?

And she shivered, holding both legs close to her mouth, and feeling the warm misery of her doomed hip.

She sat for a couple more hours, neither sleeping nor feeling the slightest need for sleep. Finally she rose and used the bathroom, and after a long careful look through the windows, she ordered the door to open and stepped outside, picking a reasonable direction and walking stiffly and quickly on the weakened leg.

Opera emerged from the shadows, startling her.

"If you want to escape," he whispered, "I can help. Let me help you, please."

The face was handsome in the moonlight, young in every fashion. He must have guessed her mood, she realized, and she didn't allow herself to become upset. Help was important, she reasoned. Even essential. She had to find her way across a vast and very strange alien world. "I want to get back into orbit," she told him, "and find another starship. We saw several. They looked almost ready to embark." Bigger than the *Kyber*, and obviously faster. No doubt designed to move even deeper into the endless wilderness.

"I'm not surprised," Opera told her. "And I understand."

She paused, staring at him before asking, "How did you guess?"

"Living forever inside our heads . . . That's just a mess of metaphysical nonsense, isn't it? You know you'll die tomorrow. Bits of your brain will vanish inside us, made part of us, and not vice versa. I think it sounds like an awful way to die, certainly for someone like you—"

"Can you really help me?"

"This way," he told her. "Come on."

They walked for an age, crossing the paddock and finally reaching the wide tube where the skimmers shot past with a rush of air. Opera touched a simple control, then said, "It won't be long," and smiled at her. Just for a moment. "You know, I almost gave up on you. I thought I must have read you wrong. You didn't strike me as someone who'd go quietly to her death. . . ."

She had a vague fleeting memory of the senior Opera. Gazing at the young face, she could recall a big warm hand shaking her hand, and a similar voice saying, "It's very good to meet you, Pico. At last!"

"I bet one of the new starships will want you." The young Opera was telling her, "You're right. They're bigger ships, and they've got better facilities. Since they'll be gone even longer, they've been given the best possible medical equipment. That hip and your general body should respond to treatments—"

"I have experience," she whispered.

"Pardon me?"

"Experience." She nodded with conviction. "I can offer a crew plenty of valuable experience."

"They'd be idiots not to take you."

A skimmer slowed and stopped before them. Opera made the windows opaque—"So nobody can see you"—and punched in their destination, Pico making herself comfortable.

"Here we go," he chuckled, and they accelerated away.

There was an excitement to all of this, an adventure like every other. Pico realized that she was scared, but in a good, familiar way. Life and death. Both possibilities seemed balanced on a very narrow fulcrum, and she found herself smiling, rubbing her hip with a slow hand.

They were moving fast, following Opera's instructions.

"A circuitous route," he explained. "We want to make our whereabouts less obvious. All right?"

"Fine."

"Are you comfortable?"

"Yes," she allowed. "Basically."

Then she was thinking about the others—the other survivors from the *Kyber*—wondering how many of them were having second or third thoughts. The long journey home had been spent in cold-sleep, but there had been intervals when two or three of them were awakened to do normal maintenance. Not once did anyone even joke about taking the ship elsewhere. Nobody had asked, "Why do we have to go to Earth?" The obvious question had eluded them, and at the time, she had assumed it was because there were no doubters. Besides herself, that is. The rest believed this would be the natural conclusion to full and satisfied lives; they were returning home to a new life and an appreciative audience. How could any sane compilation think otherwise?

Yet she found herself wondering.

Why no jokes?

If they hadn't had doubts, wouldn't they have made jokes?

Eight others had survived the mission. Yet none were as close to Pico as she had been to Tyson. They had saved each other's proverbial skin many times, and she did feel a sudden deep empathy for them, remembering how they had boarded nine separate shuttles after kisses and hugs and a few careful tears, each of them struggling with the proper things to say. But what could anyone say at such a moment? Particularly when you believed that your companions were of one mind and, in some fashion, happy. . . .

Pico said, "I wonder about the others," and intended to leave it at that. To say nothing more.

"The others?"

"From the *Kyber*. My friends." She paused and swallowed, then said softly, "Maybe I could contact them."

"No," he responded.

She jerked her head, watching Opera's profile.

"That would make it easy to catch you." His voice was quite sensible and measured. "Besides," he added, "can't they make up their own minds? Like you have?"

She nodded, thinking that was reasonable. Sure.

He waited a long moment, then said, "Perhaps you'd like to talk about something else?"

"Like what?"

He eyed Pico, then broke into a wide smile. "If I'm not going to inherit a slice of your mind, leave me another story. Tell . . . I don't know. Tell me about your favorite single place. Not a world, but some favorite patch of ground on any world. If you could be anywhere now, where would it be? And with whom?"

Pico felt the skimmer turning, following the tube. She didn't have to consider the question—her answer seemed obvious to her —but the pause was to collect herself, weighing how to begin and what to tell.

"In the mountains on Erindi Three," she said, "the air thins enough to be breathed safely, and it's really quite pretty. The scenery, I mean."

"I've seen holos of the place. It is lovely."

"Not just lovely." She was surprised by her authority, her self-assured voice telling him, "There's a strange sense of peace there. You don't get that from holos. Supposedly it's produced by the weather and the vegetation. . . . They make showers of negative ions, some say. . . . And it's the colors, too. A subtle interplay of shades and shadows. All very one-of-a-kind."

"Of course," he said carefully.

She shut her eyes, seeing the place with almost perfect clarity. A summer storm had swept overhead, charging the glorious atmosphere even further, leaving everyone in the party invigorated. She and Tyson, Midge, and several others had decided to swim in a deep blue pool near their campsite. The terrain itself was rugged, black rocks erupting from the blue-green vegetation. The valley's little river poured into a gorge and the pool, and the people did the same. Tyson was first, naturally. He laughed and bounced in the icy water, screaming loud enough to make a flock of razor-bats take flight. This was only the third solar system they had visited, and they were still young in every sense. It seemed to them that every world would be this much fun.

She recalled—and described—diving feetfirst. She was last into the pool, having inherited a lot of caution from her parents. Tyson had teased her, calling her a coward and then worse, then showing where to aim. "Right here! It's deep here! Come on, coward! Take a chance!"

The water was startlingly cold, and there wasn't much of it beneath the shiny flowing surface. She struck and hit the packed sand below, and the impact made her groan, then shout. Tyson had lied, and she chased the bastard around the pool, screaming and finally clawing at his broad back until she'd driven him up the gorge walls, him laughing and once, losing strength with all the laughing, almost tumbling down on top of her.

She told Opera everything.

At first, it seemed like an accident. All her filters were off; she admitted everything without hesitation. Then she told herself that the man was saving her life and deserved the whole story. That's when she was describing the lovemaking between her and Tyson. That night. It was their first time, and maybe the best time. They did it on a bed of mosses, perched on the rim of the gorge, and she tried to paint a vivid word picture for her audience, including smells and the textures and the sight of the double moons overhead, colored a strange living pink and moving fast.

Their skimmer ride seemed to be taking a long time, she thought once she was finished. She mentioned this to Opera, and he nodded soberly. Otherwise, he made no comment.

I won't be disembodied tomorrow, she told herself.

Then she added, *Today, I mean today.*

She felt certain now. Secure. She was glad for this chance and for this dear new friend, and it was too bad she'd have to leave so quickly, escaping into the relative safety of space. Perhaps there were more people like Opera . . . people who would be kind to her, appreciating her circumstances and desires . . . supportive and interesting companions in their own right. . . .

And suddenly the skimmer was slowing, preparing to stop.

When Opera said, "Almost there," she felt completely at ease. Entirely calm. She shut her eyes and saw the raw, wild mountains on Erindi 3, storm clouds gathering and flashes of lightning piercing the howling winds. She summoned a different day, and saw Tyson standing against the storms, smiling, beckoning for her to climb up to him just as the first cold, fat raindrops smacked against her face.

The skimmer's hatch opened with a hiss.

Sunlight streamed inside, and she thought: *Dawn. By now, sure . . .*

Opera rose and stepped outside, then held a hand out to Pico. She took it with both of hers and said, "Thank you" while rising, looking past him and seeing the paddock and the familiar faces, the green ground and the giant tent with its doorways opened now, various birds flying inside and out again . . . and Pico most surprised by how little she was surprised, Opera still holding her hands, and his flesh dry, the hand perfectly calm.

The autodocs stood waiting for orders.

This time, Pico had been carried from the skimmer, riding cradled in a robot's arms. She had taken just a few faltering steps before half-crumbling. Exhaustion was to blame. Not fear. At least it didn't feel like fear, she told herself. Everyone told her to take it easy, to enjoy her comfort; and now, finding herself flanked by autodocs, her exhaustion worsened. She thought she might die before the cutting began, too tired now to pump her own blood or fire her neurons or even breathe.

Opera was standing nearby, almost smiling, his pleasure serene and chilly and without regrets.

He hadn't said a word since they left the skimmer.

Several others told her to sit, offering her a padded seat with built-in channels to catch any flowing blood. Pico took an uneasy step toward the seat, then paused and straightened her back, saying, "I'm thirsty," softly, her words sounding thoroughly parched.

"Pardon?" they asked.

"I want to drink . . . some water, please. . . ?"

Faces turned, hunting for a cup and water.

It was Opera who said, "Will the pond do?" Then he came forward, extending an arm and telling everyone else, "It won't take long. Give us a moment, will you?"

Pico and Opera walked alone.

Last night's ducks were sleeping and lazily feeding. Pico looked at their metallic green heads, so lovely that she ached at seeing them, and she tried to miss nothing. She tried to concentrate so hard that time itself would compress, seconds turning to hours, and her life in that way prolonged.

Opera was speaking, asking her, "Do you want to hear why?"

She shook her head, not caring in the slightest.

"But you must be wondering why. I fool you into believing that I'm your ally, and I manipulate you—"

"Why?" she sputtered. "So tell me."

"Because," he allowed, "it helps the process. It helps your integration into us. I gave you a chance for doubts and helped you think you were fleeing, convinced you that you'd be free . . . and now you're angry and scared and intensely alive. It's that intensity that we want. It makes the neurological grafts take hold. It's a trick that we learned since the *Kyber* left Earth. Some compilations tried to escape, and when they were caught and finally incorporated along with their anger—"

"Except, I'm not angry," she lied, gazing at his self-satisfied grin.

"A nervous system in flux," he said. "I volunteered, by the way."

She thought of hitting him. Could she kill him somehow?

But instead, she turned and asked, "Why this way? Why not just let me slip away, then catch me at the spaceport?"

"You were going to drink," he reminded her. "Drink."

She knelt despite her hip's pain, knees sinking into the muddy bank and her lips pursing, taking in a long warmish thread of muddy water, and then her face lifting, the water spilling across her chin and chest, and her mouth unable to close tight.

"Nothing angers," he said, "like the betrayal of someone you trust."

True enough, she thought. Suddenly she could see Tyson leaving her alone on the ocean floor, his private fears too much, and his answer being to kill himself while dressed up in apparent bravery. A kind of betrayal, wasn't that? To both of them, and it still hurt. . . .

"Are you still thirsty?" asked Opera.

"Yes," she whispered.

"Then drink. Go on."

She knelt again, taking a bulging mouthful and swirling it with her tongue. Yet she couldn't make herself swallow, and after a moment, it began leaking out from her lips and down her front again. Making a mess, she realized. Muddy, warm, ugly water, and she couldn't remember how it felt to be thirsty. Such a little thing, and ordinary, and she couldn't remember it.

"Come on, then," said Opera.

She looked at him.

He took her arm and began lifting her, a small smiling voice saying, "You've done very well, Pico. You have. The truth is that everyone is very proud of you."

She was on her feet again and walking, not sure when she had begun moving her legs. She wanted to poison her thoughts with her hatred of these awful people, and for a little while, she could think of nothing else. She would make her mind bilious and cancerous, poisoning all of these bastards and finally destroying them. That's what she would do, she promised herself. Except, suddenly she was sitting on the padded chair, autodocs coming close with their bright humming limbs; and there was so much stored in her mind—worlds and people, emotions heaped on emotions—and she didn't have the time she would need to poison herself.

Which proved something, she realized.

Sitting still now.

Sitting still and silent. At ease. Her front drenched and stained brown, but her open eyes calm and dry.

DECENCY

THE VENERABLE old Hubble telescope saw it first.

A silvery splash moving against the stars, the object proved enormous—larger than some worlds—and it was faster than anything human-built, still out among the comets but coming, the first touch of cold light just beginning to brake its terrific fall.

"It's a light sail," astronomers announced, giddy as children, drunk by many means. "Definitely artificial. Probably automated. No crew, minimal mass. Photons move the thing, and even accounting for deceleration, it's going to make a quick flyby of the Earth."

By the time the sail crossed Saturn's orbit, a three-inch reflector cost its weight in platinum. Amateur astronomers were quitting their day jobs in order to spend nights plotting trajectories. Novice astronomers, some armed with nothing but binoculars or rifle sights, risked frostbite for the privilege of a glimpse. But it was the professionals who remained the most excited: every top-flight facility in the northern hemisphere studied the object, measuring its mass, its albedo, its vibrations, and its damage—ragged mile-wide punctures scattered across its vast surface, probably stemming from collisions with interstellar comets. The sail's likely point of origin was a distant G-class sun; its voyage must have taken a thousand years, perhaps more. Astronomers tried to contact the automated pilot. Portions of the radio spectrum were cleared voluntarily for better listening. Yet nothing was heard, ever. The only sign of a pilot was a subtle, perhaps accidental, twisting of the sail, the pressure of sunlight altering its course, the anticipated flyby of the Earth becoming an impact event.

Insubstantial as a soap bubble, the sail offered little risk to people or property. Astronomers said so. Military and political people agreed with them. And despite Hollywood conventions, there was no great panic among the public. No riots. No religious upheavals. A few timid souls took vacations to New Zealand and Australia, but just as many southerners came north to watch the spectacle. There were a few ugly moments involving the susceptible and the emotionally troubled; but generally people responded with curiosity, a useful fatalism, and the gentle nervousness that comes with a storm front or a much-anticipated football game.

The world watched the impact. Some people used television, others bundled up and stepped outdoors. In the end, the entire northern sky was shrouded with the brilliant sail. In the end, as the Earth's gravity embraced it, scientists began to find structures within its thin, thin fabric. Like a spiderweb, but infinitely more complex, there were fibers and veins that led to a central region — a square mile of indecipherable machinery — and the very last images showed damaged machines, the sail's tiny heart wounded by a series of swift murderous collisions.

The impact itself was beautiful. Ghostly fires marked where the leading edge bit into the stratosphere. Without sound or fuss, the sail evaporated into a gentle rain of atomized metals. But the spiderweb structures were more durable, weathering the impact, tens of thousands of miles of material falling over three continents and as many oceans, folding and fracturing on their way down, the most massive portions able to kill sparrows and crack a few windows and roof tiles.

No planes were flying at the time, as a precaution. Few people were driving. Subsequent figures showed that human death rates had dropped for that critical hour, a worldly caution in effect; then they lifted afterward, parties and carelessness taking their inevitable toll.

The sail's central region detached itself at the end, then broke into still smaller portions. One portion crashed along the shore of Lake Superior. The Fox affiliate in Duluth sent a crew, beating the military by twenty minutes. The only witness to the historic event was a temperamental bull moose. Only when it was driven off did the crew realize that the sail wasn't an automated probe. A solitary crew member lay within a fractured diamond shell, assorted life-support equipment heaped on all sides. Despite wounds and the fiery crash, it was alive—an organism built for gravity, air, and liquid water. A trembling camera showed the world its first genuine alien sprawled out on the forest floor, a dozen jointed limbs reaching for its severed web, and some kind of mouth generating a clear, strong, and pitiful wail that was heard in a billion homes.

A horrible piercing wail.

The scream of a soul in perfect agony.

Caleb was one of the guards supplied by the U.S. Marines.

Large in a buttery way, with close-cropped hair and tiny suspicious eyes, Caleb was the kind of fellow who would resemble a guard even without his uniform or bulky side arm. His service record was flawless. Of average intellect and little creativity, nonetheless he possessed a double dose of what, for lack of a better word, could be called shrewdness.

Working the security perimeter, he helped control access to the alien. *The bug,* as he dubbed it, without a shred of originality. Twice in the first two days he caught unauthorized civilians attempting to slip inside—one using a false ID, the other hiding inside bales of computer paper. Late on the third day he found a fellow guard trying to smuggle out a piece of the bug's shell. "It's a chunk of diamond," was the man's pitiful defense. "Think what it's worth, Caleb. And I'll give you half . . . what do you say. . . ?"

Nothing. He saw no reason to respond, handcuffing the man —a sometime acquaintance—then walking him back toward the abrupt little city that had sprung up on the lakeshore. Double-walled tents were kept erect with pressurized air and webs of rope, each tent lit and heated, the rumble of generators and compressors making the scene appear busier than it was. Most people were asleep; it was three in the morning. A quarter moon hung overhead, the January stars like gemstones, brighter and more perfect than the battered diamond shard that rode against Caleb's hip. But the sky barely earned a glance, and despite the monumental events of the last weeks and days, the guard felt no great fortune for being where he was. His job was to deliver the criminal to his superiors, which he did, and he did it without distraction, acting with a rigorous professionalism.

The duty officer, overworked and in lousy spirits, didn't want the shard. "You take it back to the science people," he ordered. "I'll call ahead. They'll be watching for you."

Mistrust came with the job; Caleb expected nothing less from his superior.

The bug was at the center of the city, under a converted circus tent. Adjacent tents and trailers housed the scientists and their machinery. One facility was reserved for the press, but it was almost empty, what with the hour and the lack of fresh events. Overflow equipment was stored at the back of the tent, half-unpacked and waiting to be claimed by experts still coming from the ends of the world. Despite the constant drone of moving air, Caleb could hear the bug now and again. A wail, a whimper. Then another, deeper wail. Just for a moment, the sound caused him to turn his head, listening now, feeling something that he couldn't name, something without a clear source. An emotion, liquid and intense, made him pay close attention. But then the bug fell silent, or at least it was quieter than the man-made wind, and the guard was left feeling empty, a little cold, confused and secretly embarrassed.

He was supposed to meet a Dr. Lee in the press tent; those were his orders, but nobody was waiting for him.

Caleb stood under a swaying fluorescent light, removing the diamond shard from his pocket and examining it for the first time. Cosmic dust and brutal radiations had worn at it; he'd seen prettier diamonds dangling from men's ears. What made it valuable? Why care half this much about the bug? The Earth had never been in danger. The sail's lone passenger was dying. Everyone who visited it said it was just a matter of time. To the limits of his vision, Caleb could see nothing that would significantly change people's lives. Scientists would build and destroy reputations. Maybe some fancy new machines would come from their work. Maybe. But the young man from central Missouri understood that life would go on as it always had, and so why get all worked up in the first place?

"You've got something for me?"

Caleb looked up, finding a middle-aged woman walking toward him. A very tired, red-eyed woman. She was one of the nation's top surgeons, although he didn't know or particularly care.

"I'll take that for you—"

"Sorry, ma'am." He had read her ID tag, adding, "I'm expecting Marvin Lee. Material studies."

"I know. But Marvin's busy, and I like the press tent's coffee. Since I was coming this way, I volunteered."

"But I can't give it to you. Ma'am." Caleb could see how the shard had been stolen in the first place.

Red eyes rolled, amused with his paranoia.

Not for the first time, he felt frustration. No sense of protocol here; no respect for sensible rules. The name on the ID was Hilton. Showing none of his feeling, Caleb said, "Perhaps you could take me to him, Dr. Hilton. If it's no trouble."

"I guess." She poured black coffee into a Styrofoam cup, a knowing little smile appearing. "Now I get it. You're after a trip to the big tent, aren't you?"

Hadn't he just said that?

A sly wink, and she said, "Come on then. I'll take you."

They left the press tent, the doctor without a coat and the guard not bothering to zip his up. A twenty-yard walk, then they entered the bug's enormous tent, three sets of sealed doors opening for them. The last pair of guards waved them on without a look. Caleb smelled liquor, for just a moment, and as he stepped through the door he was wondering whom to warn about this serious breach of the rules —

— and there was a horrible, horrible wail.

Caleb stopped in midstride, his breath coming up short, a bolt of electricity making his spine straighten up and his face reflexively twist as if in agony.

Turning, showing the oddest half-grin, Dr. Hilton inquired, "Is something wrong?"

It took him a moment to say, "No, I'm fine."

"But it's your first time here, isn't it?"

What was her point?

"You've heard stories about it, haven't you?"

"Some."

"And you're curious. You want to see it for yourself."

"Not particularly," he answered, with conviction.

Yet she didn't believe him. She seemed to enjoy herself. "Marvin's on the other side. Stay with me."

Caleb obeyed. Walking between banks of instruments, he noticed that the technicians wore bulky, heavily padded headphones to blunt the screams. Now and again, at unpredictable moments, the bug would roar, and again Caleb would pause, feeling a little ill for that terrible moment when the air itself seemed to rip apart. Then just as suddenly there was silence, save for the clicking machines and hushed, respectful voices. In silence, Caleb found himself wondering if the guards drank because of the sounds. Not that he could condone it, but he could anticipate their excuse. Then he stepped off a floor of particle boards, onto rocky earth punctuated with tree stumps, and in the middle of that cleared patch of forest, stretched out on its apparent back, was the very famous bug. Not close enough to touch, but nearly so. Not quite dead, but not quite alive, either.

There was some kind of face on a wounded appendage, a silent mouth left open, and what seemed to be eyes that were huge and strange and haunted. Dark liquid centers stared helplessly at the tent's high ceiling. It was no bug, Caleb realized. It didn't resemble an insect, or any mammal, for that matter. Were those legs? Or arms? Did it eat with that flexible mouth? And how did it breathe? Practical questions kept offering themselves, but he didn't ask any of them. Instead, he turned to the surgeon, dumbfounded. "Why bring me here?" he inquired.

She was puzzled. "I'm sorry, isn't that what you wanted? I assumed seeing Marvin was an excuse."

Not at all.

"You know," she informed him, "anyone else would give up a gland to be here. To stand with us."

True. He didn't quite see why, but he knew it was true.

Another pair of guards watched them from nearby. They knew the doctor. They had seen her come and go dozens of times, struggling to help her patient. In the course of three days, they had watched her face darken, her humor growing cynical, and her confidence languishing as every effort failed. They felt sorry for her. Maybe that was why they allowed Caleb to stand too close to government property. The soldier lacked clearance, but he was with Hilton, and he was safe looking, and how could this tiny indiscretion hurt? It made no sense to be hard-asses. Glancing at their watches, they measured the minutes before their shift ended . . . and once more that gruesome critter gave a big roar. . . !

"It's in pain," Caleb muttered afterward.

The doctor looked at him, then away. "Are you sure?"

What a strange response. Of course it was in pain. He searched for the usual trappings of hospitals and illness. Where were the dangling bags of medicine and food? "Are you giving it morphine?" he asked, fully expecting to be told, "Of course."

But instead Hilton said, "Why? Why morphine?"

As if speaking to an idiot, Caleb said each word with care. "In order to stop the pain, naturally."

"Except morphine is an intricate, highly specific compound. It kills the hurt in Marines, but probably not in aliens." She waited a moment, then gestured. "You've got more in common—biochemically speaking—with these birch trees. Or a flu virus, for that matter."

He didn't understand, and he said so.

"This creature has DNA," she explained, "but its genetic codes are all different. It makes different kinds of amino acids, and very unusual proteins. Enzymes nothing like ours. And who knows what kinds of neurotransmitters."

The alien's mouth opened, and Caleb braced himself.

It closed, and he sighed.

"We've found organs," said Hilton, sipping her coffee. "Some we know, some we don't. Three hearts, but two are punctured. Dead. The scar tissue shows radiation tracks. Count them, and we get an estimate of the tissue's age. A thousand years, maybe. Which means it was injured when it flew through a dust storm, probably on its way out of the last solar system."

The alien was about the size of a good riding horse. It seemed larger only because of its peculiar flattened shape. The wounds were surgically precise holes, wisps of dust having pierced diamond as well as flesh. Knowing what ballistic wounds meant, he asked, "How is it even alive?"

"Implanted machinery, in part. Most of the machinery isn't working, but what does is repairing some tissues, some organs." She took a big swallow of coffee. "But its wounds may not have been the worst news. Marvin and my other esteemed colleagues think that the cosmic buckshot crippled most of the sail's subsystems. The reactors, for instance. There were three of them, a city block square each, thick as a playing card. Without power, the creature had no choice but to turn *everything* off, including itself. A desperation cryogenic freeze, probably for most of the voyage. And it didn't wake until it was over our heads, almost. Its one maneuver might have been a doomed skydiver's attempt to strike a mound of soft hay."

Caleb turned and asked, "Will it live?"

Hilton was tiring of the game. "Eventually, no. There's talk about another freeze, but we can't even freeze humans yet."

"I said it was in pain, and you said, 'Are you sure?' "

"It's not us. We can't measure its moods, or how it feels. Empirical evidence is lacking—"

As if to debate the point, the alien screamed again. The eyes kept shaking afterward, the closing mouth making a low wet sound. Watching the eyes, Caleb asked, "Do you think it means, 'Hi, how are you?' "

Hilton didn't respond. She didn't have time.

Again the alien's mouth opened, black eyes rippling as the air was torn apart; and Caleb, hands to his ears and undistracted by nasty gray abstractions, knew exactly what that horrible noise meant.

Not a doubt in him, his decision already made.

For three days and several hours, a worldwide controversy had been brewing, sweeping aside almost every other human concern.

What should be done with the alien?

Everyone who would care knew about the wounds and screams. Almost everyone had seen those first horrid tapes of the creature, and they'd watched the twice-daily news conferences, including Dr. Hilton's extended briefings. No more network cameras were being allowed inside the central tent, on the dubious ground of cleanliness. (How did you infect such an odd creature with ordinary human pathogens?) But the suffering continued, without pause, and it was obvious that the people in charge were overmatched. At least according to those on the outside.

The United Nations should take over, or some trustworthy civilian agency. Said many.

But which organization would be best?

And assuming another caretaker, what kinds of goals would it try to accomplish?

Some observers wanted billions spent in a crash program, nothing more important now than the alien's total recovery. Others argued for a kind death, then a quick disposal of the body, all evidence of the tragedy erased in case a second sail-creature came searching for its friend. But the Earth was littered with wreckage; people couldn't hope to salvage every incriminating fiber. That led others to argue that nothing should be done, allowing Nature and God their relentless course. And should death come, the body could be preserved in some honorable way, studied or not, and should more aliens arrive in some distant age —unlikely as that seemed—they could see that people were decent, had done their best, and no blame could possibly be fixed to them.

Anne Hilton despised all those options. She wanted to heal her patient, but crash programs were clumsy and expensive, and she was a pragmatic doctor who realized that human patients would suffer as a result, no money left for their mortal ills. Besides, she doubted if there was time. The fiery crash had plainly damaged the tissue-repairing systems. And worse, there was no easy way to give the creature its simplest needs. Its oxygen use was falling.

Nitrogen levels were building in the slow, clear blood. Teams of biochemists had synthesized a few simple sugars, amino acids, and other possible metabolites; yet the creature's success with each was uneven, the intravenous feedings canceled for now.

The truth told, Hilton's patient was collapsing at every level, and all that remained for the doctor was some of the oldest, most venerable skills.

Patience.

Prayer.

And whatever happened: "Do no harm."

For the next days, months, and years, Dr. Anne Hilton would wrestle with her memories, trying to decide why she had acted as she did that morning. Why get coffee at that particular moment? Why offer to retrieve the diamond shard? And why invite Caleb on that impromptu tour?

The last question had many answers. She had assumed that he wanted a tour, that he was being stubborn about the shard for no other reason. And because he was a Marine, he represented authority, order, and ignorance. She'd already had several collisions with his sort, politicians and other outsiders without enough mental activity to form a worthy thought. Maybe she'd hoped that shocking him would help her mood. She'd assumed that he was a big thoughtless lump of a man, the very worst kind. . . ! Imagine. Stationed here for three days, guarding something wondrous, and precious, yet he didn't have the feeblest grasp of what was happening. . . !

The last scream done, Caleb asked, "Where's its brain?"

She glanced at him, noticing a change in his eyes.

"Doctor?" he asked. "Do you know where it does its thinking?"

She was suddenly tired of dispensing free knowledge, yet something in his voice made her answer. A sip of coffee, an abbreviated gesture. Then she said, "Below the face. Inside what you'd call its chest," and with that she turned away.

She should have watched him.

She could have been more alert, like any good doctor, reading symptoms and predicting the worst.

But an associate was approaching, some nonvital problem needing her best guess. She didn't guess that anything was wrong until she saw her associate's face change. One moment he was smiling. Then he became suddenly confused. Then, horrified. And only after that did she bother to ask herself why that Marine would want to know where to find the brain.

Too late, she wheeled around.

Too late and too slow, she couldn't hope to stop him, or even slow him. Caleb had removed his side arm from its holster, one hand holding the other's wrist, the first shot delivered to the chest's exact center, missing the brain by an inch. Security cameras on all sides recorded the event, in aching detail. The alien managed to lift one limb, two slender fingers reaching for the gun. Perhaps it was defending itself. Or perhaps, as others have argued, it simply was trying to adjust its killer's aim. Either way, the gesture was useless. And Hilton was superfluous. Caleb emptied his clip in short order, achieving a perfectly spaced set of holes. Two bullets managed to do what bits of relativistic dust couldn't, devastating a mind older than civilization. And the eyes, never human yet obviously full of intelligence, stared up at the tent's high ceiling, in thanks, perhaps, seeing whatever it is that only the doomed can see.

There was a trial.

The charge, after all the outcry and legal tap dancing, was reduced to felony destruction of federal property. Caleb offered no coordinated defense. His attorneys tried to argue for some kind of alien mind control, probably wishing for the benefit of the doubt. But Caleb fired them for trying it, then went on the stand to testify on his own behalf. In a quiet, firm voice, he described his upbringing in the Ozarks and the beloved uncle who had helped raise him, taking him hunting and fishing, instructing him in the moral codes of the decent man.

" 'Aim to kill,' he taught me. 'Don't be cruel to any creature, no matter how lowborn.' " Caleb stared at the camera, not a dab of doubt entering his steady voice. "When I see suffering, and when there's no hope, I put an end to it. Because that's what's right." He gave examples of his work: Small game. A lame horse. And dogs, including an arthritic Labrador that he'd raised from a pup. Yet that wasn't nearly enough reason, and he knew it. He paused for a long moment, wiping his forehead with his right palm. Then with a different voice, he said, "I was a senior, in high school, and my uncle got the cancer. In his lungs, his bones. Everywhere." He was quieter, if anything. Firmer. More in control, if that was possible. "It wasn't the cancer that killed him. His best shotgun did. His doctor and the sheriff talked it over, deciding that he must have held the twelve gauge up like this, then tripped the trigger like this." An imaginary gun lay in his outstretched arms, the geometry difficult even for a healthy oversized man. For the first time, the voice broke. But not badly and not for long. "People didn't ask questions," Caleb explained, arms dropping. "They knew what my uncle was feeling. What he wanted. They knew how we were, the two of us. And where I come from, decent people treat people just as good as they'd treat a sick farm cat. Dying stinks, but it might as well be done fast. And that's all I've got to say about that."

He was sentenced to five years of hard labor, serving every month without incident, without complaint, obeying the strict rules well enough that the prison guards voted him to be a model citizen of their intense little community.

Released, Caleb returned to Missouri, taking over the daily operations of the impoverished family farm.

Networks and news services pleaded for interviews; none were granted.

Some idiots tried sneaking onto his property. They were met by dogs and a silent ex-Marine—lean as a fence post now—and the famous shotgun always cradled in his wiry long arms.

He never spoke to trespassers.

His dogs made his views known.

Eventually, people tired of running in the woods. Public opinions began to soften. The alien had been dying, it was decided. Nothing good could have been done for it. And if the Marine wasn't right in what he did, at least he'd acted according to his conscience.

Caleb won his privacy.

There were years when no one came uninvited.

Then it was a bright spring day twenty-some years after the killing, and a small convoy drove in past the warning signs, through the tall barbed-wire gates, and right up to the simple farmhouse. As it happened, a Marine colonel had been selected to oversee the operation. Flanked by government people, he met with the middle-aged farmer, and with a crisp no-nonsense voice said, "Pack your bags, soldier. But I'll warn you, you don't need to bring much."

"Where am I going?"

"I'll give you one guess."

Something had happened; that much was obvious. With a tight, irritated voice, Caleb told the colonel, "I want you all off my land. Now."

"Goddamn! You really don't know, do you?" The colonel gave a big laugh, saying, "Nothing else is on the news anymore."

"I don't have a television," said Caleb.

"Or a family anymore. And precious few friends." He spoke as if he'd just read the man's file. Then he pointed skyward, adding, "I just assumed you'd have seen it. After dusk is a good time—"

"I get to bed early," was Caleb's excuse. Then a sudden hard chill struck him. He leaned against his doorjamb, thinking that he understood, the fight suddenly starting to leave him. "There's another sail, isn't there? That's what this is all about."

"One sail? Oh, that's wonderful!" All the government men were giggling. "Make it three hundred and eighteen sails, and that's just *today's* count!"

"An armada of them," said someone.

"Gorgeous, gorgeous," said another, with feeling.

Caleb tried to gather himself. Then with a calm, almost inaudible voice, he asked, "But what do you want with me?"

"We don't want you," was the quick reply.

No?

"*They* do." The colonel kept smiling. "*They* asked specifically for *you*, soldier."

He knew why. Not a doubt in him.

Caleb muttered, "Just a minute," and dropped back into the house, as if to get ready.

The colonel waited for a couple seconds, then knew better. He burst through the door and tried to guess where Caleb would have gone. Upstairs? No, there was an ominous *click* from somewhere on his right. Caleb was in a utility room, his shotgun loaded and cocked, the double barrels struggling to reach his long forehead; and the colonel grabbed the gun's butt and trigger, shouting, "No! Wait!" Then half a dozen government men were helping him, dark suits left rumpled and torn. But they wrestled the shotgun away from their charge, and the colonel stood over him, asking, "What were you thinking? Why in hell would you—?"

"I killed one of theirs," Caleb said. "Now they want their revenge. Isn't that it?"

"Not close." The colonel was too breathless to put much into his laugh. "In fact, I don't think you could be more wrong, soldier. The last thing they want to kill is you. . . !"

Caleb was packed into a new shuttle and taken to orbit, an ungainly lunar tug carrying him the rest of the way. There was a new moon in a high, safe orbit. One of the sail creatures had captured a modest nickel-iron asteroid and brought it there. Healthy and whole, the creature scarcely resembled its dead brother. Its vast sail was self-repairing, and it possessed an astonishing grace, superseding the most delicate butterfly. Partially folded, riding the captive asteroid, it swallowed the tug, guiding it into a docking facility built recently from the native ores. Other tugs had brought up dignitaries, scientists, and a complete medical team. Everyone had gathered in the central room. As the onetime guard drifted into view, there was applause—polite but not quite enthusiastic—and from some of the faces, envy. Incandescent green envy.

Anne Hilton was among that number.

Old and long retired, she was present at the request of the sail creatures. Caleb didn't recognize her at first glance. She shook his hand, tried smiling, then introduced him to each member of her team. "We're just advisers," she informed him. "Most of the work will be done by our host."

Caleb flinched, just for a moment.

Their "host" didn't resemble the first alien, save for the artificial trappings. Sail creatures were an assemblage of sentient species. Perhaps dozens of them. Caleb had seen photographs of this particular species: fishlike; human-sized; blackish gills flanking an unreadable carpish mouth. It had disgusted him at first glance, and the memory of it disgusted him now.

Dr. Hilton asked, "Would you like to meet her?"

He spoke honestly, saying, "Not particularly."

"But she wants to meet you." A cutting smile, then she promised, "I'll take you to her. Come on."

They had done this before, more than two decades ago. She had taken him to meet an alien, and for at least this moment she could feel superior in the same way. In charge.

There was a narrow tunnel with handholds, toeholds.

Suddenly they were alone, and with a soft, careful voice, Caleb confessed, "I don't understand. Why *me*?"

"Why not you?" Hilton growled.

"I'm not smart. Or clever. Not compared to everyone else up here, I'm not."

She lifted her eyebrows, watching him.

"These aliens should pick a scientist. Someone who cares about stars and planets. . . ."

"You're going to be young again." Hilton said the words as if delivering a curse. "It'll take her some time to learn our genetics, but she's promised me that she can reverse the aging process. A twenty-year-old body again."

"I know."

"As for being smart," she said, "don't worry. She's going to tease your neurons into dividing, like inside a baby's head. By the time you leave us, you'll be in the top ninety-nine percentile among humans. And as creative as can be."

He nodded, already aware of the general plan.

Then they were near the entrance to *her* chamber. Hilton stopped, one hand resting on Caleb's nearer arm, a firm and level voice telling him, "I would do anything—almost—for the chance to go where you're going. To live for aeons, to see all those wondrous places!"

In a quiet, almost conspiratorial tone, he said, "I'll tell her to take you instead of me."

Hilton knew that he meant it, and she grew even angrier.

Then again, Caleb asked, "Why *me?*"

"They think they know you, I guess. They've been studying our telecommunications noise for years, and you certainly earned their attention." Her withered face puckered, tasting something sour. "You acted out of a kind of morality. You didn't hesitate, and you didn't make excuses. Then you accepted the hardships of prison, and the hardships that came afterward. Being able to live alone like you did . . . well, that's a rare talent for our species, and it's invaluable. . . ."

He gave a little nod, a sigh.

"These creatures don't treasure intelligence," she exclaimed. "That's something they can grow, in vats. The same with imagination. But there's some quality in you that makes you worth taking. . . ."

A dull ocher button would open the hatch.

Hilton reached for it, and her hand was intercepted, frail bones restrained by an unconscious strength.

Caleb put his face close to hers, and whispered.

"What I did for that alien," he confessed, "I would have done for a dog." She opened her mouth, but said nothing. After a moment, he continued: "Or a bug. Or *anything.*"

She stared at him, pulling at her hand until he abruptly let go.

"Time to get this business started," Caleb announced.

With an elbow, he smacked the button. There was a hiss, a little wind blowing as the hatch pulled open, carrying with it the smell of warm water and things unnamed.

He turned and left her.

And she hugged herself as if cold, and she watched him, her mouth open and nothing to say, the ex-Marine growing small with the distance as her bewilderment grew vast and bitter and black.

THE REMORAS

UEE LEE'S apartment covered several hectares within one of the human districts, some thousand kilometers beneath the ship's hull. It wasn't a luxury unit by any measure. Truly wealthy people owned as much as a cubic kilometer for themselves and their entourages. But it had been her home since she had come on board, for more centuries than she could count, its hallways and large rooms as comfortable to her as her own body.

The garden room was a favorite. She was enjoying its charms one afternoon, lying nude beneath a false sky and sun, eyes closed and nothing to hear but the splash of fountains and the prattle of little birds. Suddenly her apartment interrupted the peace, announcing a visitor. "He has come for Perri, miss. He claims it's most urgent."

"Perri isn't here," she replied, soft gray eyes opening. "Unless he's hiding from both of us, I suppose."

"No, miss. He is not." A brief pause, then the voice said, "I have explained this to the man, but he refuses to leave. His name is Orleans. He claims that Perri owes him a considerable sum of money."

What had her husband done now? Quee Lee could guess,

halfway smiling as she sat upright. *Oh, Perri . . . won't you learn. . . ?*
She would have to dismiss this Orleans fellow herself, spooking
him with a good hard stare. She rose and dressed in an emerald
sarong, then walked the length of her apartment, never hurrying,
commanding the front door to open at the last moment but leaving the security screen intact. And she was ready for someone
odd. Even someone sordid, knowing Perri. Yet she didn't expect
to see a shiny lifesuit more than two meters tall and nearly half
as wide, and she had never imagined such a face gazing down at
her with mismatched eyes. It took her a long moment to realize
this was a Remora. An authentic Remora was standing in the
public walkway, his vivid round face watching her. The flesh was
orange with diffuse black blotches that might or might not be
cancers, and a lipless, toothless mouth seemed to flow into a grin.
What would bring a Remora here? They never, never came down
here. . . !

"I'm Orleans." The voice was sudden and deep, slightly muted
by the security screen. It came from a speaker hidden somewhere
on the thick neck, telling her, "I need help, miss. I'm sorry to dis-
turb you . . . but you see, I'm desperate. I don't know where else
to turn."

Quee Lee knew about Remoras. She had seen them and even
spoken to a few, although those conversations were aeons ago and
she couldn't remember their substance. Such strange creatures.
Stranger than most aliens, even if they possessed human souls. . . .

"Miss?"

Quee Lee thought of herself as being a good person. Yet she
couldn't help but feel repelled, the floor rolling beneath her and
her breath stopping short. Orleans was a human being, one of her
own species. True, his genetics had been transformed by hard
radiations. And yes, he normally lived apart from ordinary people
like her. But inside him was a human mind, tough and potentially
immortal. Quee Lee blinked and remembered that she had compassion as well as charity for everyone, even the most alien . . . and
she managed to sputter, "Come in." She said, "If you wish, please
do," and with that invitation, her apartment deactivated the invisible screen.

"Thank you, miss." The Remora walked slowly, almost clum-
sily, his lifesuit making a harsh grinding noise in the knees and
hips. That wasn't normal, she realized. Orleans should be graceful, his suit powerful, serving him as an elaborate exoskeleton.

"Would you like anything?" she asked foolishly. Out of habit.

"No, thank you," he replied, his voice nothing but pleasant.

Of course. Remoras ate and drank only self-made concoctions. They were permanently sealed inside their lifesuits, functioning as perfectly self-contained organisms. Food was synthesized, water recycled, and they possessed a religious sense of purity and independence.

"I don't wish to bother you, miss. I'll be brief."

His politeness was a minor surprise. Remoras typically were distant, even arrogant. But Orleans continued to smile, watching her. One eye was a muscular pit filled with thick black hairs, and she assumed those hairs were light-sensitive. Like an insect's compound eye, each one might build part of an image. By contrast, its mate was ordinary, white and fishy with a foggy black center. Mutations could do astonishing things. An accelerated, partly controlled evolution was occurring inside that suit, even while Orleans stood before her, boots stomping on the stone floor, a single spark arcing toward her.

Orleans said, "I know this is embarrassing for you—"

"No, no," she offered.

"—and it makes me uncomfortable, too. I wouldn't have come down here if it wasn't necessary."

"Perri's gone," she repeated, "and I don't know when he'll be back. I'm sorry."

"Actually," said Orleans, "I was hoping he would be gone."

"Did you?"

"Though I'd have come either way."

Quee Lee's apartment, loyal and watchful, wouldn't allow anything nasty to happen to her. She took a step forward, closing some of the distance. "This is about money being owed? Is that right?"

"Yes, miss."

"For what, if I might ask?"

Orleans didn't explain in clear terms. "Think of it as an old gambling debt." More was involved, he implied. "A very old debt, I'm afraid, and Perri's refused me a thousand times."

She could imagine it. Her husband had his share of failings, incompetence and a self-serving attitude among them. She loved Perri in a controlled way, but his flaws were obvious. "I'm sorry," she replied, "but I'm not responsible for his debts." She made herself sound hard, knowing it was best. "I hope you didn't come all this way because you heard he was married." Married to a woman of some means, she thought to herself. In secret.

"No, no, no!" The grotesque face seemed injured. Both eyes became larger, and a thin tongue, white as ice, licked at the lipless edge of the mouth. "Honestly, we don't follow the news about passengers. I just assumed Perri was living with someone. I know him, you see . . . my hope was to come and make my case to whomever I found, winning a comrade. An ally. Someone who might become my advocate." A hopeful pause, then he said, "When Perri does come here, will you explain to him what's right and what is not? Can you, please?" Another pause, then he added, "Even a lowly Remora knows the difference between right and wrong, miss."

That wasn't fair, calling himself lowly. And he seemed to be painting her as some flavor of bigot, which she wasn't. She didn't look at him as lowly, and morality wasn't her private possession. Both of them were human, after all. Their souls were linked by a charming and handsome manipulative user . . . by her darling husband . . . and Quee Lee felt a sudden anger directed at Perri, almost shuddering in front of this stranger.

"Miss?"

"How much?" she asked. "How much does he owe you, and how soon will you need it?"

Orleans answered the second question first, lifting an arm with a sickly whine coming from his shoulder. "Can you hear it?" he asked. As if she were deaf. "My seals need to be replaced, or at least refurbished. Yesterday, if possible." The arm bent, and the elbow whined. "I already spent my savings rebuilding my reactor."

Quee Lee knew enough about lifesuits to appreciate his circumstances. Remoras worked on the ship's hull, standing in the open for hours and days at a time. A broken seal was a disaster. Any tiny opening would kill most of his body, and his suffering mind would fall into a protective coma. Left exposed and vulnerable, Orleans would be at the mercy of radiation storms and comet showers. Yes, she understood. A balky suit was an unacceptable hazard on top of lesser hazards, and what could she say?

She felt a deep empathy for the man.

Orleans seemed to take a breath, then he said, "Perri owes me fifty-two thousand credits, miss."

"I see." She swallowed and said, "My name is Quee Lee."

"Quee Lee," he repeated. "Yes, miss."

"As soon as Perri comes home, I'll discuss this with him. I promise you."

"I would be grateful if you did."

"I will."

The ugly mouth opened, and she saw blotches of green and gray-blue against a milky throat. Those were cancers or perhaps bizarre new organs. She couldn't believe she was in the company of a Remora—the strangest sort of human—yet despite every myth, despite tales of courage and even recklessness, Orleans appeared almost fragile. He even looked scared, she realized. That wet orange face shook as if in despair, then came the awful grinding noise as he turned away, telling her, "Thank you, Quee Lee. For your time and patience, and for everything."

Fifty-two thousand credits!

She could have screamed. She would scream when she was alone, she promised herself. Perri had done this man a great disservice, and he'd hear about it when he graced her with his company again. A patient person, yes, and she could tolerate most of his flaws. But not now. Fifty thousand credits was no fortune, and it would allow Orleans to refurbish his lifesuit, making him whole and healthy again. Perhaps she could get in touch with Perri first, speeding up the process. . . ?

Orleans was through her front door, turning to say good-bye. False sunshine made his suit shine, and his faceplate darkened to where she couldn't see his features anymore. He might have any face, and what did a face mean? Waving back at him, sick to her stomach, she calculated what fifty-two thousand credits meant in concrete terms, to her . . .

. . . wondering if she should. . . ?

But no, she decided. She just lacked the required compassion. She was a particle short, if that, ordering the security screen to engage again, helping to mute that horrid grinding of joints as the Remora shuffled off for home.

The ship had many names, many designations, but to its long-term passengers and crew it was referred to as *the ship*. No other starship could be confused for it. Not in volume, nor in history.

The ship was old by every measure. A vanished humanoid race had built it, probably before life arose on Earth, then abandoned it for no obvious reason. Experts claimed it had begun as a sunless world, one of the countless jupiters that sprinkled the cosmos. The builders had used the world's own hydrogen to fuel enormous engines, accelerating it over millions of years while stripping away its gaseous exterior. Today's ship was the leftover core, much modified by its builders and humans. Its metal and rock interior was laced with passageways and sealed environments, fuel tanks, and various ports. There was room enough for hundreds of billions of passengers, though there were only a fraction that number now. And its hull was a special armor made from hyperfibers, kilometers thick and tough enough to withstand most high-velocity impacts.

The ship had come from outside the galaxy, passing into human space long ago. It was claimed as salvage, explored by various means, then refurbished to the best of its new owners' abilities. A corporation was formed; a promotion was born. The ancient engines were coaxed to life, changing the ship's course. Then tickets were sold, both to humans and alien species. Novelty and adventure were the lures. One circuit around the Milky Way; a half-million-year voyage touring the star-rich spiral arms. It was a terrific span, even for immortal humans. But people like Quee Lee had enough money and patience. That's why she purchased her apartment with a portion of her savings. This voyage wouldn't remain novel for long, she knew. Three or four circuits at most, and then what? People would want something else new and glancingly dangerous. Wasn't that the way it always was?

Quee Lee had no natural life span. Her ancestors had improved themselves in a thousand ways, erasing the aging process. Fragile DNAs were replaced with better genetic machinery. Tailoring allowed a wide range of useful proteins and enzymes and powerful repair mechanisms. Immune systems were nearly perfect; diseases were extinct. Normal life couldn't damage a person in any measurable way. And even a tragic accident wouldn't need to be fatal, Quee Lee's body and mind able to withstand frightening amounts of abuse.

But Remoras, despite those same gifts, did not live ordinary lives. They worked on the open hull, each of them encased in a lifesuit. The suits afforded extra protection and a standard environment, each one possessing a small fusion plant and redundant recycling systems. Hull life was dangerous in the best times. The ship's shields and laser watchdogs couldn't stop every bit of interstellar grit. And every large impact meant someone had to make repairs. The ship's builders had used sophisticated robots, but they proved too tired after several billions of years on the job. It was better to promote—or demote—members of the human crew. The original scheme was to share the job, brief stints fairly dispersed. Even the captains were to don the lifesuits, stepping into the open when it was safest, patching craters with fresh-made hyperfibers. . . .

Fairness didn't last. A kind of subculture arose, and the first Remoras took the hull as their province. Those early Remoras learned how to survive the huge radiation loads. They trained themselves and their offspring to control their damaged bodies.

Tough genetics mutated, and they embraced their mutations. If an eye was struck blind, perhaps by some queer cancer, then a good Remora would evolve a new eye. Perhaps a hair was light-sensitive, and its owner, purely by force of will, would culture that hair and interface it with the surviving optic nerve, producing an eye more durable than the one it replaced. Or so Quee Lee had heard, in passing, from people who acted as if they knew about such things.

Remoras, she had been told, were happy to look grotesque. In their culture, strange faces and novel organs were the measures of success. And since disaster could happen anytime, without warning, it was unusual for any Remora to live long. At least in her sense of long. Orleans could be a fourth or fifth generation Remora, for all she knew. A child barely fifty centuries old. *For all she knew.* Which was almost nothing, she realized, returning to her garden room and undressing, lying down with her eyes closed and the light baking her. Remoras were important, even essential people, yet she felt wholly ignorant. And ignorance was wrong, she knew. Not as wrong as owing one of them money, but still. . . .

This life of hers seemed so ordinary, set next to Orleans's life. Comfortable and ordinary, and she almost felt ashamed.

Perri failed to come home that next day, and the next. Then it was ten days, Quee Lee having sent messages to his usual haunts and no reply. She had been careful not to explain why she wanted him. And this was nothing too unusual, Perri probably wandering somewhere new and Quee Lee skilled at waiting, her days accented with visits from friends and parties thrown for any small reason. It was her normal life, never anything but pleasant; yet she found herself thinking about Orleans, imagining him walking on the open hull with his seals breaking, his strange body starting to boil away . . . that poor man. . . !

Taking the money to Orleans was an easy decision. Quee Lee had more than enough. It didn't seem like a large sum until she had it converted into black-and-white chips. But wasn't it better to have Perri owing her instead of owing a Remora? She was in a better place to recoup the debt; and besides, she doubted that her husband could raise that money now. He probably had a number of debts, to humans and aliens both; and for the nth time, she wondered how she'd ever let Perri charm her. What was she thinking, agreeing to this crazy union?

Quee Lee was old even by immortal measures. She was so old she could barely remember her youth, her tough neurons unable to embrace her entire life. Maybe that's why Perri had seemed like a blessing. He was ridiculously young and wore his youth well, gladly sharing his enthusiasms and energies. He was a good, untaxing lover; he could listen when it was important; and he had never tried milking Quee Lee of her money. Besides, he was a challenge. No doubt about it. Maybe her friends didn't approve of him—a few close ones were openly critical—but to a woman of her vintage, in the middle of a five-thousand-century voyage, Perri was something fresh and new and remarkable. And Quee Lee's old friends, quite suddenly, seemed a little fossilized by comparison.

"I love to travel," Perri had explained, his gently handsome face capable of endless smiles. "I was born on the ship, did you know? Just weeks after my parents came on board. They were riding only as far as a colony world, but I stayed behind. My choice." He had laughed, eyes gazing into the false sky of her ceiling. "Do you know what I want to do? I want to see the entire ship, walk every hallway and cavern. I want to explore every body of water, meet every sort of alien—"

"Really?"

"—and even visit their quarters. Their homes." Another laugh and that infectious smile. "I just came back from a low-gravity district, sixteen thousand kilometers below. There's a kind of spidery creature down there. You should see them, love! I can't do them justice by telling you they're graceful, and seeing holos isn't much better."

She had been impressed. Who else did she know who could tolerate aliens, what with their strange odors and their impenetrable minds? Perri was remarkable, no doubt about it. Even her most critical friends admitted that much, and despite their grumbles, they'd want to hear the latest Perri adventure as told by his wife.

"I'll stay on board forever, if I can manage it."

She had laughed, asking, "Can you afford it?"

"Badly," he had admitted. "But I'm paid up through this circuit, at least. Minus day-by-day expenses, but that's all right. Believe me, when you've got millions of wealthy souls in one place, there's always a means of making a living."

"Legal means?"

"Glancingly so." He had a rogue's humor, all right. Yet later, in a more sober mood, he had admitted, "I do have enemies, my love. I'm warning you. Like anyone, I've made my share of mistakes—my youthful indiscretions—but at least I'm honest about them."

Indiscretions, perhaps. Yet he had done nothing to earn her animosity.

"We should marry," Perri had proposed. "Why not? We like each other's company, yet we seem to weather our time apart, too. What do you think? Frankly, I don't think you need a partner who shadows you day and night. Do you, Quee Lee?"

She didn't. True enough.

"A small tidy marriage, complete with rules," he had assured her. "I get a home base, and you have your privacy, plus my considerable entertainment value." A big long laugh, then he had added, "I promise. You'll be the first to hear my latest tales. And I'll never be any kind of leech, darling. With you, I will be the perfect gentleman."

Quee Lee carried the credit chips in a secret pouch, traveling to the tube-car station and riding one of the vertical tubes toward the hull. She had looked up the name *Orleans* in the crew listings. The only Orleans lived at Port Beta, no mention of him being a Remora or not. The ports were vast facilities where taxi craft docked with the ship, bringing new passengers from nearby alien worlds. It was easier to accelerate and decelerate those kilometer-long needles. The ship's own engines did nothing but make the occasional course correction, avoiding dust clouds while keeping them on their circular course.

It had been forever since Quee Lee had visited a port. And today there wasn't even a taxi to be seen, all of them off hunting for more paying customers. The non-Remora crew—the captains, mates, and so on—had little work at the moment, apparently hiding from her. She stood at the bottom of the port—a lofty cylinder capped with a kilometer-thick hatch of top-grade hyperfibers. The only other tourists were aliens, some kind of fishy species encased in bubbles of liquid water or ammonia. The bubbles rolled past her. It was like standing in a school of small tuna, their sharp chatter audible and Quee Lee unable to decipher any of it. Were they mocking her? She had no clue, and it made her all the more frustrated. They could be making terrible fun of her. All at once, she felt lost and more than a little homesick.

By contrast, the first Remora seemed normal. Walking without any grinding sounds, it covered ground at an amazing pace. Quee Lee had to run to catch it. To catch her. Something about the lifesuit was feminine, and a female voice responded to Quee Lee's shouts.

"What what what?" asked the Remora. "I'm busy!"

Gasping, Quee Lee asked, "Do you know Orleans?"

"Orleans?"

"I need to find him. It's quite important." Then she wondered if something terrible had happened, her arriving too late—

"I do know someone named Orleans, yes." The face had comma-shaped eyes, huge and black and bulging, and the mouth blended into a slitlike nose. Her skin was silvery, odd bunched fibers running beneath the surface. Black hair showed along the top of the faceplate, except at second glance it wasn't hair. It looked more like ropes soaked in oil, the strands wagging with a slow stately pace.

The mouth smiled. The normal-sounding voice said, "Actually, Orleans is one of my closest friends!"

True? Or was she making a joke?

"I really have to find him," Quee Lee confessed. "Can you help me?"

"Can I help you?" The strange mouth smiled, gray pseudo-teeth looking big as thumbnails, the gums as silver as her skin. "I'll take you to him. Does that constitute help?" And Quee Lee found herself following, walking onto a lifting disk without railing, the Remora standing in the center and waving to the old woman. "Come closer. Orleans is up there." A skyward gesture. "A good long way, and I don't think you'd want to try it alone. Would you?"

"Relax," Orleans advised.

She thought she was relaxed, except then she found herself nodding, breathing deeply and feeling a tension as it evaporated. The ascent had taken ages, it seemed. Save for the rush of air moving past her ears, it had been soundless. The disk had no sides at all—a clear violation of safety regulations—and Quee Lee had grasped one of the Remora's shiny arms, needing a handhold, surprised to feel rough spots in the hyperfiber. Minuscule impacts had left craters too tiny to see. Remoras, she had realized, were very much like the ship itself—enclosed biospheres taking abuse as they streaked through space.

"Better?" asked Orleans.

"Yes. Better." A thirty-kilometer ride through the port, holding tight to a Remora. And now this. She and Orleans were inside some tiny room not five hundred meters from the vacuum. Did Orleans live here? She nearly asked, looking at the bare walls and stubby furniture, deciding it was too spare, too ascetic to be anyone's home. Even his. Instead, she asked him, "How are *you?*"

"Tired. Fresh off my shift, and devastated."

The face had changed. The orange pigments were softer now,

and both eyes were the same sickening hair-filled pits. How clear
was his vision? How did he transplant cells from one eye to the
other? There had to be mechanisms, reliable tricks . . . and she
found herself feeling ignorant and glad of it. . . .

"What do you want, Quee Lee?"

She swallowed. "Perri came home, and I brought what he owes
you."

Orleans looked surprised, then the cool voice said, "Good.
Wonderful!"

She produced the chips, his shiny palm accepting them. The
elbow gave a harsh growl, and she said, "I hope this helps."

"My mood already is improved," he promised.

What else? She wasn't sure what to say now.

Then Orleans told her, "I should thank you somehow. Can I
give you something for your trouble? How about a tour?" One eye
actually winked at her, hairs contracting into their pit and nothing
left visible but a tiny red pore. "A tour," he repeated. "A walk outside? We'll find you a lifesuit. We keep them here in case a captain
comes for an inspection." A big deep laugh, then he added, "Once
every thousand years, they do! Whether we need it or not!"

What was he saying? She had heard him, and she hadn't.

A smile and another wink, and he said, "I'm serious. Would you
like to go for a little stroll?"

"I've never . . . I don't know. . . !"

"Safe as safe can be." Whatever that meant. "Listen, this is the
safest place for a jaunt. We're behind the leading face, which
means impacts are nearly impossible. But we're not close to the
engines and their radiations, either." Another laugh, and he
added, "Oh, you'll get a dose of radiation, but nothing important.
You're tough, Quee Lee. Does your fancy apartment have an
autodoc?"

"Of course."

"Well, then."

She wasn't scared, at least in any direct way. What Quee Lee
felt was excitement and fear born of excitement, nothing in her
experience to compare with what was happening. She was a
creature of habits, rigorous and ancient habits, and she had no
way to know how she'd respond *out there*. No habit had prepared
her for this moment.

"Here," said her gracious host. "Come in here."

No excuse occurred to her. They were in a deep closet full of
lifesuits — this was some kind of locker room, apparently — and she
let Orleans select one and dismantle it with his growling joints. "It

opens and closes, unlike mine," he explained. "It doesn't have all the redundant systems, either. Otherwise, it's the same."

On went the legs, the torso and arms and helmet; she banged the helmet against the low ceiling, then struck the wall with her first step.

"Follow me," Orleans advised, "and keep it slow."

Wise words. They entered some sort of tunnel that zigzagged toward space, ancient stairs fashioned for a nearly human gait. Each bend had an invisible field that held back the ship's thinning atmosphere. They began speaking by radio, voices close, and she noticed how she could feel through the suit, its pseudoneurons interfacing with her own. Here gravity was stronger than Earth-standard, yet despite her added bulk she moved with ease, limbs humming, her helmet striking the ceiling as she climbed. Thump, and thump. She couldn't help herself.

Orleans laughed pleasantly, the sound close and intimate. "You're doing fine, Quee Lee. Relax."

Hearing her name gave her a dilute courage.

"Remember," he said, "your servomotors are potent. Lifesuits make motions large. Don't overcontrol, and don't act cocky."

She wanted to succeed. More than anything in recent memory, she wanted everything as close to perfect as possible.

"Concentrate," he said.

Then he told her, "That's better, yes."

They came to a final turn, then a hatch, Orleans pausing and turning, his syrupy mouth making a preposterous smile. "Here we are. We'll go outside for just a little while, okay?" A pause, then he added, "When you go home, tell your husband what you've done. Amaze him!"

"I will," she whispered.

And he opened the hatch with an arm—the abrasive sounds audible across the radio, but distant—and a bright colored glow washed over them. "Beautiful," the Remora observed. "Isn't it beautiful, Quee Lee?"

Perri didn't return home for several more weeks, and when he arrived—"I was rafting Cloud Canyon, love, and didn't get your messages!"—Quee Lee realized that she wasn't going to tell him about her adventure. Nor about the money. She'd wait for a better time, a weak moment, when Perri's guard was down. "What's so important, love? You sounded urgent." She told him it was nothing, that she'd missed him and been worried. How was the rafting? Who went with him? Perri told her, "Tweewits. Big hulking baboons, in essence." He smiled until she smiled, too. He looked thin and tired; but that night, with minimal prompting, he found the energy to make love to her twice. And the second time was special enough that she was left wondering how she could so willingly live without sex for long periods. It could be the most amazing pleasure.

Perri slept, dreaming of artificial rivers roaring through artificial canyons; and Quee Lee sat up in bed, in the dark, whispering for her apartment to show her the view above Port Beta. She had it projected into her ceiling, twenty meters overhead, the shimmering aurora changing colors as force fields wrestled with every kind of space-born hazard.

"What do you think, Quee Lee?"

Orleans had asked the question, and she answered it again, in a soft awed voice. "Lovely." She shut her eyes, remembering how the hull itself had stretched off into the distance, flat and gray, bland yet somehow serene. "It is lovely."

"And even better up front, on the prow," her companion had maintained. "The fields there are thicker, stronger. And the big lasers keep hitting the comets tens of millions of kilometers from us, softening them up for us." He had given a little laugh, telling her, "You can almost feel the ship moving when you look up from the prow. Honest."

She had shivered inside her lifesuit, more out of pleasure than fear. Few passengers ever came out on the hull. They were breaking rules, no doubt. Even inside the taxi ships, you were protected by a hull. But not up there. Up there she'd felt exposed, practically naked. And maybe Orleans had measured her mood, watching her face with the flickering pulses, finally asking her, "Do you know the story of the first Remora?"

Did she? She wasn't certain.

He told it, his voice smooth and quiet. "Her name was Wune," he began. "On Earth, it's rumored, she was a criminal, a registered habitual criminal. Signing on as a crewmate helped her escape a stint of psychological realignment —"

"What crimes?"

"Do they matter?" A shake of the round head. "Bad ones, and that's too much said. The point is that Wune came here without rank, glad for the opportunity, and like any good mate, she took her turns out on the hull."

Quee Lee had nodded, staring off at the far horizon.

"She was pretty, like you. Between shifts, she did typical typicals. She explored the ship and had affairs of the heart and grieved the affairs that went badly. Like you, Quee Lee, she was smart. And after just a few centuries on board, Wune could see the trends. She saw how the captains were avoiding their shifts on the hull. And how certain people, guilty of small offenses, were pushed into double-shifts in their stead. All so that our captains didn't have to accept the tiniest, fairest risks."

Status. Rank. Privilege. She could understand these things, probably too well.

"Wune rebelled," Orleans had said, pride in the voice. "But instead of overthrowing the system, she conquered by embracing it. By transforming what she embraced." A soft laugh. "This life-suit of mine? She built its prototype with its semiforever seals and the hyperefficient recyke systems. She made a suit that she'd never have to leave, then she began to live on the hull, in the open, sometimes alone for years at a time."

"Alone?"

"A prophet's contemplative life." A fond glance at the smooth gray terrain. "She stopped having her body purged of cancers and other damage. She let her face—her beautiful face—become speckled with dead tissues. Then she taught herself to manage her mutations, with discipline and strength. Eventually, she picked a few friends without status, teaching them her tricks and explaining the peace and purpose she had found while living up here, contemplating the universe without obstructions."

Without obstructions, indeed!

"A few hundred became the First Generation. Attrition convinced our great captains to allow children, and the Second Generation numbered in the thousands. By the Third, we were officially responsible for the ship's exterior and the deadliest parts of its engines. We had achieved a quiet conquest of a world-sized realm, and today we number in the low millions!"

She remembered sighing, asking, "What happened to Wune?"

"A heroic death," he had replied. "A comet swarm was approaching. A repair team was caught on the prow, their shuttle dead and useless—"

"Why were they there if a swarm was coming?"

"Patching a crater, of course. Remember. The prow can withstand almost any likely blow, but if comets were to strike on top of one another, unlikely as that sounds—"

"A disaster," she muttered.

"For the passengers below, yes." A strange slow smile. "Wune died trying to bring them a fresh shuttle. She was vaporized under a chunk of ice and rock, in an instant."

"I'm sorry." Whispered.

"Wune was my great-great-grandmother," the man had added. "And no, she didn't name us Remoras. That originally was an insult, some captain responsible. Remoras are ugly fish that cling to sharks. Not a pleasing image, but Wune embraced the word. To us it means spiritual fulfillment, independence, and a powerful sense of self. Do you know what I am, Quee Lee? I'm a god inside this suit of mine. I rule in ways you can't appreciate. You can't imagine how it is, having utter control over my body, my self. . . !"

She had stared at him, unable to speak.

A shiny hand had lifted, thick fingers against his faceplate. "My eyes? You're fascinated by my eyes, aren't you?"

A tiny nod. "Yes."

"Do you know how I sculpted them?"

"No."

"Tell me, Quee Lee. How do you close your hand?"

She had made a fist, as if to show him how.

"But which neurons fire? Which muscles contract?" A mild, patient laugh, then he had added, "How can you manage something that you can't describe in full?"

She had said, "It's habit, I guess. . . ."

"Exactly!" A larger laugh. "I have habits, too. For instance, I can willfully spread mutations using metastasized cells. I personally have thousands of years of practice, plus all those useful mechanisms that I inherited from Wune and the others. It's as natural as your making the fist."

"But my hand doesn't change its real shape," she had countered.

"Transformation is my habit, and it's why my life is so much richer than yours." He had given her a wink just then, saying, "I can't count the times I've reevolved my eyes."

Quee Lee looked up at her bedroom ceiling now, at a curtain of blue glows dissolving into pink. In her mind, she replayed the moment.

"You think Remoras are vile, ugly monsters," Orleans had said. "Now don't deny it. I won't let you deny it."

She hadn't made a sound.

"When you saw me standing at your door? When you saw that a Remora had come to *your* home? All of that ordinary blood of yours drained out of your face. You looked so terribly pale and weak, Quee Lee. Horrified!"

She couldn't deny it. Not then or now.

"Which of us has the richer life, Quee Lee? And be objective. Is it you or is it me?"

She pulled her bedsheets over herself, shaking a little bit.

"You or me?"

"Me," she whispered, but in that word was doubt. Just the flavor of it. Then Perri stirred, rolling toward her with his face trying to waken. Quee Lee had a last glance at the projected sky, then had it quelched. Then Perri was grinning, blinking, and reaching for her, asking:

"Can't you sleep, love?"

"No," she admitted. Then she said, "Come here, darling."

"Well, well," he laughed. "Aren't you in a mood?"

Absolutely. A feverish mood, her mind leaping from subject to subject, without order, every thought intense and sudden, Perri on top of her and her old-fashioned eyes gazing up at the darkened ceiling, still seeing the powerful surges of changing colors that obscured the bright dusting of stars.

They took a second honeymoon, Quee Lee's treat. They traveled halfway around the ship, visiting a famous resort beside a small tropical sea; and for several months, they enjoyed the scenery and beaches, bone-white sands dropping into azure waters where fancy corals and fancier fishes lived. Every night brought a different sky, the ship supplying stored images of nebulas and strange suns; and they made love in the oddest places, in odd ways, strangers sometimes coming upon them and pausing to watch.

Yet she felt detached somehow, hovering overhead like an observer. Did Remoras have sex? she wondered. And if so, how? And how did they make their children? One day, Perri strapped on a gill and swam alone to the reef, leaving Quee Lee free to do research. Remoran sex, if it could be called that, was managed with electrical stimulation through the suits themselves. Reproduction was something else, children conceived in vitro, samples of their parents' genetics married and grown inside a hyperfiber envelope. The envelope was expanded as needed. Birth came with the first independent fusion plant. What an incredible way to live, she realized; but then again, there were many human societies that seemed bizarre. Some refused immortality. Some had married computers or lived in a narcotic haze. There were many, many spiritual splinter groups . . . only she couldn't learn much about the Remoran faith. Was their faith secret? And if so, why had she been allowed a glimpse of their private world?

Perri remained pleasant and attentive.

"I know this is work for you," she told him, "and you've been a delight, darling. Old women appreciate these attentions."

"Oh, you're not old!" A wink and smile, and he pulled her close. "And it's not work at all. Believe me!"

They returned home soon afterward, and Quee Lee was disappointed with her apartment. It was just as she remembered it, and the sameness was depressing. Even the garden room failed to brighten her mood . . . and she found herself wondering if she'd ever lived anywhere but here, the stone walls cold and closing in on her.

Perri asked, "What's the matter, love?"

She said nothing.

"Can I help, darling?"

"I forgot to tell you something," she began. "A friend of yours visited . . . oh, it was almost a year ago."

The roguish charm surfaced, reliable and nonplussed. "Which friend?"

"Orleans."

And Perri didn't respond at first, hearing the name and not allowing his expression to change. He stood motionless, not quite looking at her; and Quee Lee noticed a weakness in the mouth and something glassy about the smiling eyes. She felt uneasy, almost asking him what was wrong. Then Perri said, "What did Orleans want?" His voice was too soft, almost a whisper. A sideways glance, and he muttered, "Orleans came here?" He couldn't quite believe what she was saying. . . .

"You owed him some money," she replied.

Perri didn't speak, didn't seem to hear anything.

"Perri?"

He swallowed and said, "Owed?"

"I paid him."

"But . . . but what happened. . . ?"

She told him and she didn't. She mentioned the old seals and some other salient details, then in the middle of her explanation, all at once, something obvious and awful occurred to her. What if there hadn't been a debt? She gasped, asking, "You did owe him the money, didn't you?"

"How much did you say it was?"

She told him again.

He nodded. He swallowed and straightened his back, then managed to say, "I'll pay you back . . . as soon as possible. . . ."

"Is there any hurry?" She took his hand, telling him, "I haven't made noise until now, have I? Don't worry." A pause. "I just wonder how you could owe him so much?"

Perri shook his head. "I'll give you five thousand now, maybe six . . . and I'll raise the rest. Soon as I can, I promise."

She said, "Fine."

"I'm sorry," he muttered.

"How do you know a Remora?"

He seemed momentarily confused by the question. Then he managed to say, "You know me. A taste for the exotic, and all that."

"You lost the money gambling? Is that what happened?"

"I'd nearly forgotten, it was so long ago." He summoned a smile and some of the old charm. "You should know, darling . . . those Remoras aren't anything like you and me. Be very careful with them, please."

She didn't mention her jaunt on the hull. Everything was old news anyway, and why had she brought it up in the first place? Perri kept promising to pay her back. He announced he was leaving tomorrow, needing to find some nameless people who owed him. The best he could manage was fifteen hundred credits. "A weak down payment, I know." Quee Lee thought of reassuring him—he seemed painfully nervous—but instead she simply told him, "Have a good trip, and come home soon."

He was a darling man when vulnerable. "Soon," he promised, walking out the front door. And an hour later, Quee Lee left too, telling herself that she was going to the hull again to confront her husband's old friend. What was this mysterious debt? Why did it bother him so much? But somewhere during the long tube-car ride, before she reached Port Beta, she realized that a confrontation would just further embarrass Perri, and what cause would that serve?

"What now?" she whispered to herself.

Another walk on the hull, of course. If Orleans would allow it. If he had the time, she hoped, and the inclination.

His face had turned blue, and the eyes were larger. The pits were filled with black hairs that shone in the light, something about them distinctly amused. "I guess we could go for a stroll," said the cool voice. They were standing in the same locker room, or one just like it; Quee Lee was unsure about directions. "We could," said Orleans, "but if you want to bend the rules, why bend little ones? Why not pick the hefty ones?"

She watched the mouth smile down at her, two little tusks showing in its corners. "What do you mean?" she asked.

"Of course it'll take time," he warned. "A few months, maybe a few years . . . "

She had centuries, if she wanted.

"I know you," said Orleans. "You've gotten curious about me, about *us*. Orleans moved an arm, not so much as a hum coming from the refurbished joints. "We'll make you an honorary Remora, if you're willing. We'll borrow a lifesuit, set you inside it, then transform you partway in a hurry-up fashion."

"You can? How?"

"Oh, aimed doses of radiation. Plus we'll give you some useful mutations. I'll wrap up some genes inside smart cancers, and they'll migrate to the right spots and grow. . . ."

She was frightened and intrigued, her heart kicking harder.

"It won't happen overnight, of course. And it depends on how much you want done." A pause. "Of course you should know that it's not strictly legal. The captains have this attitude about putting passengers a little bit at risk."

"How much risk is there?"

Orleans said, "The transformation is easy enough, in principle. I'll call up our records, make sure of the fine points." A pause and a narrowing of the eyes. "We'll keep you asleep throughout. Intravenous feedings. That's best. You'll lie down with one body, then waken with a new one. A better one, I'd like to think. How much risk? Almost none, believe me."

She felt numb. Small and weak and numb.

"You won't be a true Remora. Your basic genetics won't be touched, I promise. But someone looking at you will think you're genuine."

For an instant, with utter clarity, Quee Lee saw herself alone on the great gray hull, walking the path of the first Remora.

"Are you interested?"

"Maybe. I am."

"You'll need a lot of interest before we can start," he warned. "We have expenses to consider, and I'll be putting my crew at risk. If the captains find out, it's a suspension without pay." He paused, then said, "Are you listening to me?"

"It's going to cost money," she whispered.

Orleans gave a figure.

And Quee Lee was braced for a larger sum, two hundred thousand credits still large but not unbearable. She wouldn't be able to take as many trips to fancy resorts, true. Yet how could a lazy, prosaic resort compare with what she was being offered?

"You've done this before?" she asked.

He waited a moment, then said, "Not for a long time, no."

She didn't ask what seemed quite obvious, thinking of Perri and secretly smiling to herself.

"Take time," Orleans counseled. "Feel sure."

But she had already decided.

"Quee Lee?"

She looked at him, asking, "Can I have your eyes? Can you wrap them up in a smart cancer for me?"

"Certainly!" A great fluid smile emerged, framed with tusks. "Pick and choose as you wish. Anything you wish."

"The eyes," she muttered.

"They're yours," he declared, giving a little wink.

Arrangements had to be made, and what surprised her most — what she enjoyed more than the anticipation — was the subterfuge, taking money from her savings and leaving no destination, telling her apartment that she would be gone for an indeterminate time. At least a year, and perhaps much longer. Orleans hadn't put a cap on her stay with them, and what if she liked the Remoran life? Why not keep her possibilities open?

"If Perri returns?" asked the apartment.

He was to have free reign of the place, naturally. She thought she'd made herself clear —

"No, miss," the voice interrupted. "What do I tell him, if anything?"

"Tell him . . . tell him that I've gone exploring."

"Exploring?"

"Tell him it's my turn for a change," she declared; and she left without as much as a backward glance.

Orleans found help from the same female Remora, the one who had taken Quee Lee to him twice now. Her comma-shaped eyes hadn't changed, but the mouth was smaller and the gray teeth had turned black as obsidian. Quee Lee lay between them as they worked, their faces smiling but the voices tight and shrill. Not for the first time, she realized she wasn't hearing their real voices. The suits themselves were translating their wet mutterings, which is why throats and mouths could change so much without having any audible effect.

"Are you comfortable?" asked the woman. But before Quee Lee could reply, she asked, "Any last questions?"

Quee Lee was encased in the lifesuit, a sudden panic taking hold of her. "When I go home . . . when I'm done . . . how fast can I. . . ?"

"Can you?"

"Return to my normal self."

"Cure the damage, you mean." The woman laughed gently, her expression changing from one unreadable state to another. "I don't think there's a firm answer, dear. Do you have an autodoc in your apartment? Good. Let it excise the bad and help you grow your own organs over again. As if you'd suffered a bad accident. . . ." A brief pause. "It should take what, Orleans? Six months to be cured?"

The man said nothing, busy with certain controls inside her suit's helmet. Quee Lee could just see his face above and behind her.

"Six months and you can walk in public again."

"I don't mean it that way," Quee Lee countered, swallowed now. A pressure was building against her chest, panic becoming terror. She wanted nothing now but to be home again.

"Listen," said Orleans, then he said nothing.

Finally Quee Lee whispered, "What?"

He knelt beside her, saying, "You'll be fine. I promise."

His old confidence was missing. Perhaps he hadn't believed she would go through with this adventure. Perhaps the offer had been some kind of bluff, something no sane person would find appealing, and now he'd invent some excuse to stop everything —

—but he said, "Seals tight and ready."

"Tight and ready," echoed the woman.

Smiles appeared on both faces, though neither inspired confidence. Then Orleans was explaining: "There's only a slight, slight chance that you won't return to normal. If you should get hit by too much radiation, precipitating too many novel mutations . . . well, the strangeness can get buried too deeply. A thousand autodocs couldn't root it all out of you."

"Vestigial organs," the woman added. "Odd blemishes and the like."

"It won't happen," said Orleans.

"It won't," Quee Lee agreed.

A feeding nipple appeared before her mouth. "Suck and sleep," Orleans told her.

She swallowed some sort of chemical broth, and the woman was saying, "No, it would take ten or fifteen centuries to make lasting marks. Unless—"

Orleans said something, snapping at her.

She laughed with a bitter sound, saying, "Oh, she's asleep. . . !"

And Quee Lee was asleep. She found herself in a dreamless, timeless void, her body being pricked with needles—little white pains marking every smart cancer—and it was as if nothing else existed in the universe but Quee Lee, floating in that perfect blackness while she was remade.

"How long?"

"Not so long. Seven months, almost."

Seven months. Quee Lee tried to blink and couldn't, couldn't shut the lids of her eyes. Then she tried touching her face, lifting a heavy hand and setting the palm on her faceplate, finally remembering her suit. "Is it done?" she muttered, her voice sloppy and slow. "Am I done now?"

"You're never done," Orleans laughed. "Haven't you been paying attention?"

She saw a figure, blurred but familiar.

"How do you feel, Quee Lee?"

Strange. Through and through, she felt very strange.

"That's normal enough," the voice offered. "Another couple months, and you'll be perfect. Have patience."

She was a patient person, she remembered. And now her eyes seemed to shut of their own volition, her mind sleeping again. But this time Quee Lee dreamed, she and Perri and Orleans all at the beach together. She saw them sunning on the bone-white sand, and she even felt the heat of the false sun, felt it baking hot down to her rebuilt bones.

She woke, muttering, "Orleans? Orleans?"

"Here I am."

Her vision was improved now. She found herself breathing normally, her wrong-shaped mouth struggling with each word and her suit managing an accurate translation.

"How do I look?" she asked.

Orleans smiled and said, "Lovely."

His face was blue-black, perhaps. When she sat up, looking at the plain gray locker room, she realized how the colors had shifted. Her new eyes perceived the world differently, sensitive to the same spectrum but in novel ways. She slowly climbed to her feet, then asked, "How long?"

"Nine months, fourteen days."

No, she wasn't finished. But the transformation had reached a stable point, she sensed, and it was wonderful to be mobile again. She managed a few tentative steps. She made clumsy fists with her too-thick hands. Lifting the fists, she gazed at them, wondering how they would look beneath the hyperfiber.

"Want to see yourself?" Orleans asked.

Now? Was she ready?

Her friend smiled, tusks glinting in the room's weak light. He offered a large mirror, and she bent to put her face close enough . . . finding a remade face staring up at her, a sloppy mouth full of mirror-colored teeth and a pair of hairy pits for eyes. She managed a deep breath and shivered. Her skin was lovely, golden or at least appearing golden to her. It was covered with hard white lumps, and her nose was a slender beak. She wished she could touch herself, hands stroking her faceplate. Only Remoras could never touch their own flesh. . . .

"If you feel strong enough," he offered, "you can go with me. My crew and I are going on a patching mission, out to the prow."

"When?"

"Now, actually." He lowered the mirror. "The others are waiting in the shuttle. Stay here for a couple more days, or come now."

"Now," she whispered.

"Good." He nodded, telling her, "They want to meet you. They're curious what sort of person becomes a Remora."

A person who doesn't want to be locked up in a bland gray room, she thought to herself, smiling now with her mirrored teeth.

They had all kinds of faces, all unique, myriad eyes and twisting mouths and flesh of every color. She counted fifteen Remoras, plus Orleans, and Quee Lee worked to learn names and get to know her new friends. The shuttle ride was like a party, a strange informal party, and she had never known happier people, listening to Remoran jokes and how they teased one another, and how they sometimes teased her. In friendly ways, of course. They asked about her apartment—how big; how fancy; how much—and about her long life. Was it as boring as it sounded? Quee Lee laughed at herself while she nodded, saying, "No, nothing changes very much. The centuries have their way of running together, sure."

One Remora—a large masculine voice and a contorted blue face—asked the others, "Why do people pay fortunes to ride the ship, then do everything possible to hide deep inside it? Why don't they ever step outside and have a little look at where we're going?"

The cabin erupted in laughter, the observation an obvious favorite.

"Immortals are cowards," said the woman beside Quee Lee.

"Fools," said a second woman, the one with comma-shaped eyes. "Most of them, at least."

Quee Lee felt uneasy, but just temporarily. She turned and looked through a filthy window, the smooth changeless landscape below and the glowing sky as she remembered it. The view soothed her. Eventually, she shut her eyes and slept, waking when

Orleans shouted something about being close to their destination. "Decelerating now!" he called from the cockpit.

They were slowing. Dropping. Looking at her friends, she saw a variety of smiles meant for her. The Remoras beside her took her hands, everyone starting to pray. "No comets today," they begged. "And plenty tomorrow because we want overtime."

The shuttle slowed to nothing, then settled.

Orleans strode back to Quee Lee, his mood suddenly serious. "Stay close," he warned, "but don't get in our way, either."

The hyperfiber was thickest here, on the prow, better than one hundred kilometers deep, and its surface had been browned by the ceaseless radiations. A soft dry dust clung to the lifesuits, and everything was lit up by the aurora and flashes of laser light. Quee Lee followed the others, listening to their chatter. She ate a little meal of Remoran soup—her first conscious meal—feeling the soup moving down her throat, trying to map her new architecture. Her stomach seemed the same, but did she have two hearts? It seemed that the beats were wrong. Two hearts nestled side by side. She found Orleans and approached him. "I wish I could pull off my suit, just once. Just for a minute." She told him, "I keep wondering how all of me looks."

Orleans glanced at her, then away. He said, "No."

"No?"

"Remoras don't remove their suits. Ever."

There was anger in the voice and a deep chilling silence from the others. Quee Lee looked about, then swallowed. "I'm not a Remora," she finally said. "I don't understand. . . ."

Silence persisted, quick looks exchanged.

"I'm going to climb out of this . . . eventually. . . !"

"But don't say it now," Orleans warned. A softer, more tempered voice informed her, "We have taboos. Maybe we seem too rough to have them—"

"No," she muttered.

"—yet we do. These lifesuits are as much a part of our bodies as our guts and eyes, and being a Remora, a true Remora, is a sacred pledge that you take for your entire life."

The comma-eyed woman approached, saying, "It's an insult to remove your suit. A sacrilege."

"Contemptible," said someone else. "Or worse."

Then Orleans, perhaps guessing Quee Lee's thoughts, made a show of touching her, and she felt the hand through her suit. "Not that you're anything but our guest, of course. Of course." He paused, then said, "We have our beliefs, that's all."

"Ideals," said the woman.

"And contempt for those we don't like. Do you understand?" She couldn't, but she made understanding sounds just the same. Obviously she had uncovered a sore spot.

Then came a new silence, and she found herself marching through the dust, wishing someone would make angry sounds again. Silence was the worst kind of anger. From now on, she vowed, she would be careful about everything she said. Every word.

The crater was vast and rough and only partway patched. Previous crew had brought giant tanks and the machinery used to make the patch. It was something of an art form, pouring the fresh liquid hyperfiber and carefully curing it. Each shift added another hundred meters to the smooth crater floor. Orleans stood with Quee Lee at the top, explaining the job. This would be a double shift, and she was free to watch. "But not too closely," he warned her again, the tone vaguely parental. "Stay out of our way."

She promised. For that first half-day, she was happy to sit on the crater's lip, on a ridge of tortured and useless hyperfiber, imagining the comet that must have made this mess. Not large, she knew. A large one would have blasted a crater too big to see at a glance, and forty crews would be laboring here. But it hadn't been a small one, either. It must have slipped past the lasers, part of a swarm. She watched the red beams cutting across the sky, their heat producing new colors in the aurora. Her new eyes saw amazing details. Shock waves as violet phosphorescence; swirls of orange and crimson and snowy white. A beautiful deadly sky, wasn't it? Suddenly the lasers fired faster, a spiderweb of beams overhead, and she realized that a swarm was ahead of the ship, pinpointed by the navigators somewhere below them . . . tens of millions of kilometers ahead, mud and ice and rock closing fast. . . !

The lasers fired even faster, and she bowed her head.

There was an impact, at least one. She saw the flash and felt a faint rumble dampened by the hull, a portion of those energies absorbed and converted into useful power. Impacts were fuel, of a sort. And the residual gases would be concentrated and pumped inside, helping to replace the inevitable loss of volatiles as the ship continued on its great trek.

The ship was an organism feeding on the galaxy.

It was a familiar image, almost cliché, yet suddenly it seemed quite fresh. Even profound. Quee Lee laughed to herself, looking out over the browning plain while turning her attentions inward.

She was aware of her breathing and the bump-bumping of wrong hearts, and she sensed changes with every little motion. Her body had an odd indecipherable quality. She could feel every fiber in her muscles, every twitch and every stillness. She had never been so alive, so self-aware, and she found herself laughing with a giddy amazement.

If she was a true Remora, she thought, then she would be a world unto herself. A world like the ship, only smaller, its organic parts enclosed in armor and forever in flux. Like the passengers below, the cells of her body were changing. She thought she could nearly feel herself evolving . . . and how did Orleans control it? It would be astonishing if she could reevolve sight, for instance . . . gaining eyes unique to herself, never having existed before and never to exist again. . . !

What if she stayed with these people?

The possibility suddenly occurred to her, taking her by surprise.

What if she took whatever pledge was necessary, embracing all of their taboos and proving that she belonged with them? Did such things happen? Did adventurous passengers try converting—?

The sky turned red, lasers firing and every red line aimed at a point directly overhead. The silent barrage was focused on some substantial chunk of ice and grit, vaporizing its surface and cracking its heart. Then the beams separated, assaulting the bigger pieces and then the smaller ones. It was an enormous drama, her exhilaration married to terror . . . her watching the aurora brightening as force fields killed the momentum of the surviving grit and atomic dust. The sky was a vivid orange, and sudden tiny impacts kicked up the dusts around her. Something struck her leg, a flash of light followed by a dim pain . . . and she wondered if she was dead, then how badly she was wounded. Then she blinked and saw the little crater etched above her knee. A blemish, if that. And suddenly the meteor shower was finished.

Quee Lee rose to her feet, shaking with nervous energy.

She began picking her way down the crater slope. Orleans's commands were forgotten; she needed to speak to him. She had insights and compliments to share, nearly tripping with her excitement, finally reaching the work site and gasping, her air stale from her exertions. She could taste herself in her breaths, the flavor unfamiliar, thick and a little sweet.

"Orleans!" she cried out.

"You're not supposed to be here," groused one woman.

The comma-eyed woman said, "Stay right there. Orleans is coming, and don't move!"

A lake of fresh hyperfiber was cooling and curing as she stood beside it. A thin skin had formed, the surface utterly flat and silvery. Mirrorlike. Quee Lee could see the sky reflected in it, and she leaned forward, knowing she shouldn't. She risked falling in order to see herself once again. The nearby Remoras watched her, saying nothing. They smiled as she grabbed a lump of old hyperfiber, positioning herself, and the lasers flashed again, making everything bright as day.

She didn't see her face.

Or rather, she did. But it wasn't the face she expected, the face from Orleans's convenient mirror. Here was the old Quee Lee, mouth ajar, those pretty and ordinary eyes opened wide in amazement.

She gasped, knowing everything. A near-fortune paid, and nothing in return. Nothing here had been real. This was an enormous and cruel sick joke; and now the Remoras were laughing, hands on their untouchable bellies and their awful faces contorted, ready to rip apart from the sheer brutal joy of the moment. . . !

"Your mirror wasn't a mirror, was it? It synthesized that image, didn't it?" She kept asking questions, not waiting for a response. "And you drugged me, didn't you? That's why everything still looks and feels wrong."

Orleans said, "Exactly. Yes."

Quee Lee remained inside her lifesuit, just the two of them flying back to Port Beta. He would see her on her way home. The rest of the crew was working, and Orleans would return and finish his shift. After her discovery, everyone agreed there was no point in keeping her on the prow.

"You owe me money," she managed.

Orleans's face remained blue-black. His tusks framed a calm icy smile. "Money? Whose money?"

"I paid you for a service, and you never met the terms."

"I don't know about any money," he laughed.

"I'll report you," she snapped, trying to use all of her venom. "I'll go to the captains—"

"—and embarrass yourself further." He was confident, even cocky. "Our transaction would be labeled illegal, not to mention disgusting. The captains will be thoroughly disgusted, believe me." Another laugh. "Besides, what can anyone prove? You gave someone your money, but nobody will trace it to any of us. Believe me."

She had never felt more ashamed, crossing her arms and trying to wish herself home again.

"The drug will wear off soon," he promised. "You'll feel like yourself again. Don't worry."

Softly, in a breathless little voice, she asked, "How long have I been gone?"

Silence.

"It hasn't been months, has it?"

"More like three days." A nod inside the helmet. "The same drug distorts your sense of time, if you get enough of it."

She felt ill to her stomach.

"You'll be back home in no time, Quee Lee."

She was shaking and holding herself.

The Remora glanced at her for a long moment, something resembling remorse in his expression. Or was she misreading the signs?

"You aren't spiritual people," she snapped. It was the best insult she could manage, and she spoke with certainty. "You're crude, disgusting monsters. You couldn't live below if you had the chance, and this is where you belong."

Orleans said nothing, merely watching her.

Finally he looked ahead, gazing at the endless gray landscape. "We try to follow our founder's path. We try to be spiritual." A shrug. "Some of us do better than others, of course. We're only human."

She whispered, "Why?"

Again he looked at her, asking, "Why what?"

"Why have you done this to me?"

Orleans seemed to breathe and hold the breath, finally exhaling. "Oh, Quee Lee," he said, "you haven't been paying attention, have you?"

What did he mean?

He grasped her helmet, pulling her face up next to his face. She saw nothing but the eyes, each black hair moving and nameless fluids circulating through them, and she heard the voice saying, "This has never, never been about you, Quee Lee. Not you. Not for one instant."

And she understood—perhaps she had always known—struck mute and her skin going cold, and finally, after everything, she found herself starting to weep.

Perri was already home, by chance.

"I was worried about you," he confessed, sitting in the garden room with honest relief on his face. "The apartment said you were going to be gone for a year or more. I was scared for you."

"Well," she said, "I'm back."

Her husband tried not to appear suspicious, and he worked hard not to ask certain questions. She could see him holding the questions inside himself. She watched him decide to try the old charm, smiling now and saying, "So you went exploring?"

"Not really."

"Where?"

"Cloud Canyon," she lied. She had practiced the lie all the way from Port Beta, yet it sounded false now. She was halfway startled when her husband said:

"Did you go into it?"

"Partway, then I decided not to risk it. I rented a boat, but I couldn't make myself step on board."

Perri grinned happily, unable to hide his relief. A deep breath was exhaled, then he said, "By the way, I've raised almost eight thousand credits already. I've already put them in your account."

"Fine."

"I'll find the rest, too."

"It can wait," she offered.

Relief blended into confusion. "Are you all right, darling?"

"I'm tired," she allowed.

"You look tired."

"Let's go to bed, shall we?"

Perri was compliant, making love to her and falling into a deep sleep, as exhausted as Quee Lee. But she insisted on staying awake, sliding into her private bathroom and giving her autodoc a drop of Perri's seed. "I want to know if there's anything odd," she told it.

"Yes, miss."

"And scan him, will you? Without waking him."

The machine set to work. Almost instantly, Quee Lee was being shown lists of abnormal genes and vestigial organs. She didn't bother to read them. She closed her eyes, remembering what little Orleans had told her after he had admitted that she wasn't anything more than an incidental bystander. "Perri was born Remora, and he left us. A long time ago, by our count, and that's a huge taboo."

"Leaving the fold?" she had said.

"Every so often, one of us visits his home while he's gone. We slip a little dust into our joints, making them grind, and we do a pity-play to whomever we find."

Her husband had lied to her from the first, about everything.

"Sometimes we'll trick her into giving even more money," he had boasted. "Just like we've done with you."

And she had asked, "Why?"

"Why do you think?" he had responded.

Vengeance, of a sort. Of course.

"Eventually," Orleans had declared, "everyone's going to know about Perri. He'll run out of hiding places, and money, and he'll have to come back to us. We just don't want it to happen too soon, you know? It's too much fun as it is."

Now she opened her eyes, gazing at the lists of abnormalities. It had to be work for him to appear human, to cope with those weird Remoran genetics. He wasn't merely someone who had lived on the hull for a few years, no. He was a full-blooded Remora who had done the unthinkable, removing his suit and living below, safe from the mortal dangers of the universe. Quee Lee was the latest of his ignorant lovers, and she knew precisely why he had selected her. More than money, she had offered him a useful naiveté and a sheltered ignorance . . . and wasn't she well within her rights to confront him, confront him and demand that he leave at once. . . ?

"Erase the lists," she said.

"Yes, miss."

She told her apartment, "Project the view from the prow, if you will. Put it on my bedroom ceiling, please."

"Of course, miss," it replied.

She stepped out of the bathroom, lasers and exploding comets overhead. She fully expected to do what Orleans anticipated, putting her mistakes behind her. She sat on the edge of her bed, on Perri's side, waiting for him to wake on his own. He would feel her gaze and open his eyes, seeing her framed by a Remoran sky . . .

. . . and she hesitated, taking a breath and holding it, glancing upward, remembering that moment on the crater's lip when she had felt a union with her body. A perfection; an intoxicating sense of self. It was induced by drugs and ignorance, yet still it had seemed true. It was a perception worth any cost, she realized; and she imagined Perri's future, hounded by the Remoras, losing every human friend, left with no choice but the hull and his left-behind life. . . .

She looked at him, the peaceful face stirring.

Compassion. Pity. Not love, but there was something not far from love making her feel for the fallen Remora.

"What if. . . ?" she whispered, beginning to smile.

And Perri smiled in turn, eyes closed and him enjoying some lazy dream that in an instant he would surely forget.

ÆON'S CHILD

PAMIR WAS a captain of consequence. His ageless frame was tall and strong, in part because passengers seemed to expect both from the ship's officers. A large, pleasantly homely face conveyed confidence and a burdensome wisdom. In uniform, he drew long looks, whether from humans or sighted aliens. And unlike most captains, he had risen in the ship's hierarchy without depending on friendships or flattery. It was said—in his presence, with all the best intentions—that Pamir could have become a Submaster by now, earning a seat at the Master Captain's table. If he would only attempt the game. . . .

"Give gifts," Washen advised. "Memorable gifts, and durable. Gifts that will say, 'Pamir,' for ten thousand years."

He knew the game but feigned ignorance. "What would I give that could impress a Submaster?"

"There's that alien weed you like to grow. The one that sings."

"The llano-vibra?"

"Is that its name?"

He nodded, removing his mirrored captain's cap, then setting it on one of the obsidian busts fixed to the table's corners. "You think I should be giving away weeds."

"Pretty ones," she said. "Why not? Offer a reason."

With genuine disgust, he admitted, "If I did what you want, it would feel so calculated—"

"Then again," Washen interrupted, "maybe you don't deserve a promotion." She was tall and strong—a captain of roughly equal rank—and she was pretty in a smooth, unconscious way. They were lovers once, but that was so long ago that neither could remember any details. Friend to friend, she argued, "A captain has to believe in calculations. How else can he do his job? Formulas for acceleration, for stress loads. For ass-kissing. If you won't respect the formulas, maybe you don't belong at the Master Captain's table."

"I agree with you." Their drinks rose from the table's center. Claiming his rain-of-tears, Pamir said, "I don't deserve anything, and can we move to other business?"

"Such as?"

"I don't know. *You* wanted to see *me*, as I recall."

"And I can't stay long," she complained. "I'm greeting a shuttle full of Y'uy'uy. Have you heard about them?" No, he hadn't. "A social species, and tiny. A couple million are coming, and if I don't wiggle my fingers at each of them, in the proper way, the whole damned nest is my enemy."

As if practicing, Washen curled and uncurled one finger.

Pamir looked across the lounge, through its long transparent wall. A red-as-blood lake sloshed against the rocks below. Some kind of alien plankton colored the water. Probably poisonous to Terran life, the plankton were feeding—directly or indirectly—some of their remarkable passengers.

"But hey, speaking of newcomers. . . !"

Pamir turned. Puzzled, alert.

"I found one for you. And he fit most of your parameters." With a large, overly dramatic motion, she handed him a memo chip. "The odd bioscan. A very odd ship. And a port of origin that practically smells phony."

The chip was a giant snowflake worn simple by countless hands, its whiteness magnified by the tired black stone of the tabletop.

"An odd ship," she repeated. "Wooden, but not like any wood I know. He sold it for scrap. I've got the recyke reports. How many times have you seen a starship built from lumber?"

Pamir reached across the table, making a fist. "Who is *he?*"

"Don't you know? You told me to watch for him."

"How long has he been here?"

"You should see yourself," Washen exclaimed. Then she laughed, shaking her drink and inhaling the gases that rose out of solution. "I don't think I've ever seen quite that face on you."

"When did this passenger come aboard?"

She tapped the memo chip, as if answers would spring forth. "More than a week ago. But I was busy, and you were off-duty, and you never told me why I should sound an alarm."

Pamir wrestled with his adrenaline, feigning self-control.

"Wood," she repeated. "Tough, weird wood. Cellulose laced with non-Terran proteins configured for strength and durability. Except it doesn't give much protection from radiation, or from impacts, and I'm surprised how fit the passenger seemed—"

"An organic ship," Pamir muttered.

"In places, yes." She sniffed her drink again, enjoying the temporary corrosion of her nervous system. "The engines had metals where you need them. And ceramics. And the guts were diamond. But there wasn't anything like hyperfiber, and the scrap value was nil—"

"A starfaring tree," Pamir offered. He consumed the rest of his drink, barely tasting the salt, wishing all the while that this was just some enormous, curious coincidence.

"I did some research for you." Again she tapped the chip. "There's a report of another ship like this one. Organic and sloppy. But it didn't stay with us. As it happens."

"Thank you," said Pamir, feeling ill.

"A sketchy, misfiled report." Washen was staring at a point behind his eyes. "I don't even know who wrote it."

Pamir lifted his cap with both hands, placing it on his head, at an angle calculated to give their passengers confidence in him. At least the human passengers. Again he said, "Thank you."

"The man calls himself Samara."

He barely heard her voice.

"Human, but not. From a colony world that exists, only we didn't pass within a thousand light-years of it."

What should he do first? It had been centuries since Pamir had considered this scenario, and he felt lost, cold, and ill, fears building between those gaping weaknesses.

"Samara immigrated without incident. You have his address."

Washen was a friend, and she was doing him a great favor. Yet he was so consumed by his troubles that when he looked at her he felt anger—a scorching, blistering, unfair rage. How could such a creature get on board? he wanted to scream. But instead of speaking, he began to tug on his violet-black epaulets, thick fingers struggling to remain gentle.

"Some advice?" said Washen. "Come to the Master Captain's dinner this year. Bring your singing weeds, call them calculations, and smile until your face hurts." She showed him a gracious smile and a flirtatious wink, both framed by her mirrored uniform and cap. "Sit beside me, if you'd like."

Pamir sighed.

All he could think of saying was, "I don't raise llano-vibra anymore."

"No?"

"Not in ages," he muttered, claiming the memo chip and again looking through the transparent wall, gazing at that strange red lake and trying not to think of death.

There were poverty wards on *the ship*, places famous for crime and madness. Samara had taken an apartment in the most notorious ward, Pamir learned—from the memo chip and from his own research. Yet the newcomer was a relatively wealthy passenger. The ship's economy was designed to be adaptable, and Samara had come prepared, offering more than just an old wooden starship to consumers. He had vials of giant molecules, intricate and irreproducible, considered art by several species. He also brought the mummified feet of another alien, collected on the homeworld and sold to grieving, grateful relatives. Plus Samara was the reputed author of a billion-word novel meant for the computer intelligences, already purchased by an onboard publisher and released to lukewarm reviews.

Whatever Samara was, he was distinctive.

A registered human; and while his bioscans were odd, nothing about them or the man seemed certifiably dangerous.

A minor captain had interviewed him; all would-be passengers enjoyed the same treatment. When he was shown his bioscan, Samara had nodded and smiled, tiny teeth flashing in a small thin-lipped mouth. Then a voice more suitable for a bird said, "Yes, yes. A consequence of my homeworld. But those bodies are inert. Take all you want and watch them. Feed them. Torture them, if you wish. But nothing will happen because they aren't alive." The bodies were tiny organic features with a passing resemblance to mitochondria. "They're produced by native organisms. They get inside us, and there's no ridding of them. Unless you want me to endure a cell-by-cell scrubbing . . . if you think this grit might pose some kind of risk. . . ."

Samara was small and almost pretty, attempting charm but not quite succeeding. If Pamir had been the interviewer, knowing nothing, he would have pressed the man for more information.

Why had he left his homeworld? What was his destination? There was ample reason to delay, pulling new tests from the bottomless bag that every captain possessed. *Just to be sure.* But that minor captain had avoided any ugliness, moving to short-term issues. "How will you live here?" he had asked.

"How will I pay my way, you mean." A songful laugh. A human hand swept through hair that seemed blond until it was touched, then for an instant, at certain angles, a bright golden-green. "I've done my research, and believe me, I plan to live cheaply. Without complaints."

Captains liked to hear promises of compliance.

"You've seen my ship," said Samara, showing a little grin. "To have come this far, and in such a vessel . . . doesn't that prove sincerity?"

It proved desperation, but the interviewer had seemed impressed with the logic, nodding and smiling in turn.

Pamir made a note to reprimand the officer, if he had the chance. Then he hunted through every shipboard record in his grasp, resurrecting the immigrant's last few days. A thousand-year passage was paid off. The cramped apartment was rented, then left empty. After a long search of security digitals—and several turf wars with security troops—Pamir pieced together portions of the man's days, including a talkative lunch with a familiar face.

"Perri," growled the captain, staring at the face.

Several hours later, Pamir was in a wealthy district, at the front door of what passed for a modest local apartment. Long ago, Perri had been a member of the crew; but he quit for the life of a gigolo, fooling an ancient lady into marrying him. It was the wife who answered the door, and Pamir thought of telling her about her husband's secret life. But he was too much the captain to act unseemly, watching her call for Perri, then kiss him before retreating just out of sight.

Perri allowed him to walk no farther than the stone hallway beyond the opened door. "What do you want, friend?"

Pamir bristled with the word *friend*. He showed the gigolo a digital image, saying, "Samara."

"I know his name."

Pamir said, "You ate with him."

"I guess I remember that, too." Perri gave a little snort, amused by the scene. "And you want to know what we talked about, right?"

"I know what you said."

The gigolo waited, trying to gauge Pamir's mood.

"He learned that you travel, that you know the ship better than anyone else—"

"Except the captains."

"Right." Transcripts had been prepared by lip-reading computers. Parts of their conversation had evaded them, but the gist of it was easy to see. "Samara asked about secret places. Private wildernesses. Locations not on the public maps."

"So what?"

"What does he want?" asked the captain.

"He didn't name his goal."

"Can you guess?"

"In this case, no."

"Where does our sewage go?"

"Down," Perri replied, then laughed and shrugged his shoulders. "Right, he asked about sewage. And you know what I said."

"There's a treatment plant, and it's off-limits. Just a jumble of machinery, you told him." Pamir was breathing in ragged wet gulps. "Big machines, old as the ship, scrubbing the water clean. And there's nothing at all to see."

Perri leaned against a polished stone wall, waiting.

"You told him there's nothing to see, then you claimed that you've never been there."

"Because I haven't been."

The captain took him by the throat, squeezing for emphasis. It was a gesture, nothing more. Humans rebuilt themselves long ago, making their bodies glancingly immortal. It took more horrific actions to cause harm. Yet a choking hand remained an effective crudeness, and so did a low angry threat. "Lie and I'll hurt you," said Pamir. "If I don't believe you, I'll ruin you. Promise."

"I didn't tell him. . . ." The gigolo spat at Pamir, then tried to slap the hand aside. "I told him nothing. . . !"

"Because you knew I was watching."

Perri tried an ineffective kick, then shrank down and moaned.

"You met with him later," said Pamir. "In secret. That's when you told Samara about what you saw—"

"I saw nothing," Perri complained.

Bones cracked inside the squirming neck.

"We didn't meet. I saw him once." Again Perri struck the hand, doing nothing. Then the hand withdrew, at its own pace. Perri swallowed, coughed. Then, "I said I wouldn't tell, and I didn't, and I don't even know what to tell. I barely saw the place—"

"Samara offered to pay you. Handsomely."

Perri glared at him, a lucid fury behind the eyes. "Even if I knew what to say, I wouldn't tell him. And did you notice? I paid for my own damn lunch!" Perri massaged his bruised neck. "I don't like Samara. I like him even less than I like you."

Pamir was genuinely surprised. "Oh, and why not?"

The gigolo had no easy response. "There's something wrong with him. Wrong." He coughed again, then fought to swallow. "He's deep water, I think. Whatever he is, he's mostly hidden. I think."

Pamir's surprise had doubled. He believed the man, despite all odds, and he felt an astonishing pleasure in the fact that two people didn't approve of this new immigrant.

"Darling?" said a woman's voice.

The hapless wife was emerging from the shadows, walking with a deliberative gait, looking at Pamir while she asked her husband:

"Are you all right, sweetness?"

Another cough, and Perri said, "Fine. I'm fine."

She stopped just short of them, her face set. "Sir, I think you should leave now." With a chilled voice, she said, "Captain or not, I want you out of my home."

As if Pamir was the villain here.

Each district had its captains' ward, usually just beneath the hull, always within one of the catacombs thought to be as ancient as the ship. Pamir, obeying tradition, kept an apartment in his own district. Relatively small, set away from the main tube line and difficult to find, it was a private realm with several hundred meters of tunnels, rooms of a hectare or two, and a whirlpool pond with colorful muscular fish in the spinning water, beds of blackpot mussels fixed to the bottom, preventing erosion for the last ten thousand years.

Before the mussels, Pamir had used freshwater corals.

Before corals, he had let the water gnaw at its basin, sculpting the greenish olivine however it wished.

The rare visitor, staring at the unkempt surroundings, liked to mention that cleaning your home wasn't a crime. After all, nobody knew if the ship's builders had lived in the catacombs. And even if these were homes, wouldn't they want the current tenants to keep them presentable?

But Pamir enjoyed the slumping oxidized walls, thank you. He loved the sense of titanic age, the possibilities of history. In the early centuries, he had spent every off-duty moment in his largest room, staring at a wall covered with crosshatched scratches, trying to decipher meanings that might not exist. It was another delicious, unanswerable mystery in a ship with more mysteries than inhabitants. In that same room, later, Pamir began culturing the delicate llano-vibra plants, mastering their byzantine genetics to create songs of fragile surreal beauty. But then he drifted away from the hobby, and the plants went wild, crossbreeding at will and losing all sense of pitch and rhythm.

A harsh incoherent wail rose when Pamir entered the room. He barely noticed, halfway running through the tangled growth, bending to touch a certain knob of rock.

The floor beside him neatly dropped out of sight.

The tube car didn't officially exist, and it used energy stolen from nonessential machinery. The hatch sealed with a hiss. As Pamir sat down, the car began to accelerate, taking him through a network of tunnels, never repeating any past course.

Sensors watched for any fool trying to follow him.

Nobody ever did.

But he imagined Samara hunched over an identical panel, watching him with a cool amoral malevolence. The image made him anxious when he was awake, then kicked its way into his dreams while he slept; and only in the last thousand-kilometer fall could Pamir genuinely rest, shaken awake with the berthing.

Pamir undressed, his uniform left hanging in the car. Then he stepped through a second hidden doorway, a screaming mist, gray and toxic, greeting him on the other side. Hands to his mouth, he pushed into the mist, eyes tearing and sinuses catching fire, his naked feet splashing through caustic puddles and over a slope of badly eroded diamond-sharp hyperfibers — a last line of defense to dissuade the curious and the feeble.

A thousand sewers fed into the district's vast purification center. Spent water, industrial wastes, and the by-products of alien biologies came roaring from orifices on all sides. The nearest sewer flowed from human places, and it was a genuine river, swift and rancid, beaten white by the ceaseless turbulence.

Years ago, Perri had ridden with that filth, his body encased in a hyperfiber suit, both hidden inside a whale's rotting carcass. Fancying himself as an adventurer, he had evaded every security system and survived the maelstrom, expecting to find great machines at work — powerful filters and distillers and atom-cracking wonders older than vertebrates, and more durable.

But instead, to his amazement, he found the Child, and with it one naked and enraged captain.

Pamir breathed between his fingers, feeling his throat swell and bleed. There was a thin and wobbly trail that he could feel more than see, and he avoided it, preferring the thin carpet of mock-fungi, gray and bristly, fed by the toxins. The sewer's roar was vast, uncomplicated. Other fluids moved in closer places, the air itself reverberating with thunderous swallowing sounds. Eventually, the mists thinned, then vanished, leaving him on the shelf where he always stopped. He lowered his burned hands. His tough genetics began to heal the flesh. Eyes blinked and teared for a few moments, reclaiming their superior vision. And he lifted his gaze, turning in a slow circle, absorbing his surroundings.

The ceiling was an inverted bowl, a peach-colored sun strung from the apex, both sun and ceiling obscured by banks of water-fat clouds. The floor was like a shattered plate—a fifty-thousand-square-kilometer plate—its shards loosely reassembled, every gap a canyon where a different sewer flowed. In the center was an ocean of sand—countless grains of scrap hyperfiber and catalytic metals—and on top of the sand was a shallow lake being perpetually drained, its overflow bound for reservoirs that would slake the thirsts of millions.

The old machines and every surface were built of hyperfiber, yet little of the wonderstuff was visible.

Life covered every surface.

Dense and vibrant.

Noisy.

Tireless.

Kilometer-long mock-vines. Mock-trees taller than starships. Mock-fungi of elegant shapes and vivid fluorescent colors. And all were linked, roots and fleshy tendrils locked together, a perfect biological embrace extending into the sewers, absorbing tainted water and lifting it, xylem pulling it through filtering gills and kidneys and more gills. Everything of use was harvested. Everything else—the filth of modern technology—was destroyed, if not on the first try then on the next, or the thousandth. However long the work took, it took; the Child was nothing if not tenacious, doing its job without complaint or failure.

As was the custom, Pamir whispered, "Hello."

The reply was diffuse and immediate, millions of mouths and other orifices exhaling as one, mangling the words, "Hello," and "Captain," and "Friend Pamir."

The ground shook under the Child's voice.

Pamir moved, head down, stepping wherever the vegetation looked soft and sturdy. His footprints didn't linger. Every trace of him was erased. Bacteria and viral bodies, skin flakes and dislodged hairs, were caught and digested. Everything but the captain himself became the Child, incorporated and annihilated, then refashioned to serve some critical task.

Several times each year, during his off-duty time, Pamir visited the Child.

Their relationship was centuries old.

Yet even now he had to remind himself that here was one inhabitant, one organism—a multitude of forms, but all linked, like the cells inside his own durable body.

Only better.

Mock-animals appeared. Mock-insects. Mock-rodents. A herd of mock-okapi. Then a mock-angel arrived, shaped like a winged human female, gliding down to a meadow of mock-grass and its rectal umbilical linking with the grass, then the Child, the gesture as automatic as breathing.

Neural bodies spoke through the angel. A feminine voice observed, "You are early, friend. This time."

Pamir tried to speak, then stopped himself, unsure how to proceed.

Cloud-colored wings lashed at the air, causing the dew to leap from the gold-green blades—a clean chill rain in reverse—and with concern on its human face, the angel asked:

"What is wrong, friend Pamir?"

Fear, pure and raw, made him shiver and hold himself.

The Child tasted fear compounds boiling from him, and each body sobbed the same question with whatever passed for a mouth:

"What is wrong?"

Again, in a thunderblast.

"What is wrong?"

Pamir cupped his hands to his dampened face, legs buckling, knees driving into a mat of sweet-scented mushrooms. Beneath them was a solvent, gray and alien, suddenly exposed to the air. The rank odor made him cough, tasting blood again. He wished he could fall unconscious, but he didn't, and he had no choice but to say, "The Monster," with a quick, almost soundless voice. "The Monster's here, and I'm sorry. Sorry."

But the Child had guessed as much; what else could be so awful?

The mock-okapi came forward, placid herbivorous faces dropping, big blue tongues lapping at the solvent as the eyes gazed through him; and the angel spoke, a small pitiful voice begging, "Will you help me?"

Spores exploded into the air, tasting of cinnamon and things unnamed.

"Please, friend Pamir, will you help me?"

Even before he said, *Of course*, he was wondering why the Child would have to ask. After everything Pamir had risked for it—happily risked, without hesitation—why did he still have to prove his devotion, and with something as thin as words?

A minor captain had handled the initial interview, tabulating each discrepancy. Then showing his absence of spirit, he made no decision, leaving the immigrant waiting in the quarantine cell while he went to his superior. And that second captain came to Pamir, asking what she should do. Both captains were bureaucrats, trained by millennia of ritual to avoid initiatives; and in another thousand years, remembering the incident through foggy time, Pamir recalled giving them a prolonged dressing-down. Why, why, why should he be brought something as minuscule as one inappropriate passenger? Kick the idiot overboard, he had said. Then, just to prove his fortitude, he amended himself, saying, "No, I'll do the kicking. Watch your monitors, and learn."

The immigrant had a fictional name and a ludicrous biography. Smaller than any adult human, he had a glancing resemblance to a child, his features emphasizing the huge green eyes and a young boy's oversized head. Yet he claimed to be an adult, both in words and under bioscans. His starship—wooden-hulled, crude, and probably unsafe for any further travel—was something he had built by himself. On a tiny little-known colony world, he claimed. From an area without humans, the captain knew, and he pressed the man-child on that subject, making him admit that the home was a lie, that his identity was fabricated, and his bioscan was exactly what it seemed to be: a collection of odd, even bizarre features scattered within a glancingly human shell.

The boyish body was camouflage.

"You're an alien," said Pamir. "Admit it. There's no harm. We like aliens. We don't even know how many kinds are riding with us." A lie. Each species was registered, regardless of intelligence. "Maybe you're a criminal on your homeworld. Such things happen. There's no shame. We're a human venture, and the crimes of your world might not make us blink. How do you know? Until you admit the truth, you can't."

"I'm not a criminal," the Child maintained, eyes watering in a shamelessly human gesture. Calculated just as the boyish face was calculated, Pamir guessed. For pity's sake, and useless. "I have never done an intentional wrong."

"Not a criminal, but a saint. Huh!" Pamir laughed, giving his victim a pitiless gaze. "We can use saints. All we can find. But you see, the rules require me to ask: Saint or not, how do you intend to pay for your passage?"

The Child's eyes closed, opened. The mouth opened, words dribbling from it. "You can have my ship—"

"Your ship is trash," the captain barked. "How it's held together this long, I don't know."

Now the green eyes were dry, but infinitely fragile.

Pamir shook his head, and he laughed. Laughter was a weapon, and he attacked with it, battering the victim before he asked another good question. "How did you learn so much about us?"

"I monitored your broadcasts," replied the Child.

"And you're alien. Just say *yes*."

"Yes."

"See? And here you sit, still safe and whole."

The Child dipped its head, soft golden hairs breaking the light into tiny rainbows.

"What sort of beast are you?" Pamir pointed a thick finger at his victim, then lied. "Give details, and you won't be punished. Just make certain they're honest details."

"I like humans."

"Which is always good to hear, and it means little." He glanced at a hidden camera, showing the two captains his professional glee. "You've gone to the trouble of manufacturing a humanlike carriage. Like me or not, the intent is to mislead me, and misleading me, sad to say, is a significant and punishable offense."

"I will do no harm," it claimed, trying tears again.

"*What* are you?"

"A refugee."

Watching the tears, Pamir wondered if they were just a little genuine. "Son," he said, "let me show you real honesty in action. We see a lot of very nice refugees, but we're a commercial vessel on a pleasure cruise, every last passenger required to pay his way. In goods. In services. In any of several abstract monetary systems."

The Child gave a studious nod, then began to stand.

"What are you doing?" Pamir barked.

"I don't know," whispered the defeated voice.

"You saw our broadcasts. Weren't you suitably warned?"

No response.

Pamir drew up a series of commands, starting the eviction procedure. Then, almost as an afterthought, he asked, "Are you certain you don't have some useful skill?"

"I have many skills."

"Fine. Name one."

The Child took several steps, finding a direction. When Pamir told it to stay there, to keep in sight, it responded by asking, "May I retrieve something from my ship?"

"But I'll be watching you," he warned. "Remember!"

Another lie. Pamir concentrated on the eviction, making sure every legal need was fulfilled. He didn't notice the Child's return, his eyes lifting with the sound of a weak breath, finding a vial of black water nestled in the boyish hands. "Can you scan this, please?" Easily, in an instant. The results showed a stew of aggressive toxins and carnivorous oxides that could have poisoned Pamir. Just the touch of them, absorbed through the skin, would have devastated his big strong ageless body; and his first thought, reading the scan, was that this foolish organism was going to threaten him. "Let me stay or I'll attack you. . . !" Something to that effect.

But there was no threat, verbal or otherwise. The Child simply lifted the vial to its mouth and drank it dry, then with ungulate teeth grown in the last few minutes, it chewed the glass to slivers and swallowed them, too.

"Huh!" Pamir exclaimed.

He tried to laugh again, saying, "Okay, you're a tough little thing. You're put together differently than me. So what?" He paused, then said, "It doesn't matter. On my authority, I'm evicting you from this vessel. Good luck to you. And good-bye—"

"I'll clean this water," the Child promised. Begged. "If you can wait for a moment—"

"Toward what end?" Pamir interrupted. "Frankly, it's not that novel. Not for shipboard entertainment. This voyage will take several hundred millennia, and you'll have to do better. Sorry."

The Child approached, its breath scalding.

"Before," it whispered, "I drank *your* water."

So what?

"After I spoke to the first captain, I tasted what you drink." A pinching of features; a visible pain. "Sour water."

Pamir said nothing, waiting.

"Your recycling systems are ill, I think."

That was a class-one secret. This district's purification system was having trouble coping with the pollutants of so many species. But the contamination, despite being real, was at such a low level that no organism, or even a bioscan, would be able to discern any problem.

"I can help you."

Quelling his emotions, Pamir built a weak smile, then swallowed and mentioned, "There is the obvious, my friend. Perhaps you can clean up the occasional liter, but multiply that by millions more, and every minute, and without time for a breath, even. . . ."

The Child had hoped to be accepted as human, or at least as an ordinary alien. Both prospects finished, it had no choice but honesty. It didn't trust Pamir—how could it trust an organism so unlike itself?—but it was out of choices, save death.

In a quiet, stolid way, it said, "I have more than this mouth."

"Is that so?"

"I can be large," it promised.

Pamir didn't respond, gathering his belongings, ready to leave.

"Once," said the Child, "I was vast."

"As big as me?"

The child realized it was being mocked, and out of either anger or fear, it grabbed Pamir under the arms and lifted him from the ground, without effort. Then with its stinking, blistering breath, it told him, "I was once as large as a world."

"Pardon me?"

"You have a word . . . if you knew me you would describe me as. . . ." A pause. "As being . . ." The face was changing, gaining color and a rocky stillness, the eyes shrinking to hot white points. "As being gaean. I am, that."

The captain kicked at the air, muttering, "What? What?"

Not believing the words, but unable to discount them, either.

"What are you?" he asked, believing that if he could hear the word again, he could dismiss this creature, perhaps with one of his reliable laughs—

—and the Child said, "Small. I am."

Weeping with its changing face.

"I have become small, and weak, and I beg you, wondrous sir, will you allow me to stay here with you?"

The Monster had arrived, and after delivering the news, Pamir remained with the Child for several days and nights. They discussed plans of action, modes of defense, and the Child began to alter its nature, still cleaning the incoming waters but pulling more and more of its flesh into fighting bodies unlike any the captain had ever seen. Mock-okapi went extinct. Mock-rodents grew poisoned fangs and spurs. And the mock-angels gave birth to griffinlike creatures, hot-blooded and enormous, gills sucking in air like ramjets as they learned to fly, great roaring flocks of them patrolling just beneath the clouds.

Somehow all that activity comforted Pamir. The Monster was close, but it hadn't yet found the Child. And even if it did, he couldn't believe that such a tiny organism would prevail here. He said as much to his companion, and the Child responded with silence. The entire cavern paused, save the rushing waters. What was it thinking? Then a few griffin voices said, "Perhaps you are right, friend Pamir," and why did it feel as if he had disappointed the creature? Since when was confidence a symptom of failure?

He boarded the tube car, starting for home.

Thinking of that long-ago interview, Pamir began to doubt himself. A more ambitious captain would have seized the opportunity, dragging the Child before a Submaster, or perhaps the Master Captain herself. The gaean would have been given official asylum, responsibilities passed along the links of command; and today, the Monster would be facing the official resolve and pooled resources of the united ship.

But then doubt shifted back on itself. What if Pamir's superiors hadn't understood the situation? They might have evicted the Child out of fear or sheer ignorance. Or what if comprehension hadn't brought resolve? Even if the Child was given asylum, security measures would have been weak at best. Captains talk. They will tell passengers any astonishing thing, just to impress. And with passengers coming and going all the time, before too long this entire arm of the galaxy would have known about the Child, and wouldn't the Monster have come regardless?

No, he'd made the only good choice. Pamir had to handle these things himself. That's why he had faked the Child's eviction. With the two other captains watching, he had said, "Gaean, my ass! I can't believe such a thing!" And to make his lie seem more real, he had launched the wooden starship toward the nearest habitable world, its propulsion system sabotaged, but without reason, since the engine failed. A few decades later, there was a flash of light against the stars, and the ship was gone, and Pamir comforted his subordinates by telling them that rules had reasons, and besides, it was his blame to wear. Not theirs.

By then, the Child was safe and comfortable in its secret home.

Using his authority and subterfuge, Pamir had wrested control of the sewers away from another captain—with that captain's secret blessing—and nobody asked why or thought to complain. Gradually, as the Child grew larger and more competent, Pamir could put the ancient machines to sleep. Insoluble problems were solved. Effluents were absorbed and simplified, and water pure to the billion-trillion levels ran from everyone's tap. And for a thousand years, with lies and the occasional bribe, Pamir was able to deflect every official who showed the least little curiosity in trash.

The Child became his friend, and more.

Intelligent. Awesome. Beautiful beyond measure. And that from an ancient human who had grown tired of stars and nebulae, human lovers and his chosen profession.

The Child was a miracle, and it looked upon the captain as its savior. When Pamir made a visit, it welcomed him by voice and with a thousand charities. It invented fruits and meaty pods, no two tasting alike. Mock-lovers took every lubricious form. Visual spectacles, in light and in fire, made Pamir forget to breathe. A trillion mouths, singing in unison, made his scraggly llano-vibra seem pathetic. From its plastic self, the Child grew astonishing bodies — sauropods that made the hyperfiber shake; dragons that spit narcotic clouds of perfume; butterflies with hectare-sized wings; and once, a living giant exactly like Pamir, complete with his face and the mirrored uniform and the perfectly tipped cap. And always, always there were multitudes of smaller butterflies and bizarre flowers and other mock-species evolved in a night and extinct before the next day's end.

Captains asked him, "What do you do with your free time? We don't see you anymore."

It didn't occur to Pamir that they missed his company. They were just nosy people, and he forgave them, shrugging his shoulders and saying, "I do a little traveling, alone. Or I stay home. Whatever suits my mood, I guess."

"That's funny," a few captains remarked. "We thought you had a new lover somewhere."

With a sly look, Washen had told him, "I thought you were ashamed of her."

Ashamed? Never. And he wouldn't use the word "lover," except perhaps in the most abstract, ethereal sense.

But leaving the Child so soon was like parting from a lover. Pamir missed its company after he was underway, and for every conscious instant after that. And because the Child disliked his confidence, he stopped feeling it, feeding a nugget of gloom until there was nothing else, a part of him terrified that the Monster — this Samara creature — would attack now, in his absence, robbing Pamir of his chance to die with his perfect friend.

Home again, slipping through the hidden entrance, Pamir first thought to contact the Child by one of several secure means. Just to know it was safe. But that was a risk in itself, and instead, with a dose of practiced discipline, he made himself sort through various messages, most of them from captains and each message more mundane than the last.

Then came a familiar face, smiling, and a sexless recorded voice saying, "Hello, Pamir."

Pamir triggered the digital by muttering, "Hello?"

"When you have extricated yourself from the Child," said Samara, "come see me. We need to speak."

Why was he surprised?

He had no right to feel surprise, a glacial chill building.

"We can meet on neutral ground. You select the place." Samara paused, smiling again, and the background slid into focus. It was sitting in a captains' lounge, and behind it, seated at a second table, was the captain who had first interviewed the Child. And Samara gave a little laugh, anticipating Pamir's reaction.

"I'll assure you of your safety," it said. "Honestly, I hold no malice toward you, sir."

Never in his enormous life had Pamir felt this alone.

This small and vulnerable.

A child-sized hand appeared, lifting a glass to thin smiling lips. "How could you hope to hide anything so large, dear Captain?" Samara asked, taking a sip of chilled water.

He couldn't hope to hide the Child, of course. Hope was a game, a makeshift shelter for ego and his pride. Captains told stories, spun gossip, and kept thorough records of every official act. And how could Pamir ever hope to keep the Child a perfect secret, belonging to no one but himself?

Full unedited maps were only available to the captains—in principle—but Samara instantly claimed to know how to find their meeting place. The ship was mapped ages ago by robots, tiny and self-replicating; they had been set free in the tunnels, doubling their numbers with each branching, using sound and radiation to peer into the volumes of chilled metal and stone around them. One robot had walked into Pamir's selected chamber, but it didn't find another exit, then turned and retreated. No human hand had ever touched that space, which was its attraction. Anything organic, down to the smallest, most desiccated spore, had to be linked to the captain or, more likely, to Samara.

As clean as medicine and persistence could make him, Pamir arrived early for their meeting. Robot tracks showed the way, nothing else marring a thin coating of gray-white dust. No contamination, claimed his bioscanner. He brightened his torch's beam. And of all things, he remembered the first time he had stepped into his apartment, four billion years of peaceful darkness broken and a weak, self-important part of himself grieving because of it.

There was a sound.

From *out there?*

"Welcome," said a voice. Familiar, and not. Neither warm nor cold. Then came a diffuse orange light that silhouetted a human figure, both of them tiny, apparently distant.

Pamir took another bioscan, unable to find the tiniest hint of anything that didn't belong to him.

The chamber was a cube, precisely fashioned and intended for no known purpose. Little more than a kilometer on a side, it seemed both vast and relentlessly claustrophobic; Pamir had to concentrate to make his legs walk, the sound of his boots crisp and steady, each footfall swallowed by the darkness.

"Welcome," said the voice once more. Louder, nearer.

Pamir hesitated, took a ragged breath, then asked:

"What do you want?"

"I want," said the Monster, "what you expect me to want. I intend to kill your friend."

There. At least it's said. . . .

Again he was walking, halfway across the square floor, then farther, still nothing organic but his own assemblage of microbes and wayward cells; yet there was a vivid glowing mass of *something*, presumably alive, and Pamir could only guess where his opponent had gotten the materials and the energy to construct it.

No, *construct* was the wrong word.

He straightened his cap, extinguished the torch, then stepped at a faster clip. Everything was Samara, he reminded himself; everything was an extension of the hidden genetics, the mammoth potentials. And still, the damned bioscanner refused to show any trace of it.

"You're kind to see me," said Samara. Its body was the same, except nude and blatantly sexless, empty hands offered and the face seemingly amused when Pamir stopped short, refusing to touch it. "I promised not to hurt you. I meant my words."

"Leave us alone," Pamir managed, his voice soft. Almost silent.

"You do call it the Child, don't you?"

"How do you know—?"

"I understand its preferences. I did come here with a certain amount of knowledge, after all." A pause. "But answer this: Whose child is it?"

Pamir watched the body step closer, no threat implied. Between the body and the glowing orange mass was a tendril, neural impulses flowing both directions, the Samara body no more than a finger to the whole.

"In all these years," asked Samara, "haven't you ever asked about its mysterious parent?"

"Aeon," Pamir replied, in reflex.

Samara repeated the name, nodding. "What else do you know? Please, tell me."

"Everything."

" 'Everything.' " It acted jovial for a long moment, then said, "You are a captain and a very good one, as I understand it. But can you tell me, in perfect honesty, that you know 'everything' about this great vessel of yours? Of course you cannot. And you can't claim perfect knowledge about the Child, either."

"You murdered Aeon," Pamir snapped. He was panting, feeling a general weakness. For an instant, he hoped Samara would murder him here, drawing the wrath of the captains. "The Child's told me the story. Everything or not, I know where you're from. I know you. And you murdered its parent."

"Well," said the body, "in those terms, yes. I'm guilty."

Pamir took a half-step forward. If he died, various computers would release files to certain trusted captains; even if they wouldn't defend the Child, at least they would have vengeance on a captain's killer.

"For my entertainment," said Samara, "and for my edification, slice off a piece of this 'everything.' Simplify. Clarify. And perhaps we can reach an accommodation." What might or might not be teeth shone inside the narrow mouth. "And if you can, hurry. It's been a long chase. I'm eager to get to the end, please."

Pamir had heard the epic dozens of times, in a wondrous array of voices. The original Child told it, then used a variety of other bodies. Singly, or together. The story appeared as written words in living wood. As lucid dreams brought on by tailored drugs. A trillion torchflies made a cold living picture, majestic and tragic, their spent bodies falling like rain over Pamir. But his preferred style was a single voice, usually an angel's, her wings embracing him along with her arms and the whispered words making him tremble, with astonishment and awe, and rage, and something indistinguishable from love.

Aeon had been a gaean in the truest, rarest sense:

A vast interlocking organism carpeting a rich world, the simplest algae and the most sophisticated mock-animals linked together in a glorious Whole.

It existed because of evolutionary accidents. A steady climate, a devoted sun, and runaway symbioses had given it birth. Neural centers arose from a gently parasitic worm; it was the worm's spores that the bioscans had found, each spore filled with the makings of an intellect. Only one world in ten thousand ever showed gaean qualities. Fewer than one in ten million generated any kind of consciousness. And according to Pamir's research, none were truly self-aware, possessing what seemed to him to be an authentic and priceless soul.

But Aeon wasn't born alone. There was a sister world, complete with an atmosphere and two small salty oceans; the two worlds were in a tidal lock, the same faces staring at each other as they turned—sixteen hours to the day—around their center of gravity. With countless eyes, night and day, Aeon watched its companion, marking the changing of its seasons, the advance and retreat of glaciers, and the eras of relative abundance when the land and swollen waters became a golden sweet green.

The moon was alive, Aeon realized. And knowing nothing else, it assumed a gaean entity.

For millennia, by many means, Aeon attempted to speak to its great neighbor. It grew forests and huge swarms of torchflies; it caused its ocean's plankton to fluoresce. Every display built symbols. Pictures of their two worlds. Abstract patterns meant to imply simple mathematics. Images of favorite bodies, favorite shores, jungles and mountains and deep cold waters. But there was no response—nothing clear and unambiguous—and Aeon was forced into more desperate means.

Winged mock-animals could fly only so high. And living balloons might reach the ends of the atmosphere, but then their gases escaped, their bodies freezing and descending again like spent leaves to the forest floor.

New ideas were needed, plainly.

Specialized, oversized neural centers were produced, generating silly notions with a smidgen of genius in the mix. That's where the idea of rockets was created. Within days, the first wood-and-flesh bodies were born and launched. And found wanting. Yet that direction became the focus of hope: new materials; new fuels; radical new methods of growth. Specialized bodies mined the crust, purifying and reshaping elements scarcely needed in the past. The first metal-gutted rockets reached space, a few achieving orbit; and then, after a supreme marshaling of resources, better rockets landed on the moon's surface, their mock-animal crews examining and deciphering, then returning home to disgorge memories of immeasurable worth, immeasurable gloom.

That other world had a thin dry impoverished atmosphere. Its poles were brutally cold while the equator baked until the land was blowing dust. Life was divided into units—into bitter and independent species—and even within one species there was competition, each body struggling for water and food, homelands and mates.

There was nothing gaean to find, nothing there to relish.

In the most fundamental sense, Aeon was alone.

Yet it could feel its neighbor's pain, the waste and daily tragedies; and after careful consideration, it saw no choice but to act.

It sent rockets by the thousands.

With the neighbor's own flesh, Aeon taught those impolite pieces how to cooperate. How to share without shame or hesitation. To build neural masses and link them together, a collective intelligence born, and eventually, a genuine self. A *soul*.

Ages passed, productive beyond measure.

The gaeans spoke, faces to faces. Aeon discovered radio waves, and later, lasers. In tandem, they fashioned a single network of mirrors and antennae, orbiting and landlocked, all watching the great emptiness engulfing tiny them.

Eventually, they heard creatures speaking, star to star to star. They realized that the universe was rich with minds. And strange minds, at that. Minuscule. Swift. Cooperative, but not in the gaean sense. And minds without number, Aeon declared, enthralled with their roar and the occasional gifts of knowledge.

The neighbor suggested that they should build a genuine link.

A physical connection to make them One.

Aeon invented the means. Why not a great bridge? No wood or metal would be strong enough. But certain ultrapure crystals, if properly cultivated and aligned, could be laid down like coral, a great strong perfect bridge accreting with the ages.

Aeon's deepest water was directly beneath its neighbor's waist. To support its end of the bridge, it grew a small continent—a mammoth hunk of living wood and hollow aluminum—and the bridge appeared as an endless tree, then as many trees, and finally as a great tube bigger around than most mountains.

Matching tubes joined in space.

There was a ceremony.

A celebration.

A grand, glorious embrace.

Aeon allowed its fellow gaean to build huge muscular pumps, and with them it took a modest quantity of ocean water, spilling it over the bitter plains.

But no more, Aeon warned. In a cautioning tone.

They would share everything, naturally. But their long-range rockets were returning with news of water. The precious stuff was common on nearby worlds, and comets were made of nothing else; and wasn't it reasonable to wait, disrupting nothing until prosperity could be won?

But the neighbor had no intention of waiting.

Without warning—without so much as a declaration of intent —it stole the floating continent. Neural pipelines and mock-animals arrived, the latter built to be warriors. Bladders full of careful poisons broke open, killing Aeon's helpless flesh; and in that instant, in retreat, it named its opponent the Monster, every other name stricken from its mind.

There was a slow, enormous war.

The pumps roared, joined by still larger pumps. Cubic kilometers of seawater flowed across the bridge, flooding deserts and creating new seas, the Monster's visible face suddenly blue as a gemstone.

Aeon tried to fight, and failed.

What did it know about competition? How could it learn treachery and cruelty, and learn them fast enough?

Now it knew why peaceful, selfless gaeans were scarce; and it wasted centuries dwelling on the unfairness of the universe, the grossness of life, intellect trying to contrive some noble gaean course.

Its ocean dropped, the pace accelerating, the continental shelves exposed and its once-verdant continents growing cold and dry. The floating continent—ancient now—rested several kilometers beneath its starting point. Sunken volcanoes stood as islands. Aeon's shores fell straight into deceptively tranquil seas. And with the new poverty came dust storms, rumbling glaciers, and brutal cold droughts without end.

The Monster prospered. Its smaller world was submerged, hidden beneath the stolen waters. Floating continents of mock-kelp fed on sunlight and fusion power. Aeon hoped it would take its fill, finally satiated, leaving the first gaean maimed but alive. And with that hope in mind, it called out for a meeting, sending diplomats across the front lines, a thousand mock-dragons escorting them to the near end of the cursed bridge.

A still newer pumping facility was beginning to work; the Monster showed it off, without shame.

The atmosphere was being absorbed, pressurized, and liquefied, then taken away. A great chill wind was blowing up the new shaft. One of the diplomats was thrown in for emphasis. How much air would be enough air? the survivors inquired. And the Monster responded with a great laugh, its nearest mouths admitting:

"I will leave nothing here but bare stone and hard vacuum."

A single diplomat asked, "But why?"

"What else would I do?" it responded, utterly amused. "We can't negotiate because I have won, and you will soon die, and why did you waste this flesh on such a ridiculous mission?"

The diplomats were killed, in a painful manner, their neural centers returned for Aeon's edification.

A few centuries later, the dying gaean managed to produce a single durable starship with its own pilot—the self-sufficient Child—and the Child fled the war, carrying a portion of its parent's memories and character, setting course for the strongest of the nearby transmissions.

Deciphering their meanings, the Child discovered thc great ship.

It changed its shape and nature, fitting expectations as well as it could manage. What choice did it have but to believe the transmissions, expecting to find a tolerant and charitable crew, and a berth for its little self?

Mercy, in whatever truncated form, had to exist in the universe.

Otherwise, why live?

Decided the Child.

Why, without mercy, should one ever bother with the smallest single breath?

Samara listened to the tale, never interrupting.

It remained silent, and Pamir realized that this was the first time that he himself had ever told the story. In any form.

Then Samara showed a wan smile, saying, "A delicious lie."

Pamir mopped at the sweat on his homely face. "What do you mean? That it never happened?"

The body shrugged its shoulders, the orange glow behind it flaring, dilating orifices belching gases that caught fire. For emphasis, probably. Then it said, "In these last days, I've come to understand your species. Tiny minds, and old. Thoughts so hardened by habit and dream that none of you seem capable of asking the obvious—"

"I'm expelling you," Pamir blurted. "I'll go to the Master Captain, if that's what it takes."

"You can't expel what you can't catch, old man."

Again, Pamir hoped to be murdered. A heroic shortsighted part of him saw no other solution.

The orange mass moved, retreating like some vast amoeba. There was a vivid sloshing as its watery self crept into hairline fissures, unmapped and uncountable. That's how it got here, the captain realized. Through the ship's cracked, aged body; and how could he evict such a creature?

Samara asked:

"Who is the Child?"

Pamir blinked, managing a breath but no answer.

"Is it that little fragment of Aeon—your dear friend—or maybe it's Aeon's world-sized creation?" The body stepped backward, pausing against the ancient wall before saying, "Perhaps both are its children. But since I arose from the first and truest child, perhaps I too should be given that name. Yes?"

"Stay away from me," Pamir whispered.

Samara responded with a strange prolonged gaze, eyes pained; then it asked another question:

"If brothers tell two stories—?"

Yes?

"—which brother will you believe?"

The body was merging with the basaltic wall. The orange glow was the weakest, coolest light imaginable.

"Which of us?" asked the vanishing mouth.

Pamir gave no answer.

"I intend to take relish in my work," Samara proclaimed. "A fair warning to you, and good-bye. Forever, I hope."

Then, darkness.

A four-billion-year night returned, undiminished by that sliver of day.

"Weapons," said Pamir, speaking as much to himself as to the Child. "I know places. Sources. *You* can't make these kinds of weapons for yourself—"

"Thank you."

"—and I can use them, too. Another pair of hands? Does that sound worthwhile?"

"Friend Pamir," the Child replied, speaking through the nearest griffin. "When it's time, I hope you leave me. I can't ask you to fight, and frankly, if you don't mind my saying, you are tiny and weak and more a burden than my fellow soldier." The voice was certain, logic and concern smeared together. "What I've asked you to do, you have done. What more can I want?"

"Let me take my chances," Pamir responded. Then, for emphasis, he promised, "It'll take more than words to keep me away from you."

The Child didn't react to the banality, except to beat the griffin's wings. Huge eyes watched him, the golden pupils pulling wide, threatening to swallow Pamir whole.

He turned, walking away.

An alien sewer flowed beside him, rushing between high canyon walls. Here the water should be clean and sweet. But as more of the Child was readied to fight, less of the wastes were being absorbed and purified. Eventually, no work would be done, and raw sewage would fall through the central sands, into a reservoir that Pamir had left empty for this day. He had recalibrated the computer overseers; years could pass, and no one needed to know what was happening. Yet that act—the sabotage of a warning system—reminded Pamir that he wasn't acting as a captain, that his first duty was no longer to the ship and its smooth, dignified operation.

Fumes lifted from the river, tickling his nose. Scorching flesh. Pamir coughed but refused to back away from the shoreline. In the torrent, camouflaged to match the brown poisons, was a sort of mock-fish, suction cups holding it to the hyperfiber bottom and its armored back visible in the deeper troughs. A new species, he thought. Then he corrected himself: *An old species, with fresh wrinkles.* The Child had mentioned it. Aeon built it during the long war. Eggs that mimicked the dead shells of plankton were carried by currents, occasionally pulled into the transworld bridge. These fish fed on moving water and simple organics, building flesh laced with unstable compounds. The dead gaean had tried to demolish the bridge with them, wanting to ignite the bodies in a single apocalyptic blast. But the Monster had anticipated the attack, no significant damage done; and afterward it had mocked Aeon for trying such a transparent, foolhardy, and useless nontrick.

What good would a few fish do now? Pamir asked himself. And he coughed, tasting blood as he turned to look at the canyon walls and sky.

The Child was transforming itself; he kept forgetting where he was.

Every vegetable mass was covered with spines and piercing threads, a thousand proven, reborn poisons waiting to be injected, another thousand fresh poisons built from alien sewage, ready to be thrown into the breach. No mock-animal, no matter how small or scarce, lacked a killing function. Fruiting bodies were filled to bursting with napalms. Bacteria generated tons of necrotic enzymes. The griffins were growing larger, swifter—and more ominous—they were resting more than training, shepherding their energies in case of a sudden attack. Even the Child's color hinted at deadly work, a blackness of flesh swallowing the soft orange light, hiding details, a velvety sameness making an attacker's job just slightly more difficult.

Pamir couldn't wander at will anymore. Even if a toxin didn't kill him, there would be damage to his skin, puncture wounds and the reflexive slashes of spring-loaded blades.

The Child was right; he was small, weak, and no doubt a burden.

Yet he had helped, undoubtedly. According to the Child, Samara had to enter through one of the orifices; the hyperfiber floor and ceiling were too dense and perfect to allow passage. That known, Pamir had ordered robots to hide sensors above and below this facility. And more robots had set booby traps in the sewers, inorganic bombs and electrified screens set to fire if they felt anything alive. And Pamir himself had climbed inside the ancient machines, behind these very canyon walls, fiddling with worn parts and the power sources, inventing at least one good way to help the Child . . . if it came to that. . . .

"What kinds of weapons?" asked a voice.

A griffin—the same huge griffin—laid a dry talon over Pamir's shoulder, in a gentle fashion. Its talons and beak were sheathed in hyperfiber, mirror-colored and sharp. Pamir had ordered them from a friendly supplier, paying for them from an official account; another lapse as a captain, and he didn't care.

"And where will you find them, friend Pamir?"

He preferred to answer the first question, offering possibilities, then admitting, "But I can't be certain. I mean, I've never actually had reason to buy this kind of gear. . . ."

The Child waited, saying nothing.

"Captains," promised Pamir, "know all the illegal markets."

"Is there something else?"

He hesitated.

"That you've forgotten to tell me, perhaps."

Feigning confusion, he said, "I told you what's important. Why wouldn't I?"

The Child knew about his meeting with Samara. But Pamir had neglected to mention the parting words, hoping it would be forgotten. And since it was anything but, and since it must have showed on his troubled face, the Child felt justified to ask, "Is there something trivial? Something silly? Why not say it and get it done with, friend Pamir?"

Like a lover admitting to an indiscretion, he blurted out, "It tried to tell a different history."

"Yes?"

"Different," he repeated.

The talon lifted. A small voice said, "I can imagine."

"I don't know what's different. All it did was make noise about a two-sided story."

"The creature's clever," the Child replied. "Remember that."

"I remember." There was no place to hide his eyes, and a sheen of cold sweat made his skin shine. "It just gave me this vague shit about brothers. . . . I don't know why—"

"Because you can imagine *anything*. You have that power, it knows full well. . . !"

Pamir had worked hard for days, forcing himself to avoid any dreaminess, keeping his liquid thoughts in safe places.

Captains—every captain—knew doubt was a killer.

A decision made, then aborted, oftentimes was worse than the simple wrong decision.

"It is cunning," said the griffin, with confidence.

Pamir gave a nod. Then after a long uncomfortable pause, he added, "I'll keep one weapon for my own use. And I will be here—"

"If you wish."

"—when Samara comes."

"It's your choice, friend Pamir."

The griffin sprang into the air, wings beating once, then again, carrying it toward a high perch where the old hyperfiber lay exposed, griffins by the hundreds in a tidy mass, doing nothing.

Something soft touched Pamir's back, and he wheeled, surprised to find a reborn angel, perfect breasts swaying before his face and its face—a lean strong lovely favorite—saying, "For you," over and over again.

Hands stroked his chest, no human hands as soft.

Then the wings extended, causing the breasts to lift, and Pamir heard himself saying, "Not now, no." He couldn't accept the gift. Not here. "Take it back. Make something useful with it." Something wicked and brutal, and fatal. "But thank you, Child. Thanks."

The angel's eyes seemed deep, hiding worlds.

It stepped into the churning waters, flesh dissolving as it moved, without pain, the beautiful body embraced and annihilated in an instant; and Pamir was left in what passed for solitude.

He took an official leave of absence.

The Submaster thought he understood, taking Pamir's hand in a gesture of pure ignorance, remarking, "Enjoy your rest. But remember, endless rest is Heaven, and Heaven is for the dead."

A low-ranking crew member sold Pamir five dozen portable lasers, homemade from stolen parts and capable of incinerating everything short of top-grade hyperfibers. As was customary, the captain told the seller that he was taking friends on a hunt, their quarry large, alien, and nonsentient. That would be the crew member's excuse, in case of trouble. Then Pamir set to work, adapting all the lasers but one for griffins' paws. He was working at home, trying to hurry, when Washen contacted him. Could they meet for drinks again? And talk?

"Talk about what?" Pamir was standing in an adjacent room, hoping to brush her aside now and for good. "I'm awfully busy, if you really want to know—"

"Your friend vanished."

"What?" He blurted the word, thinking of the Child. His first instinct was to panic, trying to piece together some story . . . the Child had decided not to fight, following their planned escape route . . . except then he realized Washen meant some other friend. . . .

"Samara," she said. "Remember him?"

Pamir exhaled through his teeth, remarking, "I don't know him."

"Either way, he's gone." Washen gave a little smile, as if some special knowledge was being shared. "And since you seemed interested in him—"

"Not him, no. I was mistaken."

She knew better but didn't press. "I heard a rumor that you're taking some time off."

"A little." No reason to lie now.

"Who's doing your jobs?"

He named captains, leaving one responsibility unaccounted for.

Washen didn't mention the obvious, a kind of tacit conspiracy begun. What did she suspect? Nothing could be as strange as the truth, he told himself; then his friend, peer, and ex-lover remarked:

"She must be astonishing."

"Who?"

"The woman. Whoever she is." A slicing look, jealousy balanced with a strange vapid pity. "But you don't even know, do you? How much you're in love. Do you even sense—"

He blanked the screen, the channel.

In a mad rush, he loaded the tube car with the lasers. Then Pamir set out for the Child, taking the most direct route, thinking hard and finally deciding that of course he loved the entity, in a fashion, and why shouldn't he admit it? Yet once he arrived, stepping through the final hatch, he couldn't say the words. He found himself facing a griffin, its eagle-eyes staring through him; and after his moment's hesitation, in a hushed voice, the Child told him:

"Samara. Is here."

Holding to form, their enemy had arrived as Drought.

Every sewer was blocked. Plugs of rubbery flesh were lodged upstream, beyond the reach of booby traps. The river below Pamir—the one from human places—had fallen to a greasy blue-green rivulet, its fish dead and dying, the Child absorbing and reallocating their bodies in the grandest kind of panic he had ever seen.

Griffins took every laser but his.

The first griffin remained behind, asking for a quick lesson.

Pamir showed how to link the laser's umbilical to the ship's power net, then he gave a demonstration, sealing the hatch with a thunderous blast. An instant later, an alarm sounded. *Something* had moved in the nearby tunnels; sensors disgorged great volumes of vague data. Pointing his laser at the dry river's source, the captain said, "It's massive. And it's setting off the booby traps."

The orifice was unlit, no motions betrayed.

The laser's barrel began to twist, correcting for Pamir's nervous tremors.

"Hide," begged a hundred small voices. "Will you, please?"

He selected a small intake port, exposed now by the drought. The griffin carried him and his laser to it, and a second griffin brought a hyperfiber suit, trim and lightweight, with a double-thick helmet and a sealed environment. Looking at his reflection in the port's hyperfiber wall, he decided that he felt as expected: Strong. Scared, but determined. And tired, yet existing outside the need for normal rest.

"Soon, do you think?"

The Child gave no answer.

Pamir relinked and calibrated his laser. The high clouds had evaporated, their moisture stored and the bare ceiling reflecting the rich blackness below. How much longer? he wondered. And asked, again. And when he asked enough times, the Child responded, its nearest face saying, "I have no way of knowing. . . ."

If Samara just waited, he thought.

If it just bided its time, weakening both of them —

— *what's that?*

Every face lifted. Something was felt. Heard. Pamir glanced at the sensors' readouts, a thousand signs of motion making his heart race.

"Now!" screamed the Child's nearest face.

A leathery, fanged face, and droplets of alien plague arced through the dry, dry air.

Not now, thought Pamir. "I'm not ready—!"

Through the closest orifice, in one titanic push, came life, unformed and full of energies bled from it as light and screaming white noise. The electrified screens were shattered. Winged monsters sprang from the plastic goo, born in flight, driving for the Child's center. And in reflex, fruits exploded. Living nets launched themselves, engulfing and slicing the enemy's bodies. Then the armed griffins, firing as a unit, evaporated the carcasses and broke the molecules, leaving an incandescent vapor that hung in the air, for an instant, before it was absorbed by a second wave of screaming winged bodies.

Pamir remembered to aim and fire, nanosecond pulses cutting. Boiling. Doing remarkably little good.

Samara was vast. Not as large as the Child, but its first assault killed as much as it lost, and it managed to absorb casualties from both sides, reshaping and reanimating the spoils, then launching those newborn troops.

Its second assault dwarfed the first.

The third nearly reached Pamir's hiding place, and he fired until he couldn't see, a haze of boiled blood hanging as a curtain before him.

"Retreat," said a voice.

The Child's? Was it?

Then came another sound. More distant, and louder. A piercing wail rose in the crimson fog. Pamir took a reflexive backward step, retreating deeper into the port, and he lifted the laser, and a long winged *something* plowed into the riverbed in front of him. Fresh cacti impaled its body. A serpentine neck extended, aiming for the port, for Pamir, falling short and dying with a musical roar.

Then a smaller beast sprang from its lifeless head, and it too was grabbed by the spines, dying in turn. But then, after a half-pause, its corpse gave birth to a pair of wings — dragonfly-style; more delicate than smoke — and the wings flapped with an astonishing vigor, Pamir watching with a mixture of astonishment and fatalism. Wings with a threadlike body between, and what could such a little thing accomplish? Hardly anything, surely.

Behind him was a griffin, unnoticed until now.

With a paw encased in hyperfiber, it swatted the dragonfly.

The blast threw it and Pamir backward, deeper into the ancient machinery. Despite the glove, the paw was shattered. Despite the battle's roar, the captain heard the griffin shouting, "Retreat," with a plaintive begging voice.

He ripped the laser's umbilical free, then ran through a maze of mirror-colored tunnels, reaching a downstream port, having enough time to replug and aim and fire for thirty seconds. He didn't need to be coached into retreating this time. "Go, go, go!" he screamed at himself. Strong, scared legs carried him past a third port. He stopped at the fourth, for just a moment, gazing at the sky and seeing a gaseous mass drifting overhead. Like a bubble, wasn't it? Detached from Samara's engorged Whole, and punctured, but somehow holding together and pushing itself along on jets of heated air. It was past him, falling with a certain stateliness, and he didn't see its explosive impact, Pamir diving underground and running again, the immortal hyperfiber shuddering and rolling around him.

He moved twenty kilometers through a sleeping purification system, then took a chance on resting. Then he ran another ten kilometers, and he had to dig his way through a damp black wall of earth to reach the surface. The false sun had been extinguished. By the Child . . . why give away free photons. . . ? Pamir could see by the light of fires, the blue electric discharges. And some brutalized little creature dragged itself to him, plugging its rectal umbilical into the Child, the voice saying, "Friend Pamir," and then, "What a fucking mess. . . !"

Nothing was going well.

Worst-case plans hadn't looked this black, and Pamir cursed himself for ever having felt optimism.

A glowing wall of unformed flesh was closing, moving like syrup down the riverbed, and the captain fired until the fumes condensed on his pitted faceplate, half-blinding him. A griffin arrived, shouting, "Hold on. Here!" And beating its wings, fighting gravity and its own exhaustion, it lifted him and his armored suit and the precious laser out of immediate danger, Samara's advance made negligible by the distance.

How long had they been fighting?

A full day, he realized. But it felt like ten minutes, or a year. He found himself bouncing between wild excitement and a drugged hunger for sleep.

The griffin took him over the flat dry sands—a sudden desert —and landed at a prearranged, marginally secure place where he could rest, and watch. It was one of the original control stations, a kilometer-tall ridge of hyperfiber covered with leathery skin and spines; and Pamir told the griffin to wait, giving it his laser and saying the obvious:

"You can do more with this than I can."

Not that it made a difference, one way or the other. He took drugs to sleep, then woke when a distant blast lit the cavern from end to end. The juncture between the two gaeans was a U-shaped line, the Child holding the interior, Samara attacking the stems in irregular unpredictable bursts, plainly striving to collapse the U into a tiny circle set in the middle of the defenseless sands.

"I don't believe this," muttered Pamir, mystified by Samara's size and its effortless success. How could the captains hope to control such an organism? "If it wants," he told himself, in a near-whisper, "it could take the whole ship for itself."

"I told you so," said a familiar voice.

A small hand touched the captain's shoulder, setting off an alarm in his armored suit.

He jumped and spun around, finding a childlike figure staring up at him. Another resurrected figure; it was identical to the body he had interrogated some thousand years ago.

"I told you," the Child repeated, a grim expression lit by the glare of lasers. "It's black-hearted and treacherous. Didn't you believe me?"

"Not well enough," he confessed.

That body was their last hope. If the Child was doomed, Pamir and this tiny totipotent construction would retreat, and the ship's sheer volume would give them places to hide. Unless of course Samara could wrest control of the ship away from its captains.

"Keep fighting," Pamir advised.

The Child never quit, but after another two days it held nothing but the central sands and Pamir's little ridge.

A single encircling attack began.

Bloodied half-dead griffins landed at the bunker, desperate for nourishment. They fed through umbilicals and their mouths, and they fired the last functioning lasers. Another great bubble rose out of Samara, pushing itself overhead, then dove and spread like an octopus, engulfing everything in its reach. The nearest semi-liquid tendril flowed up the slope, within a hundred meters of Pamir; and he could smell it—a sweet, almost delicate fragrance—and ten griffins were killed when its flesh turned explosive, the blast hotter than a sun.

The Child's lifeboat body, dressed in its own armored suit, turned and gave Pamir a little nod, then a despairing smile.

Beside them was a wall of controls.

Ancient.

Asleep.

With a captain's authority, Pamir initiated a series of commands, coaxing the machinery into wakefulness, telling the systems that things here were an awful mess, then defining Samara as a grievous toxic spill.

With a dull grinding rumble, creations older than worlds awoke.

Then busied themselves with housekeeping.

Vast and cunning, perhaps. But Samara seemed taken by surprise.

Great twisting chunks of it were sucked into the ports, chopped into smaller pieces, their water pulled free and purified while the organics were torn down to their atoms, stripped of identity and purpose, then stored in coffers until needed by *the ship*.

For several days, with an orchestrated professional brutality, Pamir fought the gaean. Samara was forced to retreat, and it shrank, and the Child grew to where it held half of the cavern's floor again.

Then the machinery faltered.

It was its age, in part. And it was because Samara slipped into the old guts, finding ways to sabotage weak systems and confound the others. The gaean war settled into a stalemate. Pamir lost control over a succession of systems. The Child attempted one last counterattack, and it failed, bodies retreating, struggling to destroy everything of use between them and the ridge.

There were no more griffins. Weaker, smaller bodies fired the unwieldy lasers, and Samara came across the bare sands, its Whole exposed and very nearly exhausted, too.

"Look," said the lifeboat body. "It's beaten, almost."

Samara was like a ring of pudding, glowing with a feeble cold light. Pamir could tell that its new bodies were coming more slowly. And none possessed the fight and fire of the originals.

But the Child was just a few hundred hectares of scales and spines laid over hyperfiber. Pamir stepped out of his bunker to take inventory, and he was struck hard, knocked flat, and left senseless. The lifeboat body dragged him back into cover. There he discovered that his helmet was cracked, and a captainly part of him tried calculating what kind of blow would be needed to split this grade of hyperfiber—

—and the Child cried out, "It's time! To go!"

A final, beaten retreat.

"Take me," begged the little body, pushing the last laser into his hands. "Will you? To the car?"

There was a hidden, secure escape route. Of course Pamir would take it out of here. Gladly, with utter devotion. Aiming a battered laser at nothing, coming around each turn of the hallway to find nothing barring their way, he took them deeper into the ridge . . . then hesitated, something feeling wrong as he turned . . . and the hallway behind him as empty as the one ahead. *Where was the Child. . . ?*

Outside, Samara was making a final charge.

Pamir heard its great wet roar, then an explosion. The last of the Child's spare flesh changed its nature, combusting with a yellowish light that rapidly faded, accomplishing little. But Pamir saw the light through a side hallway, which meant some sort of passageway to the surface. He turned and ran up a set of steep stairs, then stopped as he saw a figure silhouetted against the darkened sky. It was dressed in armor, standing on scaffolding beside a huge apparatus that shouldn't be there. A gemstone and metal apparatus, perched high on top of a makeshift fuel tank. Pamir recognized the device but couldn't find the name. He knew it, but *why* did he know it?

Mounting the last stairs, he whispered, "Oh, shit—"

This was the motor of a starship, a ship recently sold as scrap—according to records—and with a mixture of astonishment and horror, Pamir realized the obvious: If one gaean could manipulate the truth, then why couldn't every other gaean, too?

The stardrive stood tall in a vertical room—a room cut from many smaller rooms.

Nothing was above but the huge bowl-shaped ceiling.

Oblivious to the captain, the Child took a seat, gripping a simple control. Then it paused for an instant, watching a monitor, examining images of the cavern and its nemesis. Pamir dropped his laser and began to climb, able to see the Child smiling, a cold razored serenity in the eyes and the little mouth pursing, then remarking with an acidic certainty:

"Now, you die."

Pamir read the lips, then saw the Child squeeze the control.

There was a flash of light and plasmas, a sun born, jumping to the ceiling and scattering; and Pamir dove behind the Child to save himself, guessing everything in an instant, including the scope of his own dear ignorance.

Samara—the bulk of it—was turned to gas and ash.

Later that day, they found one surviving body huddling under a pile of half-melted desiccators. Like the Child, it was the original human form. But despite having lost, the gaean acted amused, cocky, and sharp-tongued. "What did you accomplish?" it asked, using a mocking voice. "Nothing, of course. More like me are coming, and they know what I know. Who cares if it takes millennia to kill *that?*"

Pamir was holding the laser, and the Child said, "Kill it."

Samara's green-gold eyes found Pamir. "The Monster is prepared for a million-year hunt." With glee, it asked, "What could be more patient than a vengeful gaean?"

The Child moved to strike it, or worse.

Pamir stopped his friend, with a warning and then the laser. "I want to hear this. Don't. Stand back." There was nowhere to plug the weapon's umbilical, but its batteries were fully charged. Turning to Samara, he asked, "Why vengeance? Tell me."

A hopeful look, then it said, "The Child lied to you—"

"No!"

Pamir fired a burst, then said, "Quiet."

"My homeworld was a simple place, yes." Samara nodded, the smile softening. "Ungaean, yes. Those parts of the story aren't too awfully wrong."

"Go on."

The creature's eyes could see that world as the words poured from it. "Perhaps its life seemed cruel to Aeon, but cruelty implies intent, doesn't it? And since there was no great linking mind, how could that world be held accountable for any crimes?"

The Child struggled not to move, not to speak.

"My world had no self, no soul, but Aeon gave it both. And it gave the world a name: The Child." A pause. "Before it became the Monster, it was Aeon's little offspring, weak and aware of its weaknesses. But stronger by the century, and more self-aware. And like every child born, it imagined its future, and how it would act differently than its parent, and maybe it would improve on Aeon's ways. . . ."

Pamir nodded as he listened.

Samara looked at the other gaean, with an expression more complex than mere disgust. "They fought, of course. And like it admits, Aeon wouldn't share its abundant waters. But more than that, other resources were rationed, and certain knowledge was forbidden. Aeon demanded oaths of fealty, then physical acts to prove the same. But no proof was adequate. The Child gave and gave of itself, begging for acceptance and winning none. With every word, every gesture, Aeon would find flaws, minuscule and oftentimes invented. And when the Child tried to claim freedom, its parent . . . Aeon . . . would curse it. . . ."

The creature was panting, emotions twisting its face.

"That bridge between them. . . ? Built by Aeon, for Aeon. To help it maintain control." A deep, wet gasp. "It sent griffins, armies of them, to teach the Child to behave—"

"Lies," spat the other gaean.

"—and Aeon put mirrors in space, bringing droughts and endless dust storms. 'I'm hurting you in order to teach you,' it would say. 'I am doing these things to help you, Child.'"

Pamir felt weak, chilled.

"And when the Child wouldn't surrender, Aeon decided to murder it. To take the poor little world for itself." A pause, a hearty smile. "But you can guess the rest, can't you? All that effort to teach the Child, and what was learned? The vagaries of misery and treachery, naturally. And the Child put each good lesson to work.

"And it won, in time. . . ."

Pamir anticipated his friend's leap, and he fired, leaving a pool of remelted hyperfiber between them.

The laser's batteries were half-drained, he noted.

"Lies," the current Child repeated. In earnest.

Pamir didn't point out the obvious: If gaeans could mold flesh however they wished, couldn't they mold memories with the same certainty? And rob their capacity to doubt the stories chiseled into their souls. . . ?

Instead, he turned to his friend, asking, "Where did you find that stardrive?"

A watery look, then resolve.

"I saw the records. It was bought by an alien." Pamir named the species, then the individual. "Do you know that alien?"

Resolve became haughtiness. "I may have met it, yes."

"How?"

Silence.

"Of course you've met it. I'm rarely here. What if you let a few select explorers come here while I'm away?" Like the faithful, cheated lover, Pamir realized that he must have imagined the unfaithfulness countless times. The Child had lied, and what's more, Pamir had lied to himself, without hesitation. "A few aliens with money, and you entertained them, and they loved you . . . and after ten centuries, you built a network of helping hands, and eyes—"

"How can it possibly matter, friend Pamir? I don't understand."

"I learned about Samara's arrival, and I came here to tell you . . . but you already knew, didn't you. . . ?"

Silence.

Despite himself, Pamir began to weep, the laser shaking in his weary aged arms.

"I don't love them, I love *you*," the Child professed, starting to reach for him. "But what if something happened to you? An accident could have happened, and I needed safeguards."

Pamir used silence now.

"Safeguards," the Child repeated, in a mutter.

The captain turned to Samara, saying, "More like you will arrive. Is that right?"

"Many," it replied. "Each more clever than the last."

"You have to kill it," the Child begged. "Hurry."

"But what if this one is dead?" He asked Samara the question, watching the green-gold eyes. "Will they threaten the ship?"

"Never. They'll want vengeance, nothing more."

He looked at the Child, its face changing, alarm building as both hands lifted, seemingly pushing against an invisible set of bars—

—and the captain announced, "All right."

He said, "I've decided what I will do."

The tears had stopped flowing. His arms held the weapon very still, two bursts were fired and the air filled with the vivid stink of evaporated flesh and steam, and the brief beginnings of twin screams cut short by the boiling of their respective tongues.

"We're chasing you. I saw the arrest warrant for myself."

"I know. I've seen it, too."

"You destroyed that entire facility. If we didn't have those water reserves, we'd already be drinking our own urine."

"I know," said Pamir. "I built up those reserves."

"Mention that at the trial," Washen advised, taking a tentative step toward the fugitive. "Whatever's happened, you need to turn yourself in and let the Submasters examine the evidence—"

"Washen? I'm guilty."

"What do you know? You're not a Submaster."

Pamir actually laughed, looking across the big room. Her home was rather like his, except cleaner. Against one wall, in a tiny root-bound pot, a tired clump of llano-vibra sang in hushed voices about everlasting love. "Are you curious about what happened down there?"

"Tell me," she demanded.

He shook his head. "Sorry. I can't."

She took another step, asking, "Will you turn yourself in to me?"

"No."

"Will you surrender to anyone?"

"Not intentionally, no."

She paused, probably wondering if she could physically restrain him. Not now, not in these circumstances. In a quiet, calculating voice, she said, "I don't see why you sneaked in here, frankly."

"I've got a gift for you."

She exhaled, entirely surprised.

"You advised me to give gifts, didn't you?"

Washen asked, "What is it?"

He laid a biovial on the nearest tabletop, then passed his laser to his other hand, yanking a memo chip from his trouser pocket. "These are the instructions." It was the same chip that she had given him, resembling a worn snowflake. "It's all pretty straightforward, really. If you're willing to help me."

"What happened down there? Give me that much."

The homely face grinned. "Study the chip. Do whatever you believe is right, but study it first. Promise?"

She nodded, then said, "You look different. I barely recognized you, at first glance."

"I'm out of uniform," he replied.

"No, it's not that." She shook her head, her expression drifting into pity and gloom. "Where will you go, Pamir?"

He said nothing.

"We won't stop hunting you."

The grin brightened. He stepped to one side and past her, making for Washen's emergency hatch. "Good-bye, darling. And thank you."

Desperate to delay him, Washen grabbed the vial, threatening to smash it if he didn't confess what was inside it.

Pamir gave a backward glance. "Flesh. Living flesh."

"Yours?"

"Yes. And theirs, too."

"Whose?" she asked.

He stepped through the open hatch.

"Who else, Pamir?"

Then the hatch closed, a blast of light melting its mechanisms; and after a moment's contemplation, Washen set down the biovial and picked up the old memo chip, tapping it as if to coax the answers to spring forth, explaining every mystery without fuss, without delay.

She called him the Child, and she called herself his mother, even when both knew that no part of her was incorporated into him. And the Child lived in his mother's home, growing faster than human children but requiring much longer to mature. His talents were baffling and incomplete. His mistakes were painful for both him and his botched creations. But he persisted with his education, imagining the future, some grand part of him eager to become vast, and powerful, and wise.

His mother-who-wasn't-his-mother told him what little she knew.

When the Child dreamed of the past—worlds he didn't know; violence beyond measure—she would comfort him, wetting his forehead with damp rags while saying, "That isn't you. You are not *them*."

Yet *they* were part of him.

Tiny, tiny bodies floated inside each of his myriad cells, giving him almost magical powers over flesh and bone.

"*They* were enemies. They came here and fought—a terrible, brutal fight—and they killed each other."

"But why, Mother?"

She didn't know, but she made guesses. Greed and jealousy, and fear. All human emotions. Then she added, "Little parts of each one survived. Not enough to remake either of them, but when combined, with human flesh as a binding agent . . . well, that's you. You."

The human was his father. The Child couldn't stop asking about him.

"I don't know where he is," said his mother, her expression grave. Sorrowful. "I don't even know if he's alive anymore."

"I'll find him," he'd promise both of them.

But one day, instead of acting happy, Mother shook her head and told him, "You won't, no. You're getting too strong, too skilled. I think it's time that you leave."

Leave what? This apartment?

"No, the ship." She showed him images of a world, young and barely living. Its sun was ruddy and big in the sky. Its oceans were thick with organics and simple bugs. "Your father left instructions. Once you were ready, he wanted you to go to a place like this to live. Do you like it?"

Not at all. In the Child's mind, it seemed ugly.

Yet then again, the prospect of embracing an entire world seemed wondrous. Even inevitable.

They went to one of the great ship's ports, to a tiny shuttle that would carry him to the new world. Kneeling before him, Mother straightened his useless clothes, and she wept, saying, "Remember. Two of your parents hated each other so thoroughly that they couldn't see anything else. They lived badly, and they hurt one another, and how do you erase their terrible crimes. . . ?"

"By living properly," he replied, with feeling.

"What does 'properly' mean?"

"With kindness to all of my parts, and to whatever life-forms that I meet along the way."

She sobbed and said, "Be good."

The eternal motherly advice.

Suddenly the child looked over her shoulder, focusing on something distant.

"A man—"

She turned.

"—was watching me. But he's gone now."

"Did he look like you?"

"Maybe." He thought harder, then said, "No, he didn't. He was much better-looking than me."

She straightened his clothes again, always smiling.

"I think you're lovely," she told him. "Just beautiful, if you ask me."

THE SHAPE OF EVERYTHING

THEY COULDN'T find him. The party had just become a party, tame scientists finally imbibing enough to act a little careless and speak their minds, every mind happy, even ecstatic. That's when someone noticed that the old man was missing. To bed already? Just when the celebration had begun? But someone else mentioned that he never slept much, and it still was early. And a little knot of technicians went to his cabin and discovered that he wasn't there, precipitating a good deal of worry about his well-being. The next oldest person in the observatory was barely seventy—young enough to be his granddaughter—and almost everyone feared for his health. His strength. Even his mind. Where could he be? they asked themselves. On a night like this . . . of all nights. . . ?

Search parties began fanning through the facility, and the security net was alerted. Cameras watched for a frail form; terminals waited for his access code. But wherever the man was, he wasn't visible or working. That much was certain after an hour of building panic.

It was one of his assistants who finally found him. She was a postdoc and maybe his favorite, although he was a difficult man to read in the best of times. What she did was recall something he'd mentioned in passing—something about the cleansing effects of raw light—and she remembered a certain tiny chamber next to the hull, built long ago and never used by the current staff. It had a window to the outside, plus old-style optics, an old-time astronomer able to peer into a simple lensing device, examining the glorious raw light coming straight from the giant mirrors themselves.

She found him drifting, one hand holding him against the optics, the long frail body looking worn out in the bad light. It looked even worse in good light, she knew. Bones like dried sticks and his flesh hanging loose, spotted with benign moles too numerous to count. The cleansing effects of light? She'd always wondered where a committed night-owl had found time and the opportunity to abuse his skin. More than a century old, and the postdoc felt her customary fear of ending up like him. Lost looks; diminished energies. And she wasn't an authentic genius like him. No residual capacities to lean against, the great long decline taking its toll—

"Yes?" said the astronomer. "What is it?"

She cleared her throat, once and again, then asked, "Are you all right, sir? We were wondering."

"I bet you were," he replied. Only then did he take his eye off the eyepiece, the haggard face grinning at her. "Well, I'm fine. Just got tired of the noise, that's all."

She didn't know how to respond. Leave now? Perhaps she should leave if he wanted quiet.

But when she turned, he said, "No," with force.

"Sir?"

"Here. Come see this."

As always, she did as she was told. She kicked across the room and used a single eye, knowing the trick but not having done this nonsense in years. Why did anyone bother with lenses? Even when this observatory was built, digitized images were the norm. The best. And besides, what she saw here was just the focused light from a single mirror—a representative sampling of the whole—meaning it was almost useless to their ongoing work. Too simple by a factor of ten million. Yet she wasn't the old man's maybe-favorite for nothing, feigning interest, squinting into the little hole until he seemed satisfied.

"It's the same as last time," he said, "and the time before. It's always the same, isn't it?"

She looked at him, nodding and saying, "Why shouldn't it be?"

"But doesn't it amaze you?" He asked the question, then he spoke before she could answer. "But not like it amazes me. Do you know why? Because you grew up expecting to see the beginning of time. When you were a little girl, this place was catching first light with its first mirrors, and by then the goal was obvious. Isn't that right?"

A little nod, and she thought of what was out there. It did amaze her, yes, and what right did he have to minimize her feelings? But it wasn't exactly the beginning of time, either. She remembered the digitized images, scrubbed clean by computers, contrasts added and the noise deleted. She could see little blobs of spiraling light—the earliest galaxies—and the best images resolved individual stars. No, it wasn't fair of him to claim a greater amazement. Not when she thought of the work she'd done, the long hours and the years invested in helping him and everyone else, a great mystery now solved, more than likely—

—and the old man was laughing, almost gently.

Was it a trick? A joke? Had he been teasing her? It wouldn't be the first time, of course.

"No, I'm not laughing at you, dear." He smiled, implanted teeth too white to be real. "I'm the amusing one. I look at you and remember someone else. Please, please don't take this wrong, but you've always reminded me of her."

He's been drinking, she realized. At least a little bit.

"A young woman, but she seemed infinitely old at the time. Seventeen years old, give or take, and nearly as beautiful as you. And the first woman I ever loved."

She said nothing.

"Can I tell you about her? Let me, then you'll be free to go back to the party. I promise. It's just a little story, a slice-of-life tale. I know you don't want to hear it—"

"Not true," she heard herself blurt.

"—but indulge me. For a few moments, please."

Of course. She held the eyepiece in one hand, feeling the residual heat left by his hand and knowing she had no choice. This was a duty, perhaps even an honor. Nodding, she looked out the thick window, watching half a dozen mammoth mirrors hanging motionless against the starry background, collecting photons from near the beginning of time . . . helping to support the theory that he, in part, had formulated. . . .

"I was eight years old at the time."

The woman's imagination strained, picturing him as a boy.

"Forever ago," he said, "or yesterday. Depending on how you count these things."

His parents sent him to a day camp in the country, and he still could remember waiting for the yellow bus that picked him up at the corner. It was a noisy, stinking bus full of loud kids, and he always sat alone near the front, as close to the driver as possible. The driver was authority, and he believed in authority when he was eight. He thought it was important not to make enemies or get into trouble. A lot of the kids were older and larger, a few of them almost thirteen, and they seemed dangerous. It was the same as school—the same as all life, he imagined—survival depending on being quiet and small, keeping in the shade of authority whenever possible.

His parents meant well. To them, the camp was a peaceful retreat with docile horses, a spring-fed swimming pool, and a staff of smiling, well-scrubbed adults. At least the brochures promised as much. The truth was that the horses were ratty and ill-tempered, and the pool's water had a suspicious odor. The staff was teenagers, one particular fellow holding sway over the others. His name was Steve or something equally ordinary—a fellow almost big, lean, and strong in a haphazard youthful way. He wore Western clothes, complete with a cowboy hat, and he smoked and chewed tobacco every waking moment. His greatest pleasure in life was bossing around children. It was Steve who introduced the future astronomer to horseback riding and archery, plus a variety of games learned from a stint with that quasi-military organization, the Boy Scouts of America.

One afternoon, on a whim, Steve divided the kids into pairs and said, "This is a tracking game. Shut up and listen." The rules were transparently simple. One person walked from a starting point, heading for the nearby trees, and every time he or she changed direction, two sticks had to be laid down, making an arrowhead to show the new direction. It was a race in time, and it shouldn't take long. Steve promised to sit on the porch of the main lodge, drinking beer and keeping track of the minutes. "And when you're done," he promised, "we'll go down to the pool and you can take your daily pees in the deep end. All right? All right!"

The astronomer's partner was maybe a year older, a boy both confident and bold, and he went first, vanishing into the green woods while Steve counted down five minutes. "Go!" He remembered running hard, reaching the woods and cool shadows, then pausing to let his eyes adjust, eventually spotting his partner in a little clearing uphill from him. The boy was kneeling in sunlight, setting a pair of sticks into position. Catching him meant walking a straight line. "That's not fair!" the boy protested. "You've got to follow the arrows!" And as if to prove his hard work and correctness, he took the astronomer back to each arrow, pointing to them with a barely restrained fury.

The other teams took longer. Once done, everyone reassembled, and Steve, using a fancy Boy Scout knife to open a new beer, said, "Five minutes head start. Set. Go!"

"And play fair," warned the astronomer's partner. "Or else!"

Of course he'd play fair. He believed in rules and authority. Yet he had an idea on his run to the woods—a legal possibility— kneeling in the shade and pointing his first arrow in a random direction. Then he started to jog, heading uphill without varying his direction. The rules were being met, after all. The other boys and rare girls were behind him when the five minutes were up. He didn't pause, barely even slowed, and eventually it felt as if he'd gone miles. He was utterly alone, and only then did he kneel and make a second arrow pointing ninety degrees to his first course. It was a big arrow, and the rules were more than satisfied.

Time passed. The angle of the sun changed. After a while he didn't feel sure about any directions, or even his approximate position. Some places looked familiar—perhaps they'd passed here on horseback—but other places resembled virgin forest. What if he couldn't find camp before the bus left? What if he had to spend tonight in the wilderness? Angry with his own cleverness, he turned and pushed straight up a likely hillside, right through the heart of thorny brush and into the open green ground above the lodge, no sight ever so lovely in his long little life.

Walking downhill, he imagined the celebration accompanying his return. But instead of relief, he found Steve sitting on a folding chair beside the mossy pool, a swimming suit instead of jeans but the hat and beer in place. Steve's response was to belch, saying, "Look what drug itself in, would you? We were thinking of getting up a search party. But I guess you ruined that fun, too. Huh?"

The astronomer's partner was even less understanding. "What happened to you?" he squealed. "You cheated! I knew you'd cheat!"

The lone sympathetic voice came from the lifeguard's chair. Her name was Wendy. She had a pretty face tanned brown, a nose whitened with cream, and big sunglasses hiding her eyes. Wendy was easily the nicest person on the staff, and when he walked past her, she made a point of saying, "I was worried. I thought you might be hurt."

"The kid's fine," Steve shouted. "Don't make a big deal out of it, Wendy, Jesus Christ!"

"And," she said, "I don't think you cheated. I don't."

She looked at Steve while she spoke, her face strong and unperturbed, and he felt there was something between them. He tasted it in the air. There was an understanding, real and precious. She glanced back down at him, the white nose shining. "You are all right, aren't you?"

"I'm fine."

"Good," she said emphatically. "I'm very glad."

Memory expands what's important and what is strange, and that's why his memories of day camp seemed to cover months, not just a single week. Every day was rich with adventures and horrors, his young body sore every night and his parents curious in a careful way. Was he enjoying himself? They had to hear that their money was well spent. But can a young boy know if he's having a wonderful time? He had never been to camp; he had no basis for comparisons. Maybe it was his fault that he wasn't having great fun. "Oh, I like it," he told them, wanting to please. His parents smiled. Was he making any new friends? He thought of Wendy. Nobody else. But instead he mentioned his partner in the tracking game, which again pleased his audience, Mom and Dad nodding and grinning, congratulating themselves for sending him to that piece of Hell.

It was Thursday when Wendy reminded everyone, "Bring your sleeping bags tomorrow, and a change of clothes, too." It was a day camp, but the last day—Friday—reached into Saturday morning. They'd eat dinner here and camp outdoors, then ride home in time for the late morning cartoons.

"We'll sleep up on the hill," Steve told them. "Coyote bait in baggies. It's going to be fun!"

"Quiet," growled Wendy. "Don't say that stuff!"

Steve grinned, stained teeth capable of a menacing air. "They know I'm kidding, girl. They're smart kids. Hell, they love me. Everyone loves me, Wendy. 'Cept you. Ever think why?"

She just shook her head, turning away.

Next morning, at first light, the astronomer woke and found himself hoping to be sick. He looked for a nameless rash, for any excuse not to go. But there were no excuses, him dressing and collecting his belongings, his mother making a snap inspection and then passing him the miraculous sum of five dollars. "For emergencies," she confided. The words seemed full of grim possibilities. No, he wouldn't spend it. He made a pact with himself. There wouldn't be any emergencies, and he'd come home alive and well.

Friday followed the usual routines. There was a horseback

ride, his stallion fat and breathing wetly. Steve rode his thunder-ing beast through the trees, trying to spook the others. Like always. Then came the morning archery contest, and the astron-omer almost broke one hard rule. He was winning, even beating one of the older boys, and he saved himself unknown horrors by sending his last arrow into the gully behind the range. Steve made him climb after it, but that was okay. He found a fine old bottle near the arrow, which made it worthwhile. Then came lunch, cold sandwiches and cheap strawberry pop. Then a round of capture the flag, followed by a long swim; and that's where Steve and most of the rest of the staff vanished. No one mentioned where to or why. Wendy sat above the pool, and she seemed uneasy. Or was he imagining things?

By evening, clouds had rolled in. Dinner was hot dogs, boiled and bland. By then Steve and the others had reappeared, laughing and shouting, moving the furniture to one side of the lodge while drinking beer from a big metal keg. There never was any chance to sleep outdoors. By dusk, it was raining, not hard but enough, and Steve told the kids to spread their bags in a corner and keep out of trouble. He already was drunk, though it would be years before the astronomer would appreciate what kind of fellow Steve was. Possessing an alcoholic's constitution, his nervous system could function despite being thoroughly pickled. Kids and non-drinkers stayed clear of him. Particularly Wendy. Meanwhile, others arrived from somewhere. They were teenagers, big and loud, and maybe there weren't many of them. Maybe they weren't even badly behaved. But to an eight-year-old from a tame, sober household, it seemed as if there were thousands of them packed into the lodge. A hi-fi played stacks of records. People danced while others drank beer and smoked, sometimes pointing to the kids huddled in their corner, making jokes and breaking into raucous laughter.

Steve would watch Wendy, sometimes cocking his cowboy hat and making his approach. But she'd spot him and shy away some-how. She'd vanish into the bathroom or around to the other side of the room, Steve becoming puzzled, walking circles and finally spotting his love all over again.

It was a great drama—a drama that must have been played out through the summer—and it had rhythms and its rules. Wendy usually placed herself near the kids, perhaps feeling protective of them. And Steve's approaches became bolder, failure having a cumulative effect on his frustration. It became late, probably not even midnight, but that was very late back then; and the party was running without pause, without even needing to breathe.

"Which," confessed the astronomer, "might be where I learned to dislike parties." Then he smiled at the postdoc, pausing, nodding to himself and the eyes losing their focus.

The postdoc wondered if the story was finished. Was that all there was to it?

Seemingly changing the subject, he told her, "We've done astonishing work here. You know, you deserve to feel proud."

"I do," she promised.

He drifted closer, and for an instant she feared he would make a clumsy romantic pass. But no, all he wanted was to peer through the eyepiece again. He squinted, watching galaxies forming in the first billion years after Creation. It was then that the universe had cooled enough and diluted itself enough to allow suns to form. But why like this? Why make galaxies of that particular size and composition? It had been a mystery for decades. Why did these oldest galaxies have a sameness of size and color? And what mechanism caused them to be arranged in enormous groups, forming distinct wall-like structures stretching for hundreds of millions of light-years?

Now they knew, or at least they thought they did.

The best clues had remained hidden. It had taken every mirror and every interlinked computer to bring them out. Black holes and cosmic strings were just part of the explanation. More important were some dim dense plasma clouds—relics of a hotter, older era—and how each cloud was aligned beside one new spiral galaxy. Cosmic strings ran through both of them, making eddies in the primordial gases, which in turn made suns. Just five years ago, researchers had determined that those earliest suns were divided into distinct sizes and colors. They came in twenty-three flavors, in essence. They ranged from orange pinpricks to blue-white giants, and what was stranger was their orderly spacing. Very odd, they seemed. Unlikely. Bizarre.

It was the old man's suggestions that had made the difference. He hadn't done the hard work—he wouldn't have known how, the youngsters much more skilled with computer simulations and high-energy physics—but he was the crazy one who suggested they were looking at the work of ancient, possibly extinct intelligences. What if the plasma clouds were organized? What if they were truly conscious? They manipulated matter and the super-strings to create the first galaxies, arranging them in space in order to fulfill a great purpose. "Just suppose," he had told everyone. "That's all I want. Just suppose."

Even the postdoc, loyal by any measure, had to wonder if the old man was losing his mind and common sense. "Why would they build galaxies?" she had asked him. "What possible role could they serve?"

But he'd had an answer waiting. "Distinct kinds of stars might imply some kind of alphabet. A code. Maybe a coherent language. The giant black holes at the center can act as anchors or reference points. Look at the galaxy from above, and you can read everything at a glance."

"Can plasmas be alive?" she had inquired.

"Perhaps. In a smaller, hotter universe, perhaps they'd evolved into intelligence. Maybe galaxies were used as elaborate transmitting devices."

"Transmitting what? And to whom?"

"I don't know, but I can guess." A long pause. "What audience? I don't think the plasmas were chatting with each other. Look at the background temperatures then. Space must have been very, very cold already. From their perspective, I mean. Building galaxies was something done just before they dissolved. Before they died. It was the end of their time, and I think their intended audience hadn't even been born yet."

It was a crazy notion, and a great one, and a few people found the craziness appealing. They did some tests, made mathematical models, and found that indeed, each galaxy had its own inherent code. The best images were just good enough to read a kind of dictionary encircling the central black holes. It was stunning news, and the first translations had answered most of the central questions. Those plasma clouds, using cosmic strings as their pens, were visible writing their autobiographies. In effect, they were telling of their births and development, sentience evolving from the heat and hard radiations. Evolving and growing aware enough to recognize a doomed future. Billions of stars constituted life stories, their authors like old men and women huddling about a waning fire, jotting down a few last notes before their great sleep.

Die they did. Nearer, younger space showed no plasmas, but the galaxies persisted for a little while. Patient observers could resurrect old meanings if they wished. But eventually the original stars aged and exploded, helping to form wild suns while spewing out carbon and oxygen and iron. And meanwhile, the central black holes swallowed anything close, the first quasars igniting, and human beings spotting those scalding lights back when this old man was a mere eight-year-old waif, attending summer camp, wholly unaware that he was the audience whom the great clouds had anticipated.

He was the new ruler of the universe. . . .

The postdoc thought of leaving, glancing at the door, wondering if she should tell the others that he was found. Found and a little drunk and babbling.

"Actually," he said, "you don't remind me of Wendy. I barely remember the girl, quite frankly."

With honesty and a certain impatience, she asked, "I don't understand. Why are you telling me this story now?"

"Because it's pleasant. Because it's important." He sighed and said, "Because I want to tell it."

She nodded and waited.

"Steve eventually caught Wendy, and by then he was titanically drunk. And I'd guess dangerous, too. In my mind he seemed awfully dangerous."

She knew those kinds of men. Too many of them, in fact.

"As it happened, she was near me when she was caught, and he shouted, 'Aren't you going to dance with me?' Poor Wendy. She had a look on her face, brave and scared at the same time. Then she made herself smile, telling him, 'I promised my friend this dance.' With that she snatched me off my sleeping bag and took me into the middle of the room, a new song beginning. I can't remember the song, but I remember dancing and how I looked at the hi-fi as we passed. Each time I looked, measuring how much time remained. There is a certain similarity between these galaxies and our old-fashioned records, and maybe that's the point of my story." A long pause, then he said, "If anyone asks, tell them that I had my inspiration while remembering an out-of-date technology. The hi-fi."

She gave a nod, thinking he was done.

But he said, "Later we went outside together. Wendy led me outdoors." A sigh and a smile. "The lodge's roof overhung a patch of dry ground, and we sat together and talked. I don't remember about what. Though I think she told me, 'We're okay if you stay with me. Steve's gutless, and good people like you scare him.'"

The postdoc said, "I see. . . ."

"No, I haven't thought about Wendy in a long time," he admitted. "It's the atmosphere tonight. It's the meanings of stars." He smiled at her with his too-white teeth. "I'm glad you're the one who found me. And just you."

She felt honored and uncomfortable.

"Everyone's so happy tonight, and why?" He told her, "It's because a great race from the dawn of time was dying. Dying and feeling the urge to leave some memory of themselves. And we're the clever ones who are going to be lionized for seeing what's obvious."

She gave a little nod.

"For all we know, the Milky Way itself began as someone's autobiography. We're built on the scrambled incoherent epic of something vast. And when our time passes, when every sun burns out, perhaps we'll leave some similar kind of record for those who follow us."

The postdoc cleared her throat, then asked, "What happened to Wendy?"

A smile grew on the weary face. "Later, much later, a friend of hers came outside and told her that Steve was asleep. Unconscious. She was safe again, and she turned to me, saying, 'Thank you for your help.' Then she gave me a little kiss on the forehead —my first kiss outside my ugly old family—and she walked with me back inside."

He paused, then said, "I remember my heart.

"I remember feeling its beat, and how I held Wendy's hand with both of mine, wishing I didn't have to let go. Wishing time would stop itself and save this moment. I kept wishing I was special enough to make time stop. And that's when I learned that I wasn't so special, and everything is eventually lost, making room for everything else. And that's not too sad. If you think about it. There's always room being made for the future, and that's altogether not a bad thing."